The New Brighton Archeological Society

BOOK ONE

• The Castle of Galomar •

Created By

Mark Andrew Smith
& Matthew Weldon

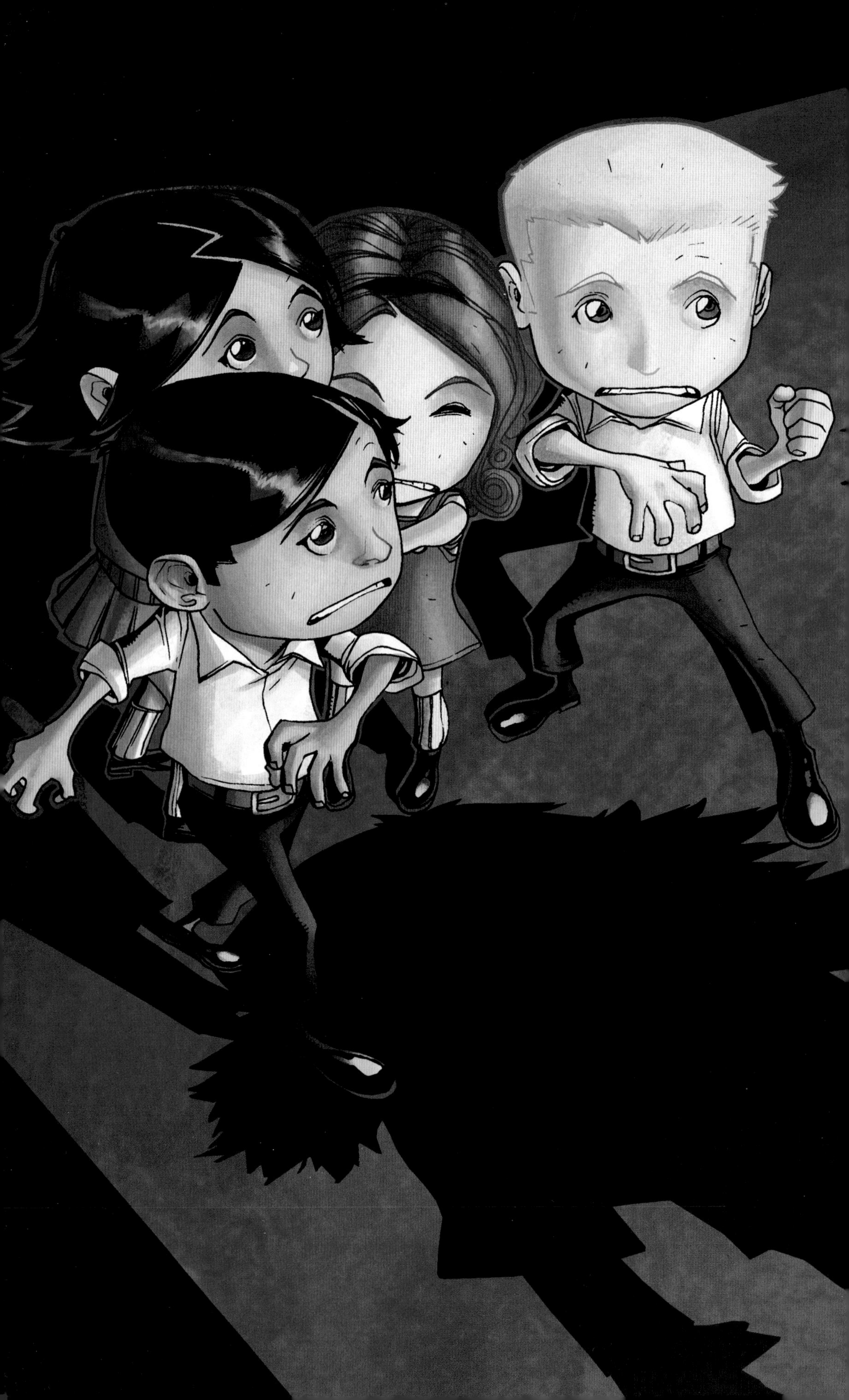

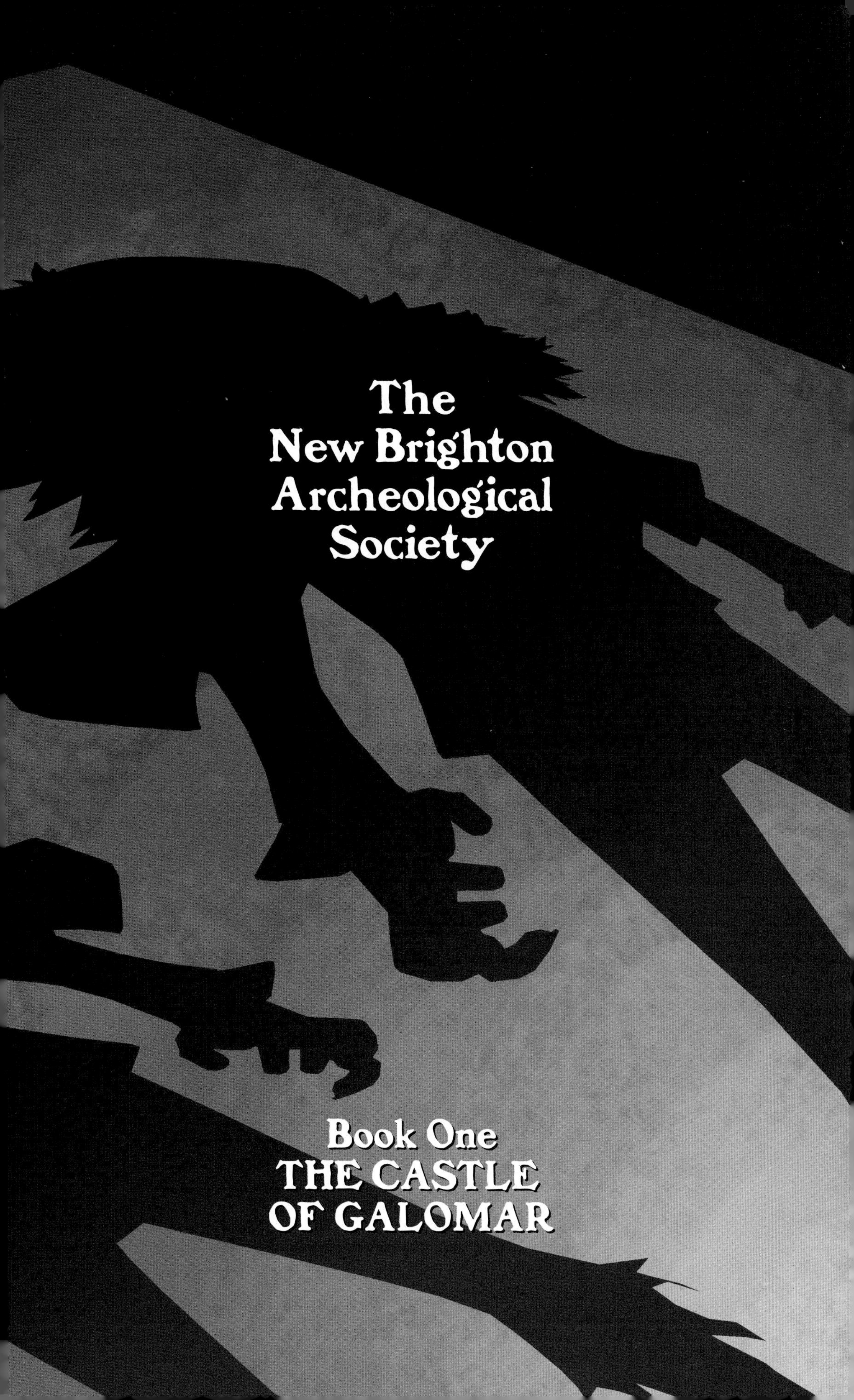
The New Brighton Archeological Society
Book One
THE CASTLE OF GALOMAR

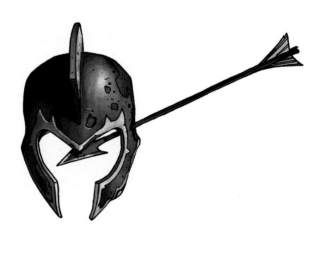

Written by:
Mark Andrew Smith

Illustrated by:
Matthew Weldon

Colored by:

Rodrigo Avilés
(Covers, front & back matter, pp. 22, 118-167)
Jacob Baake
(pp. 7-21, 23-42, 44-48)
Carlos Carrasco
(pp. 43, 49-62, 68-86, 104-117)
Bill Crabtree
(pp. 63-67)
Jessie Lam
(pp. 168-175)
Ralph Niese
(pp. 87-103)

Lettered by:
Fonografiks

New Brighton Archeological
Society Logo by:
Paul Conrad

Edited by:
D.J. Kirkbride

Production Edits by:
Thomas Mauer

Image Comics, Inc.

Robert Kirkman - *Chief Operating Officer*
Erik Larsen - *Chief Financial Officer*
Todd McFarlane - *President*
Marc Silvestri - *Chief Executive Officer*
Jim Valentino - *Vice-President*

ericstephenson - *Publisher*
Joe Keatinge - *PR & Marketing Coordinator*
Branwyn Bigglestone - *Accounts Manager*
Tyler Shainline - *Administrative Assistant*
Traci Hui - *Traffic Manager*
Allen Hui - *Production Manager*
Drew Gill - *Production Artist*
Jonathan Chan - *Production Artist*
Monica Howard - *Production Artist*

www.imagecomics.com

International Rights Representative:
Christine Jensen (christine@gfloystudio.com)

THE NEW BRIGHTON ARCHEOLOGICAL SOCIETY
ISBN: 978-1-58240-973-3
First Printing

Published by Image Comics, Inc. Office of publication:
2134 Allston Way, 2nd Floor, Berkeley, CA 94704. Copyright © 2009
Mark Andrew Smith and Matthew Weldon. All rights reserved. THE NEW
BRIGHTON ARCHEOLOGICAL SOCIETY™ (including all prominent
characters featured herein), its logo and all character likenesses are trademarks
of Mark Andrew Smith and Matthew Weldon, unless otherwise noted.

PRINTED IN CANADA

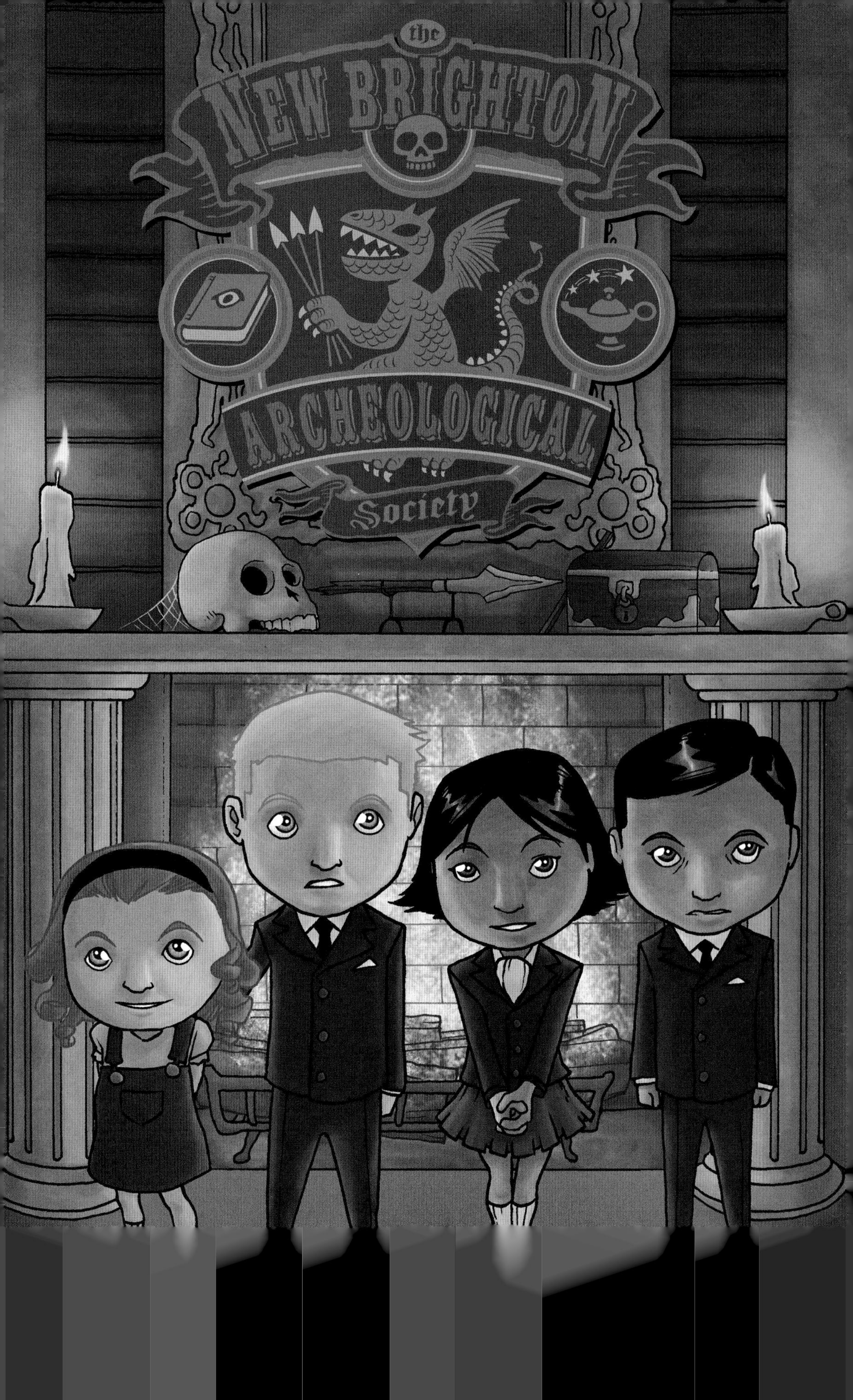

the
NEW BRIGHTON
ARCHEOLOGICAL
Society

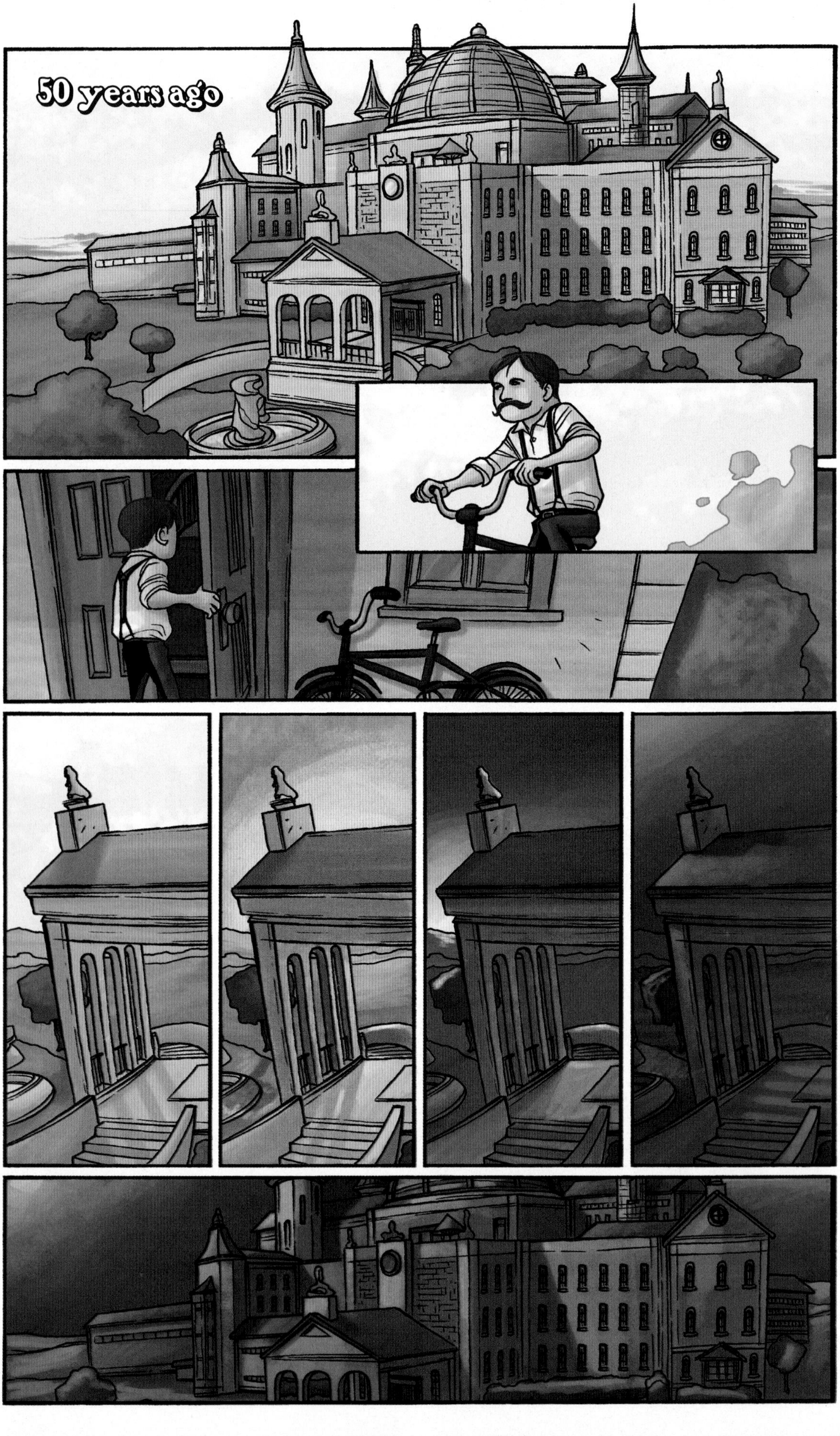
50 years ago

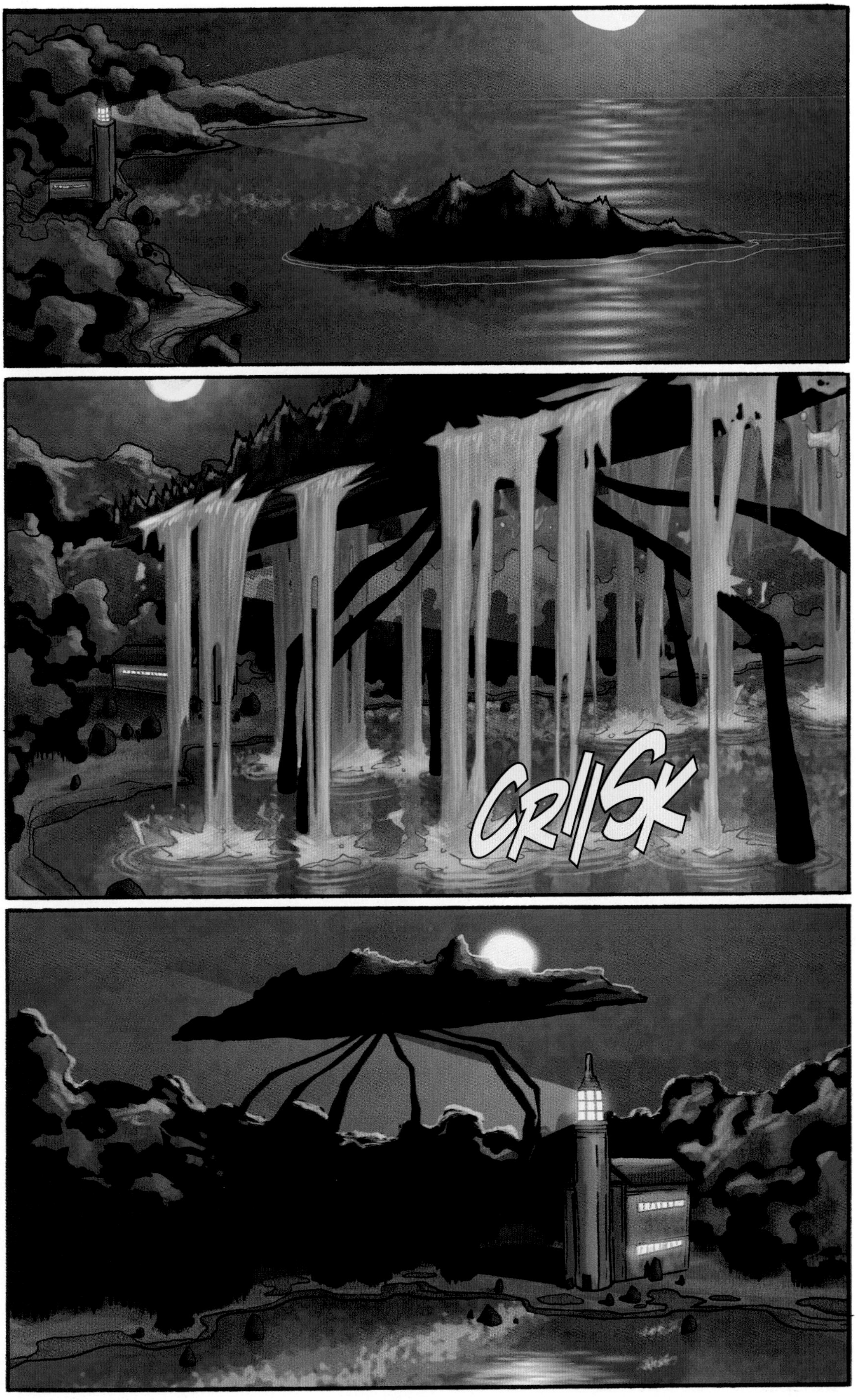
CRISK

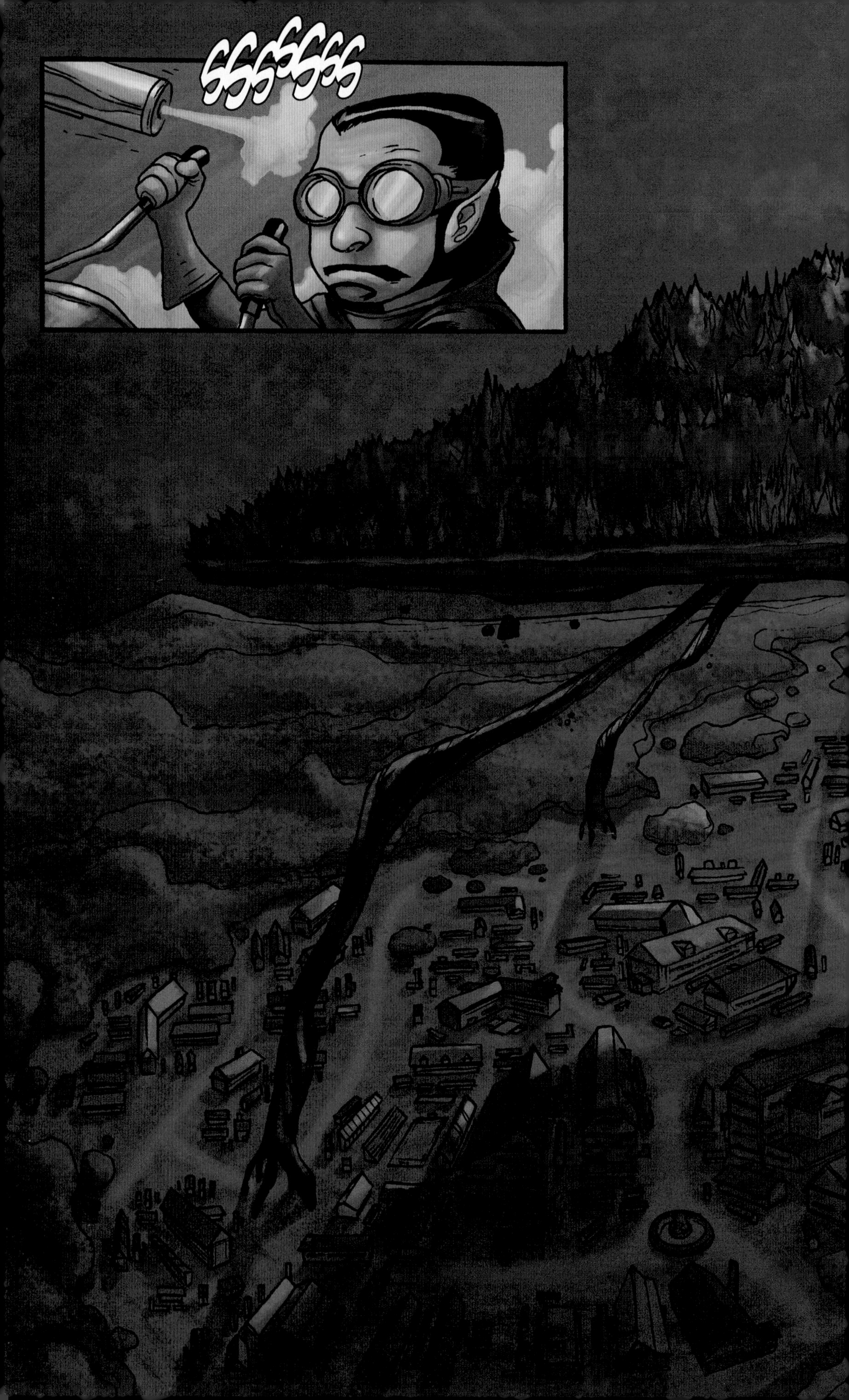
SSSSSSS

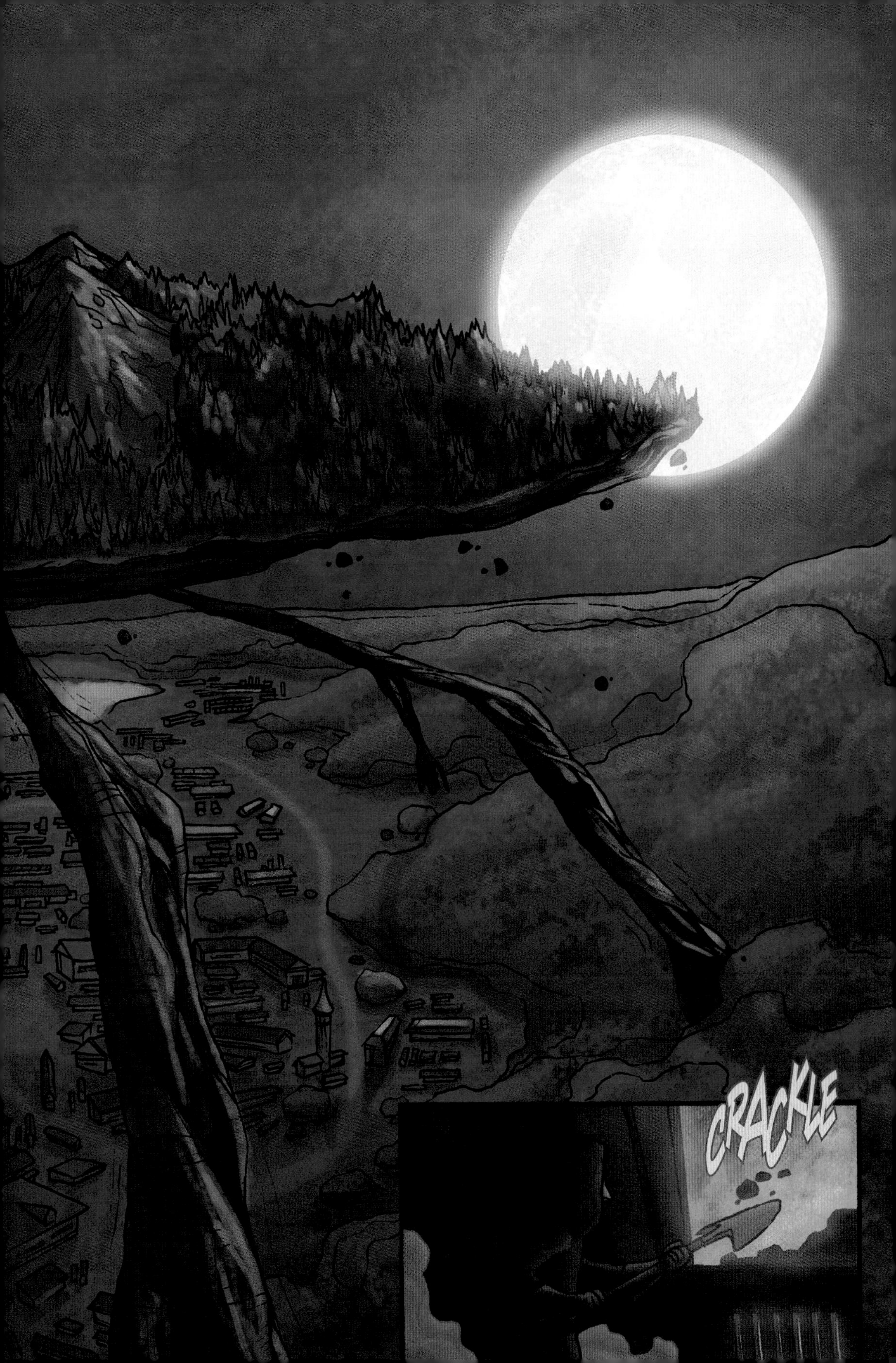
CRACKLE

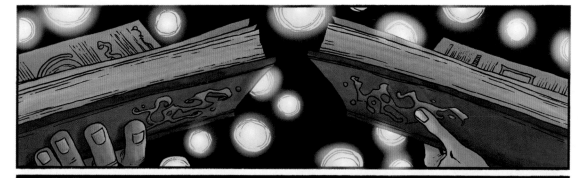

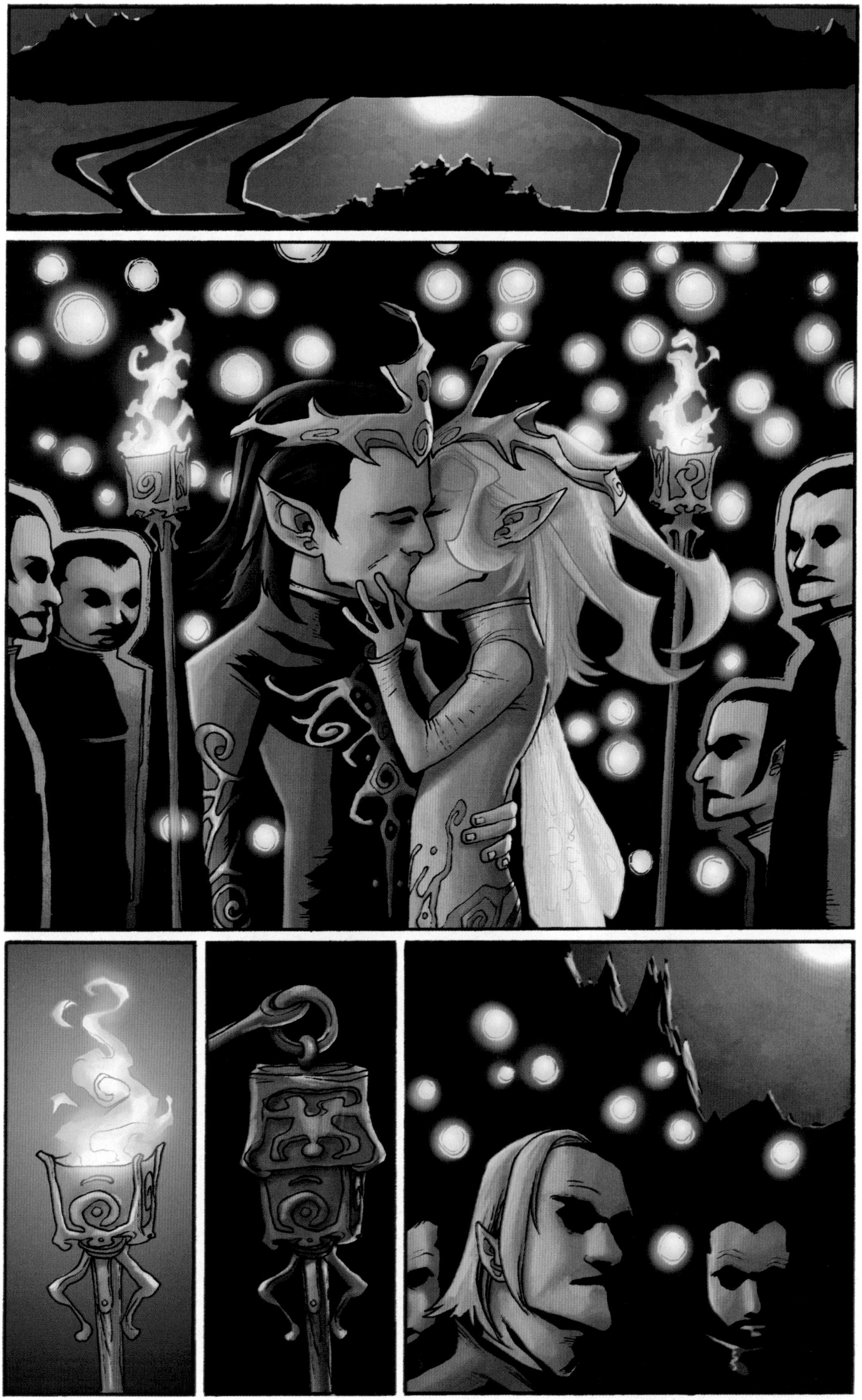

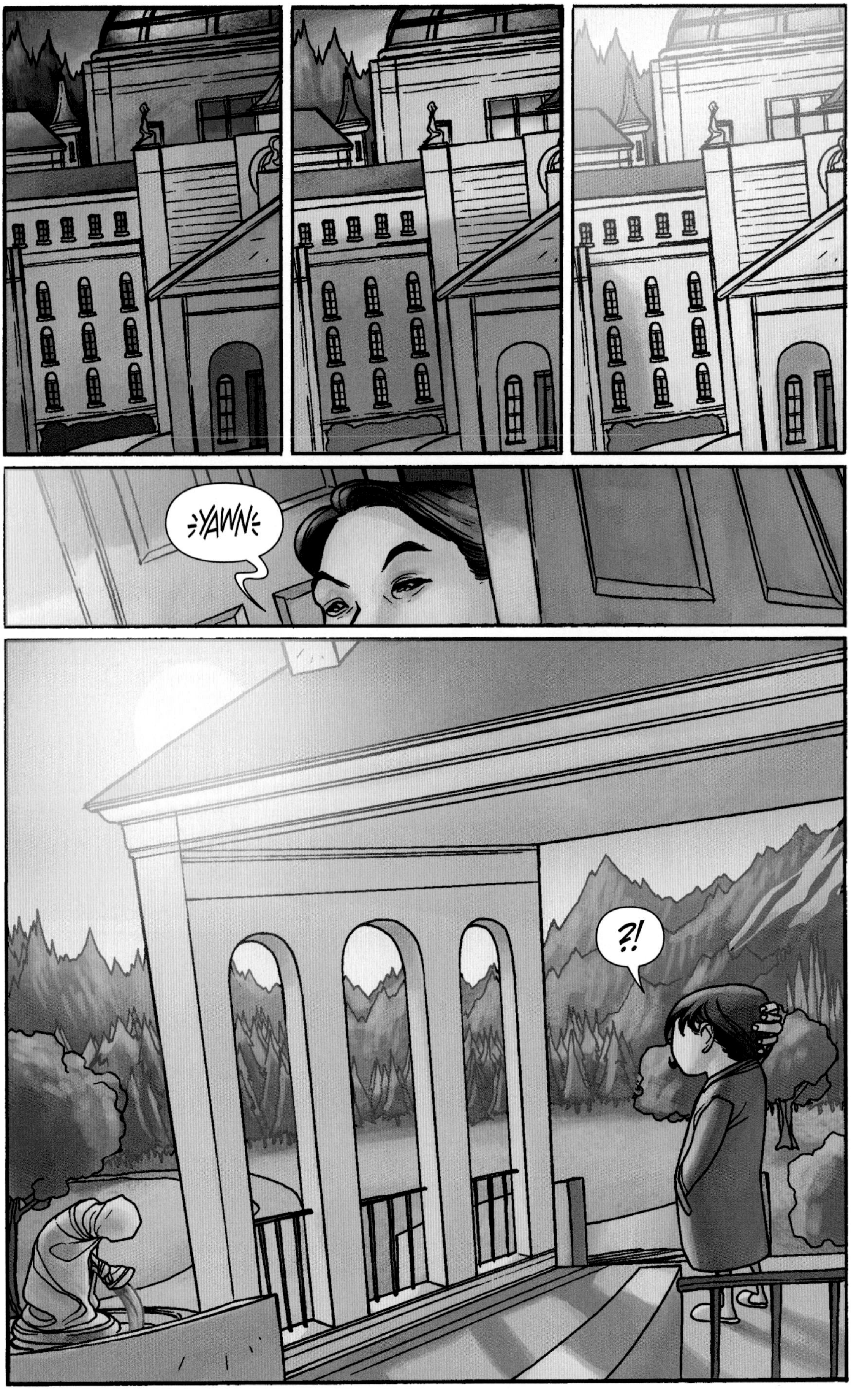
YAWN
?!

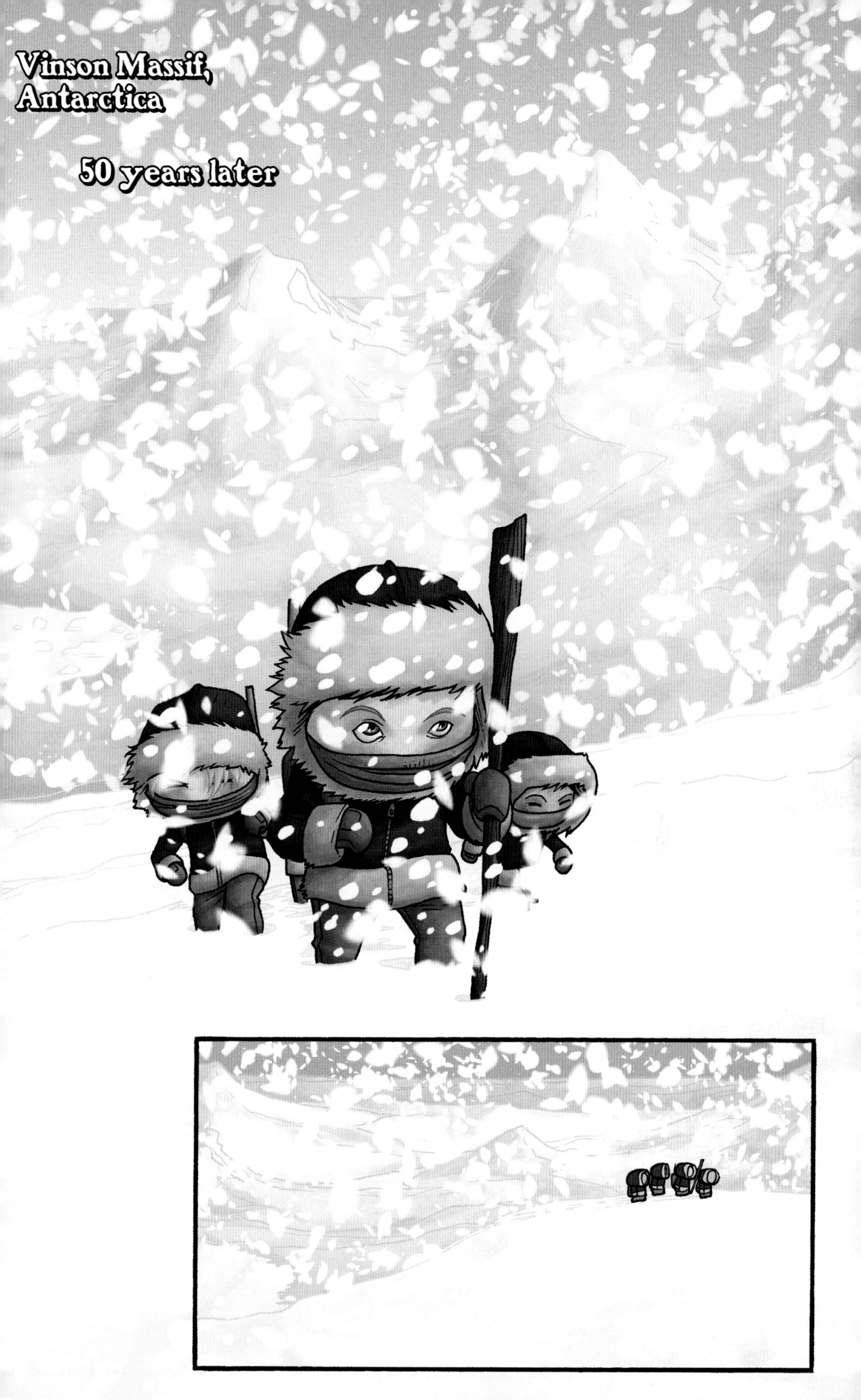
Vinson Massif,
Antarctica
50 years later

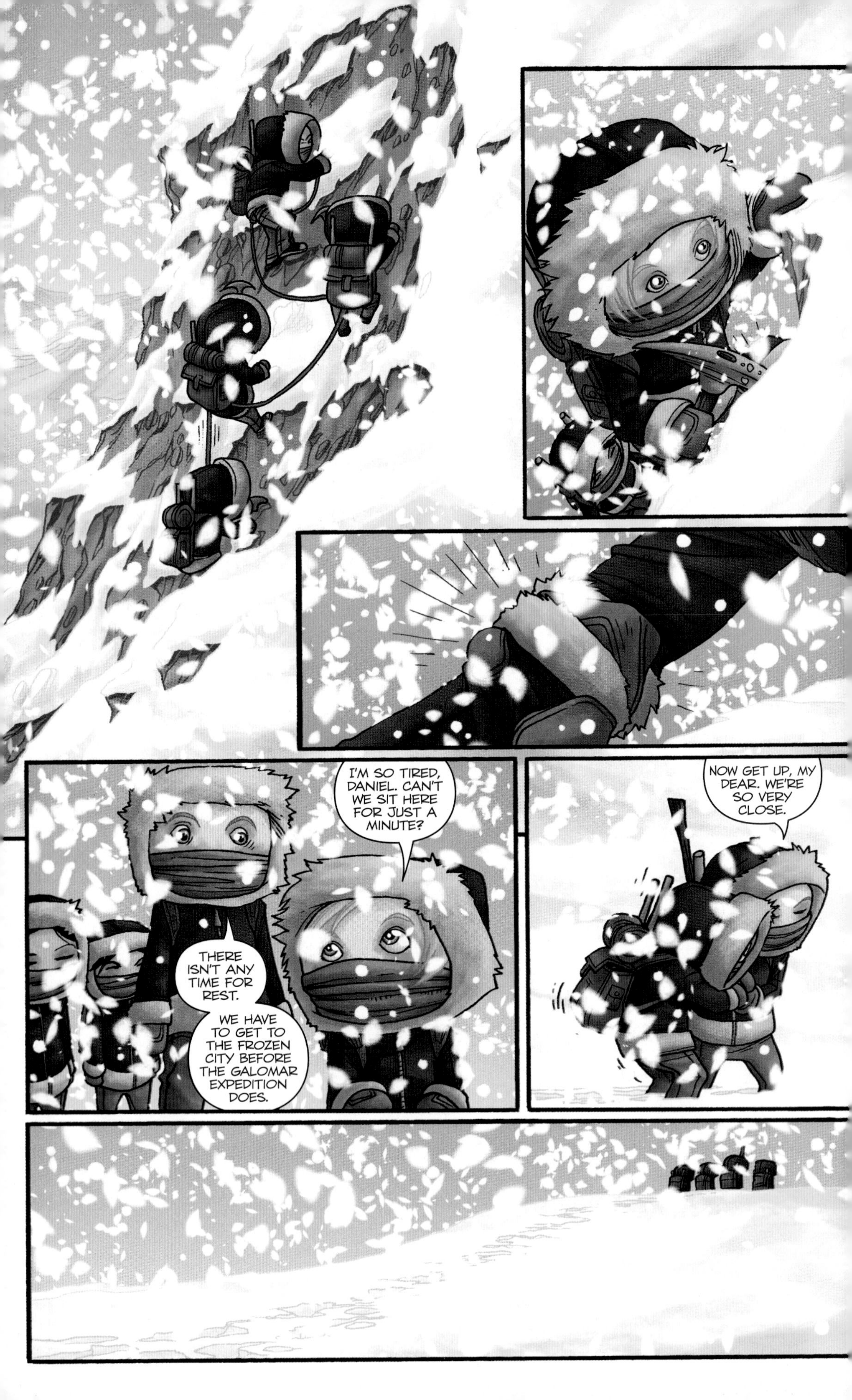
I'M SO TIRED, DANIEL. CAN'T WE SIT HERE FOR JUST A MINUTE?
THERE ISN'T ANY TIME FOR REST.
WE HAVE TO GET TO THE FROZEN CITY BEFORE THE GALOMAR EXPEDITION DOES.
NOW GET UP, MY DEAR. WE'RE SO VERY CLOSE.

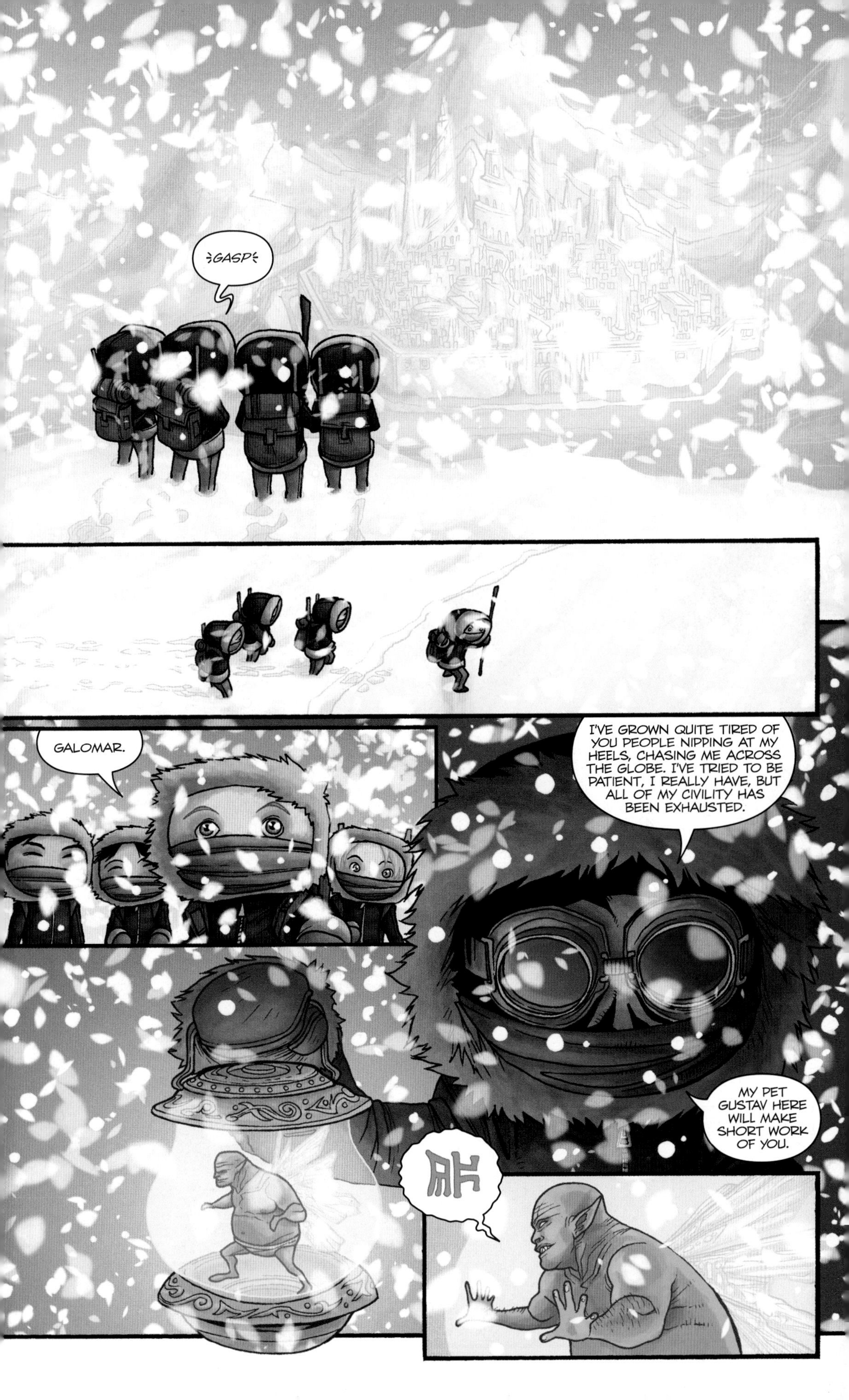

GASP
GALOMAR.
I'VE GROWN QUITE TIRED OF YOU PEOPLE NIPPING AT MY HEELS, CHASING ME ACROSS THE GLOBE. I'VE TRIED TO BE PATIENT, I REALLY HAVE, BUT ALL OF MY CIVILITY HAS BEEN EXHAUSTED.
MY PET GUSTAV HERE WILL MAKE SHORT WORK OF YOU.

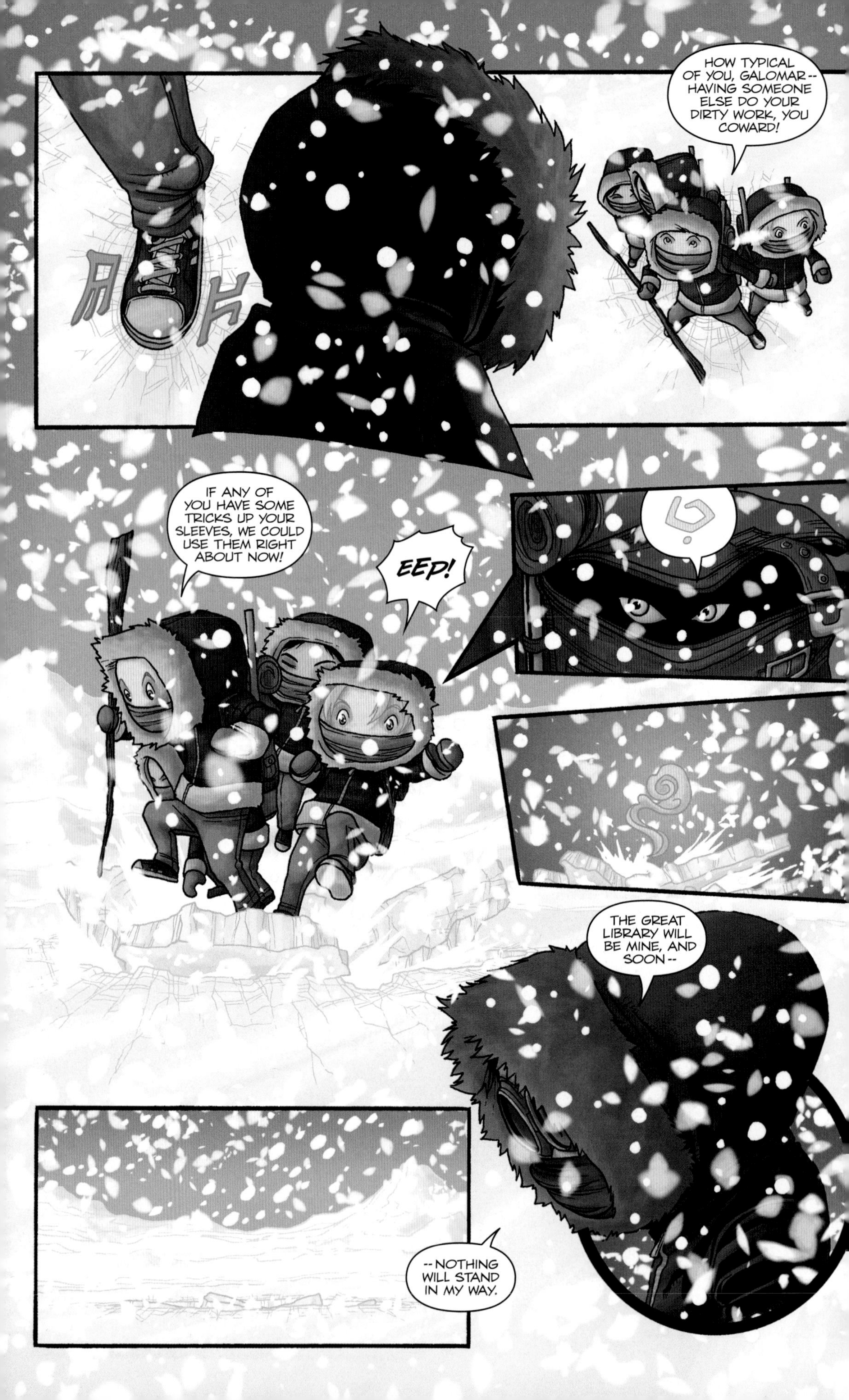
HOW TYPICAL OF YOU, GALOMAR-- HAVING SOMEONE ELSE DO YOUR DIRTY WORK, YOU COWARD!
IF ANY OF YOU HAVE SOME TRICKS UP YOUR SLEEVES, WE COULD USE THEM RIGHT ABOUT NOW!
EEP!
THE GREAT LIBRARY WILL BE MINE, AND SOON --
-- NOTHING WILL STAND IN MY WAY.

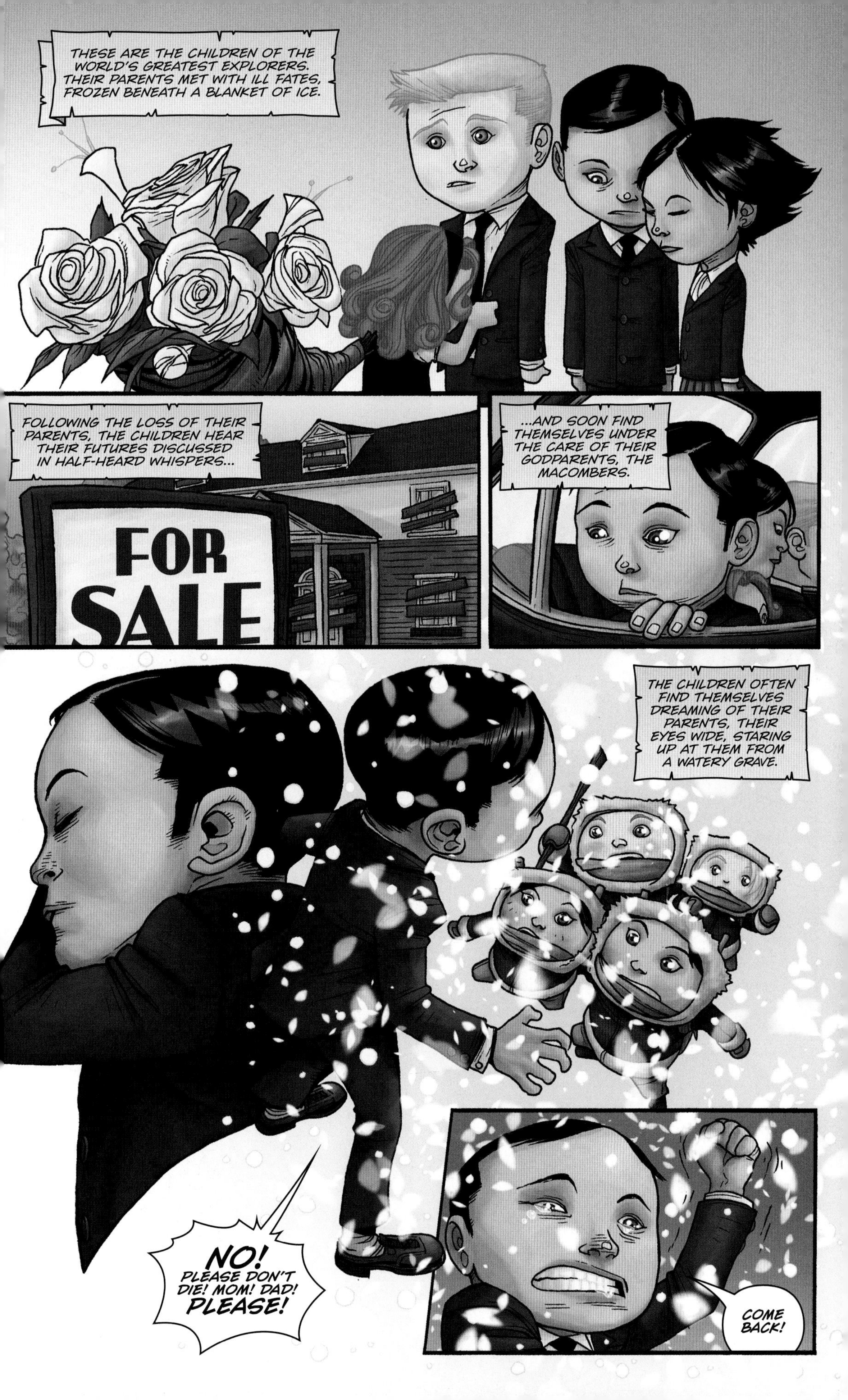

THESE ARE THE CHILDREN OF THE WORLD'S GREATEST EXPLORERS. THEIR PARENTS MET WITH ILL FATES, FROZEN BENEATH A BLANKET OF ICE.
FOLLOWING THE LOSS OF THEIR PARENTS, THE CHILDREN HEAR THEIR FUTURES DISCUSSED IN HALF-HEARD WHISPERS...
FOR SALE
...AND SOON FIND THEMSELVES UNDER THE CARE OF THEIR GODPARENTS, THE MACOMBERS.
THE CHILDREN OFTEN FIND THEMSELVES DREAMING OF THEIR PARENTS, THEIR EYES WIDE, STARING UP AT THEM FROM A WATERY GRAVE.
NO! PLEASE DON'T DIE! MOM! DAD! PLEASE!
COME BACK!

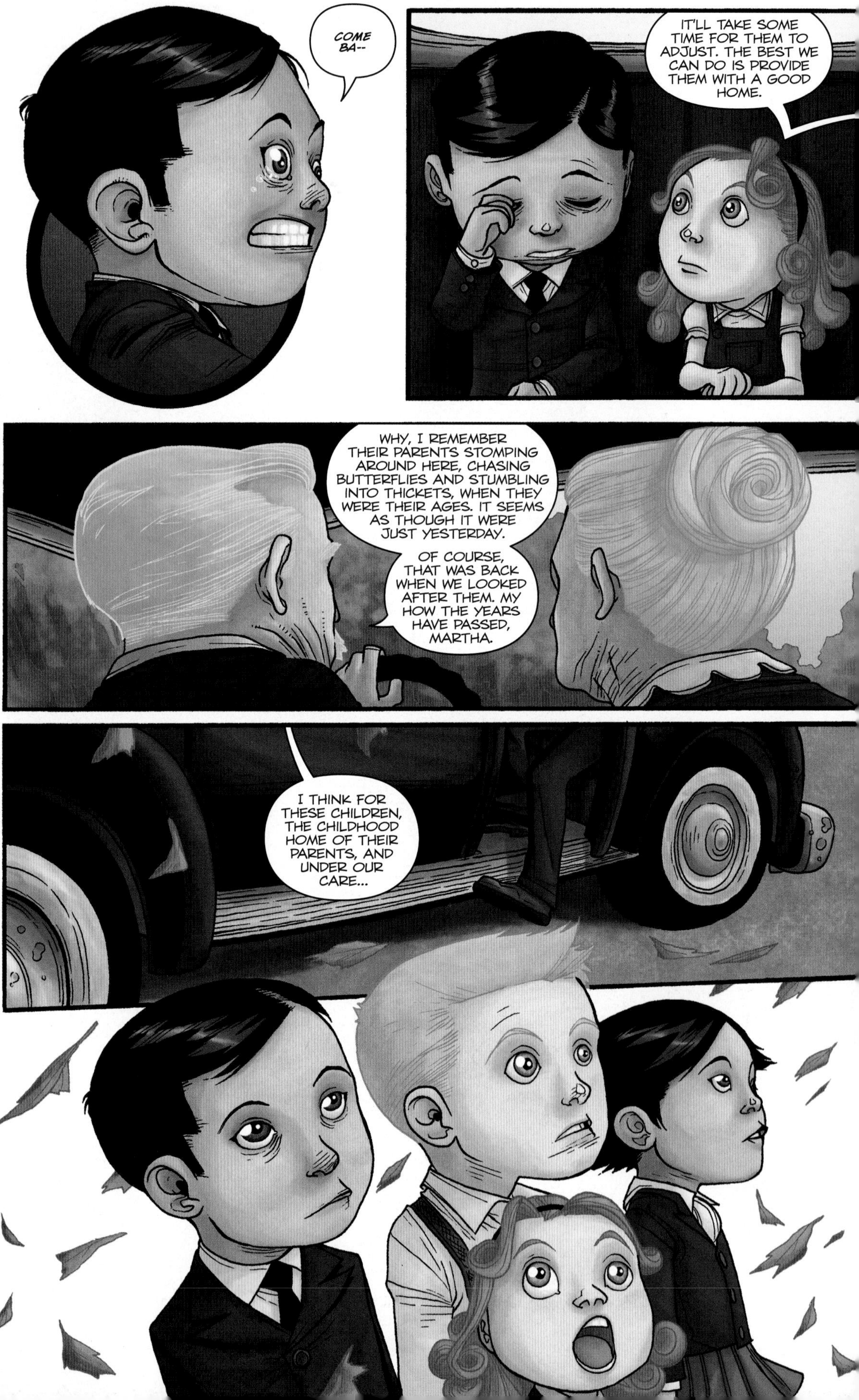
COME BA--
IT'LL TAKE SOME TIME FOR THEM TO ADJUST. THE BEST WE CAN DO IS PROVIDE THEM WITH A GOOD HOME.
WHY, I REMEMBER THEIR PARENTS STOMPING AROUND HERE, CHASING BUTTERFLIES AND STUMBLING INTO THICKETS, WHEN THEY WERE THEIR AGES. IT SEEMS AS THOUGH IT WERE JUST YESTERDAY.
OF COURSE, THAT WAS BACK WHEN WE LOOKED AFTER THEM. MY HOW THE YEARS HAVE PASSED, MARTHA.
I THINK FOR THESE CHILDREN, THE CHILDHOOD HOME OF THEIR PARENTS, AND UNDER OUR CARE...

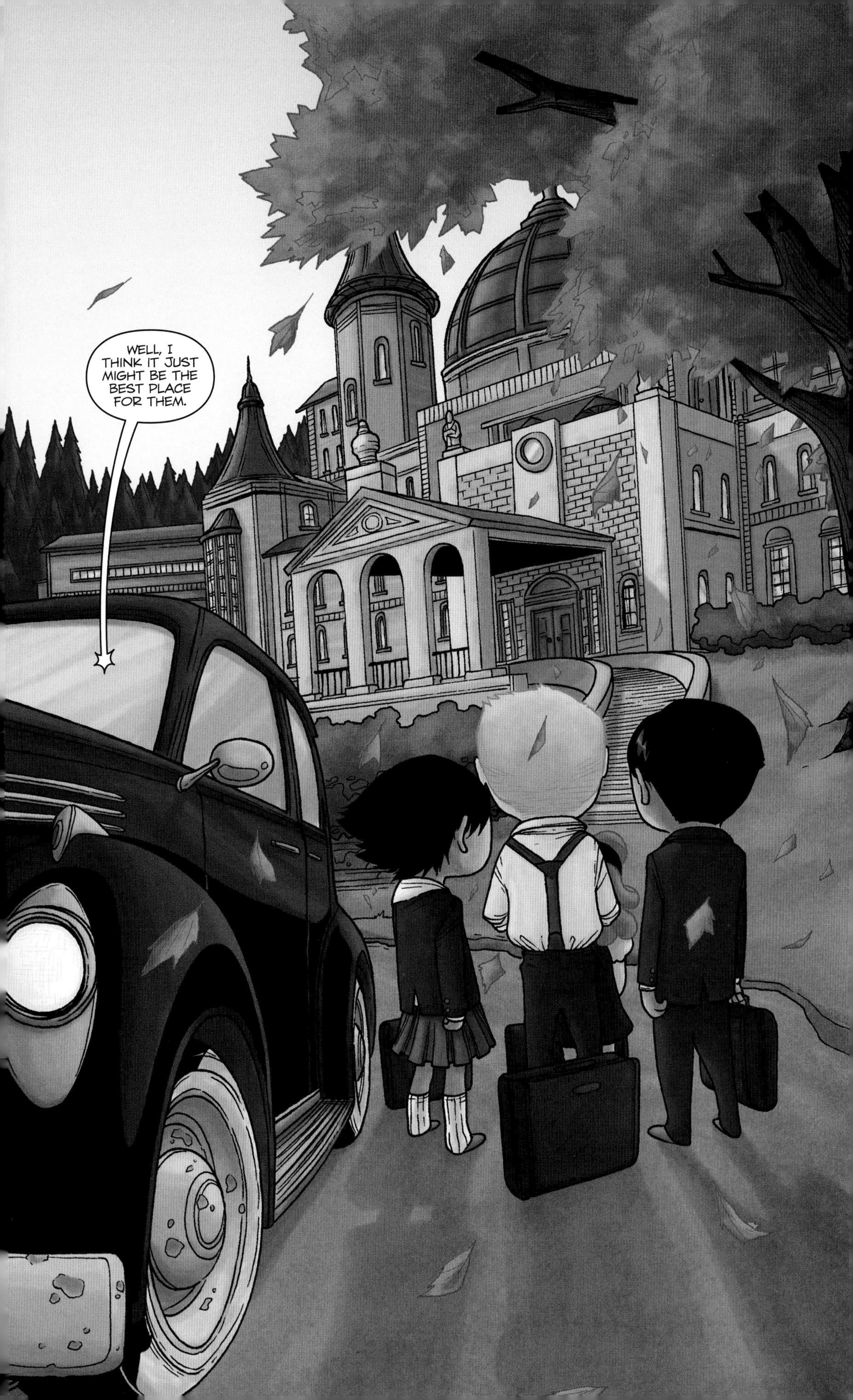
WELL, I THINK IT JUST MIGHT BE THE BEST PLACE FOR THEM.

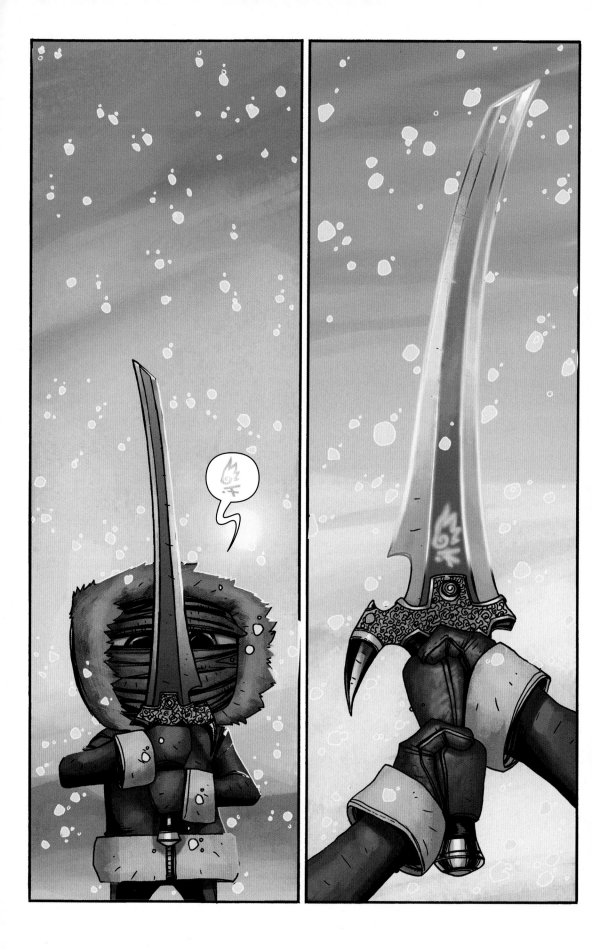

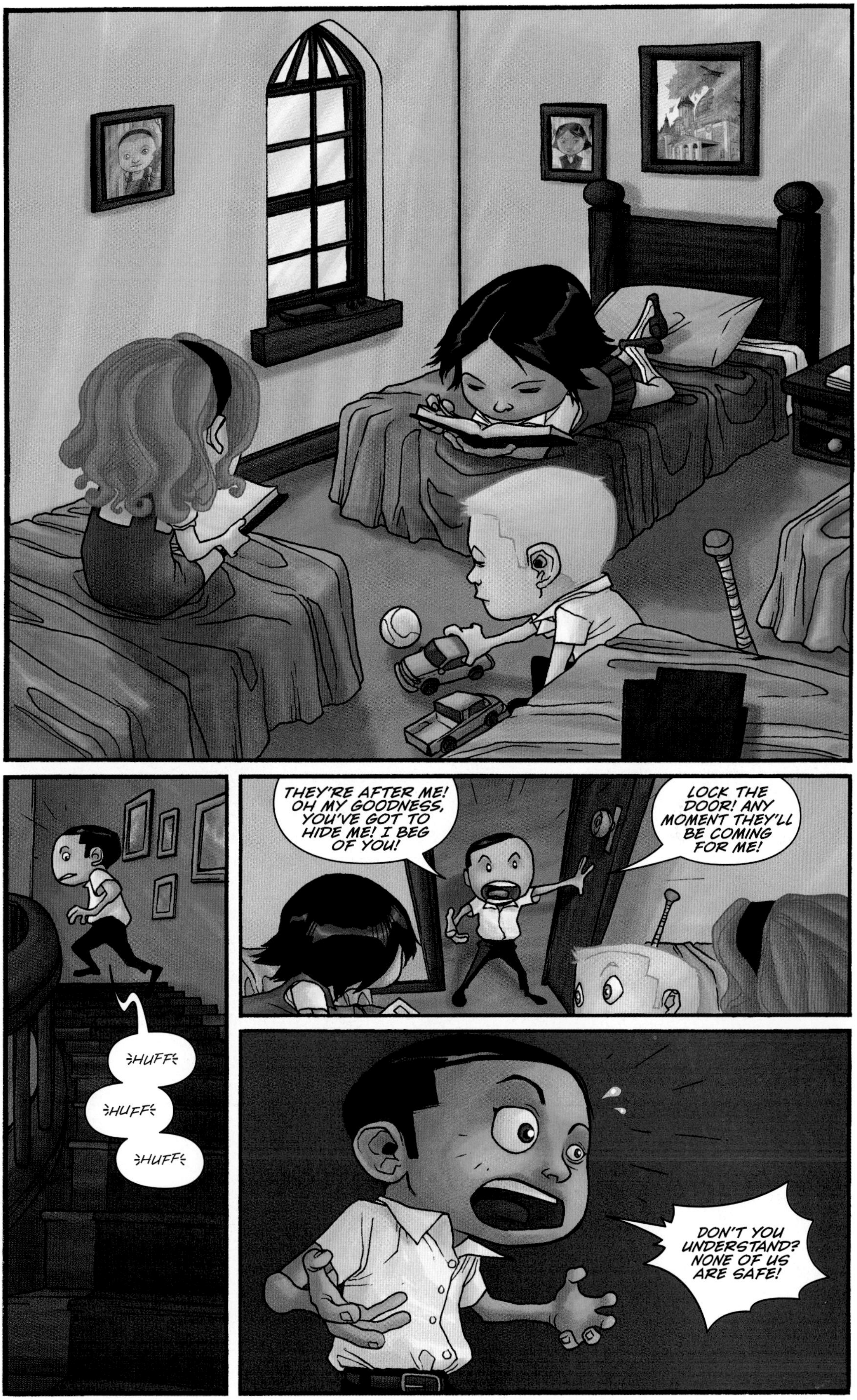
HUFF
HUFF
HUFF
THEY'RE AFTER ME! OH MY GOODNESS, YOU'VE GOT TO HIDE ME! I BEG OF YOU!
LOCK THE DOOR! ANY MOMENT THEY'LL BE COMING FOR ME!
DON'T YOU UNDERSTAND? NONE OF US ARE SAFE!

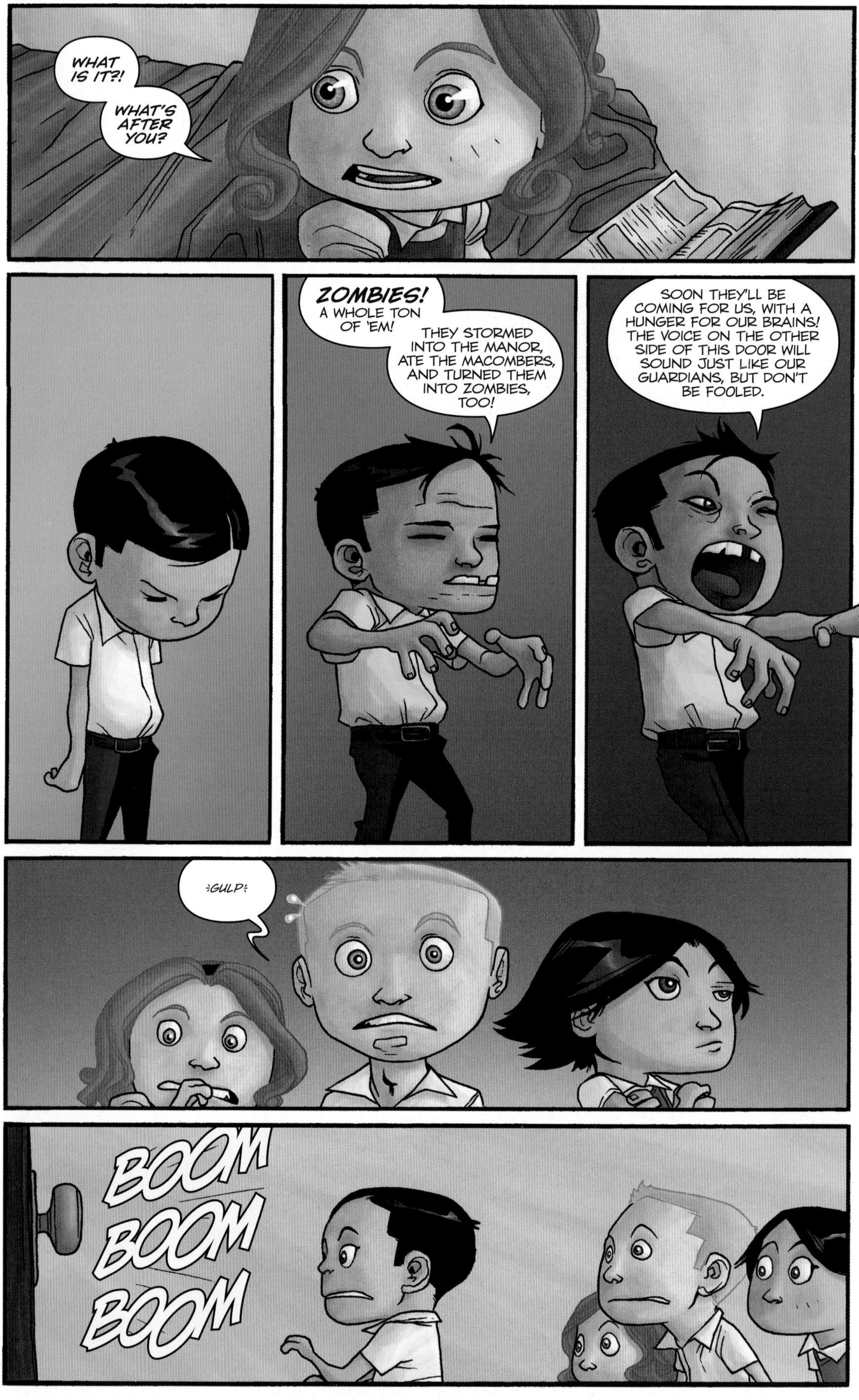
WHAT IS IT?!
WHAT'S AFTER YOU?
ZOMBIES! A WHOLE TON OF 'EM!
THEY STORMED INTO THE MANOR, ATE THE MACOMBERS, AND TURNED THEM INTO ZOMBIES, TOO!
SOON THEY'LL BE COMING FOR US, WITH A HUNGER FOR OUR BRAINS! THE VOICE ON THE OTHER SIDE OF THIS DOOR WILL SOUND JUST LIKE OUR GUARDIANS, BUT DON'T BE FOOLED.
GULP
BOOM BOOM BOOM

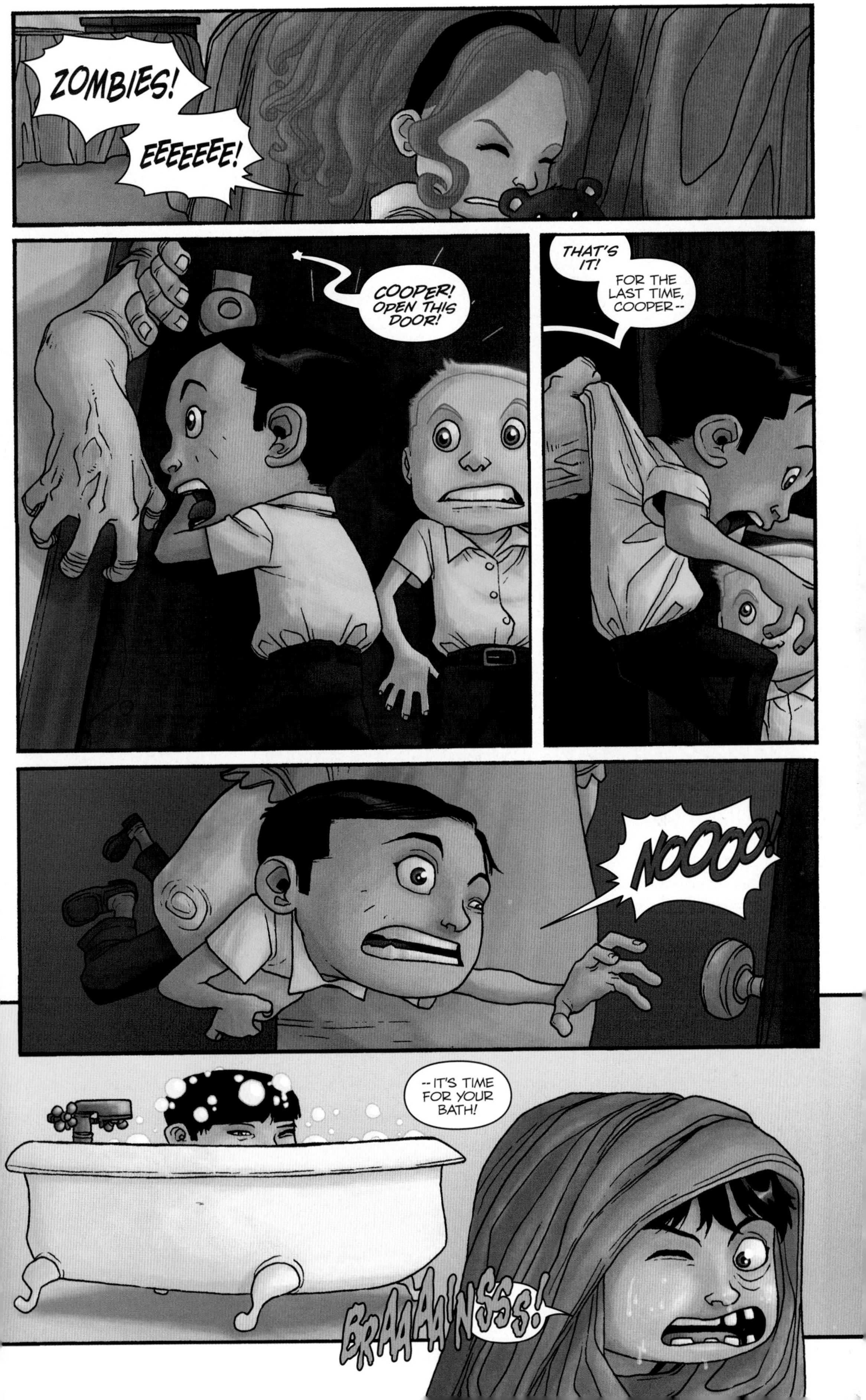

ZOMBIES!
EEEEEEE!
COOPER! OPEN THIS DOOR!
THAT'S IT!
FOR THE LAST TIME, COOPER--
NOOOO!
--IT'S TIME FOR YOUR BATH!
BRAAAAINSSS!

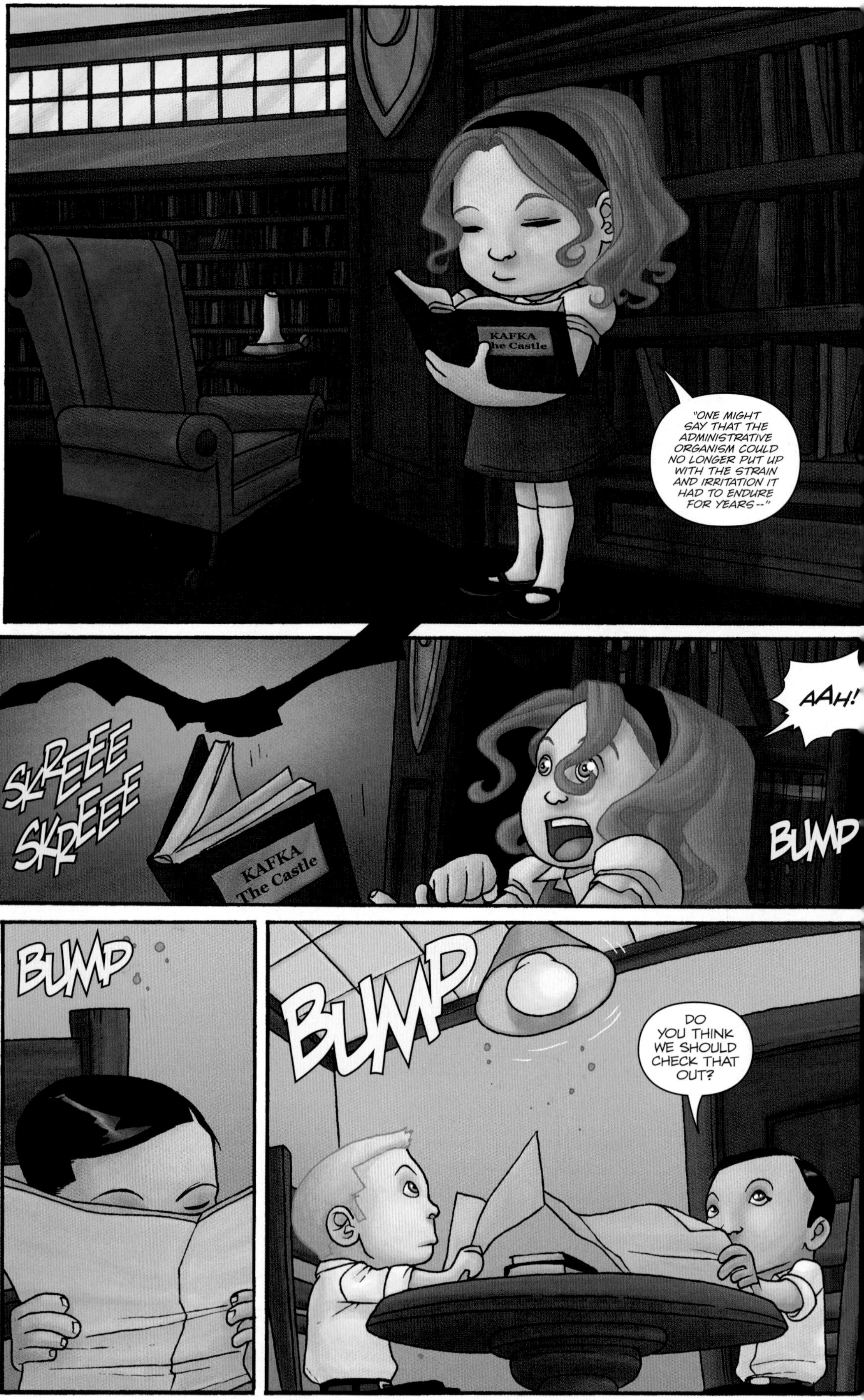
KAFKA
The Castle
"ONE MIGHT SAY THAT THE ADMINISTRATIVE ORGANISM COULD NO LONGER PUT UP WITH THE STRAIN AND IRRITATION IT HAD TO ENDURE FOR YEARS--"
SKREEEE
SKREEEE
KAFKA
The Castle
AAH!
BUMP
BUMP
BUMP
DO YOU THINK WE SHOULD CHECK THAT OUT?

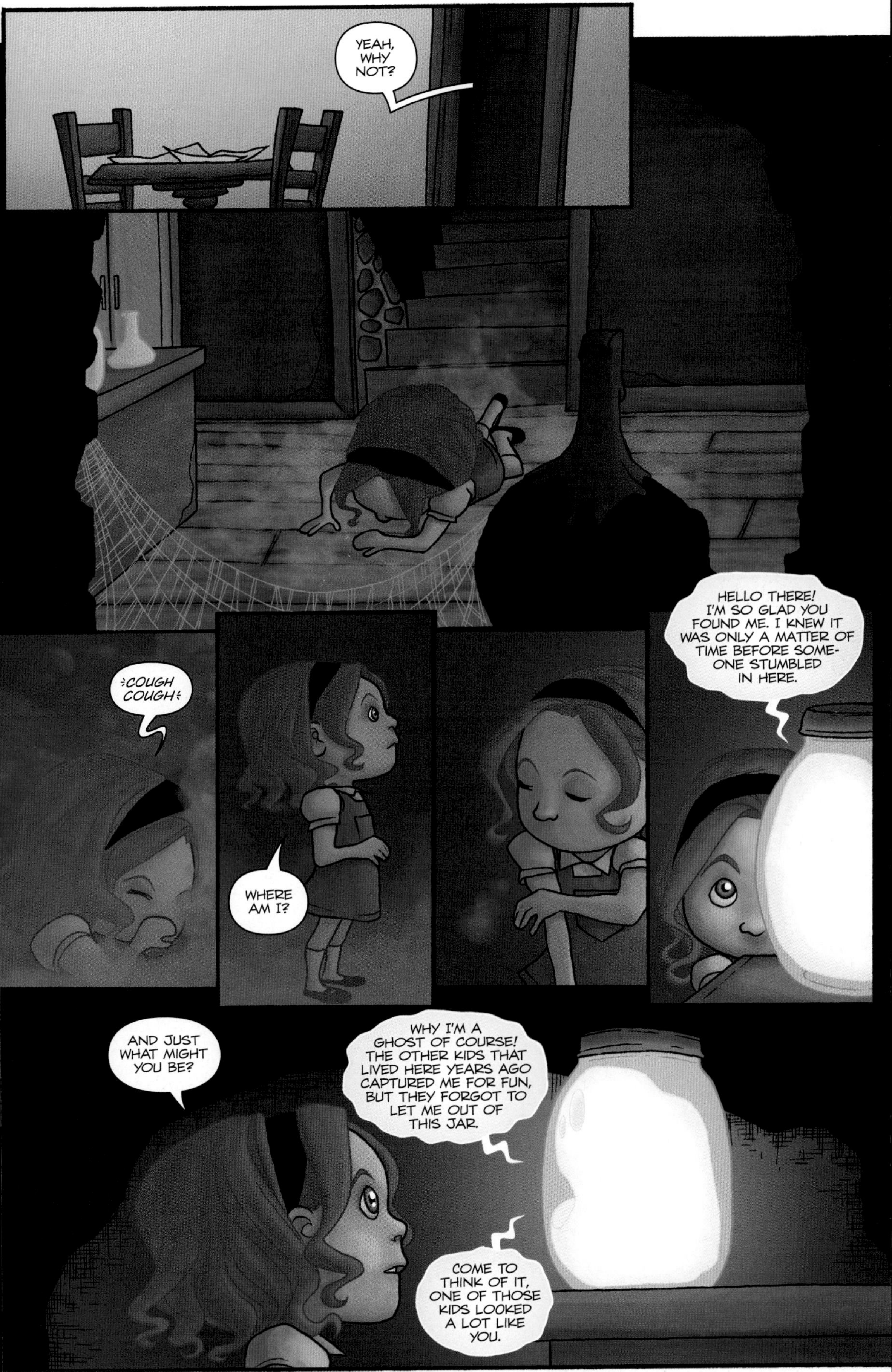
YEAH, WHY NOT?
COUGH COUGH
WHERE AM I?
HELLO THERE! I'M SO GLAD YOU FOUND ME. I KNEW IT WAS ONLY A MATTER OF TIME BEFORE SOME-ONE STUMBLED IN HERE.
AND JUST WHAT MIGHT YOU BE?
WHY I'M A GHOST OF COURSE! THE OTHER KIDS THAT LIVED HERE YEARS AGO CAPTURED ME FOR FUN, BUT THEY FORGOT TO LET ME OUT OF THIS JAR.
COME TO THINK OF IT, ONE OF THOSE KIDS LOOKED A LOT LIKE YOU.

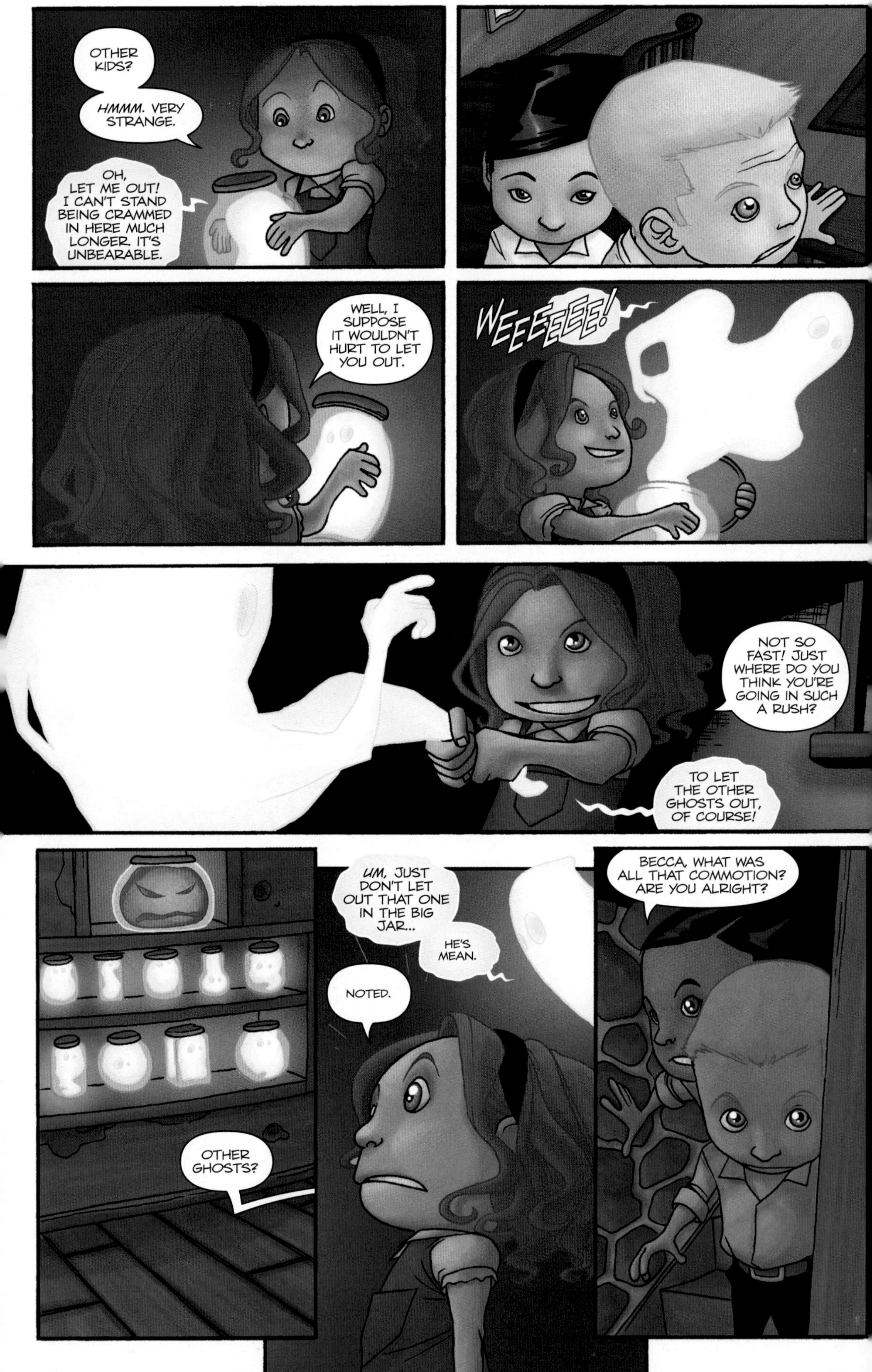
OTHER KIDS?
HMMM. VERY STRANGE.
OH, LET ME OUT! I CAN'T STAND BEING CRAMMED IN HERE MUCH LONGER. IT'S UNBEARABLE.
WELL, I SUPPOSE IT WOULDN'T HURT TO LET YOU OUT.
WEEEEEEE!
NOT SO FAST! JUST WHERE DO YOU THINK YOU'RE GOING IN SUCH A RUSH?
TO LET THE OTHER GHOSTS OUT, OF COURSE!
OTHER GHOSTS?
UM, JUST DON'T LET OUT THAT ONE IN THE BIG JAR...
HE'S MEAN.
NOTED.
BECCA, WHAT WAS ALL THAT COMMOTION? ARE YOU ALRIGHT?

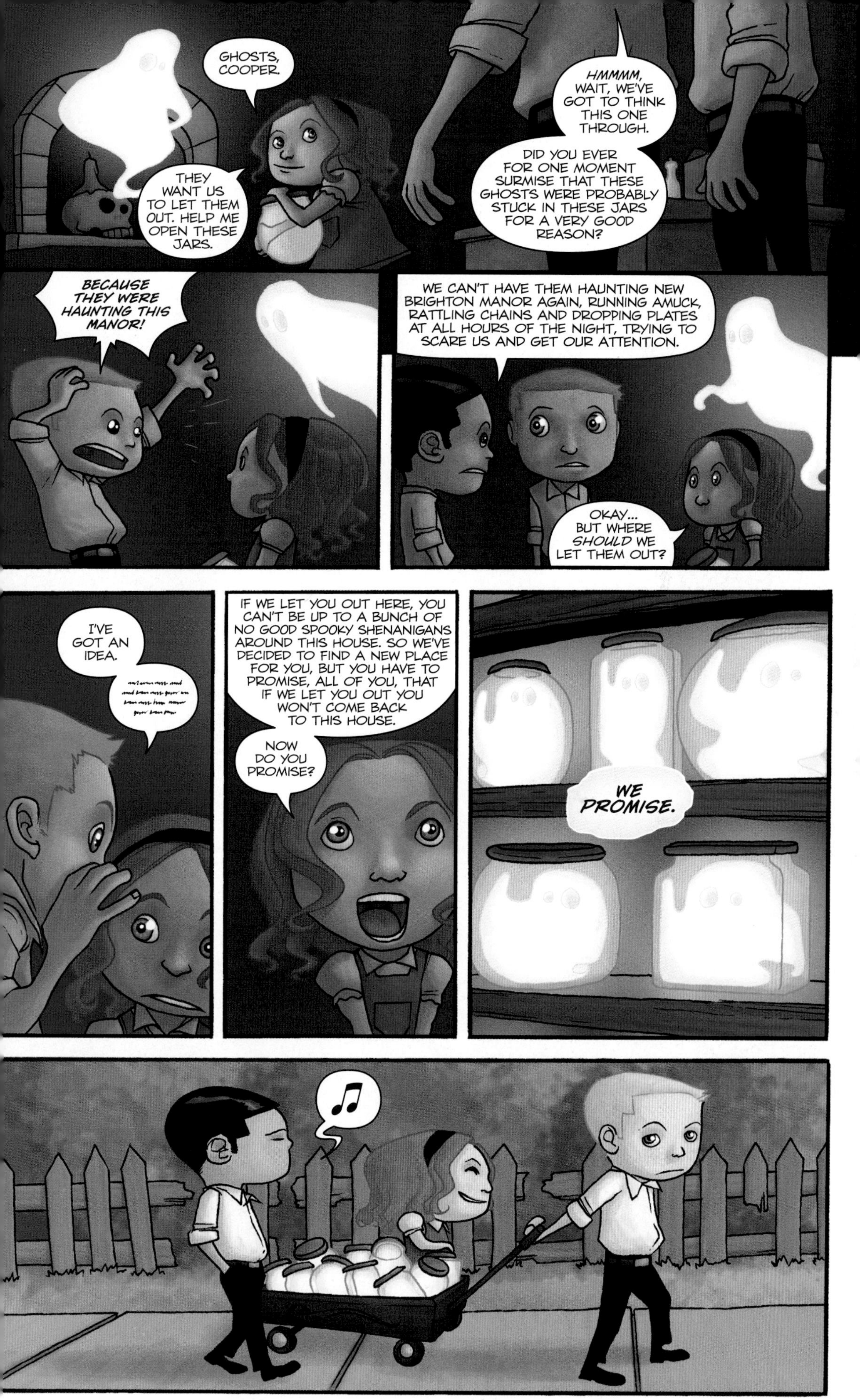
GHOSTS, COOPER.
THEY WANT US TO LET THEM OUT. HELP ME OPEN THESE JARS.
HMMMM, WAIT, WE'VE GOT TO THINK THIS ONE THROUGH.
DID YOU EVER FOR ONE MOMENT SURMISE THAT THESE GHOSTS WERE PROBABLY STUCK IN THESE JARS FOR A VERY GOOD REASON?
BECAUSE THEY WERE HAUNTING THIS MANOR!
WE CAN'T HAVE THEM HAUNTING NEW BRIGHTON MANOR AGAIN, RUNNING AMUCK, RATTLING CHAINS AND DROPPING PLATES AT ALL HOURS OF THE NIGHT, TRYING TO SCARE US AND GET OUR ATTENTION.
OKAY... BUT WHERE SHOULD WE LET THEM OUT?
I'VE GOT AN IDEA.
IF WE LET YOU OUT HERE, YOU CAN'T BE UP TO A BUNCH OF NO GOOD SPOOKY SHENANIGANS AROUND THIS HOUSE. SO WE'VE DECIDED TO FIND A NEW PLACE FOR YOU, BUT YOU HAVE TO PROMISE, ALL OF YOU, THAT IF WE LET YOU OUT YOU WON'T COME BACK TO THIS HOUSE.
NOW DO YOU PROMISE?
WE PROMISE.
♫

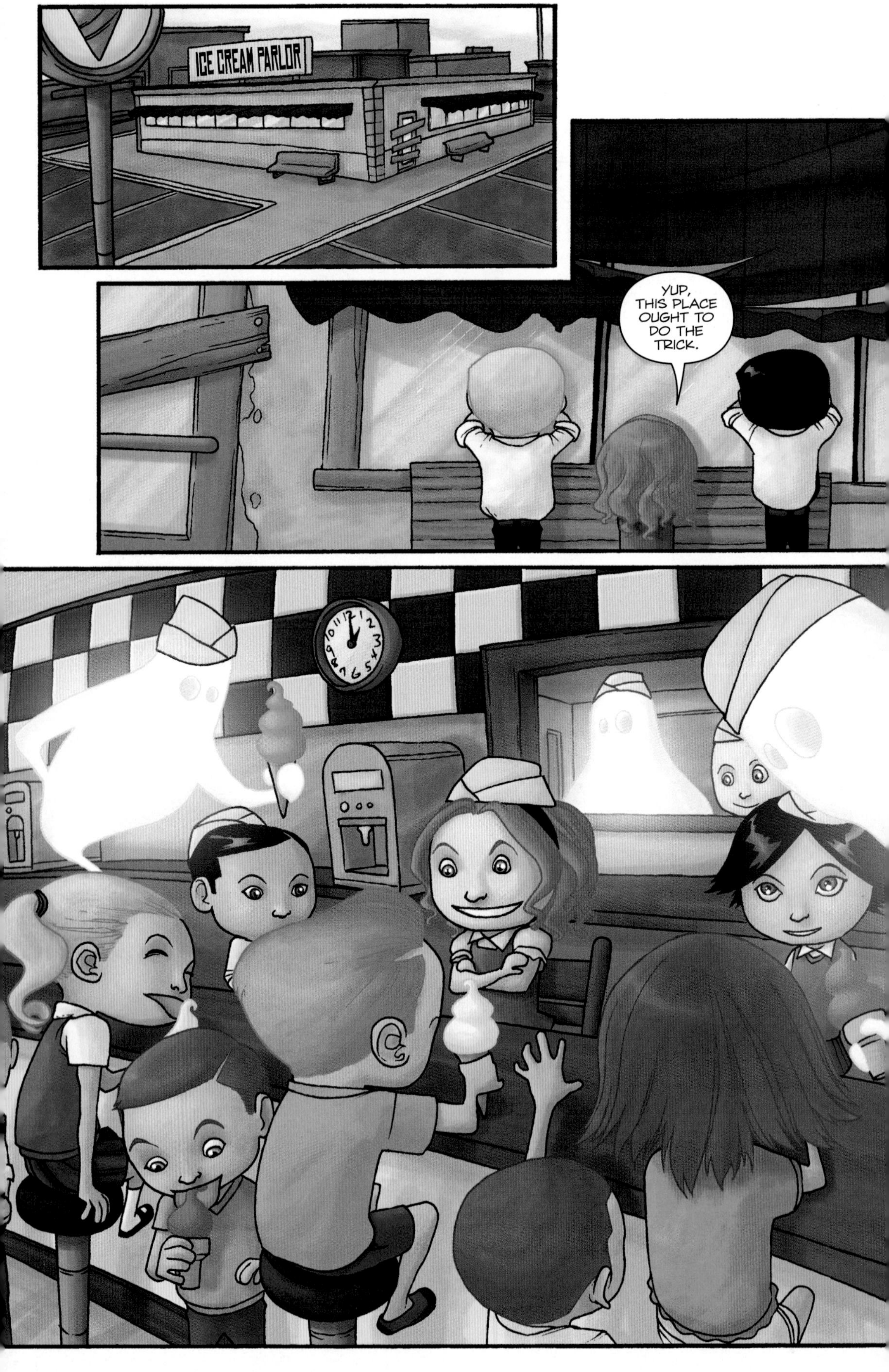
ICE CREAM PARLOR
YUP, THIS PLACE OUGHT TO DO THE TRICK.

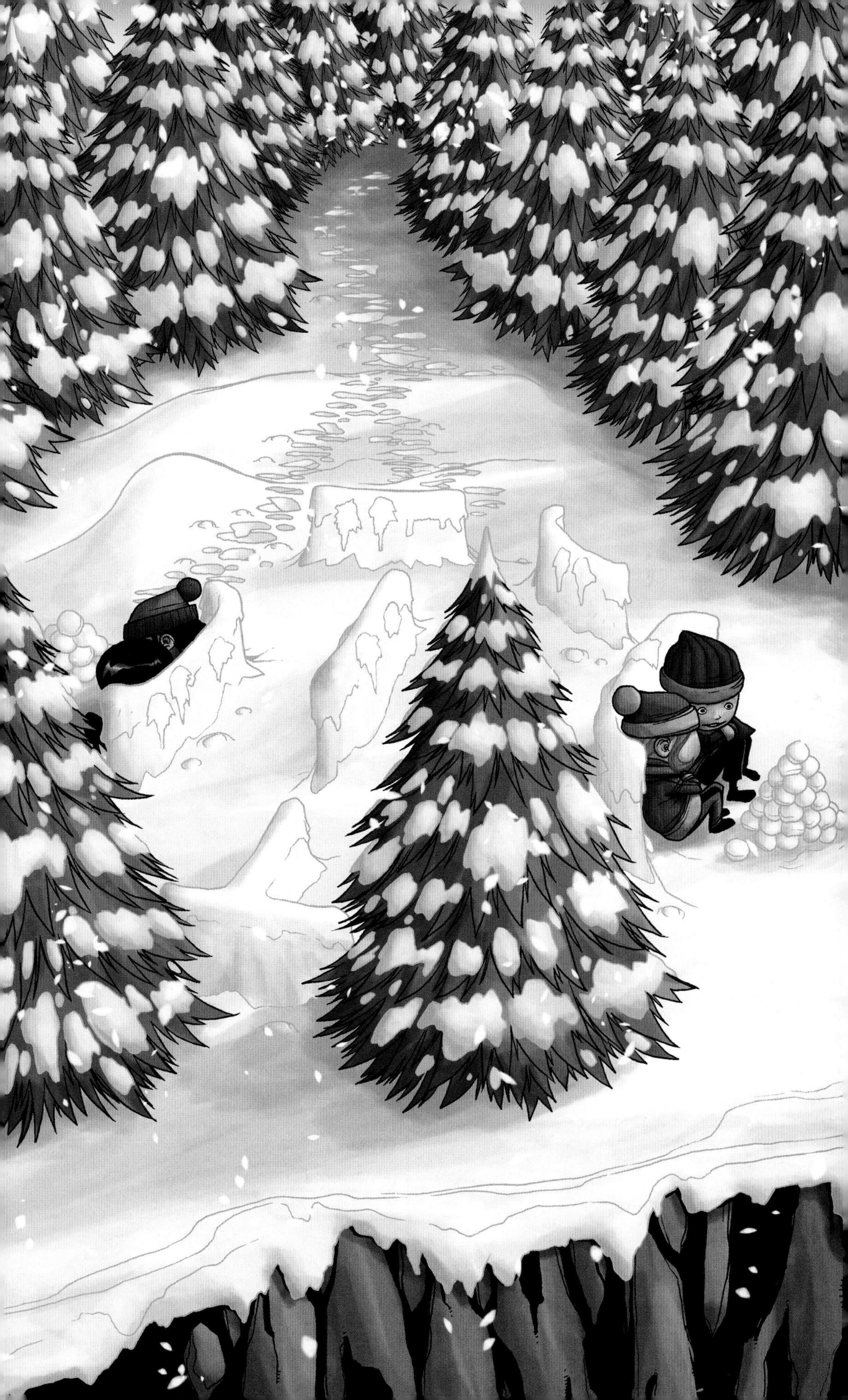

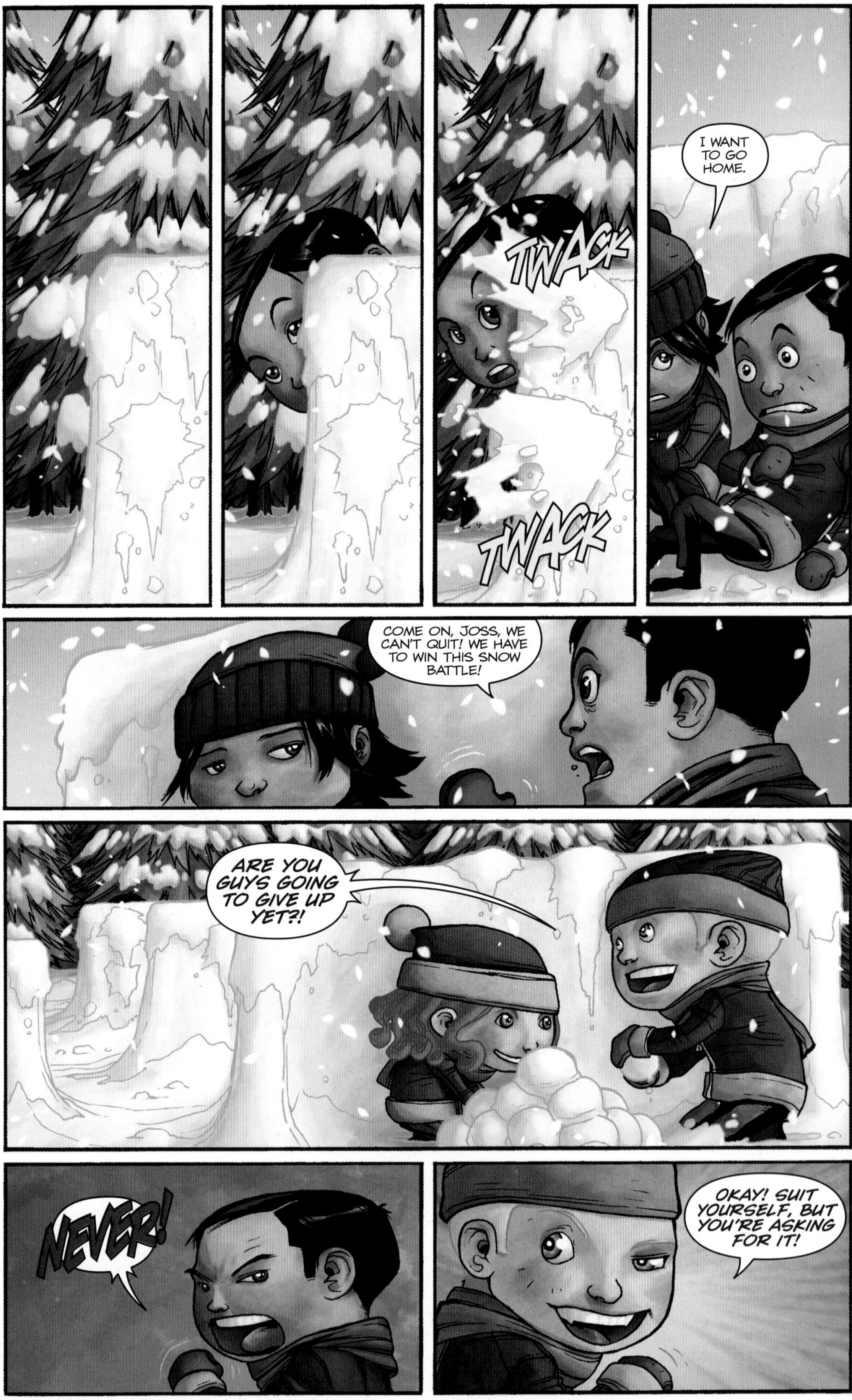

TWACK
TWACK
I WANT TO GO HOME.
COME ON, JOSS, WE CAN'T QUIT! WE HAVE TO WIN THIS SNOW BATTLE!
ARE YOU GUYS GOING TO GIVE UP YET?!
NEVER!
OKAY! SUIT YOURSELF, BUT YOU'RE ASKING FOR IT!

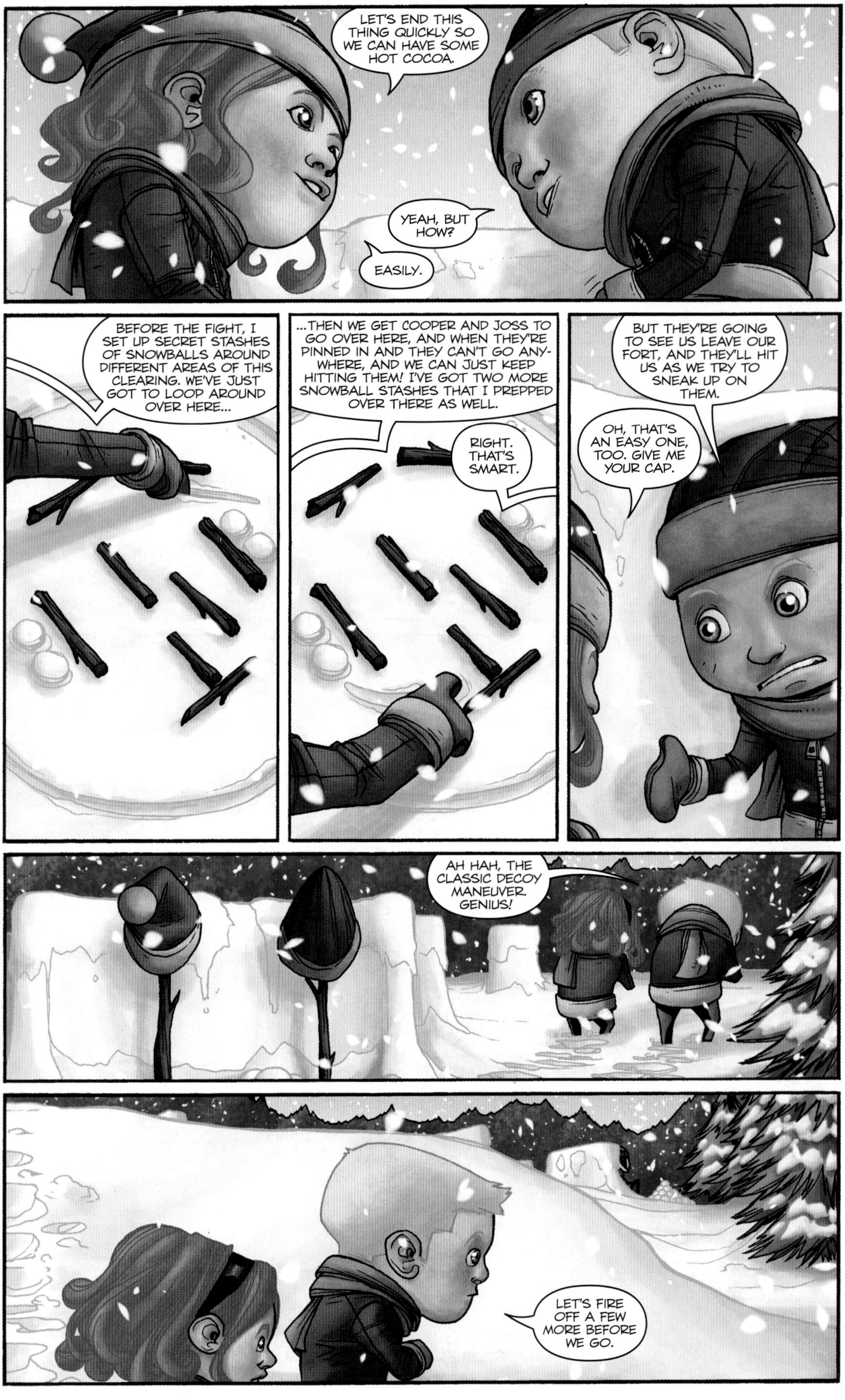
LET'S END THIS THING QUICKLY SO WE CAN HAVE SOME HOT COCOA.
YEAH, BUT HOW?
EASILY.
BEFORE THE FIGHT, I SET UP SECRET STASHES OF SNOWBALLS AROUND DIFFERENT AREAS OF THIS CLEARING. WE'VE JUST GOT TO LOOP AROUND OVER HERE...
...THEN WE GET COOPER AND JOSS TO GO OVER HERE, AND WHEN THEY'RE PINNED IN AND THEY CAN'T GO ANY-WHERE, AND WE CAN JUST KEEP HITTING THEM! I'VE GOT TWO MORE SNOWBALL STASHES THAT I PREPPED OVER THERE AS WELL.
RIGHT. THAT'S SMART.
BUT THEY'RE GOING TO SEE US LEAVE OUR FORT, AND THEY'LL HIT US AS WE TRY TO SNEAK UP ON THEM.
OH, THAT'S AN EASY ONE, TOO. GIVE ME YOUR CAP.
AH HAH, THE CLASSIC DECOY MANEUVER. GENIUS!
LET'S FIRE OFF A FEW MORE BEFORE WE GO.

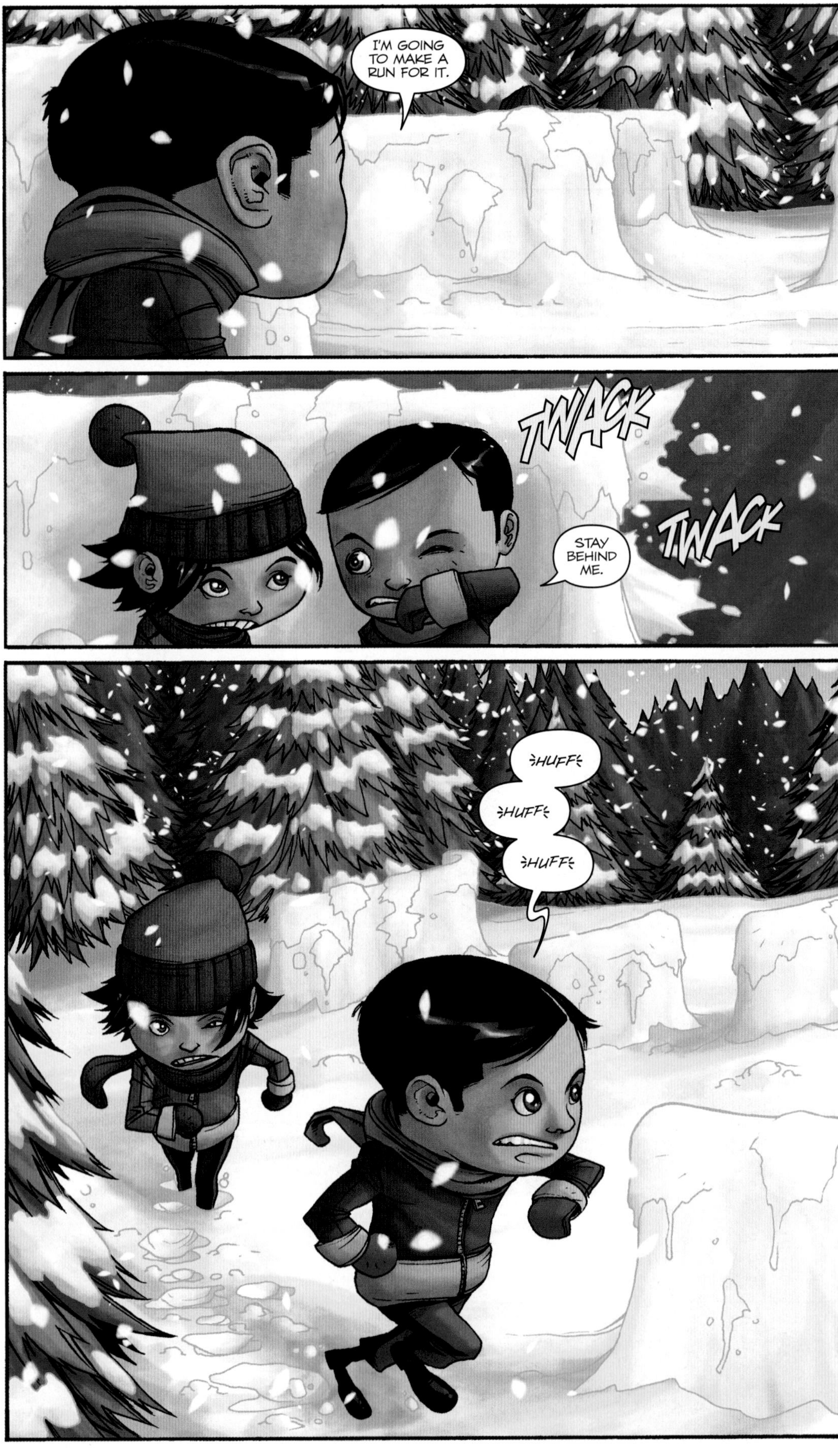

I'M GOING TO MAKE A RUN FOR IT.
TWACK
TWACK
STAY BEHIND ME.
HUFF
HUFF
HUFF

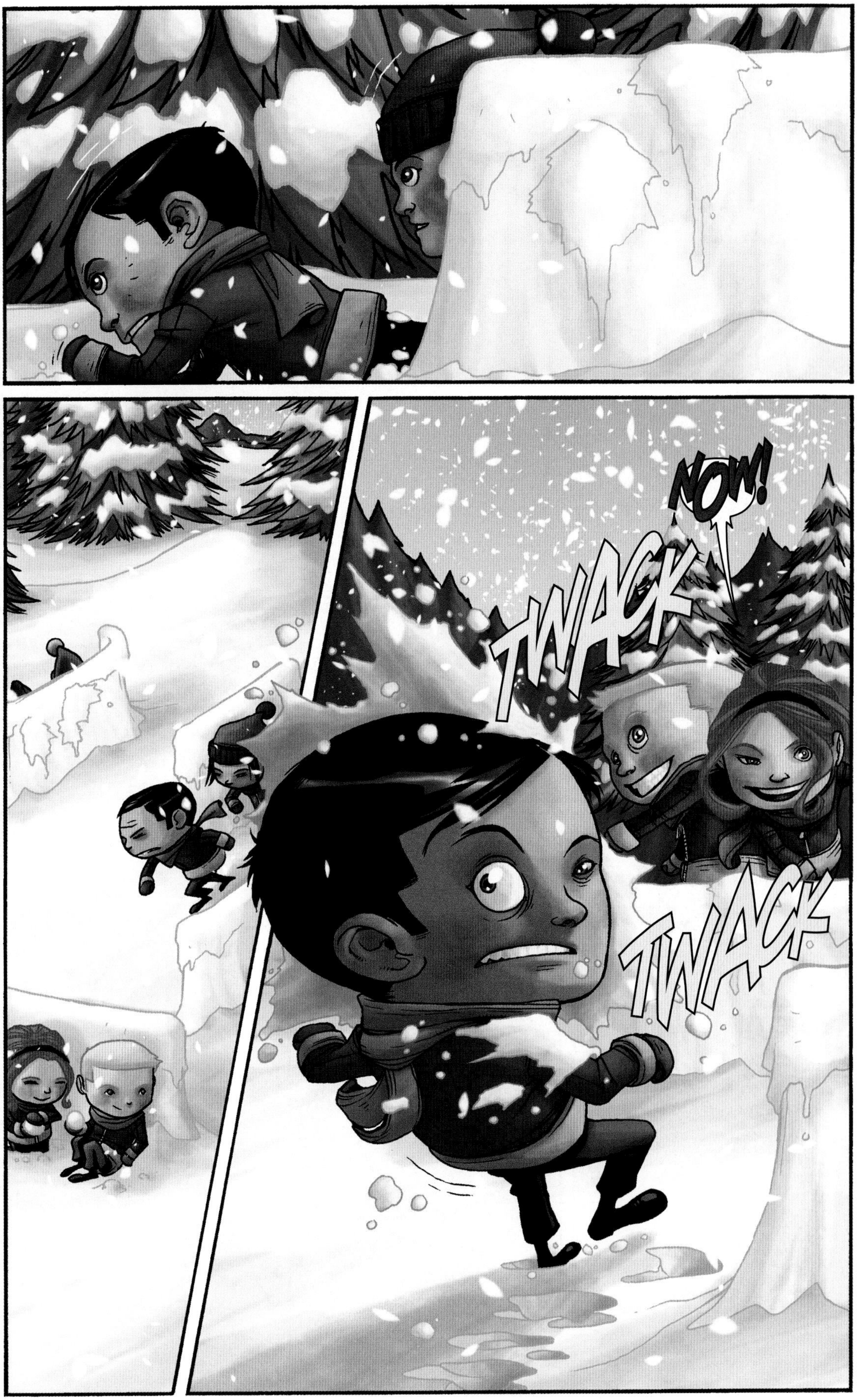
NOW!
TWACK
TWACK

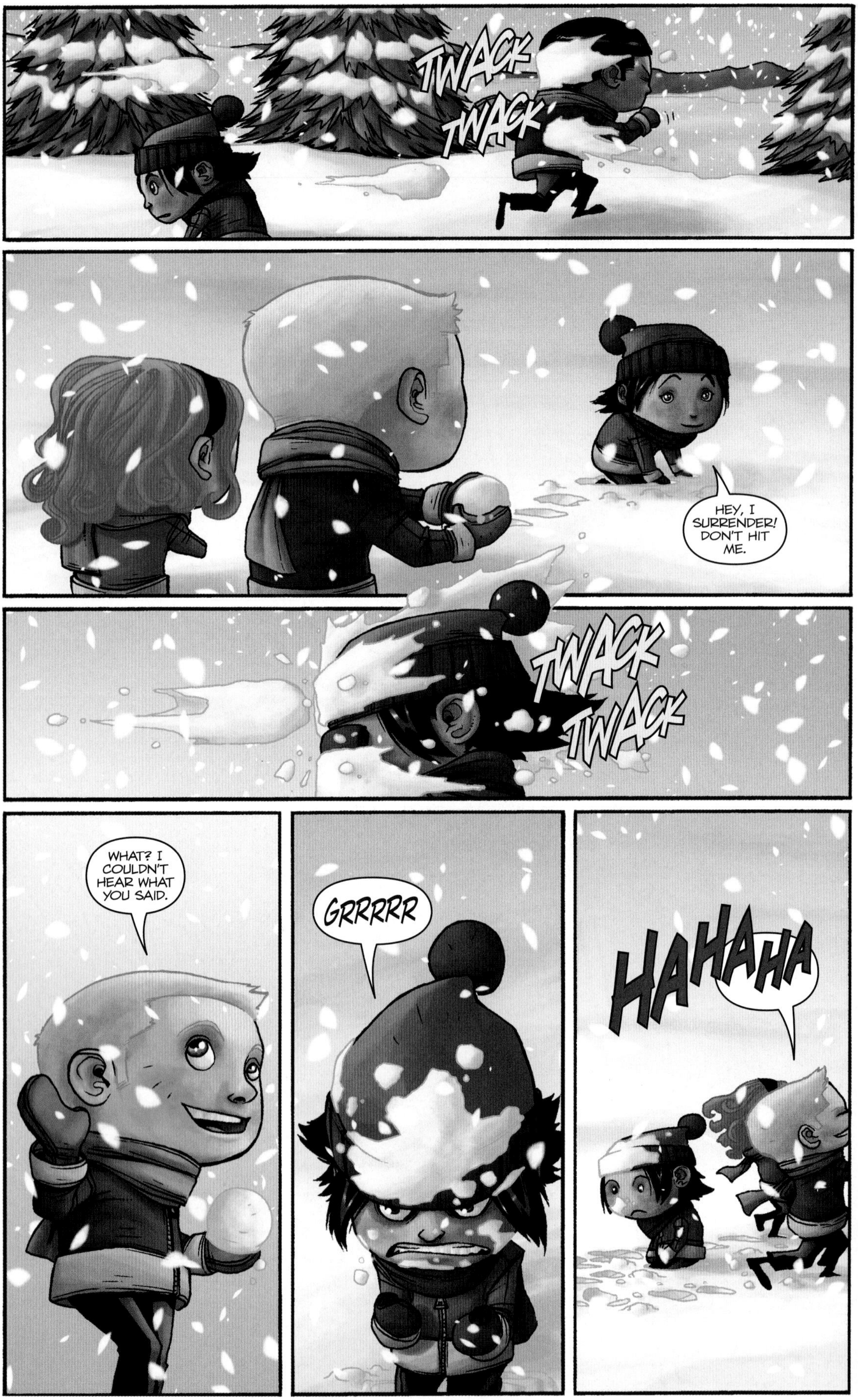
TWACK
TWACK
HEY, I SURRENDER! DON'T HIT ME.
TWACK
TWACK
WHAT? I COULDN'T HEAR WHAT YOU SAID.
GRRRRR
HAHAHA

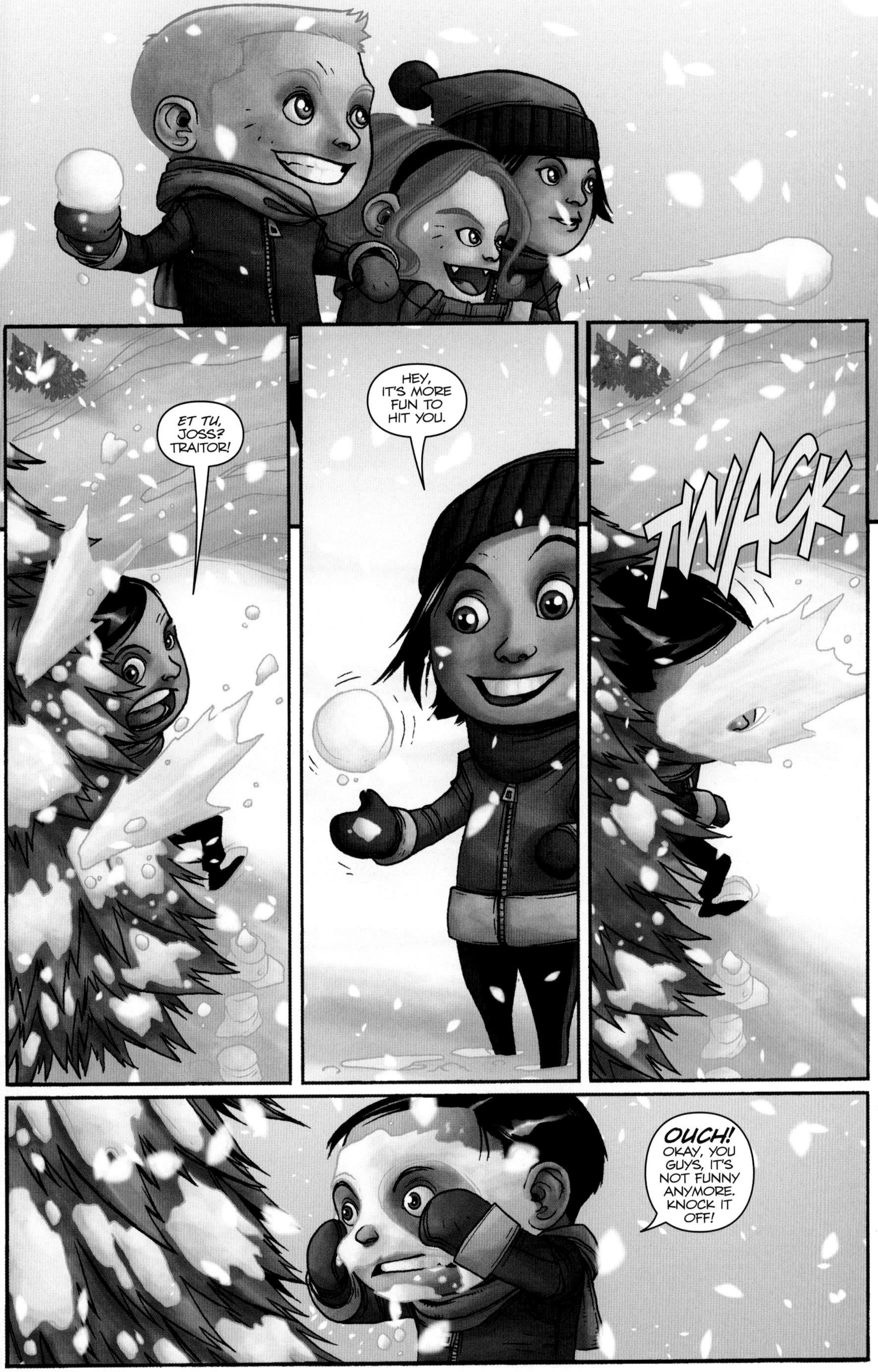
ET TU, JOSS? TRAITOR!
HEY, IT'S MORE FUN TO HIT YOU.
TWACK
OUCH! OKAY, YOU GUYS, IT'S NOT FUNNY ANYMORE. KNOCK IT OFF!

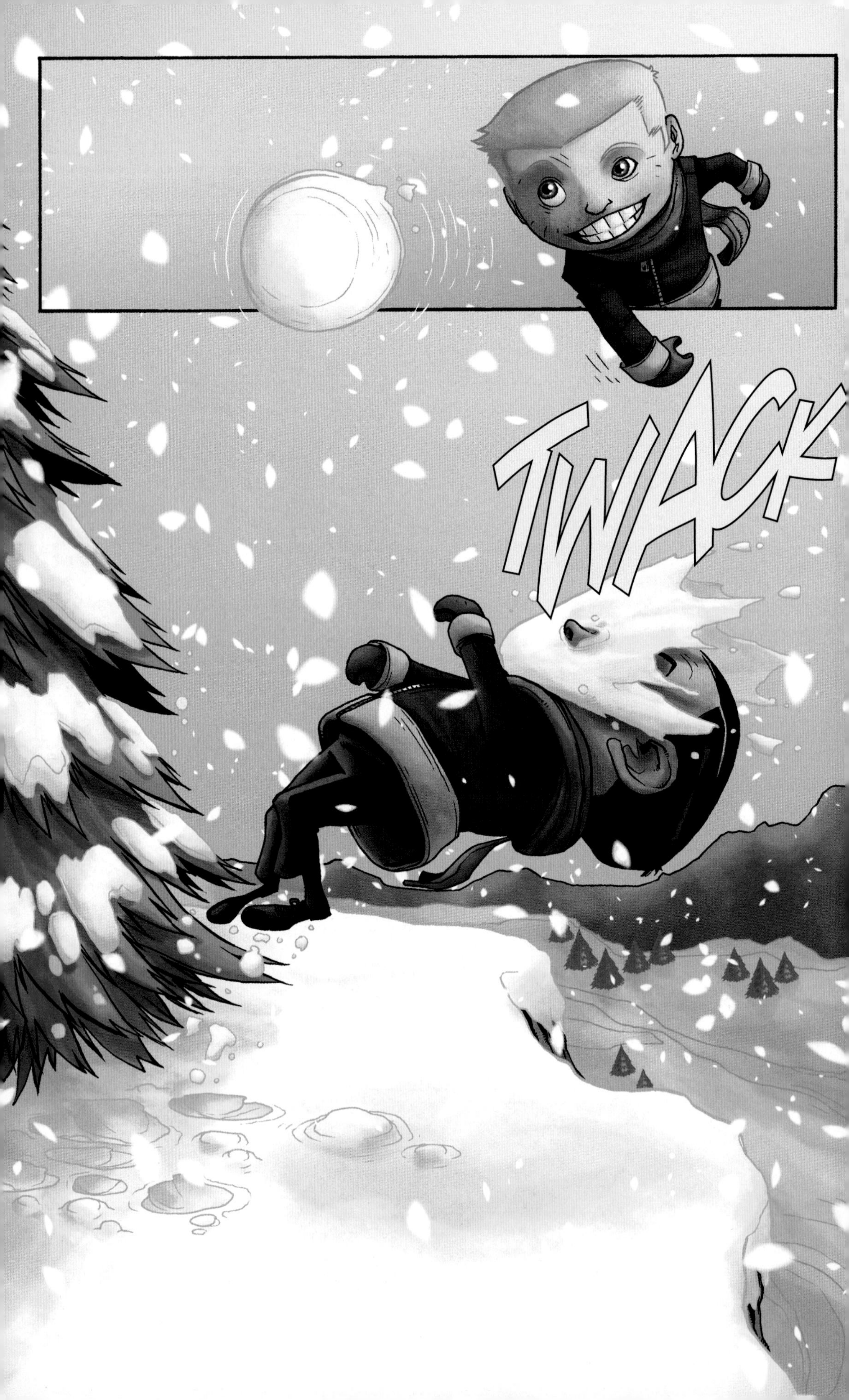
TWACK

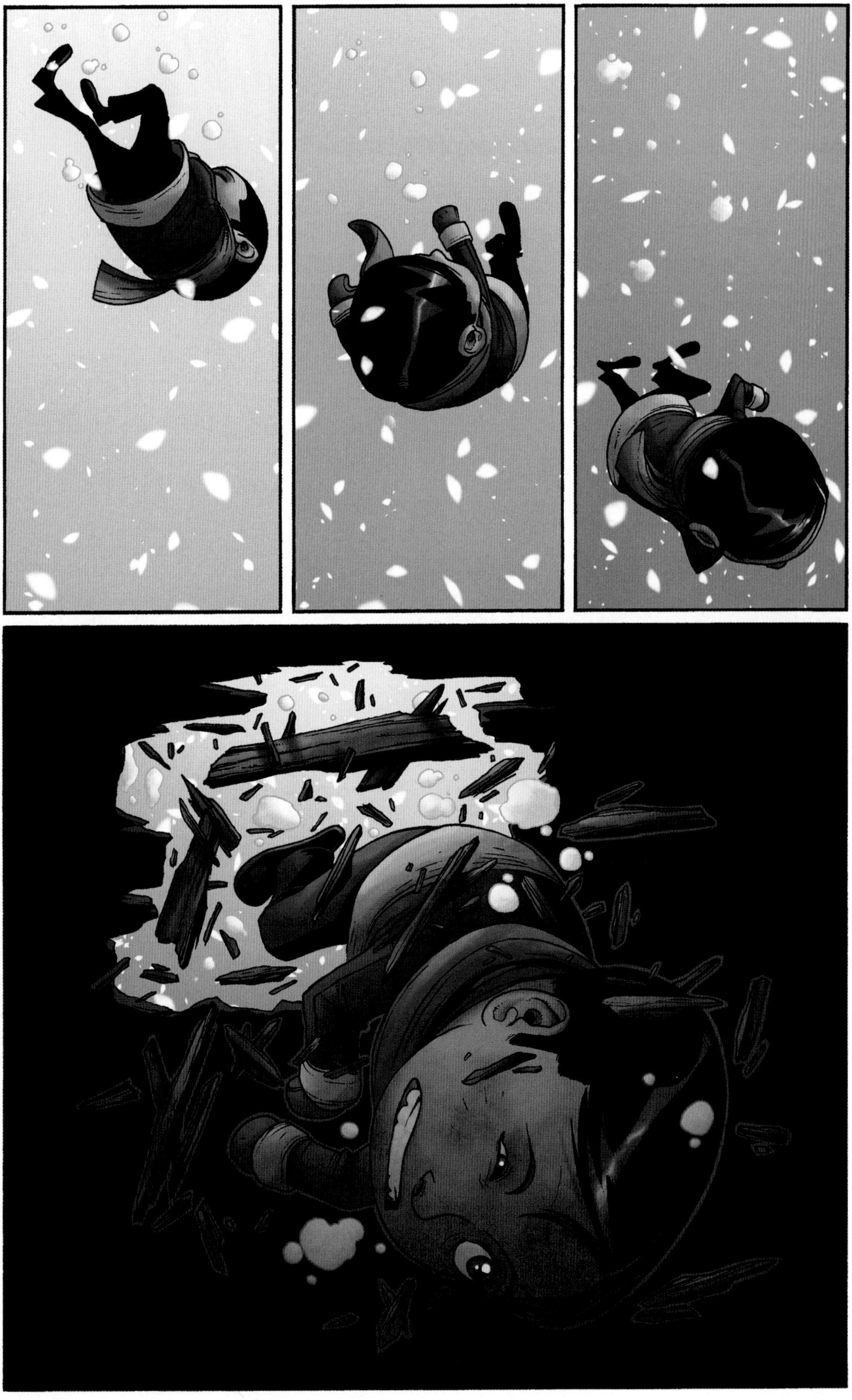

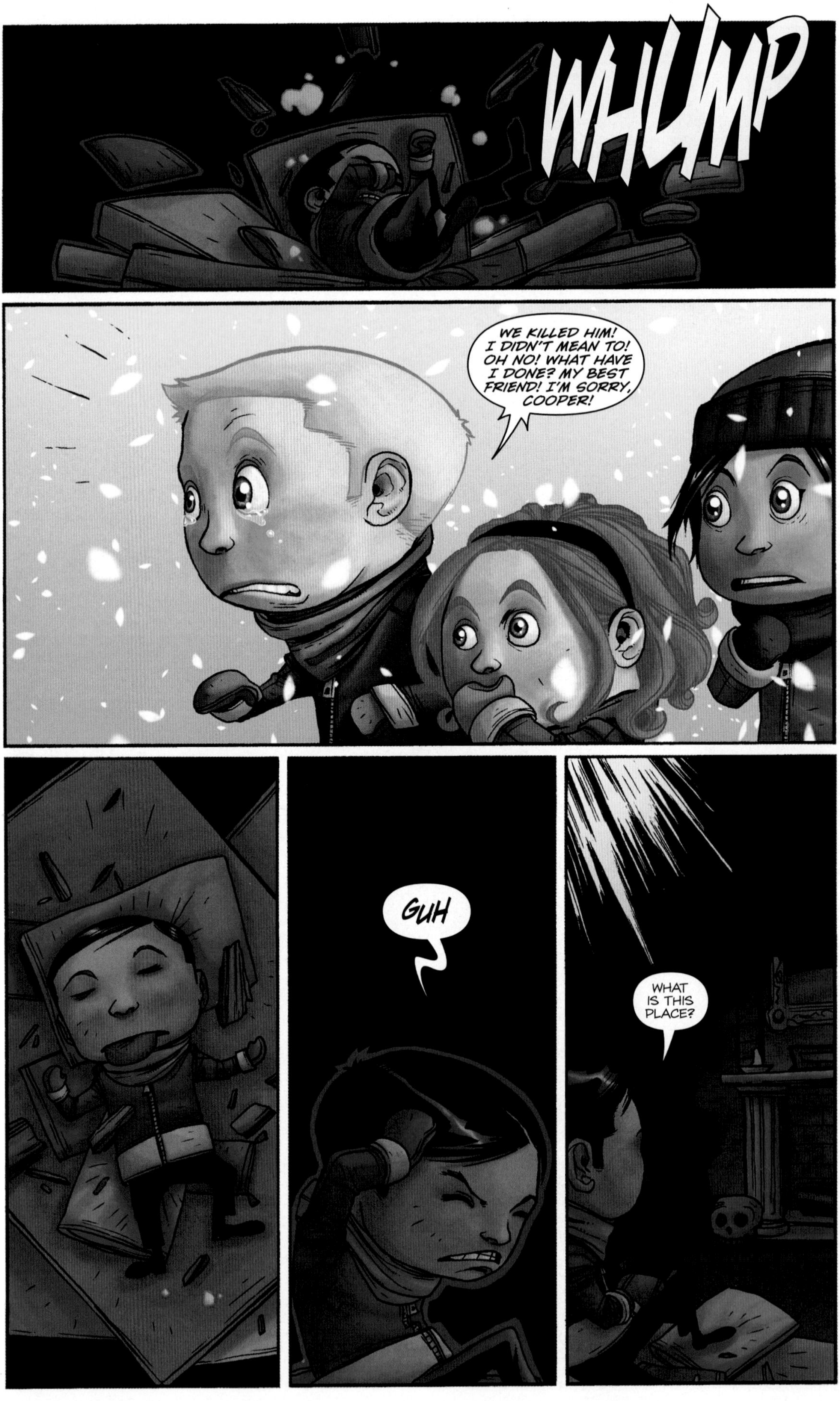
WHUMP
WE KILLED HIM! I DIDN'T MEAN TO! OH NO! WHAT HAVE I DONE? MY BEST FRIEND! I'M SORRY, COOPER!
GUH
WHAT IS THIS PLACE?

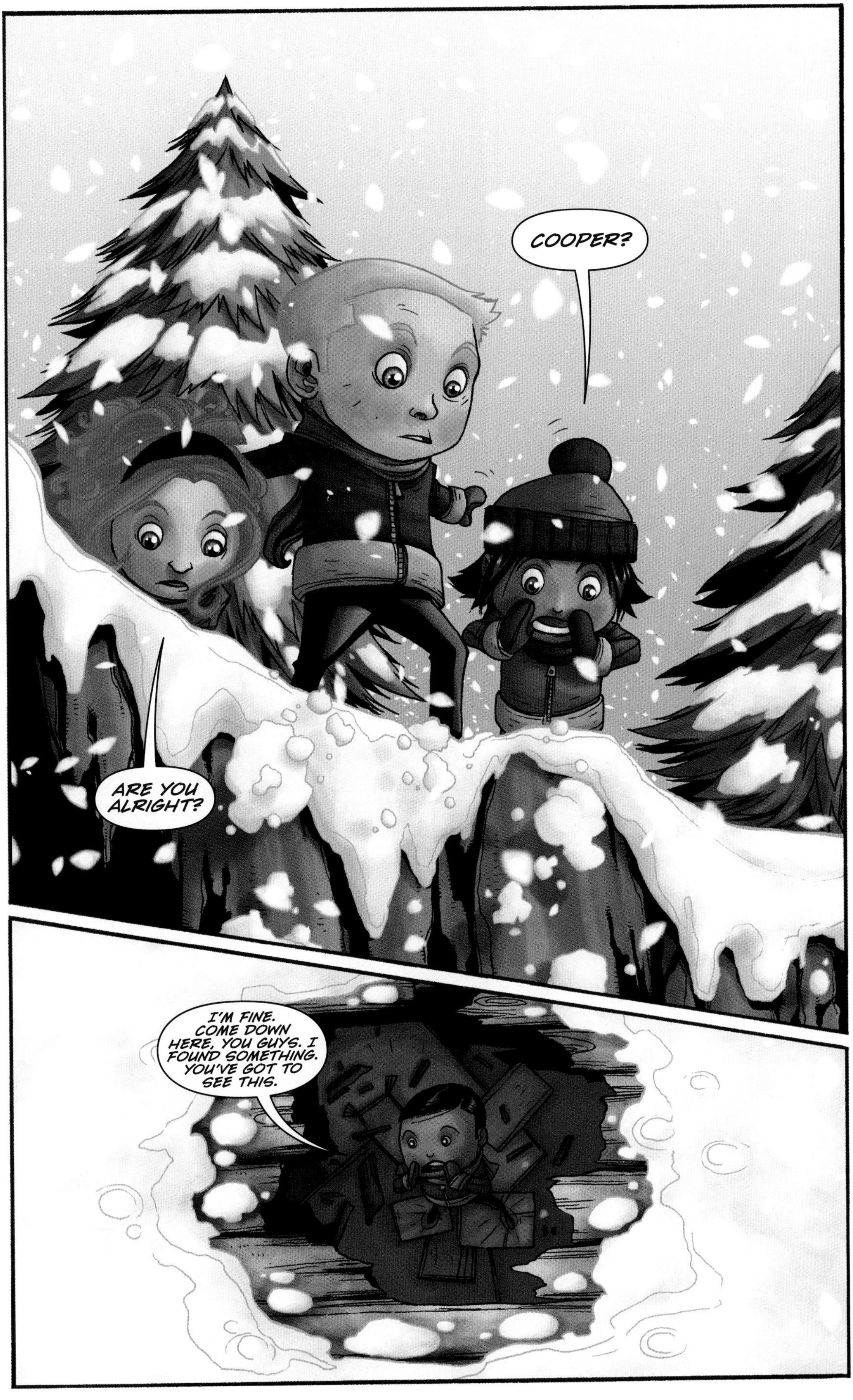
COOPER?
ARE YOU ALRIGHT?
I'M FINE. COME DOWN HERE, YOU GUYS. I FOUND SOMETHING. YOU'VE GOT TO SEE THIS.

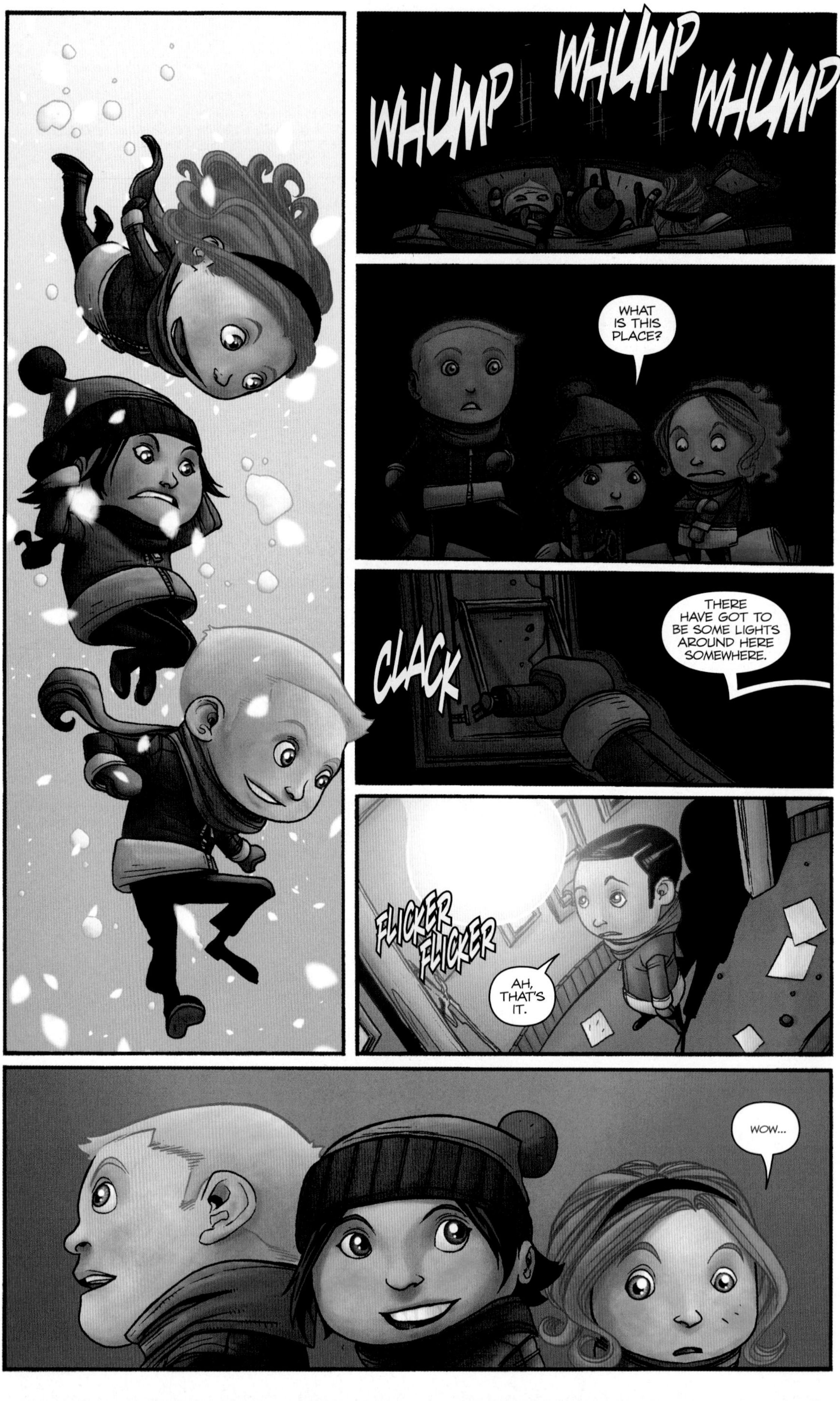
WHUMP WHUMP WHUMP
WHAT IS THIS PLACE?
CLACK
THERE HAVE GOT TO BE SOME LIGHTS AROUND HERE SOMEWHERE.
FLICKER FLICKER
AH, THAT'S IT.
WOW...

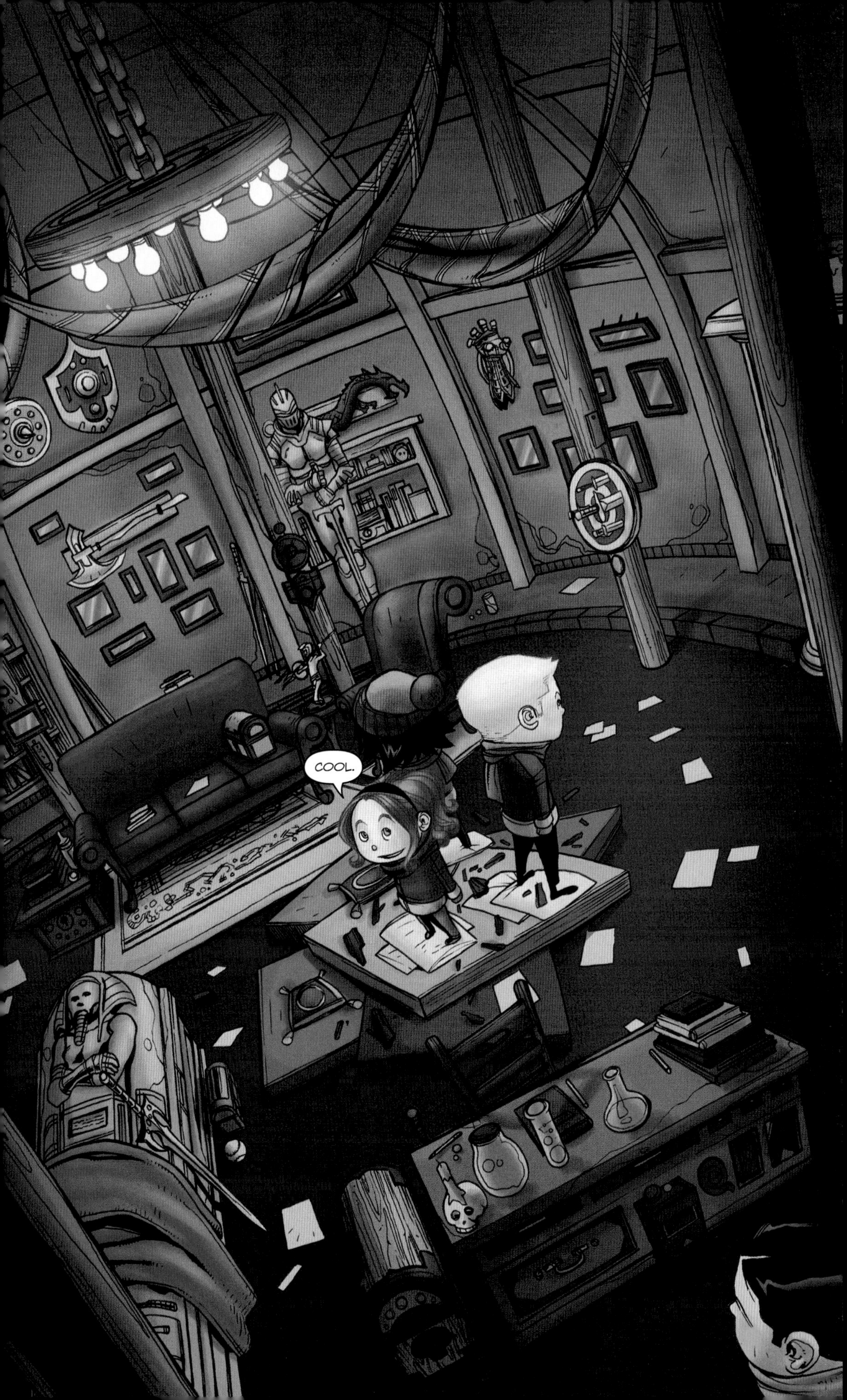
COOL.

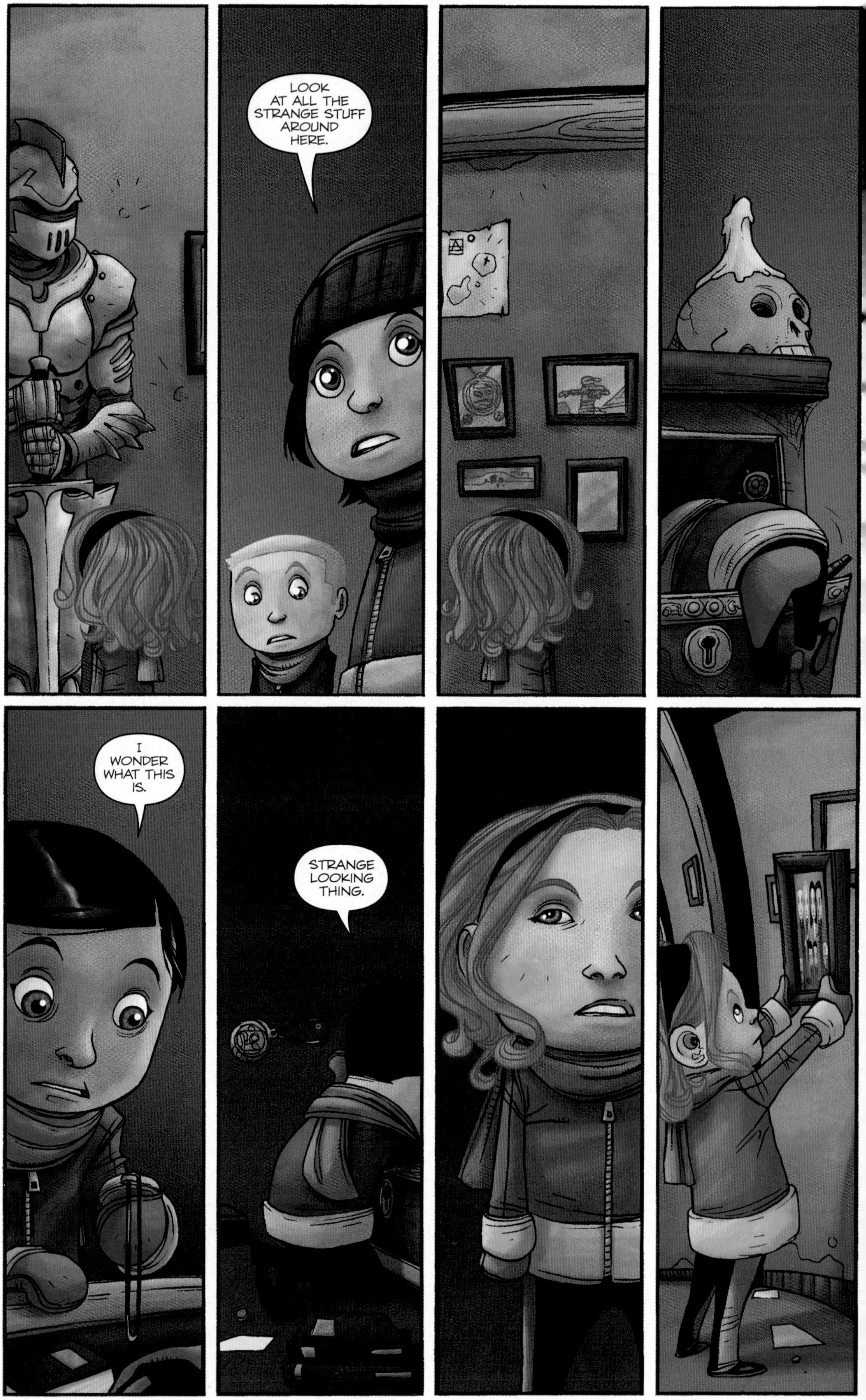
LOOK AT ALL THE STRANGE STUFF AROUND HERE.
I WONDER WHAT THIS IS.
STRANGE LOOKING THING.

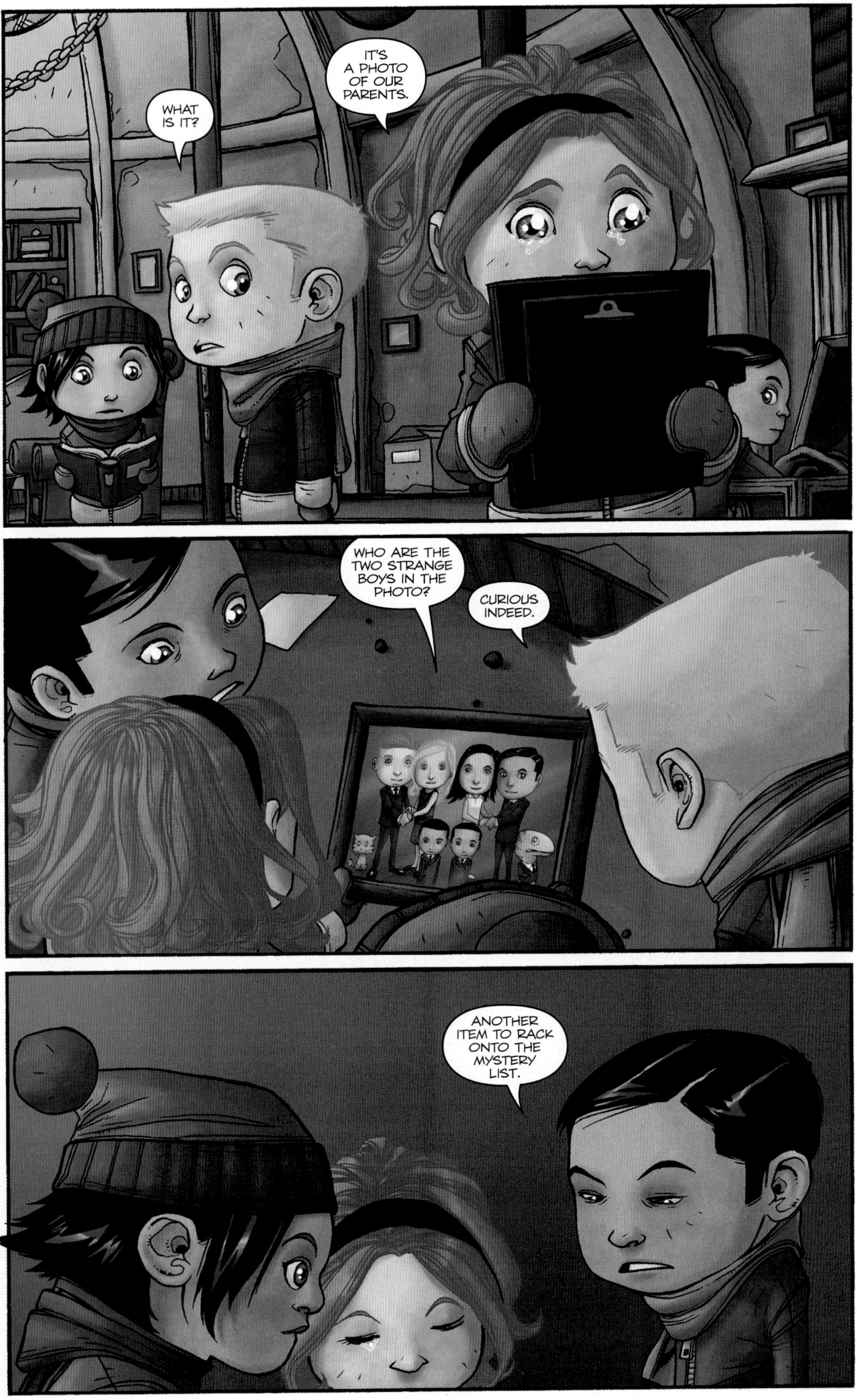
WHAT IS IT?
IT'S A PHOTO OF OUR PARENTS.
WHO ARE THE TWO STRANGE BOYS IN THE PHOTO?
CURIOUS INDEED.
ANOTHER ITEM TO RACK ONTO THE MYSTERY LIST.

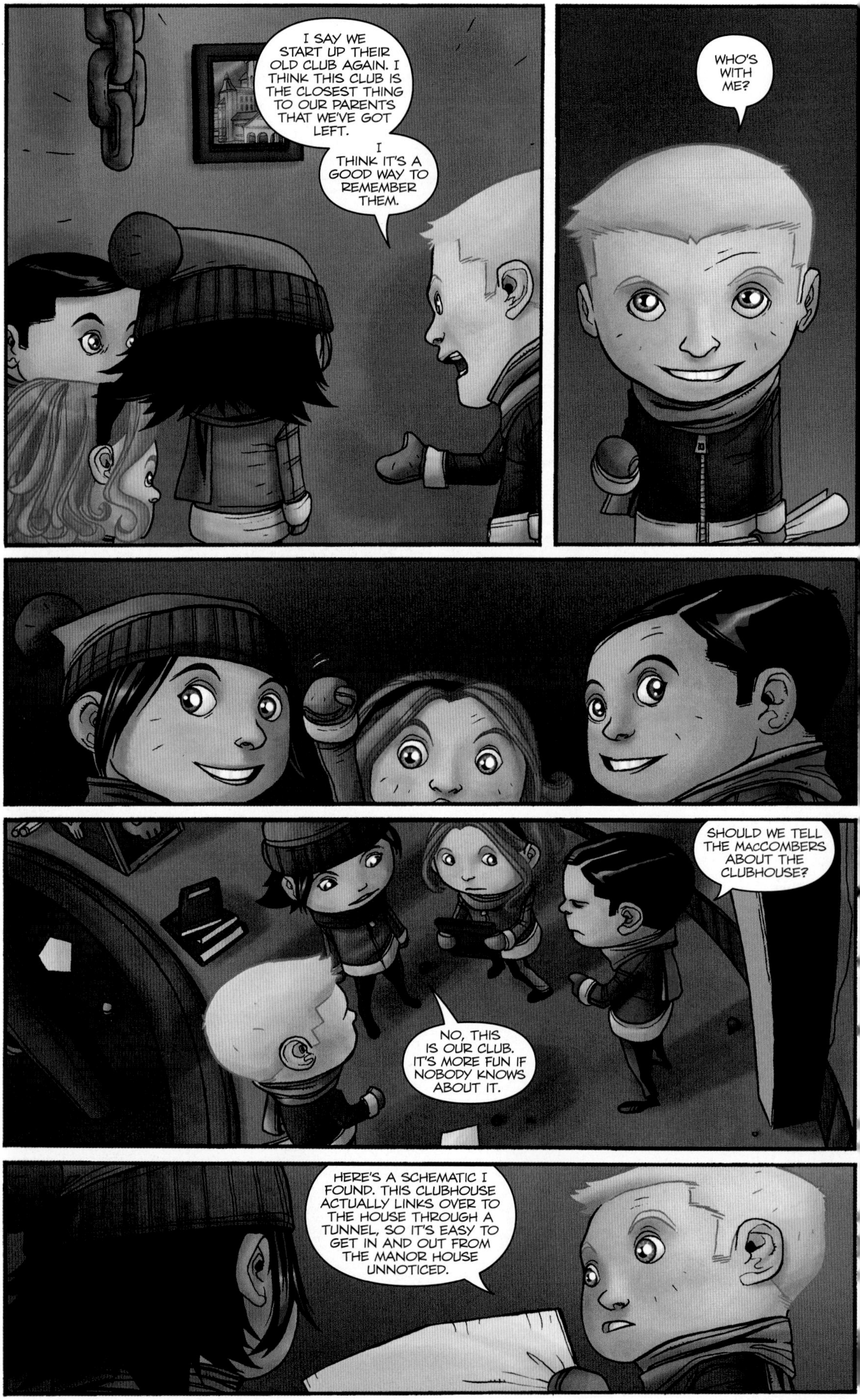
I SAY WE START UP THEIR OLD CLUB AGAIN. I THINK THIS CLUB IS THE CLOSEST THING TO OUR PARENTS THAT WE'VE GOT LEFT.
I THINK IT'S A GOOD WAY TO REMEMBER THEM.
WHO'S WITH ME?
SHOULD WE TELL THE MACCOMBERS ABOUT THE CLUBHOUSE?
NO, THIS IS OUR CLUB. IT'S MORE FUN IF NOBODY KNOWS ABOUT IT.
HERE'S A SCHEMATIC I FOUND. THIS CLUBHOUSE ACTUALLY LINKS OVER TO THE HOUSE THROUGH A TUNNEL, SO IT'S EASY TO GET IN AND OUT FROM THE MANOR HOUSE UNNOTICED.

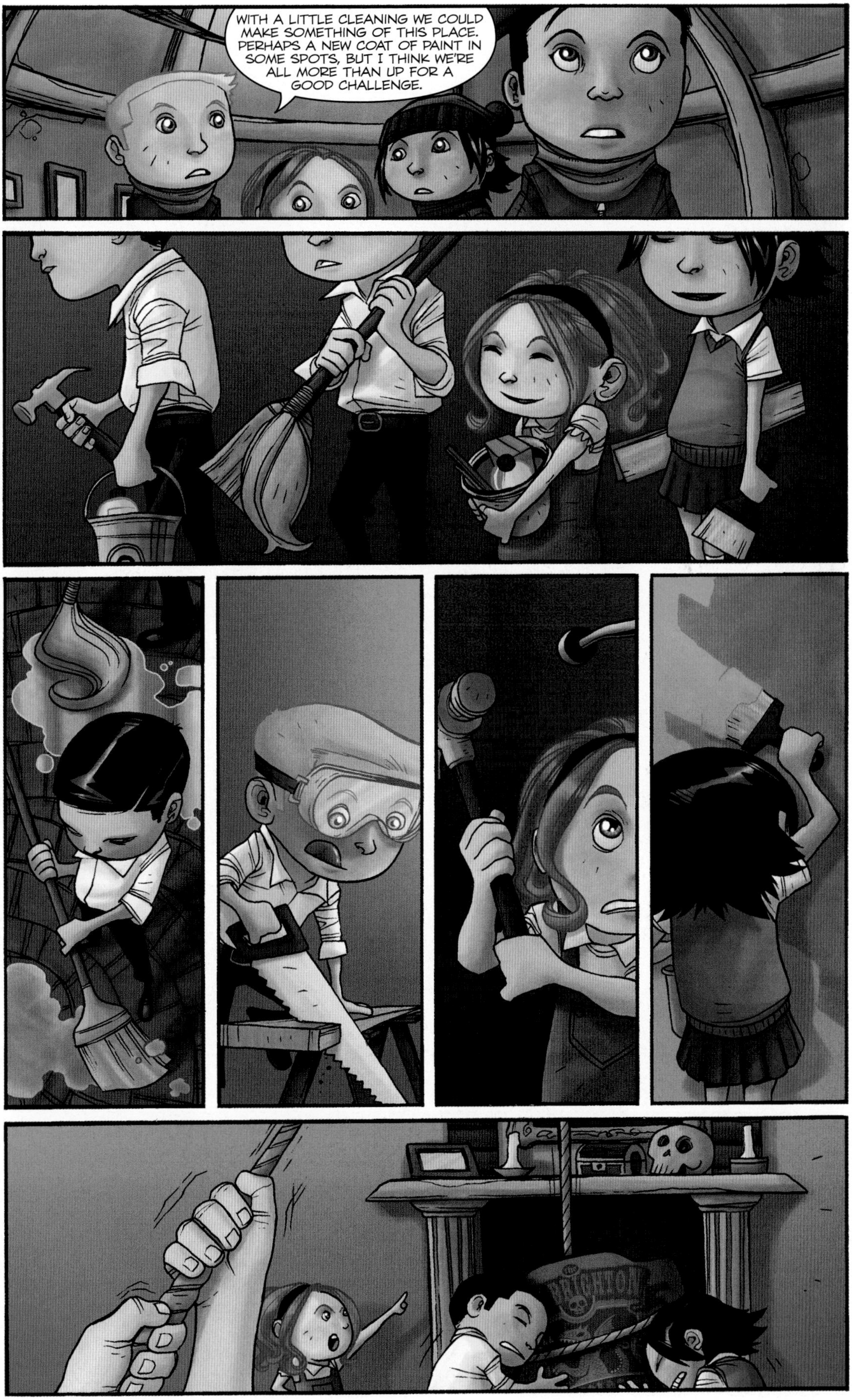
WITH A LITTLE CLEANING WE COULD MAKE SOMETHING OF THIS PLACE. PERHAPS A NEW COAT OF PAINT IN SOME SPOTS, BUT I THINK WE'RE ALL MORE THAN UP FOR A GOOD CHALLENGE.

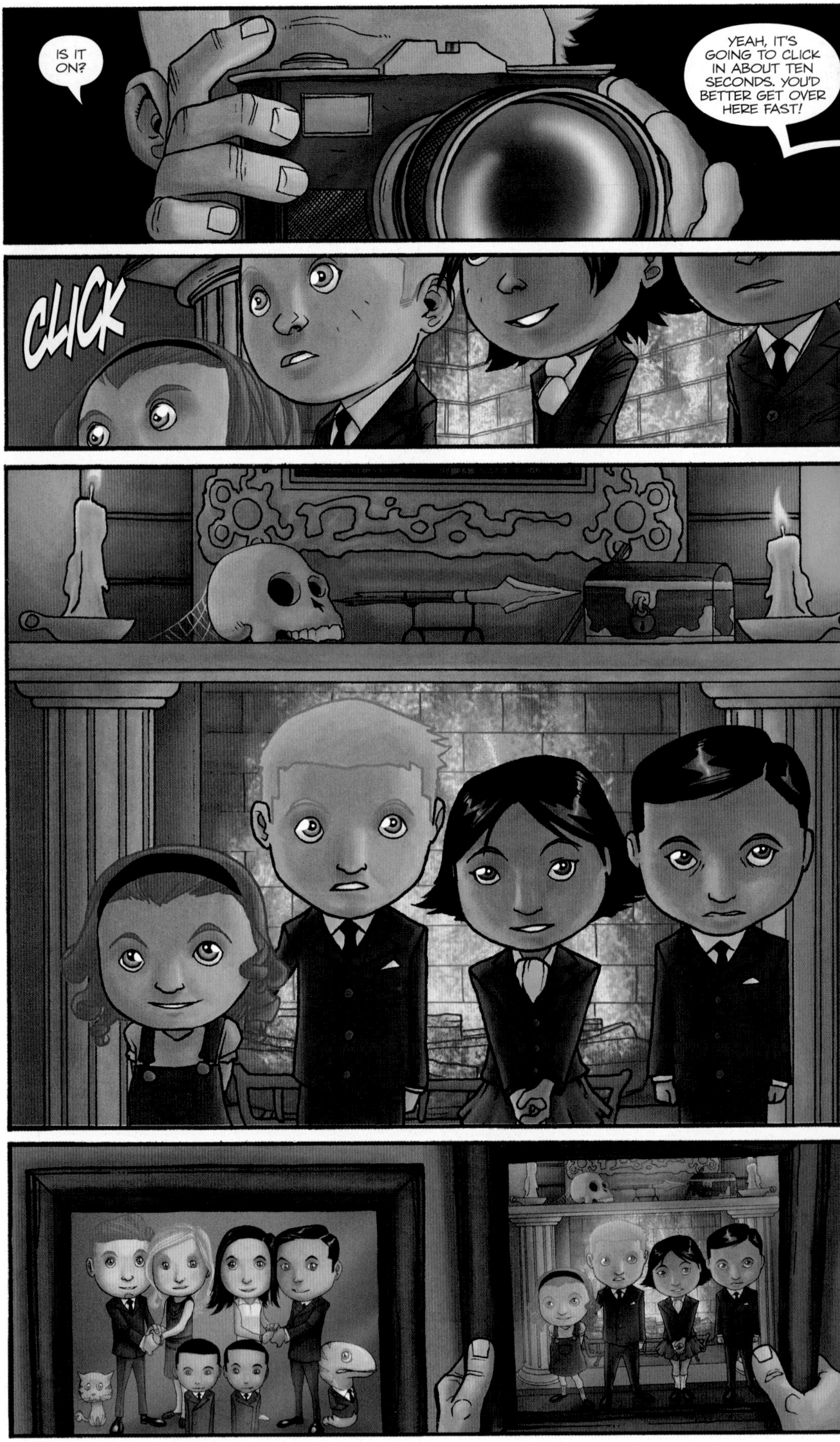
IS IT ON?
YEAH, IT'S GOING TO CLICK IN ABOUT TEN SECONDS. YOU'D BETTER GET OVER HERE FAST!
CLICK

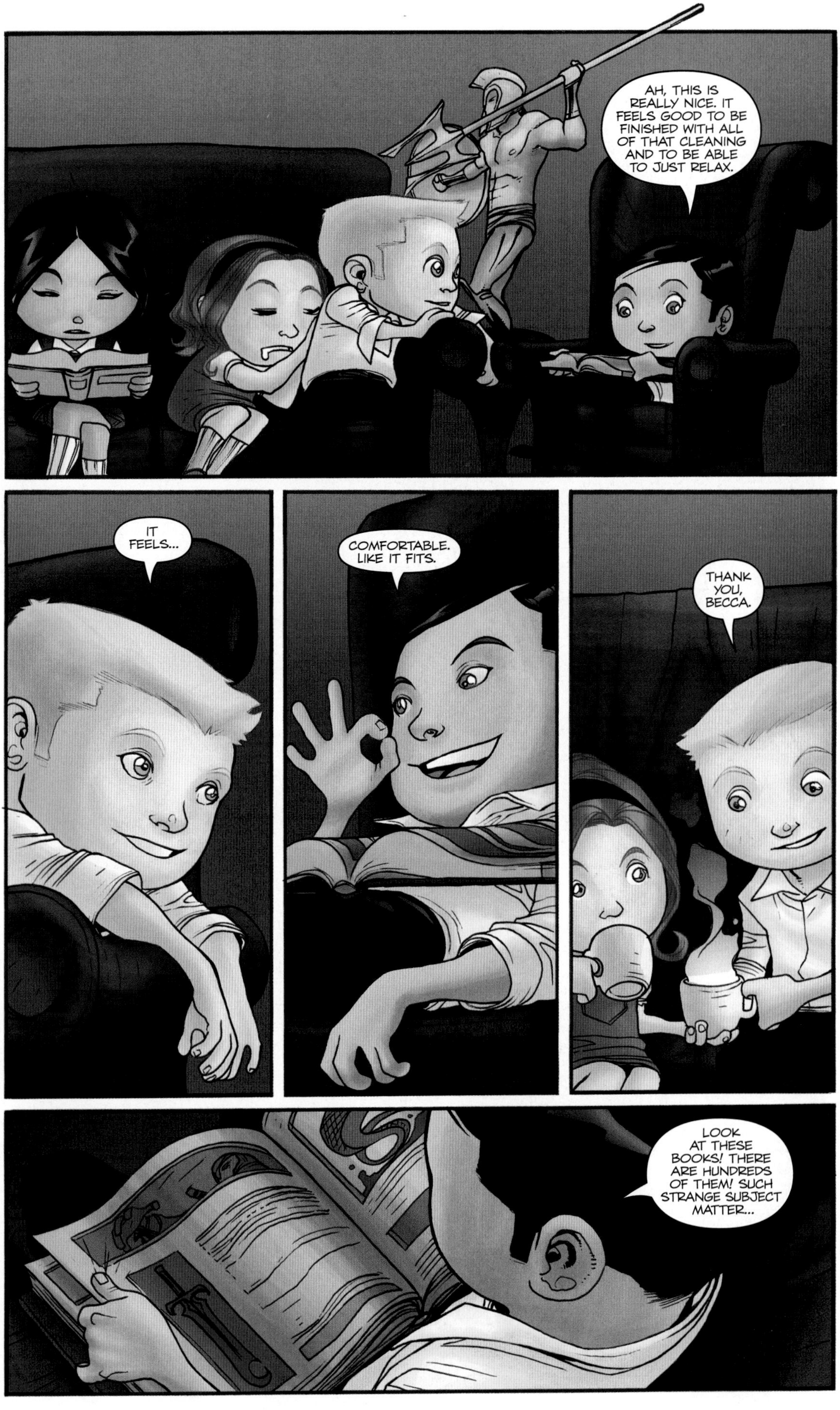
AH, THIS IS REALLY NICE. IT FEELS GOOD TO BE FINISHED WITH ALL OF THAT CLEANING AND TO BE ABLE TO JUST RELAX.
IT FEELS...
COMFORTABLE. LIKE IT FITS.
THANK YOU, BECCA.
LOOK AT THESE BOOKS! THERE ARE HUNDREDS OF THEM! SUCH STRANGE SUBJECT MATTER...

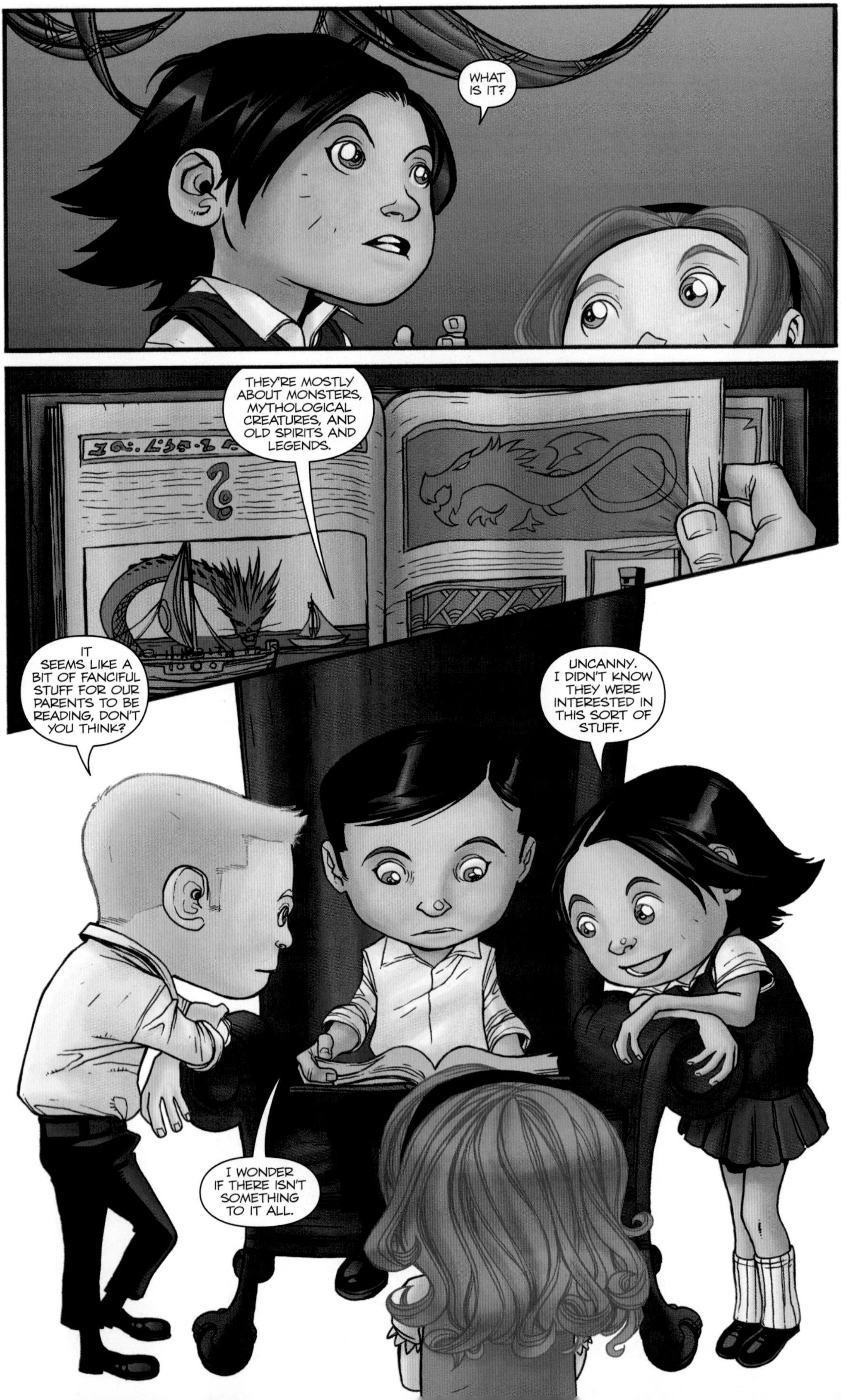
WHAT IS IT?
THEY'RE MOSTLY ABOUT MONSTERS, MYTHOLOGICAL CREATURES, AND OLD SPIRITS AND LEGENDS.
IT SEEMS LIKE A BIT OF FANCIFUL STUFF FOR OUR PARENTS TO BE READING, DON'T YOU THINK?
UNCANNY. I DIDN'T KNOW THEY WERE INTERESTED IN THIS SORT OF STUFF.
I WONDER IF THERE ISN'T SOMETHING TO IT ALL.

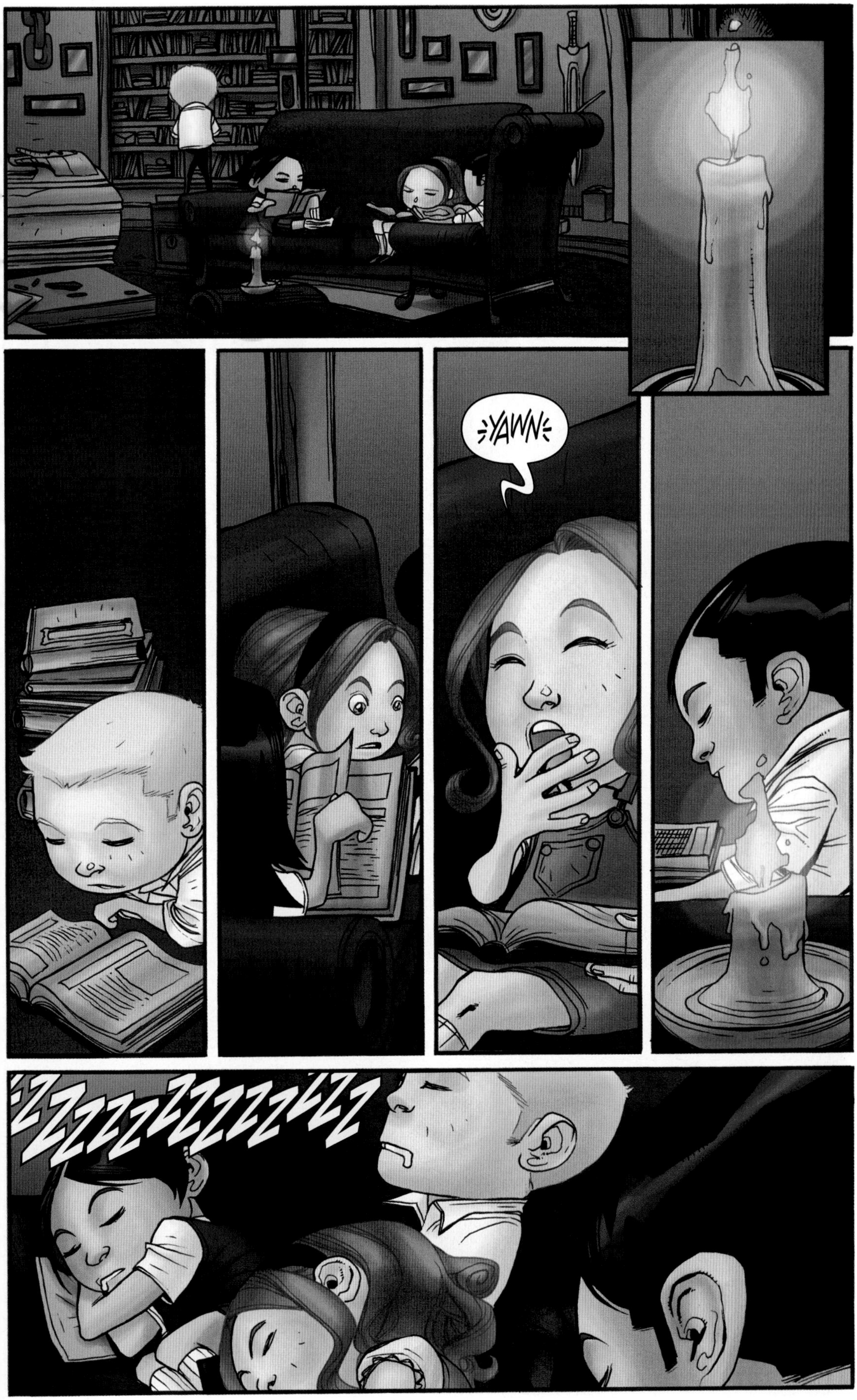
YAWN
ZZZZZZZZZZZZ

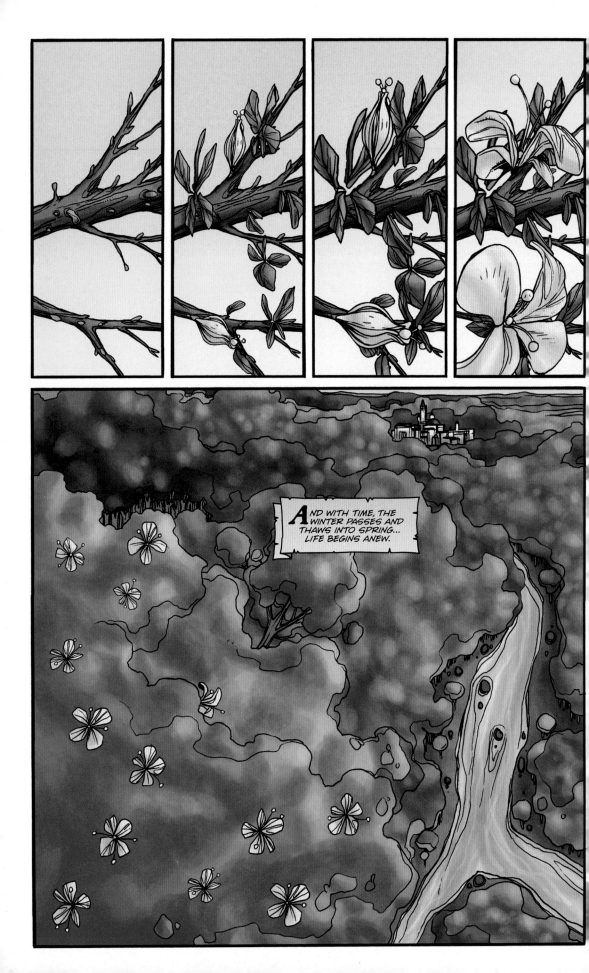

AND WITH TIME, THE WINTER PASSES AND THAWS INTO SPRING... LIFE BEGINS ANEW.

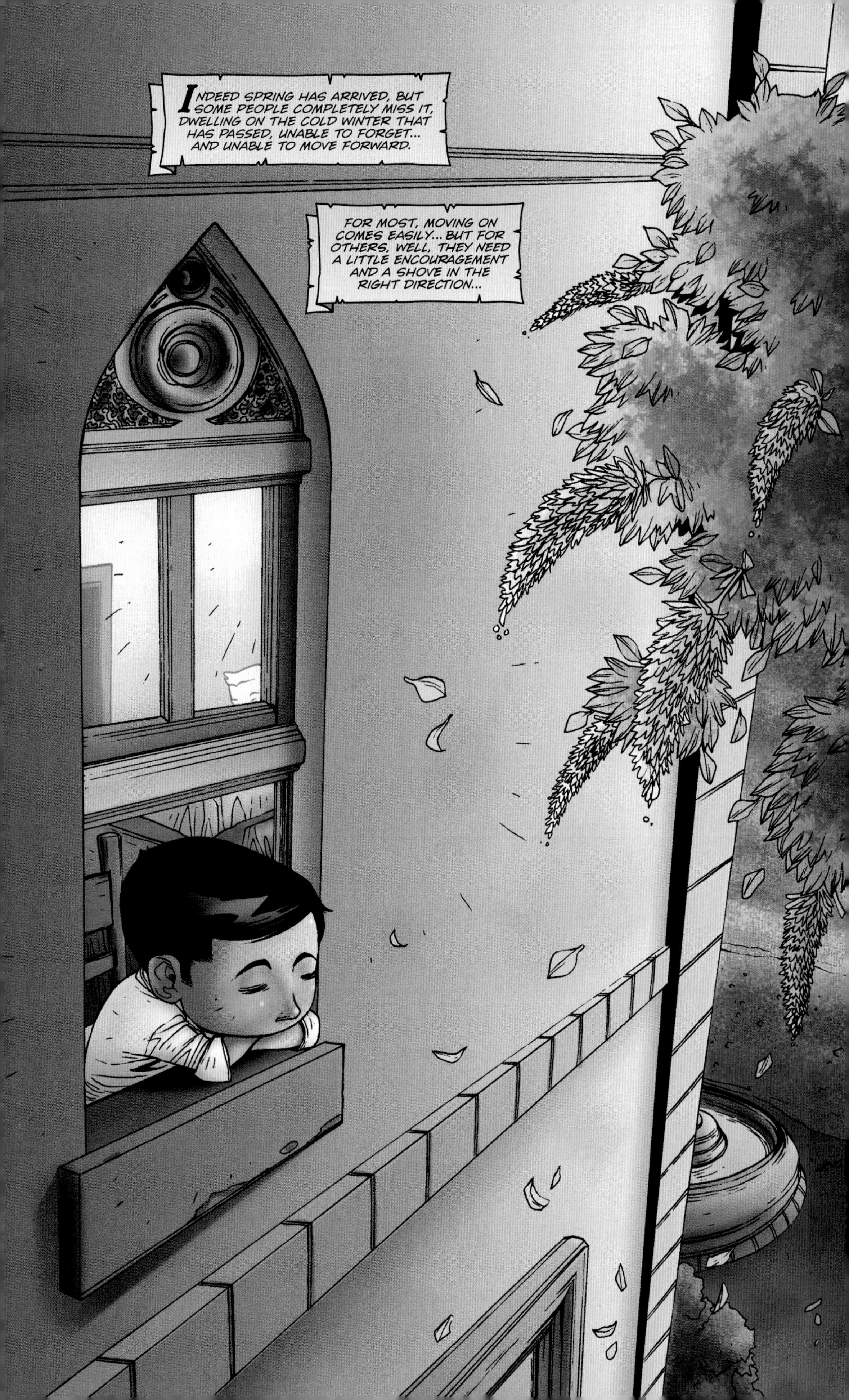
INDEED SPRING HAS ARRIVED, BUT SOME PEOPLE COMPLETELY MISS IT, DWELLING ON THE COLD WINTER THAT HAS PASSED, UNABLE TO FORGET... AND UNABLE TO MOVE FORWARD.
FOR MOST, MOVING ON COMES EASILY... BUT FOR OTHERS, WELL, THEY NEED A LITTLE ENCOURAGEMENT AND A SHOVE IN THE RIGHT DIRECTION...

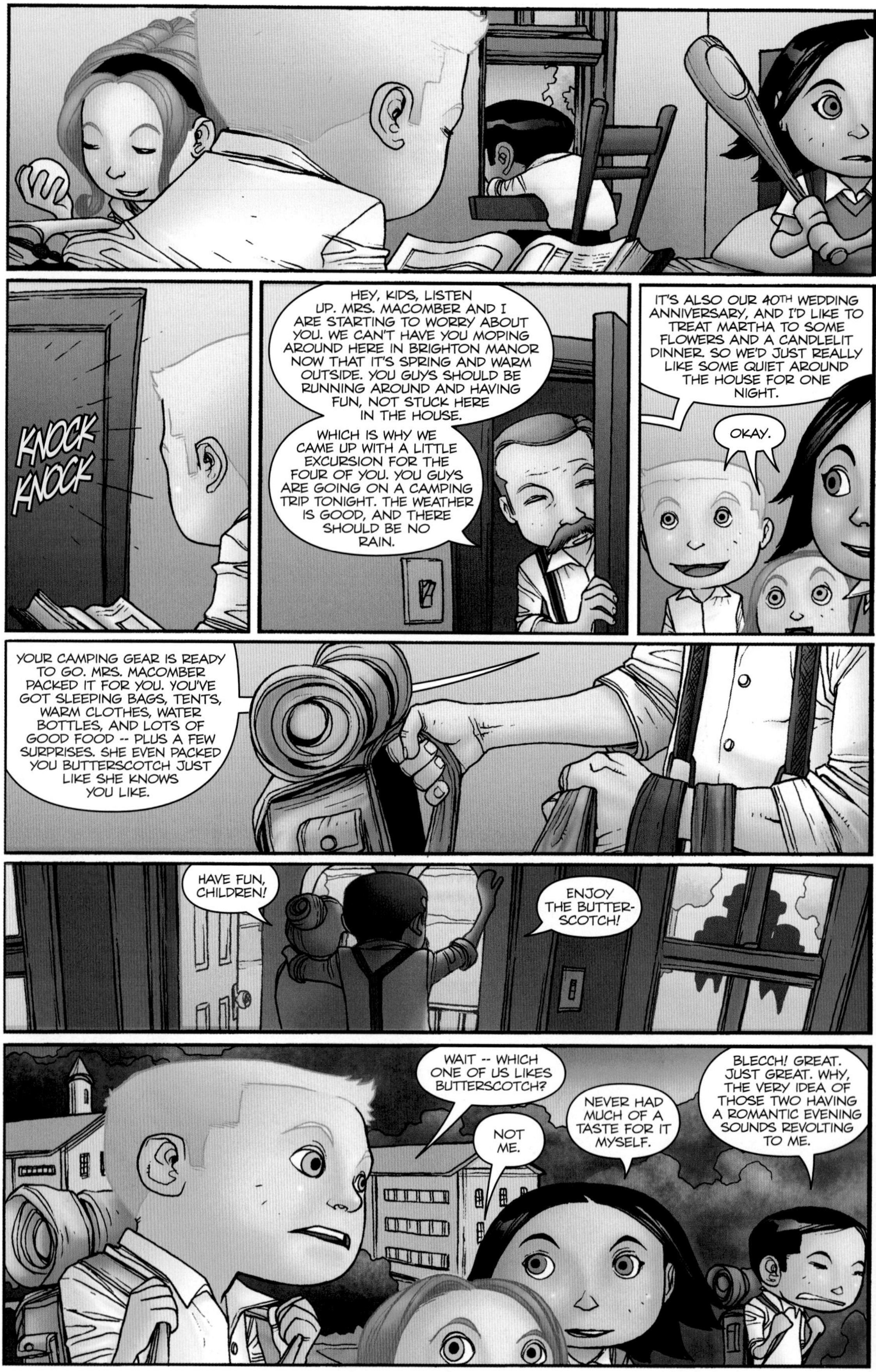
KNOCK KNOCK
HEY, KIDS, LISTEN UP. MRS. MACOMBER AND I ARE STARTING TO WORRY ABOUT YOU. WE CAN'T HAVE YOU MOPING AROUND HERE IN BRIGHTON MANOR NOW THAT IT'S SPRING AND WARM OUTSIDE. YOU GUYS SHOULD BE RUNNING AROUND AND HAVING FUN, NOT STUCK HERE IN THE HOUSE.
WHICH IS WHY WE CAME UP WITH A LITTLE EXCURSION FOR THE FOUR OF YOU. YOU GUYS ARE GOING ON A CAMPING TRIP TONIGHT. THE WEATHER IS GOOD, AND THERE SHOULD BE NO RAIN.
IT'S ALSO OUR 40TH WEDDING ANNIVERSARY, AND I'D LIKE TO TREAT MARTHA TO SOME FLOWERS AND A CANDLELIT DINNER. SO WE'D JUST REALLY LIKE SOME QUIET AROUND THE HOUSE FOR ONE NIGHT.
OKAY.
YOUR CAMPING GEAR IS READY TO GO. MRS. MACOMBER PACKED IT FOR YOU. YOU'VE GOT SLEEPING BAGS, TENTS, WARM CLOTHES, WATER BOTTLES, AND LOTS OF GOOD FOOD -- PLUS A FEW SURPRISES. SHE EVEN PACKED YOU BUTTERSCOTCH JUST LIKE SHE KNOWS YOU LIKE.
HAVE FUN, CHILDREN!
ENJOY THE BUTTER-SCOTCH!
WAIT -- WHICH ONE OF US LIKES BUTTERSCOTCH?
NOT ME.
NEVER HAD MUCH OF A TASTE FOR IT MYSELF.
BLECCH! GREAT. JUST GREAT. WHY, THE VERY IDEA OF THOSE TWO HAVING A ROMANTIC EVENING SOUNDS REVOLTING TO ME.

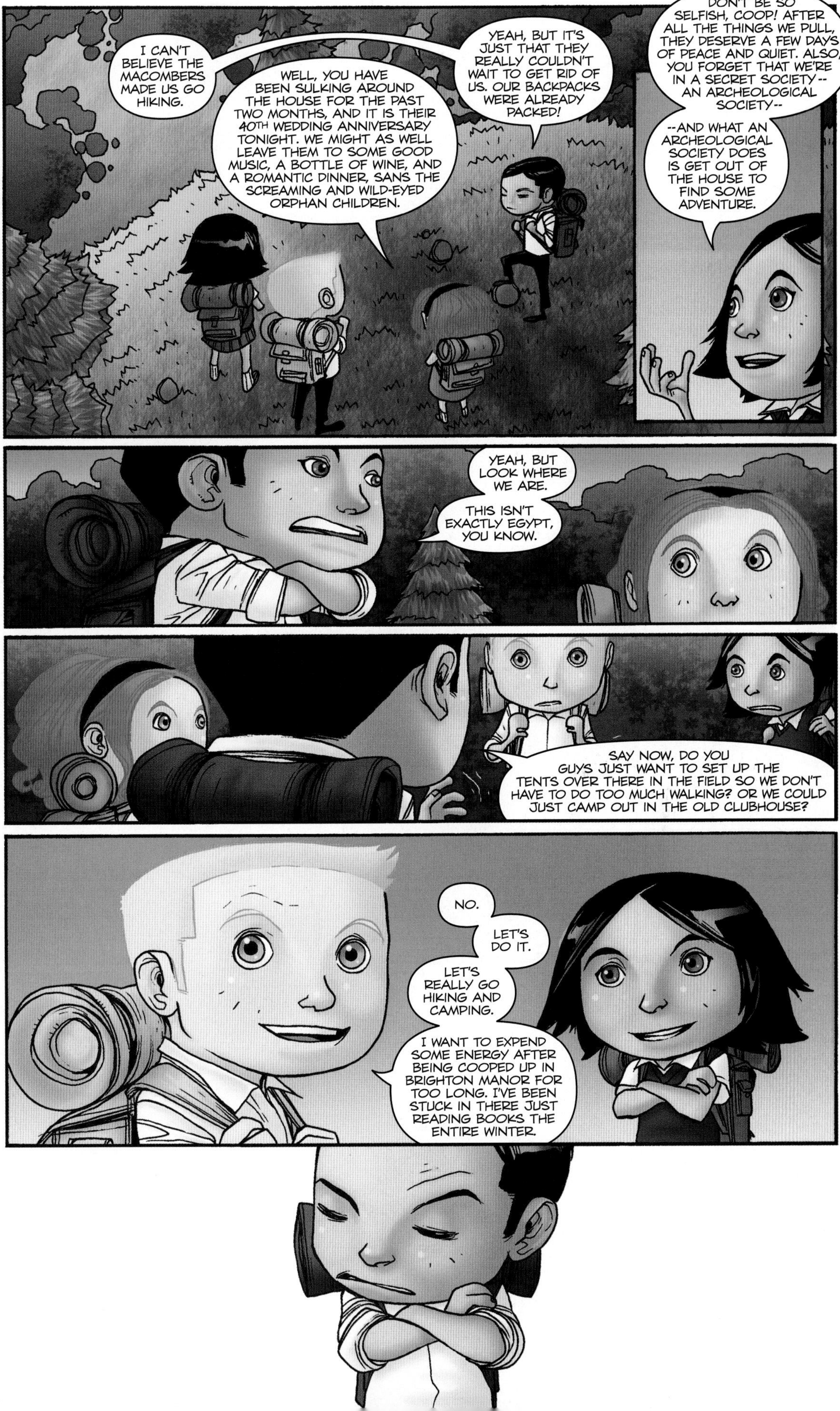
I CAN'T BELIEVE THE MACOMBERS MADE US GO HIKING.
WELL, YOU HAVE BEEN SULKING AROUND THE HOUSE FOR THE PAST TWO MONTHS, AND IT IS THEIR 40TH WEDDING ANNIVERSARY TONIGHT. WE MIGHT AS WELL LEAVE THEM TO SOME GOOD MUSIC, A BOTTLE OF WINE, AND A ROMANTIC DINNER, SANS THE SCREAMING AND WILD-EYED ORPHAN CHILDREN.
YEAH, BUT IT'S JUST THAT THEY REALLY COULDN'T WAIT TO GET RID OF US. OUR BACKPACKS WERE ALREADY PACKED!
DON'T BE SO SELFISH, COOP! AFTER ALL THE THINGS WE PULL, THEY DESERVE A FEW DAYS OF PEACE AND QUIET. ALSO, YOU FORGET THAT WE'RE IN A SECRET SOCIETY--AN ARCHEOLOGICAL SOCIETY--
--AND WHAT AN ARCHEOLOGICAL SOCIETY DOES IS GET OUT OF THE HOUSE TO FIND SOME ADVENTURE.
YEAH, BUT LOOK WHERE WE ARE.
THIS ISN'T EXACTLY EGYPT, YOU KNOW.
SAY NOW, DO YOU GUYS JUST WANT TO SET UP THE TENTS OVER THERE IN THE FIELD SO WE DON'T HAVE TO DO TOO MUCH WALKING? OR WE COULD JUST CAMP OUT IN THE OLD CLUBHOUSE?
NO.
LET'S DO IT.
LET'S REALLY GO HIKING AND CAMPING.
I WANT TO EXPEND SOME ENERGY AFTER BEING COOPED UP IN BRIGHTON MANOR FOR TOO LONG. I'VE BEEN STUCK IN THERE JUST READING BOOKS THE ENTIRE WINTER.

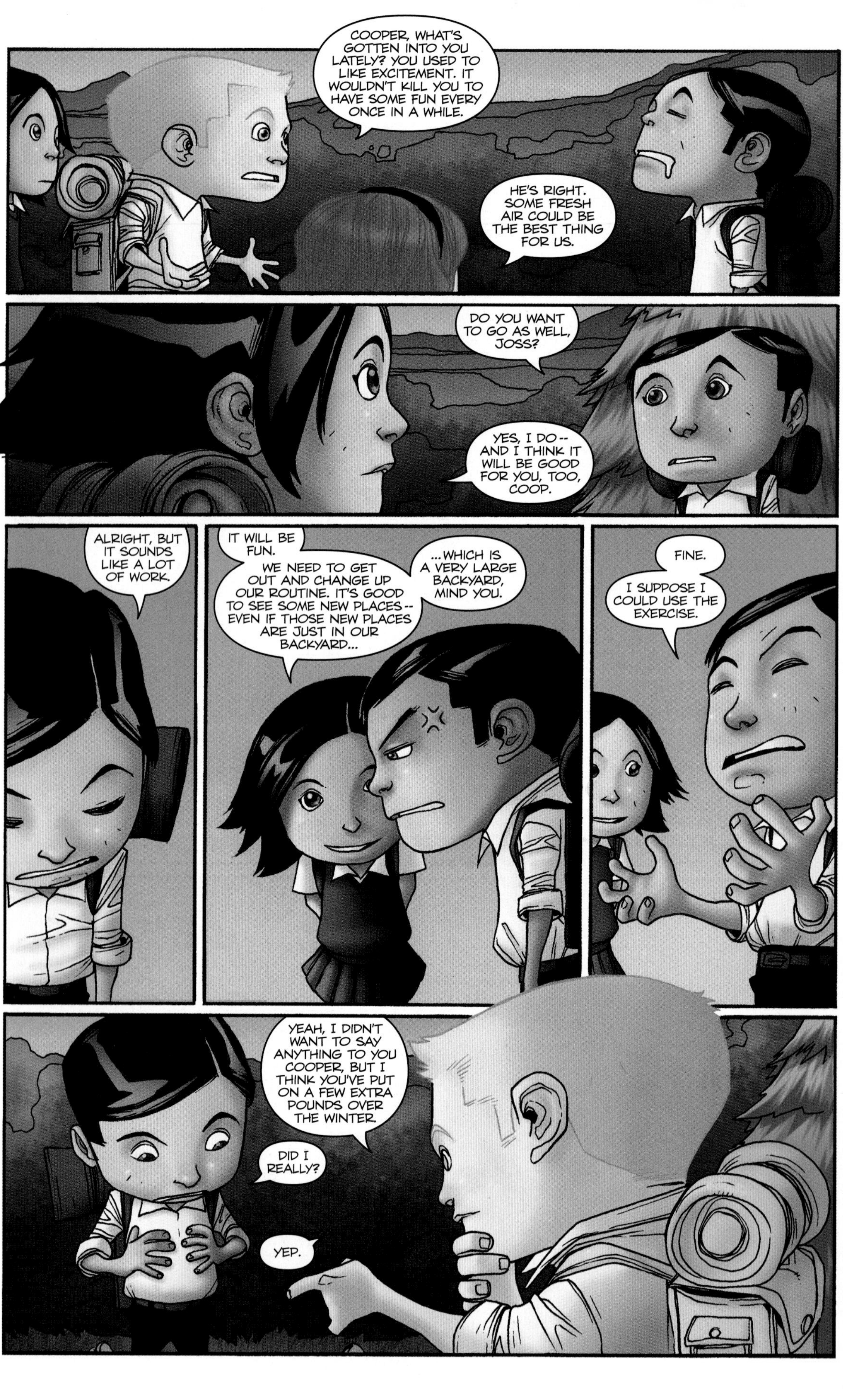
COOPER, WHAT'S GOTTEN INTO YOU LATELY? YOU USED TO LIKE EXCITEMENT. IT WOULDN'T KILL YOU TO HAVE SOME FUN EVERY ONCE IN A WHILE.
HE'S RIGHT. SOME FRESH AIR COULD BE THE BEST THING FOR US.
DO YOU WANT TO GO AS WELL, JOSS?
YES, I DO-- AND I THINK IT WILL BE GOOD FOR YOU, TOO, COOP.
ALRIGHT, BUT IT SOUNDS LIKE A LOT OF WORK.
IT WILL BE FUN.
WE NEED TO GET OUT AND CHANGE UP OUR ROUTINE. IT'S GOOD TO SEE SOME NEW PLACES-- EVEN IF THOSE NEW PLACES ARE JUST IN OUR BACKYARD...
...WHICH IS A VERY LARGE BACKYARD, MIND YOU.
FINE.
I SUPPOSE I COULD USE THE EXERCISE.
YEAH, I DIDN'T WANT TO SAY ANYTHING TO YOU COOPER, BUT I THINK YOU'VE PUT ON A FEW EXTRA POUNDS OVER THE WINTER.
DID I REALLY?
YEP.

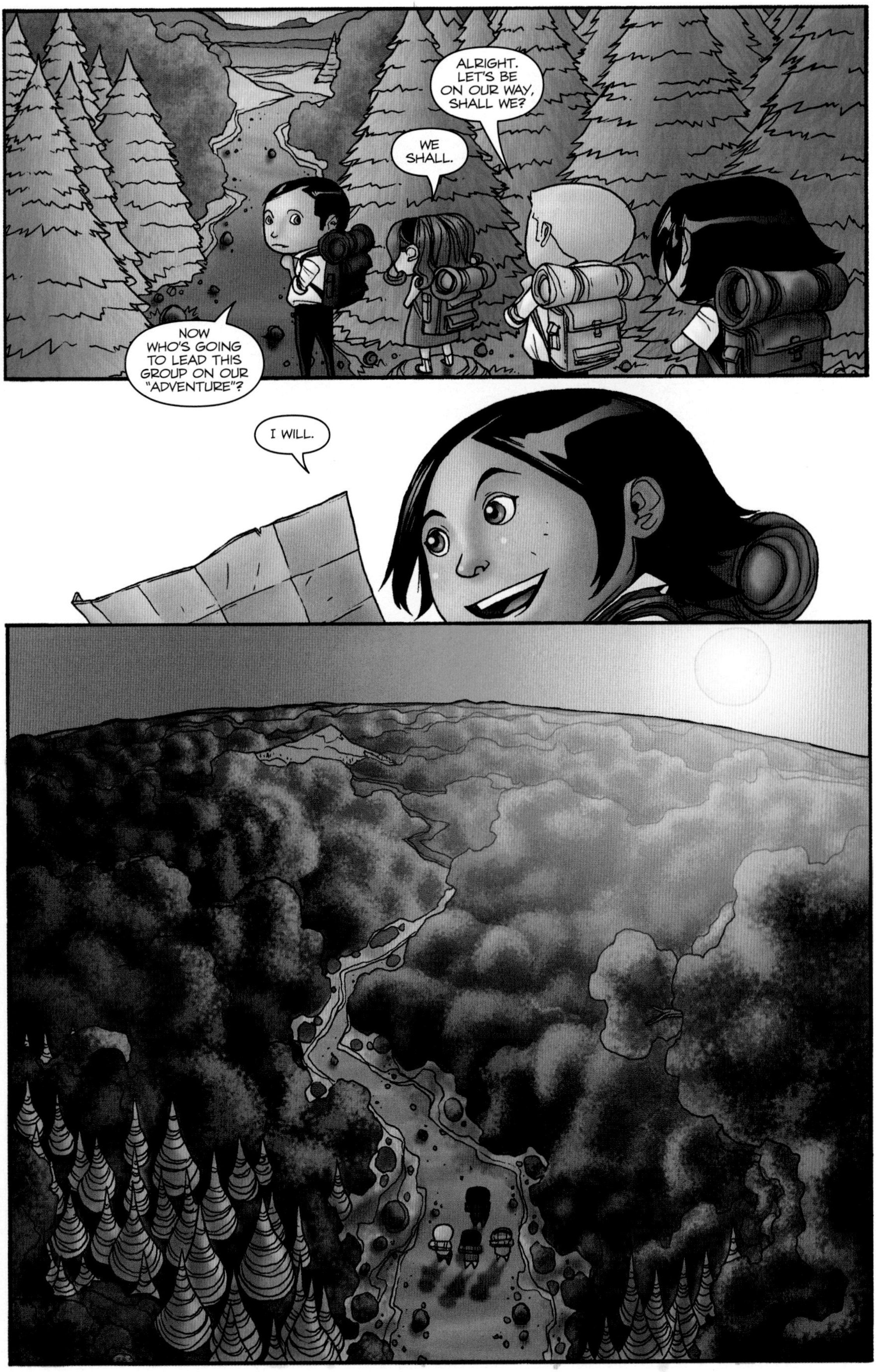
ALRIGHT. LET'S BE ON OUR WAY, SHALL WE?
WE SHALL.
NOW WHO'S GOING TO LEAD THIS GROUP ON OUR "ADVENTURE"?
I WILL.

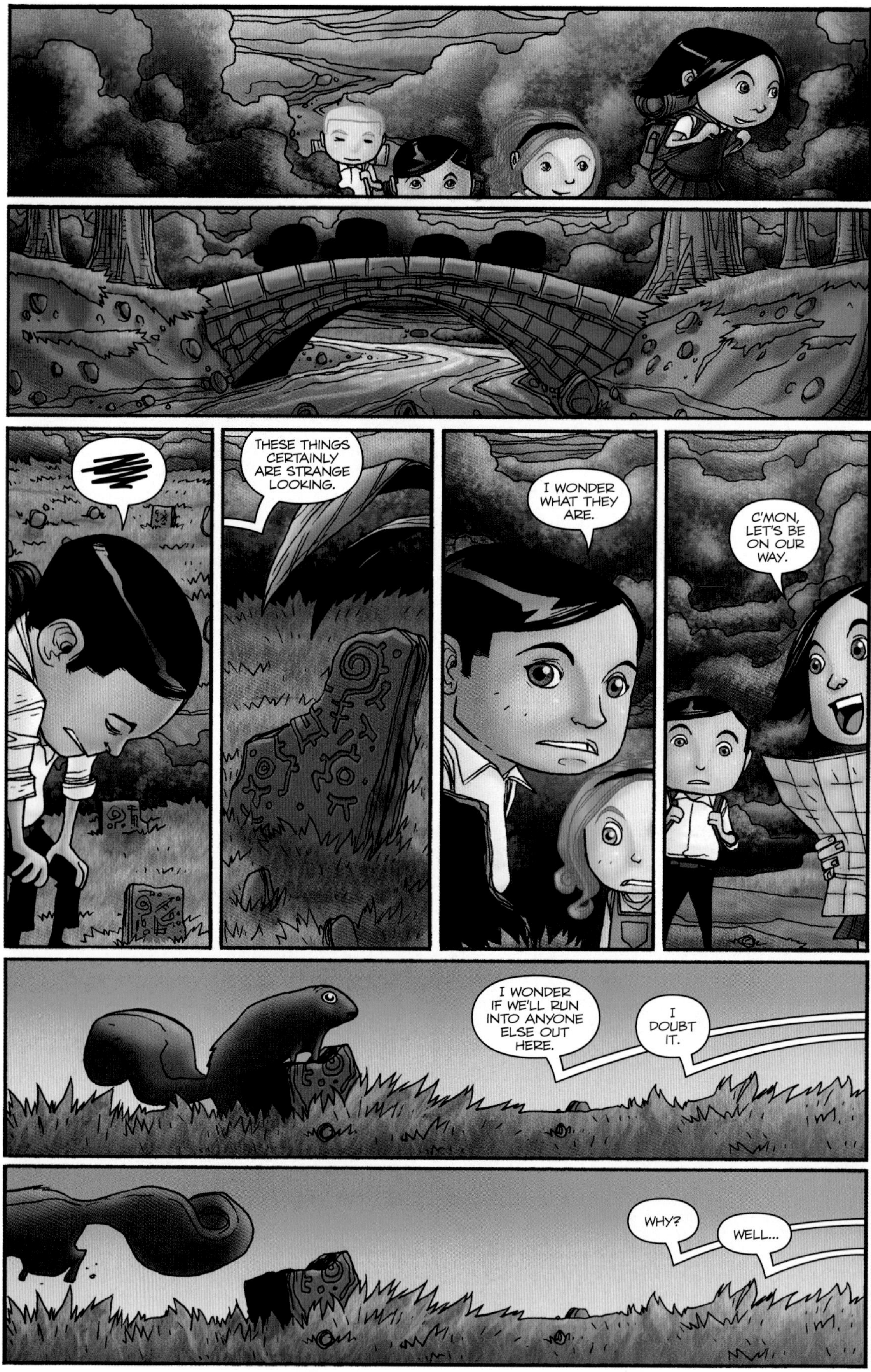
THESE THINGS CERTAINLY ARE STRANGE LOOKING.
I WONDER WHAT THEY ARE.
C'MON, LET'S BE ON OUR WAY.
I WONDER IF WE'LL RUN INTO ANYONE ELSE OUT HERE.
I DOUBT IT.
WHY?
WELL...

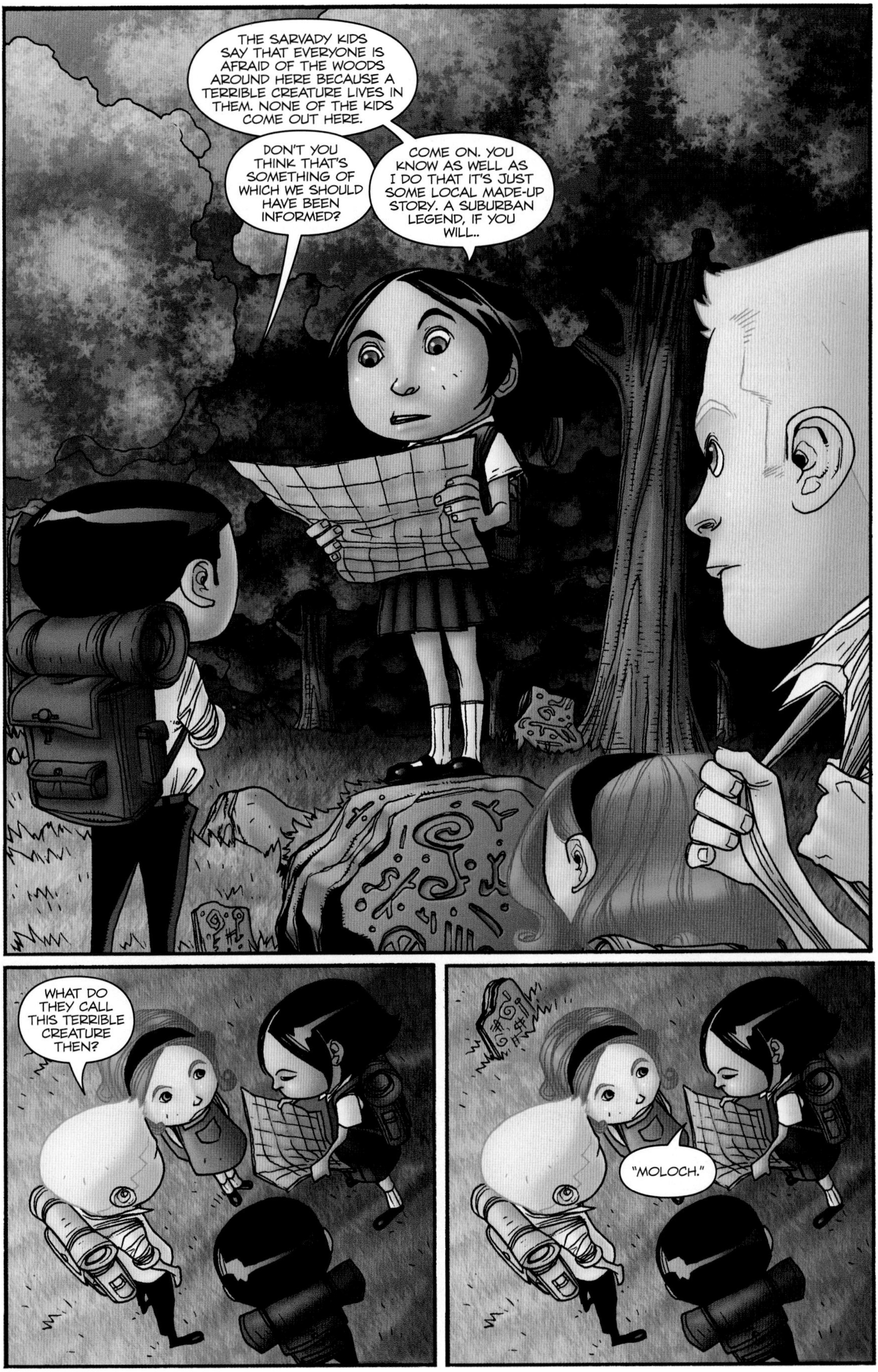
THE SARVADY KIDS SAY THAT EVERYONE IS AFRAID OF THE WOODS AROUND HERE BECAUSE A TERRIBLE CREATURE LIVES IN THEM. NONE OF THE KIDS COME OUT HERE.
DON'T YOU THINK THAT'S SOMETHING OF WHICH WE SHOULD HAVE BEEN INFORMED?
COME ON. YOU KNOW AS WELL AS I DO THAT IT'S JUST SOME LOCAL MADE-UP STORY. A SUBURBAN LEGEND, IF YOU WILL..
WHAT DO THEY CALL THIS TERRIBLE CREATURE THEN?
"MOLOCH."

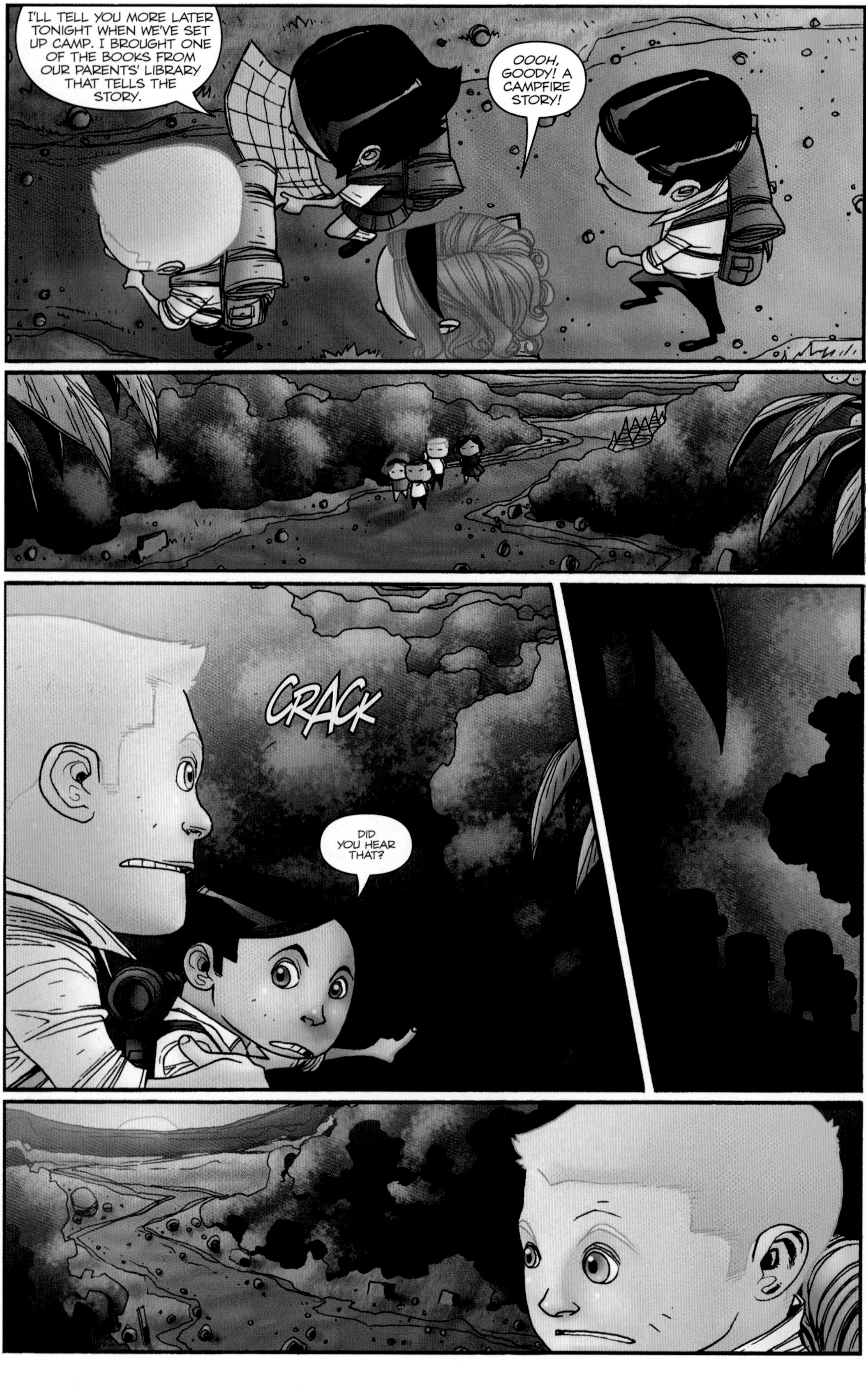
I'LL TELL YOU MORE LATER TONIGHT WHEN WE'VE SET UP CAMP. I BROUGHT ONE OF THE BOOKS FROM OUR PARENTS' LIBRARY THAT TELLS THE STORY.
OOOH, GOODY! A CAMPFIRE STORY!
CRACK
DID YOU HEAR THAT?

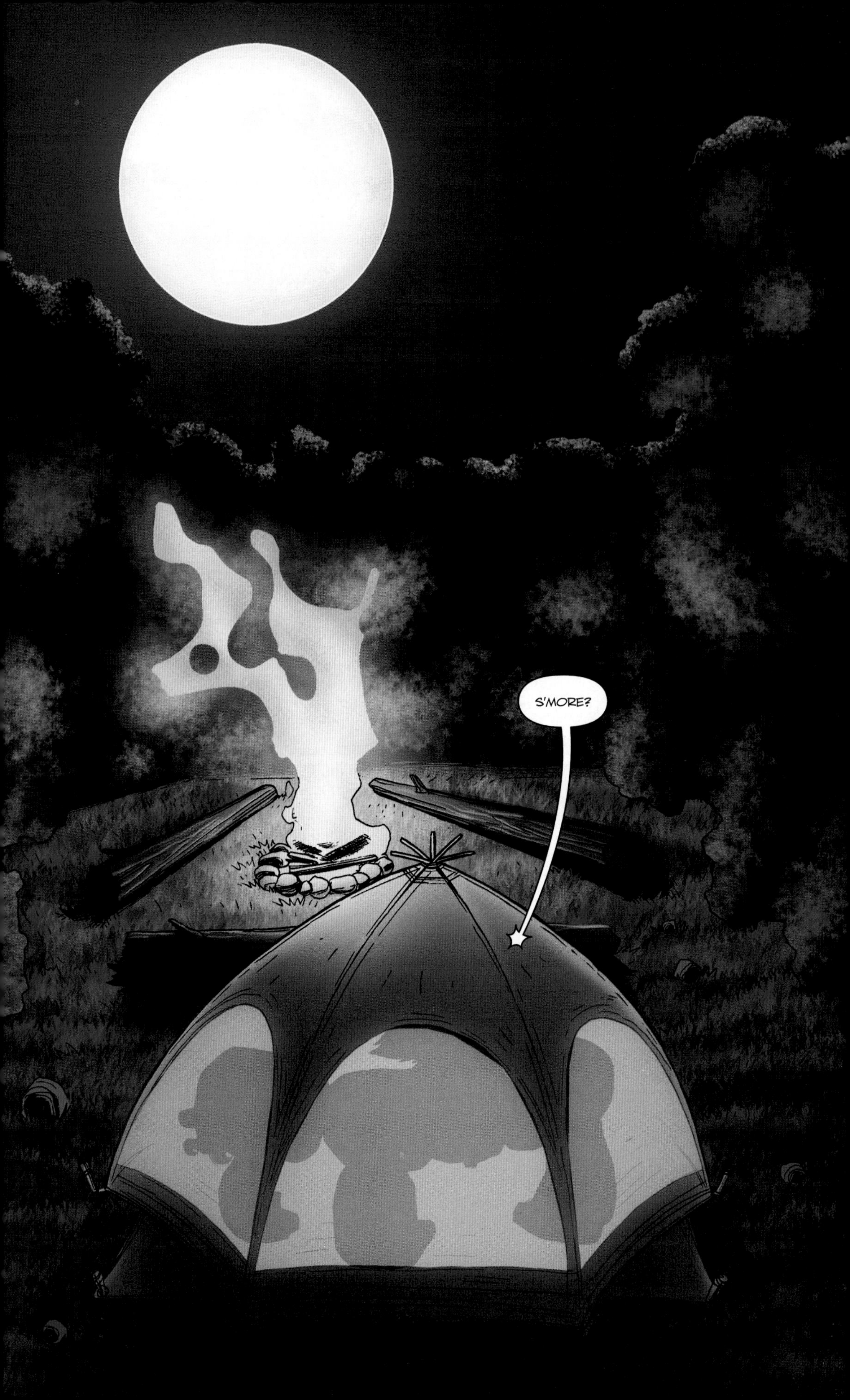
S'MORE?

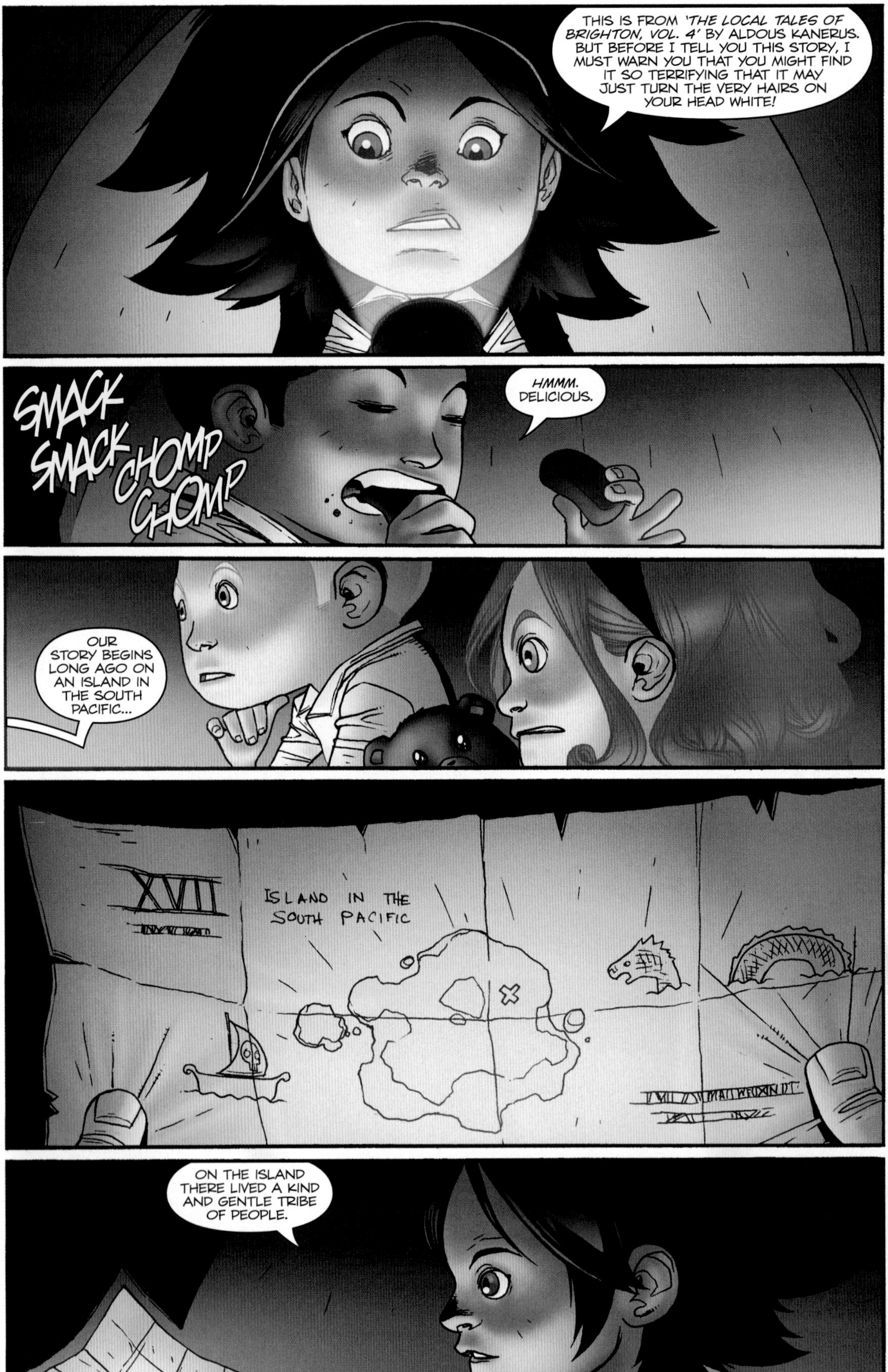

THIS IS FROM *'THE LOCAL TALES OF BRIGHTON, VOL. 4'* BY ALDOUS KANERUS. BUT BEFORE I TELL YOU THIS STORY, I MUST WARN YOU THAT YOU MIGHT FIND IT SO TERRIFYING THAT IT MAY JUST TURN THE VERY HAIRS ON YOUR HEAD WHITE!
SMACK SMACK CHOMP CHOMP
HMMM. DELICIOUS.
OUR STORY BEGINS LONG AGO ON AN ISLAND IN THE SOUTH PACIFIC...
XVII
ISLAND IN THE SOUTH PACIFIC
ON THE ISLAND THERE LIVED A KIND AND GENTLE TRIBE OF PEOPLE.

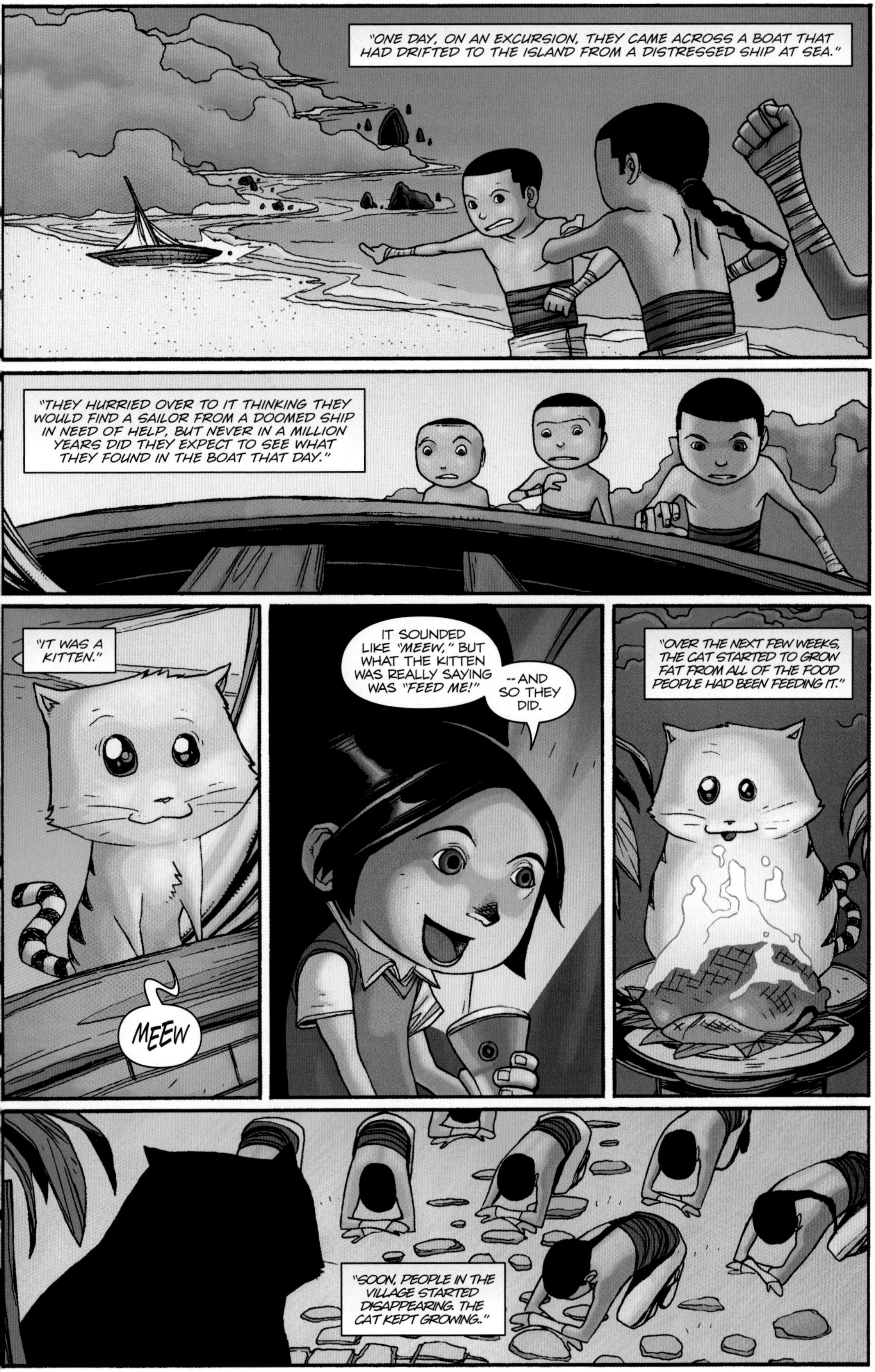
"ONE DAY, ON AN EXCURSION, THEY CAME ACROSS A BOAT THAT HAD DRIFTED TO THE ISLAND FROM A DISTRESSED SHIP AT SEA."
"THEY HURRIED OVER TO IT THINKING THEY WOULD FIND A SAILOR FROM A DOOMED SHIP IN NEED OF HELP, BUT NEVER IN A MILLION YEARS DID THEY EXPECT TO SEE WHAT THEY FOUND IN THE BOAT THAT DAY."
"IT WAS A KITTEN."
MEEW
IT SOUNDED LIKE "MEEW," BUT WHAT THE KITTEN WAS REALLY SAYING WAS "FEED ME!"
--AND SO THEY DID.
"OVER THE NEXT FEW WEEKS, THE CAT STARTED TO GROW FAT FROM ALL OF THE FOOD PEOPLE HAD BEEN FEEDING IT."
"SOON, PEOPLE IN THE VILLAGE STARTED DISAPPEARING. THE CAT KEPT GROWING.."

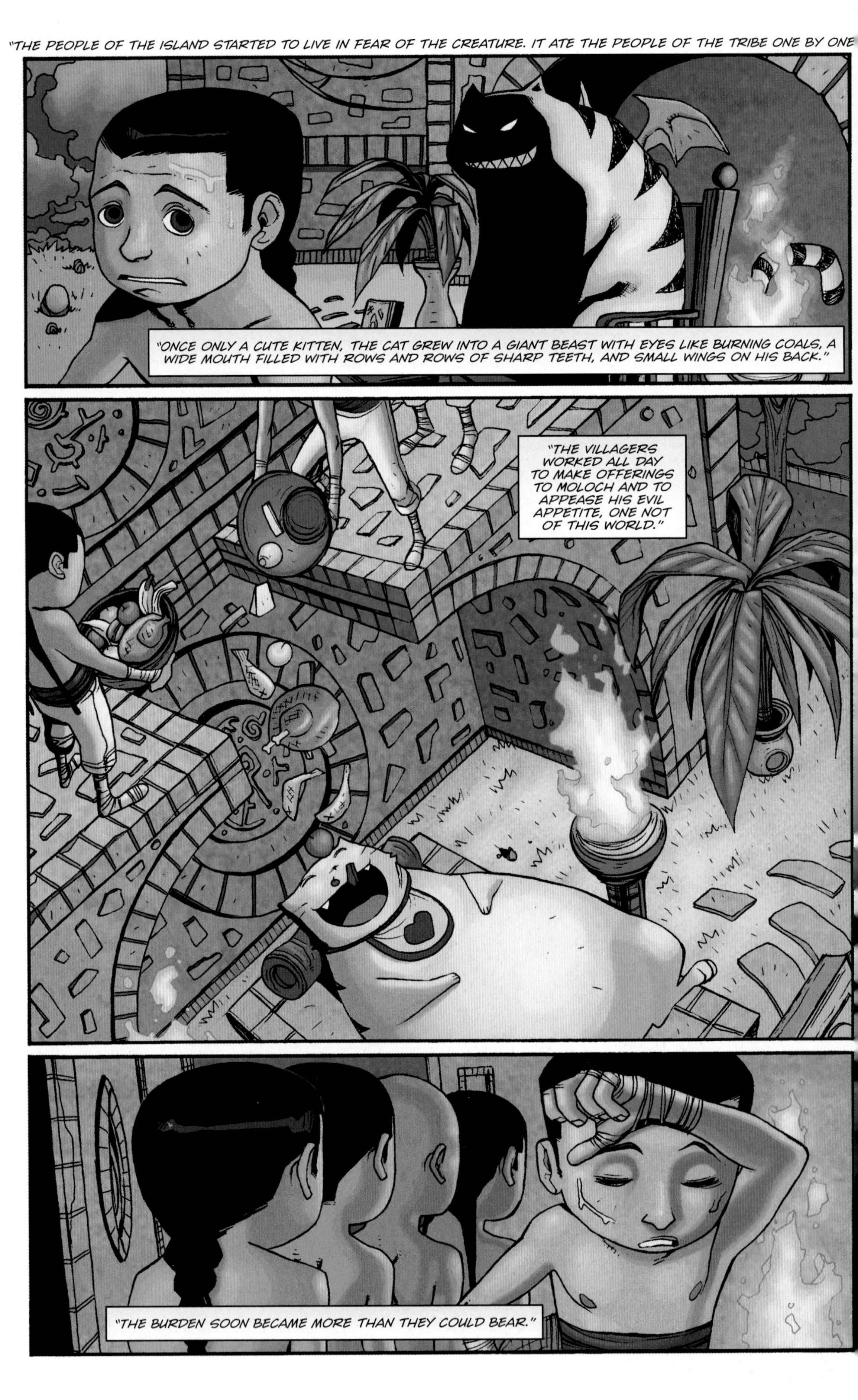
"THE PEOPLE OF THE ISLAND STARTED TO LIVE IN FEAR OF THE CREATURE. IT ATE THE PEOPLE OF THE TRIBE ONE BY ONE
"ONCE ONLY A CUTE KITTEN, THE CAT GREW INTO A GIANT BEAST WITH EYES LIKE BURNING COALS, A WIDE MOUTH FILLED WITH ROWS AND ROWS OF SHARP TEETH, AND SMALL WINGS ON HIS BACK."
"THE VILLAGERS WORKED ALL DAY TO MAKE OFFERINGS TO MOLOCH AND TO APPEASE HIS EVIL APPETITE, ONE NOT OF THIS WORLD."
"THE BURDEN SOON BECAME MORE THAN THEY COULD BEAR."

• Biographies •

Mark Andrew Smith is the writer of THE AMAZING JOY BUZZARDS, THE NEW BRIGHTON ARCHEOLOGICAL SOCIETY, AQUA LEUNG, and GLADSTONE'S SCHOOL FOR WORLD CONQUERORS.

Matthew Weldon, a Texas native, has been laboring in the field of Comic Art since 2005 and makes attempts to write on the side. He likes sports, social events, and going out of his way to obtain delicious cookies and donuts.

Born in 1986 in Chile, ***Rodrigo Avilés*** lives in the small city of Melipilla. He started drawing as a child and at twelve won a soccer ball from a drawing contest, but he didn't like soccer. Doing graffiti and comics in his adolescence, he studied illustration from 2005 to 2007 and now works as a freelance comic book colorist and illustrator.

Jacob Baake—otherwise known as Jacon P. Blake to magazines he doesn't want—is a freelance artist and colorist.

Carlos Carrasco has loved comics since he was a kid, dreaming of working on them. Now that he's living that dream, it's a lot of hard work and staying up late—but it's rewarding at the end and is still an awesome job (way better than working in a bank). He's really proud to be a part of this project and hopes you enjoy it as much as he did (at the end).

Bill Crabtree began his comics career in 2002 with FIREBREATHER from Image Comics and has colored a myriad of other titles including FANTASTIC FOUR FOES and THE IRREDEEMABLE ANT-MAN for Marvel Comics, Image Comics' SAVAGE DRAGON, YOUNGBLOOD, the Eisner nominated GODLAND, and is perhaps best known for his bold, Harvey Award nominated colors on INVINCIBLE. He lives in Portland, Oregon with his cat Vincent the super-brat.

Jessie Lam is a Toronto-based illustrator/animator who works in comics, commercials, and music videos. As a colorist, her projects include ROGOGIN: JUNKBOTZ from Image/Sunscript Studios and NEOZOIC from Red 5 Comics.

Ralph Niese resides, studies, and works in Leipzig, Germany. First published in horror comic anthologies at the tender age of sixteen, he dwelled for some time in the world of art and avant-garde music... just to return to what he dearly loves—drinking!—*uhm*, making comics, okay, kids?

Fonografiks is a studio specializing in digital lettering, graphic design, and pre-press production for comic books.

Paul Conrad's first job was as "bun boy" at his hometown Dairy Queen Brazier, but he quickly moved up the ladder to "fry guy" and finally the coveted position of "grill man." He's now a freelance artist who has worked at Pixar Animation Studios, The Walt Disney Co., Big Idea Productions, Scholastic, and Little Golden Books.

D.J. Kirkbride is an editor for Image Comics' award-winning POPGUN anthologies, KILL ALL PARENTS!, and AQUA LEUNG. Also a writer, D.J.'s currently working on some comics that will hopefully knock off socks everywhere once unleashed. A resident of Hell A, CA, D.J. has no pets nor any practical skills with real world applications.

Thomas Mauer wears many hats in comics including lettering, editing, book design, and pre-press. He currently works on books such as AWAKENING, BAD DOG, LOVE BUZZ, POPGUN, OUTLAW TERRITORY, and RAPTURE.

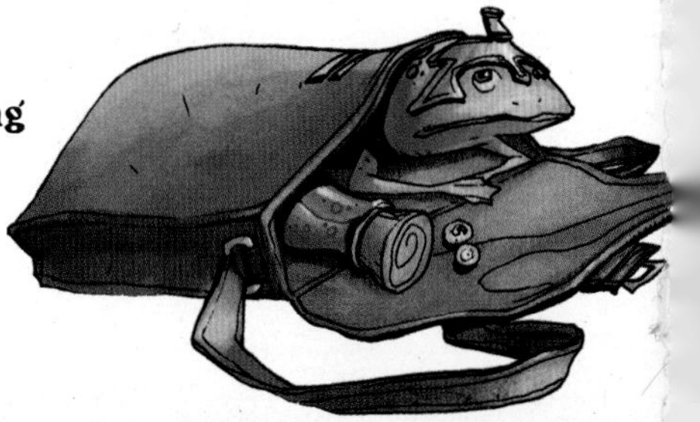

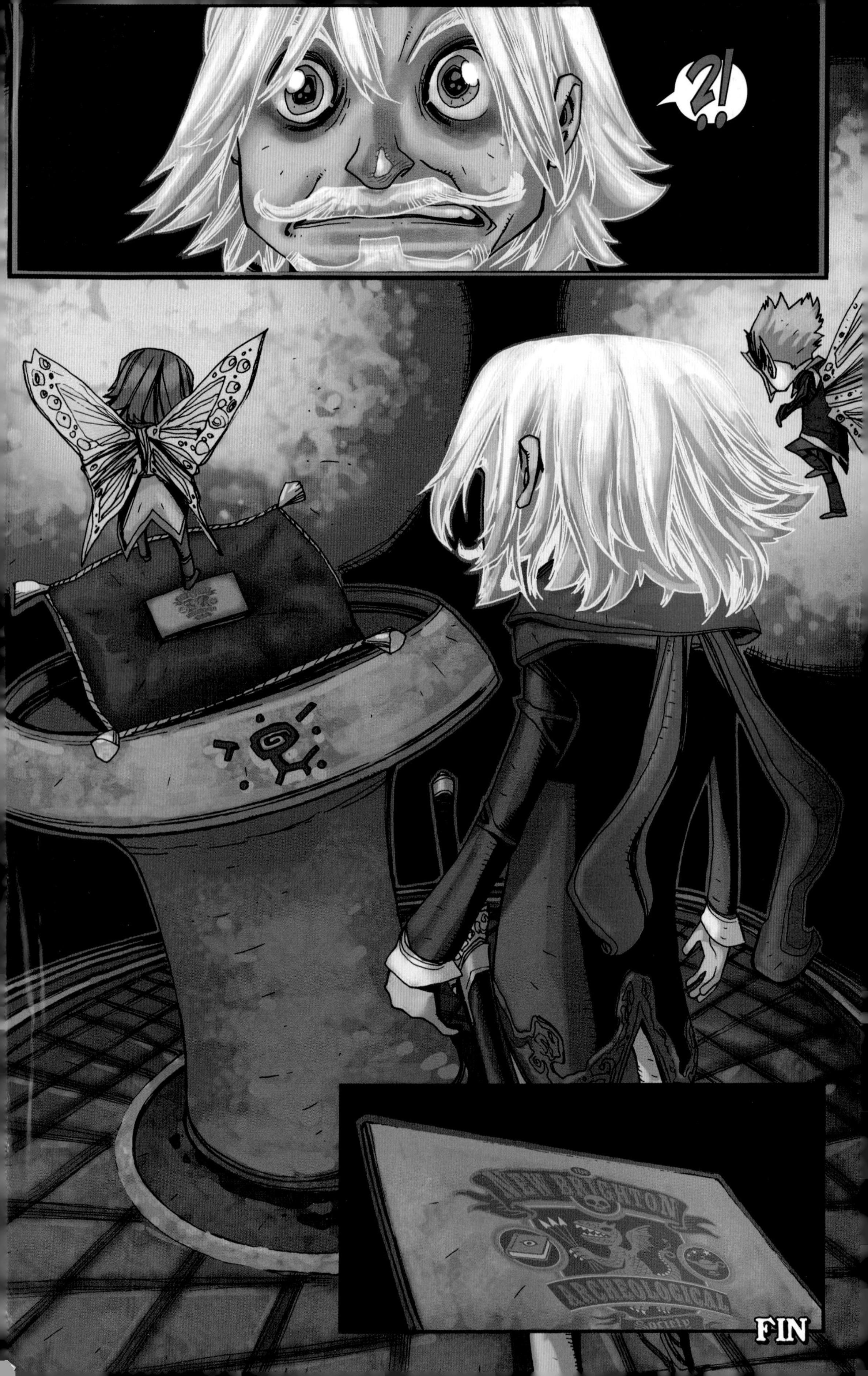
?!
NEW BRIGHTON
ARCHEOLOGICAL
Society
FIN

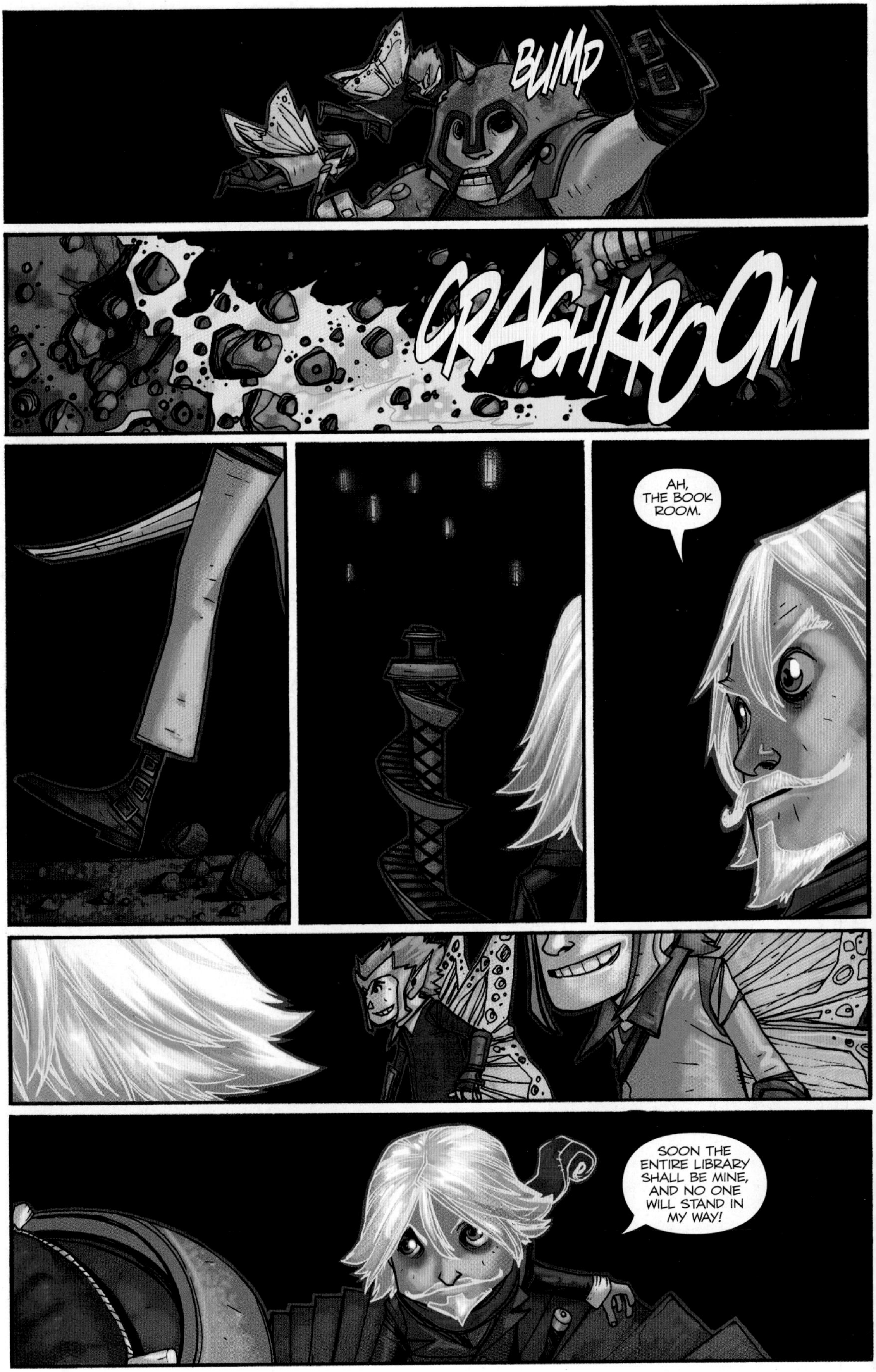
BUMP
CRASHKROOM
AH, THE BOOK ROOM.
SOON THE ENTIRE LIBRARY SHALL BE MINE, AND NO ONE WILL STAND IN MY WAY!

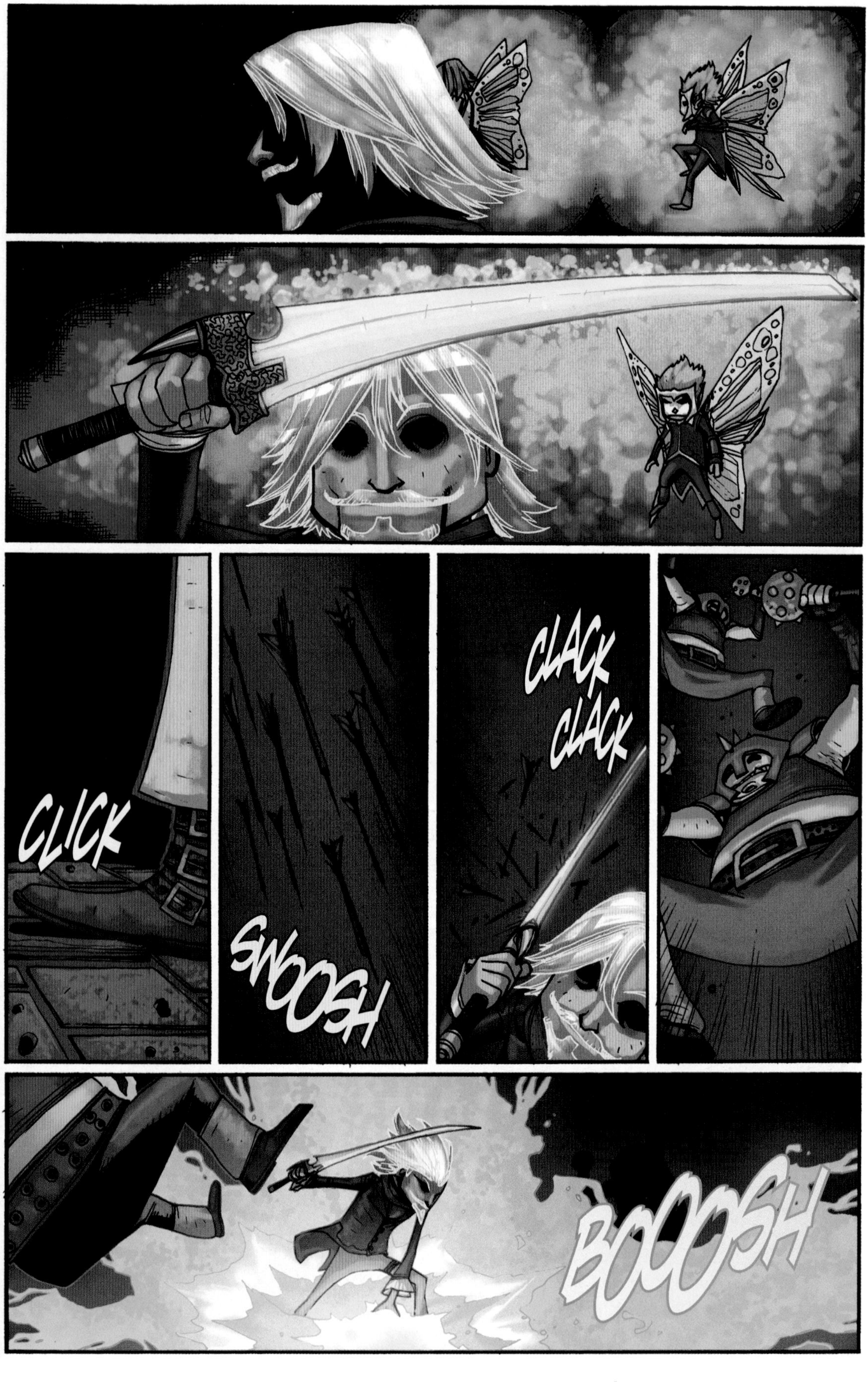
CLICK
SWOOSH
CLACK
CLACK
BOOOSH

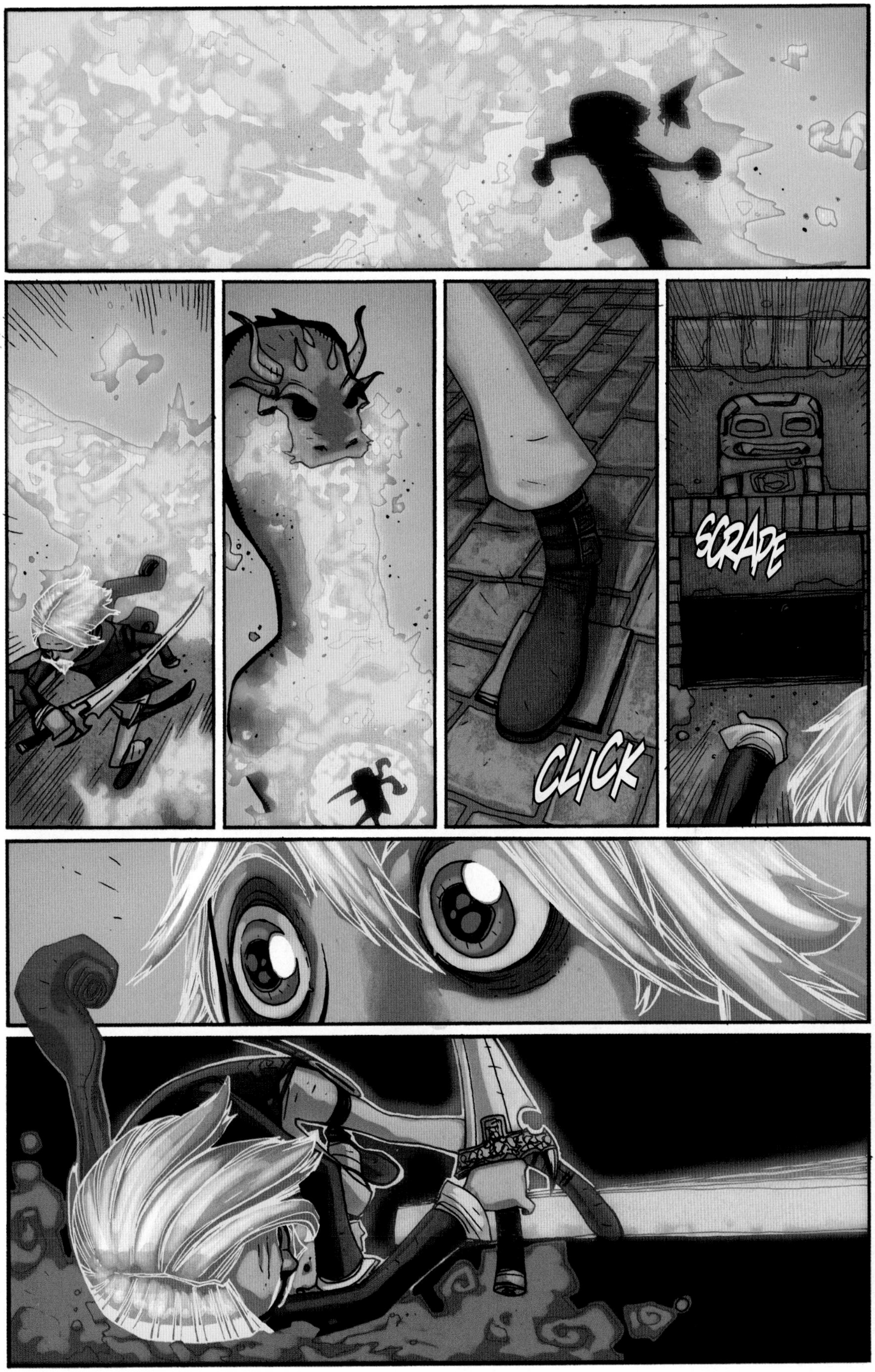
CLICK
SCRAPE

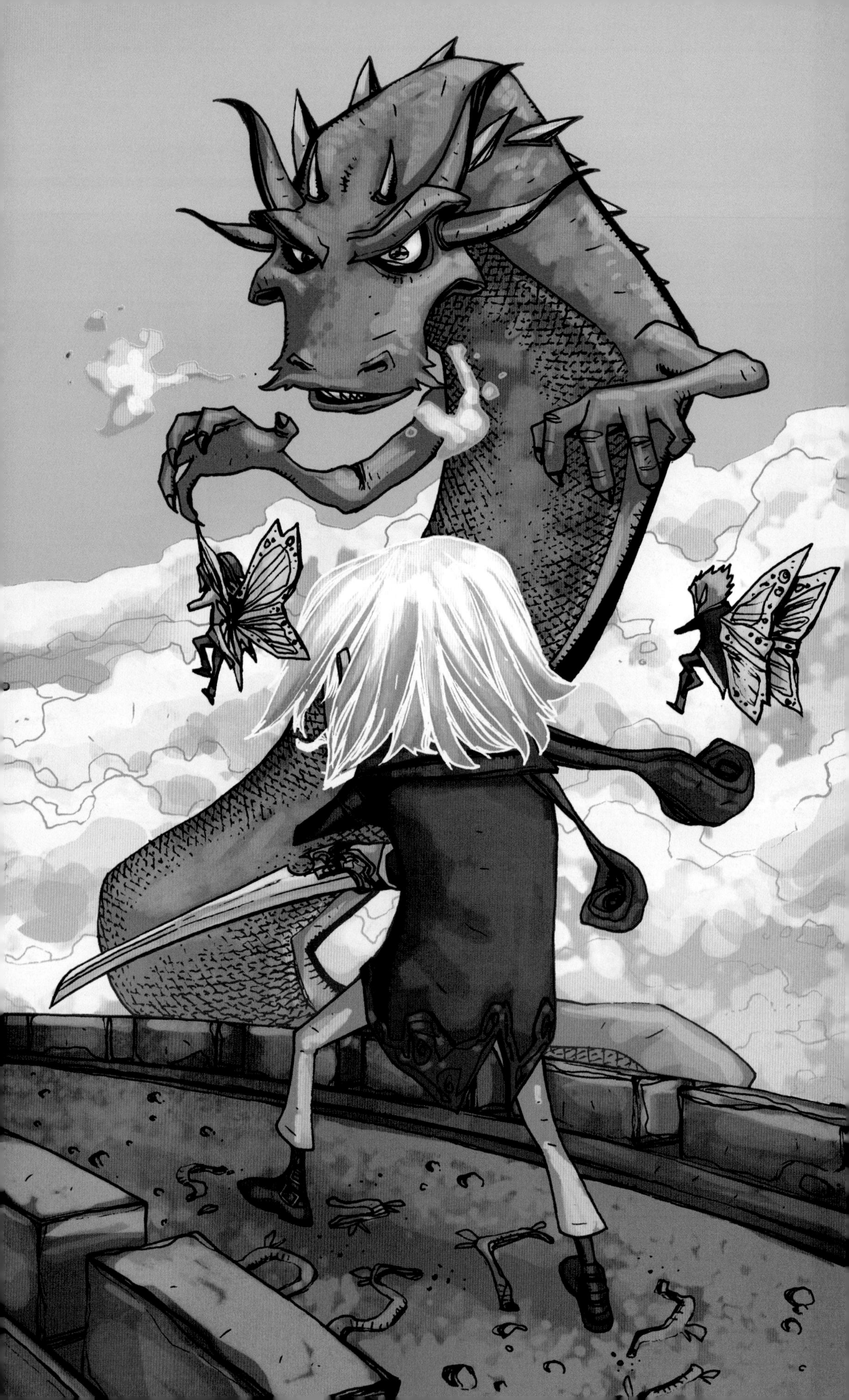

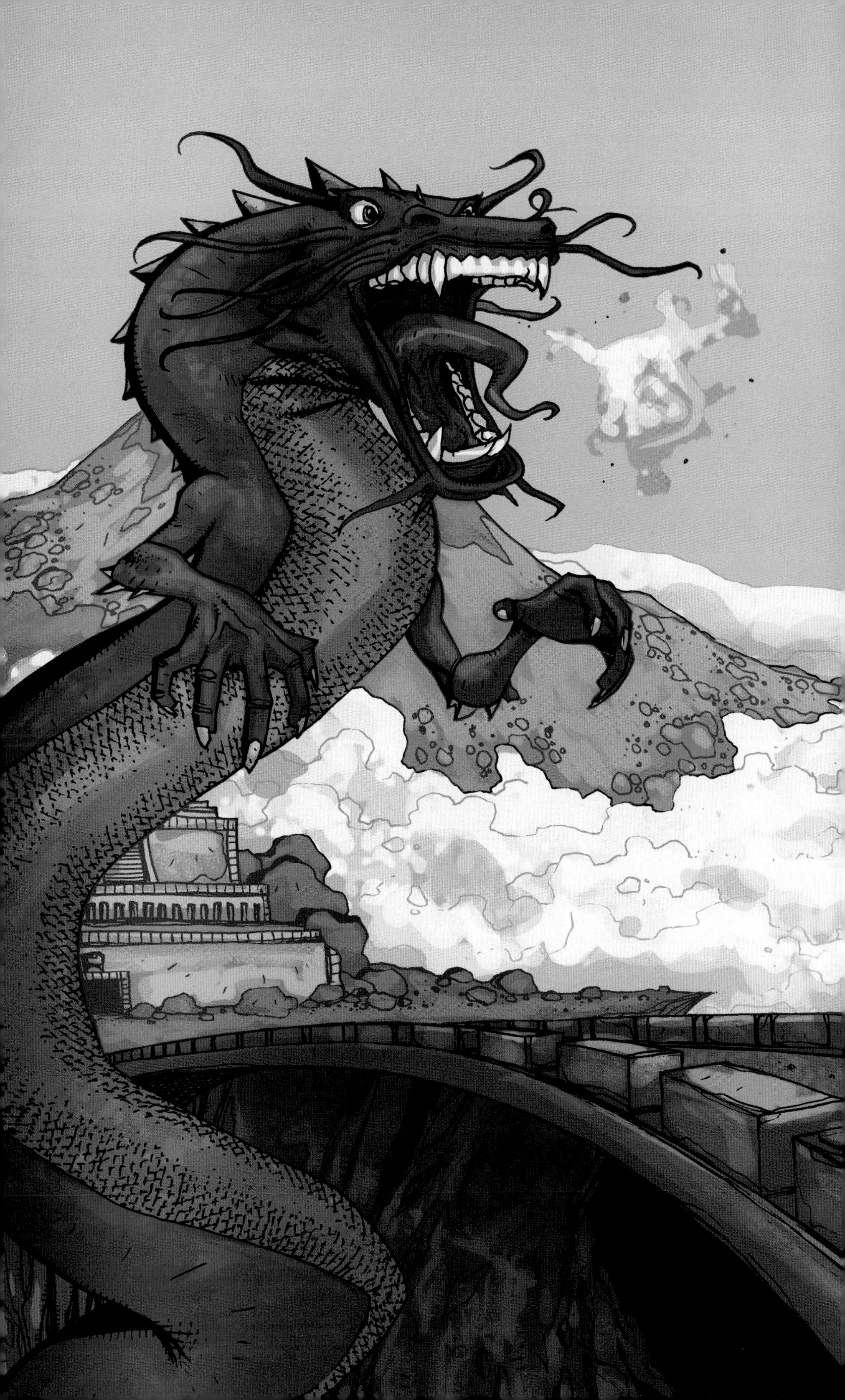

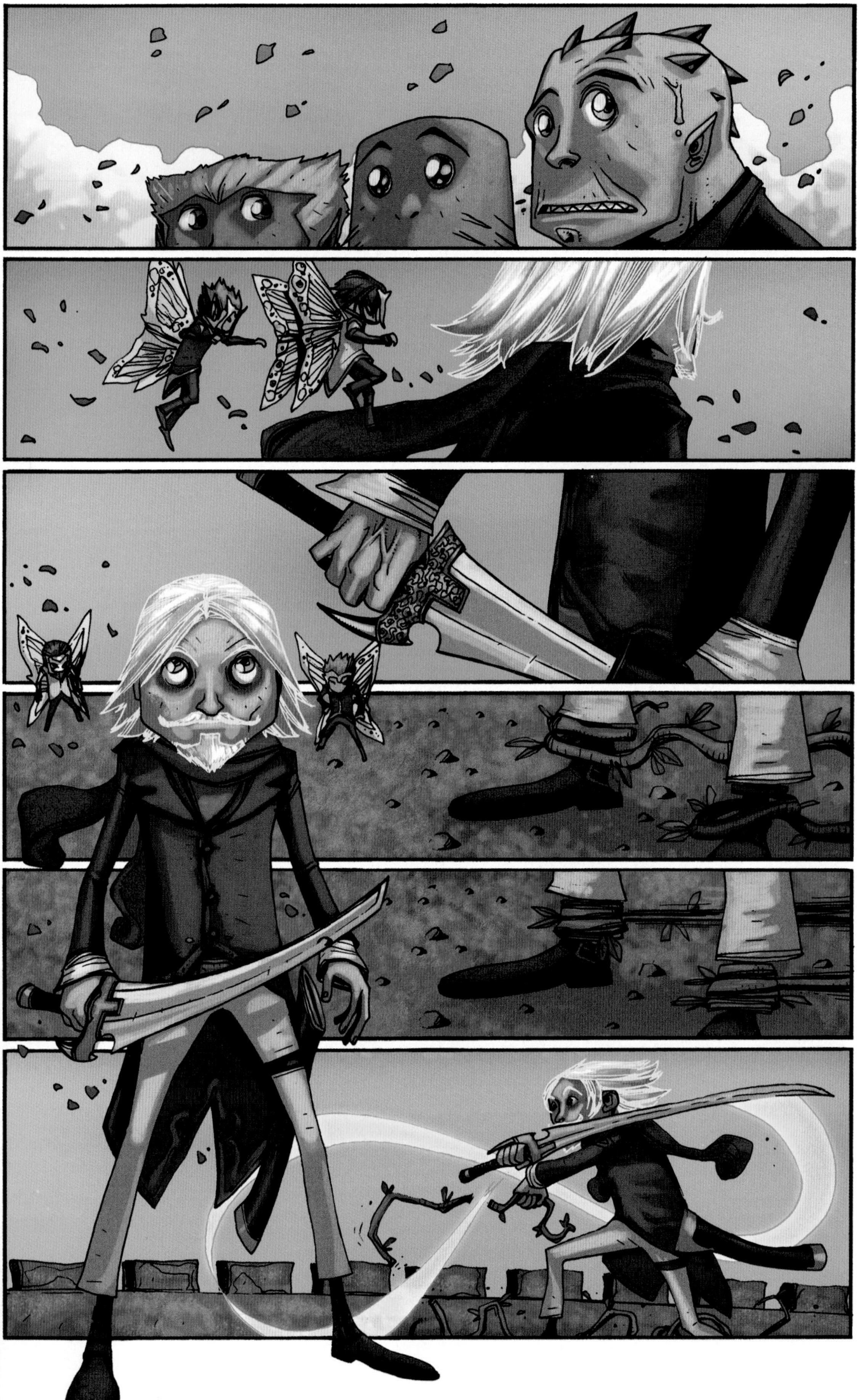

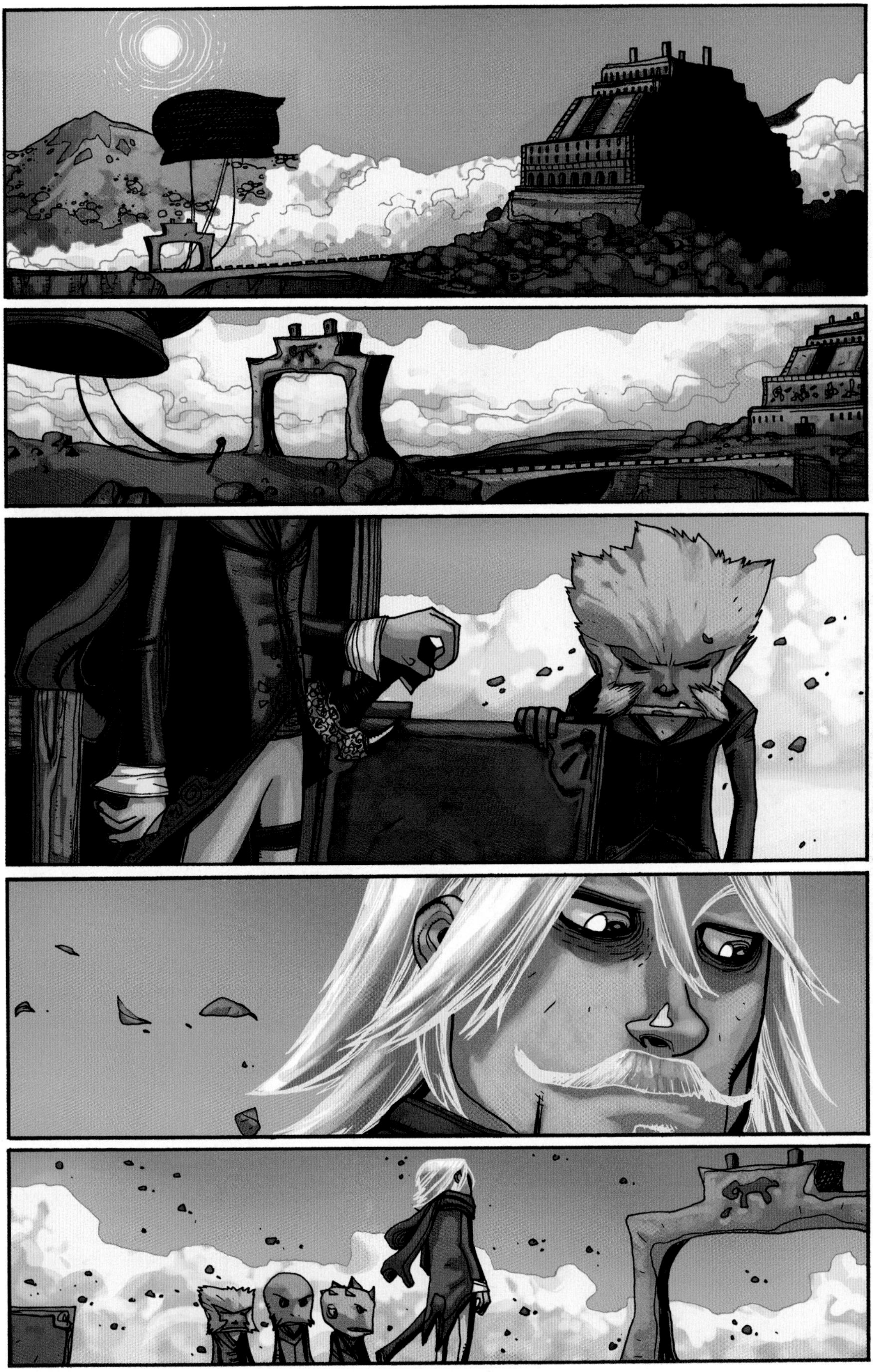

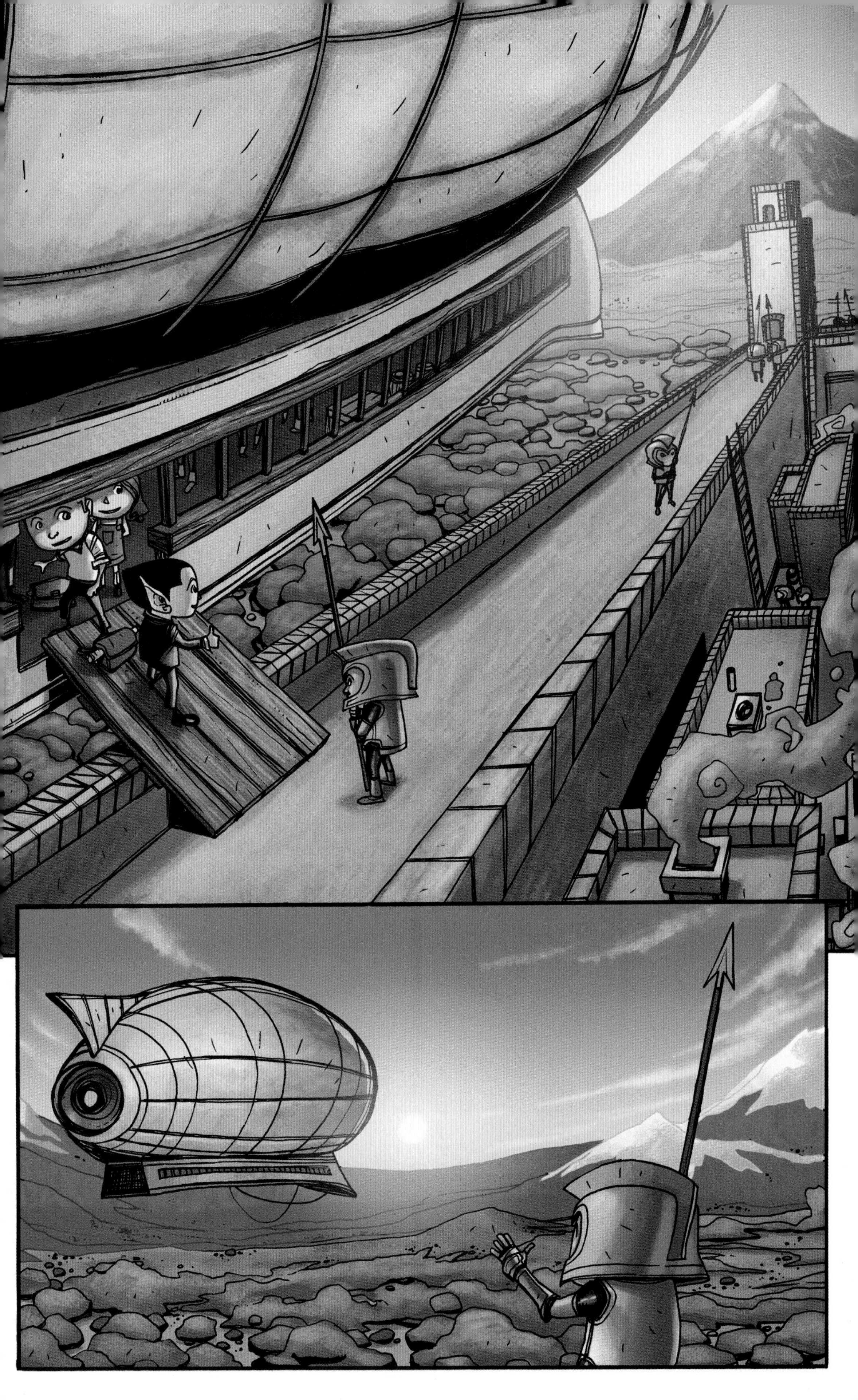

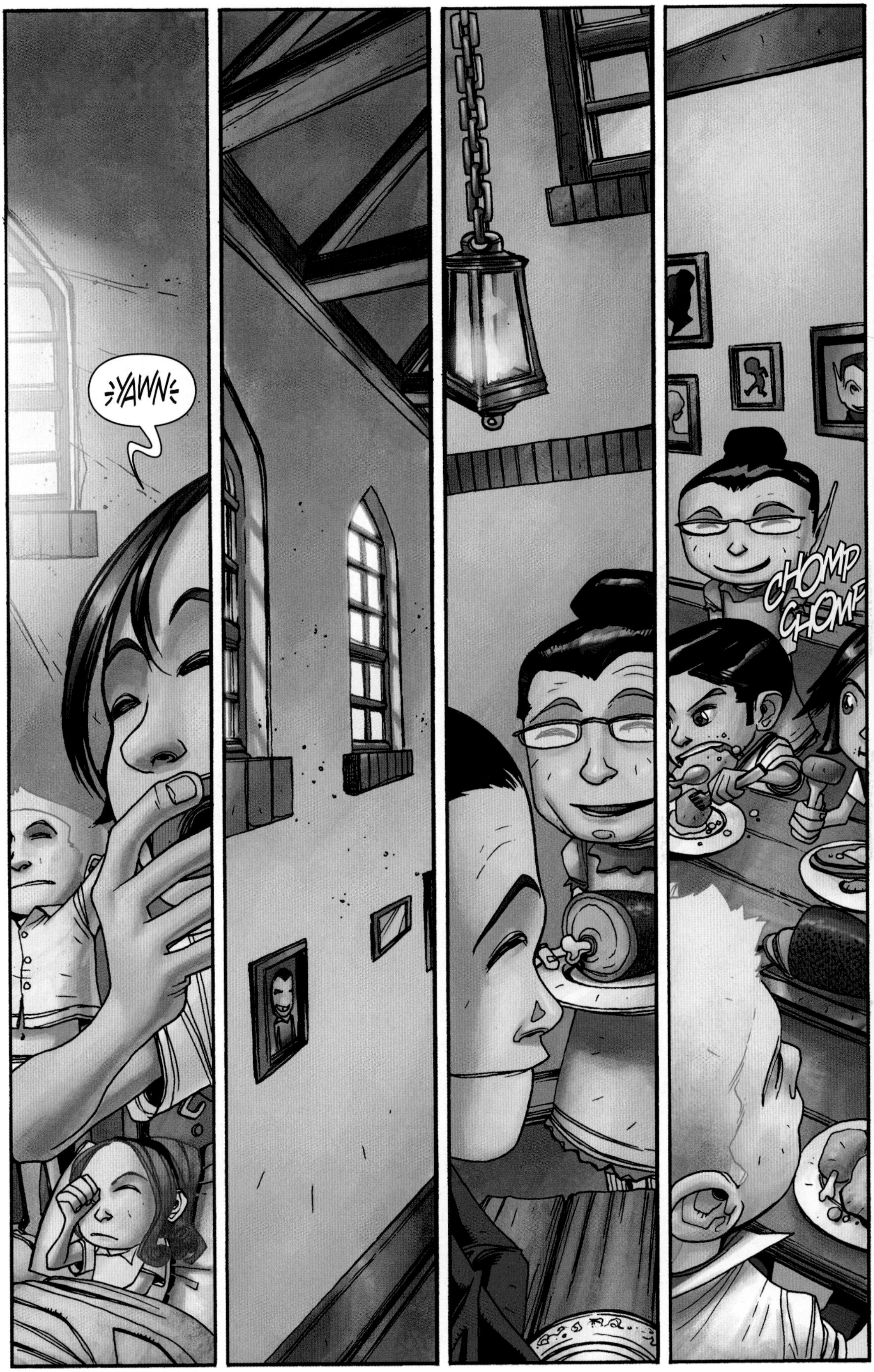
YAWN
CHOMP
CHOMP

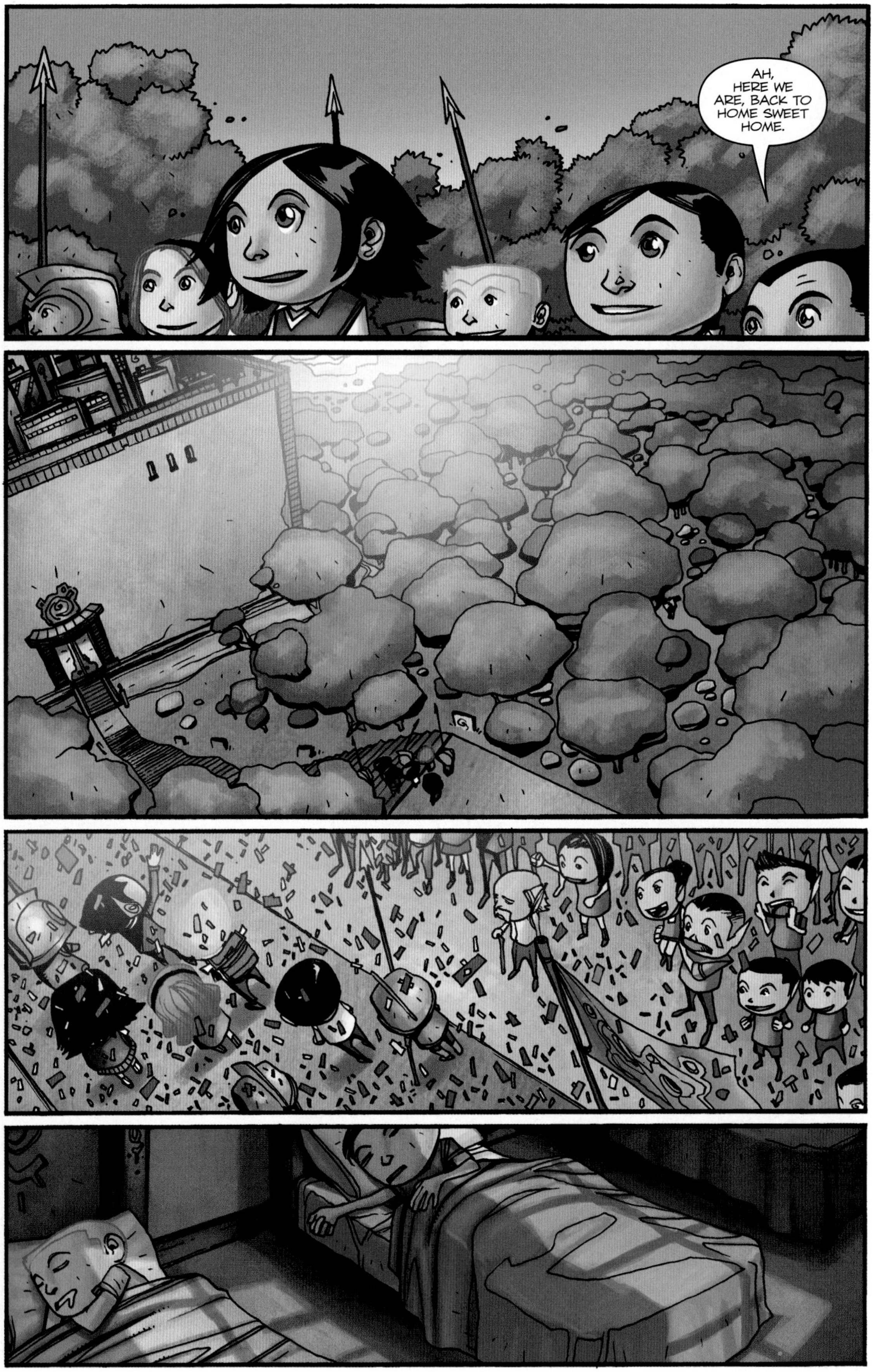
AH, HERE WE ARE, BACK TO HOME SWEET HOME.

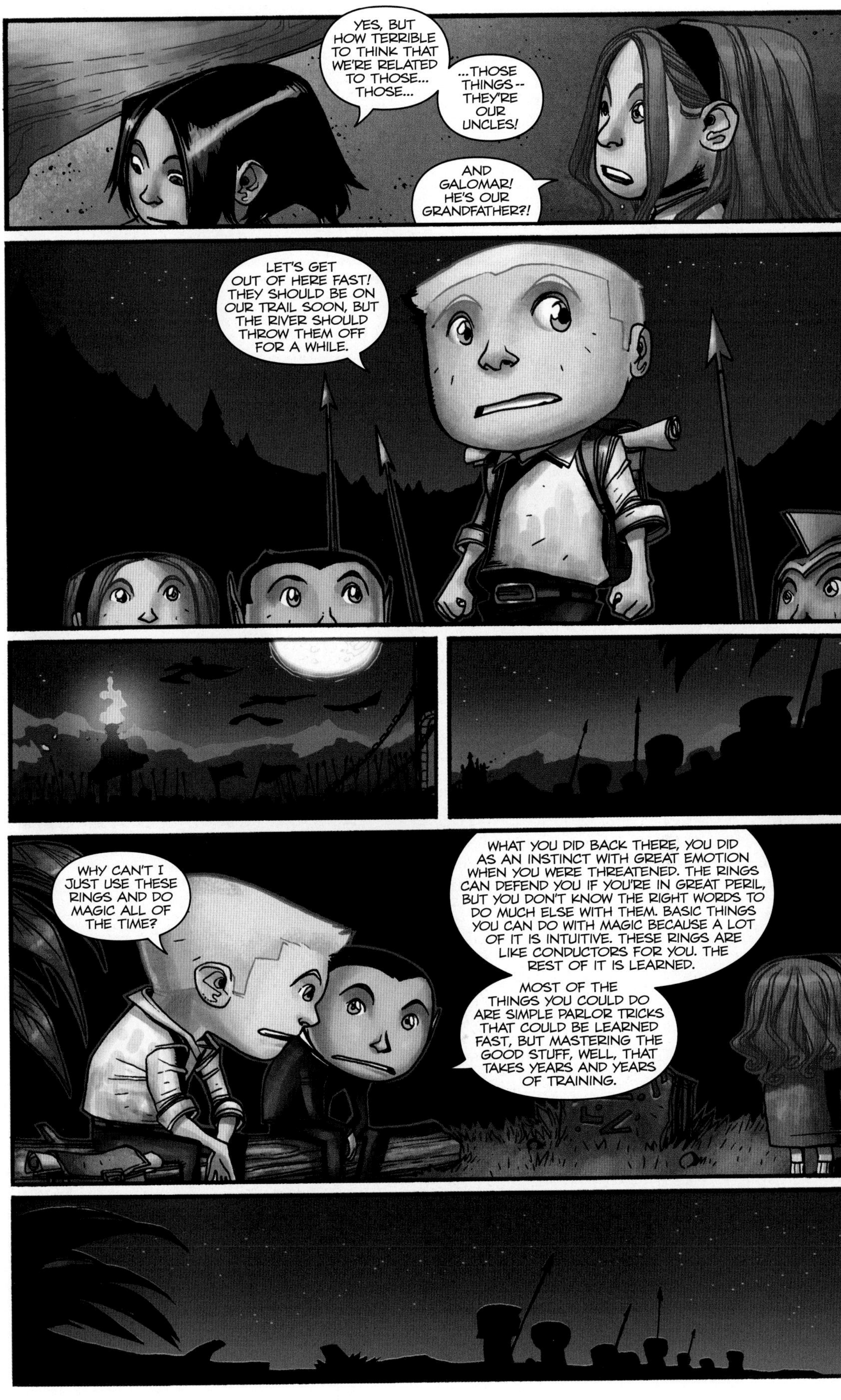
YES, BUT HOW TERRIBLE TO THINK THAT WE'RE RELATED TO THOSE... THOSE...
...THOSE THINGS-- THEY'RE OUR UNCLES!
AND GALOMAR! HE'S OUR GRANDFATHER?!
LET'S GET OUT OF HERE FAST! THEY SHOULD BE ON OUR TRAIL SOON, BUT THE RIVER SHOULD THROW THEM OFF FOR A WHILE.
WHY CAN'T I JUST USE THESE RINGS AND DO MAGIC ALL OF THE TIME?
WHAT YOU DID BACK THERE, YOU DID AS AN INSTINCT WITH GREAT EMOTION WHEN YOU WERE THREATENED. THE RINGS CAN DEFEND YOU IF YOU'RE IN GREAT PERIL, BUT YOU DON'T KNOW THE RIGHT WORDS TO DO MUCH ELSE WITH THEM. BASIC THINGS YOU CAN DO WITH MAGIC BECAUSE A LOT OF IT IS INTUITIVE. THESE RINGS ARE LIKE CONDUCTORS FOR YOU. THE REST OF IT IS LEARNED.
MOST OF THE THINGS YOU COULD DO ARE SIMPLE PARLOR TRICKS THAT COULD BE LEARNED FAST, BUT MASTERING THE GOOD STUFF, WELL, THAT TAKES YEARS AND YEARS OF TRAINING.

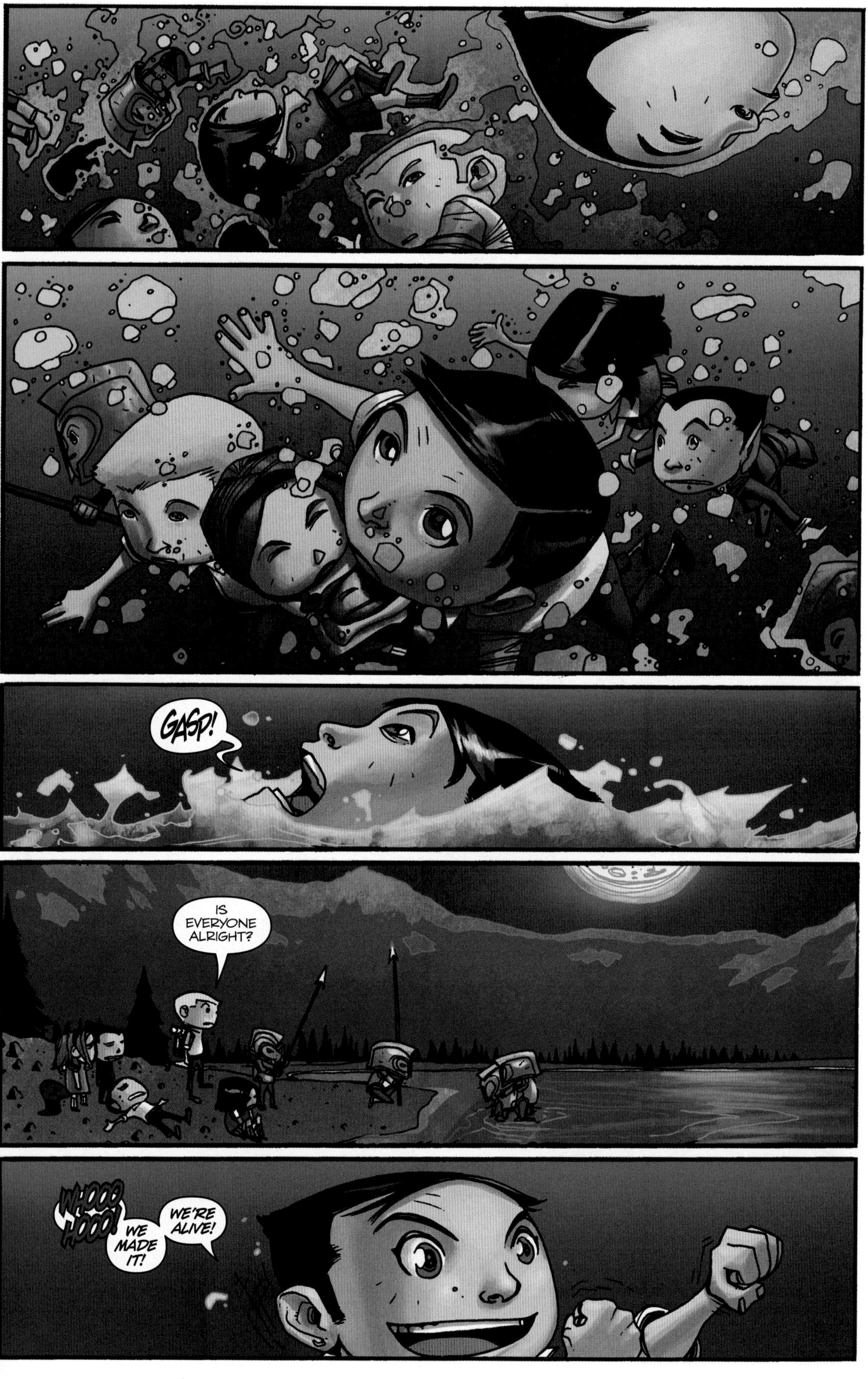
GASP!
IS EVERYONE ALRIGHT?
WHOOO HOOO!
WE MADE IT!
WE'RE ALIVE!

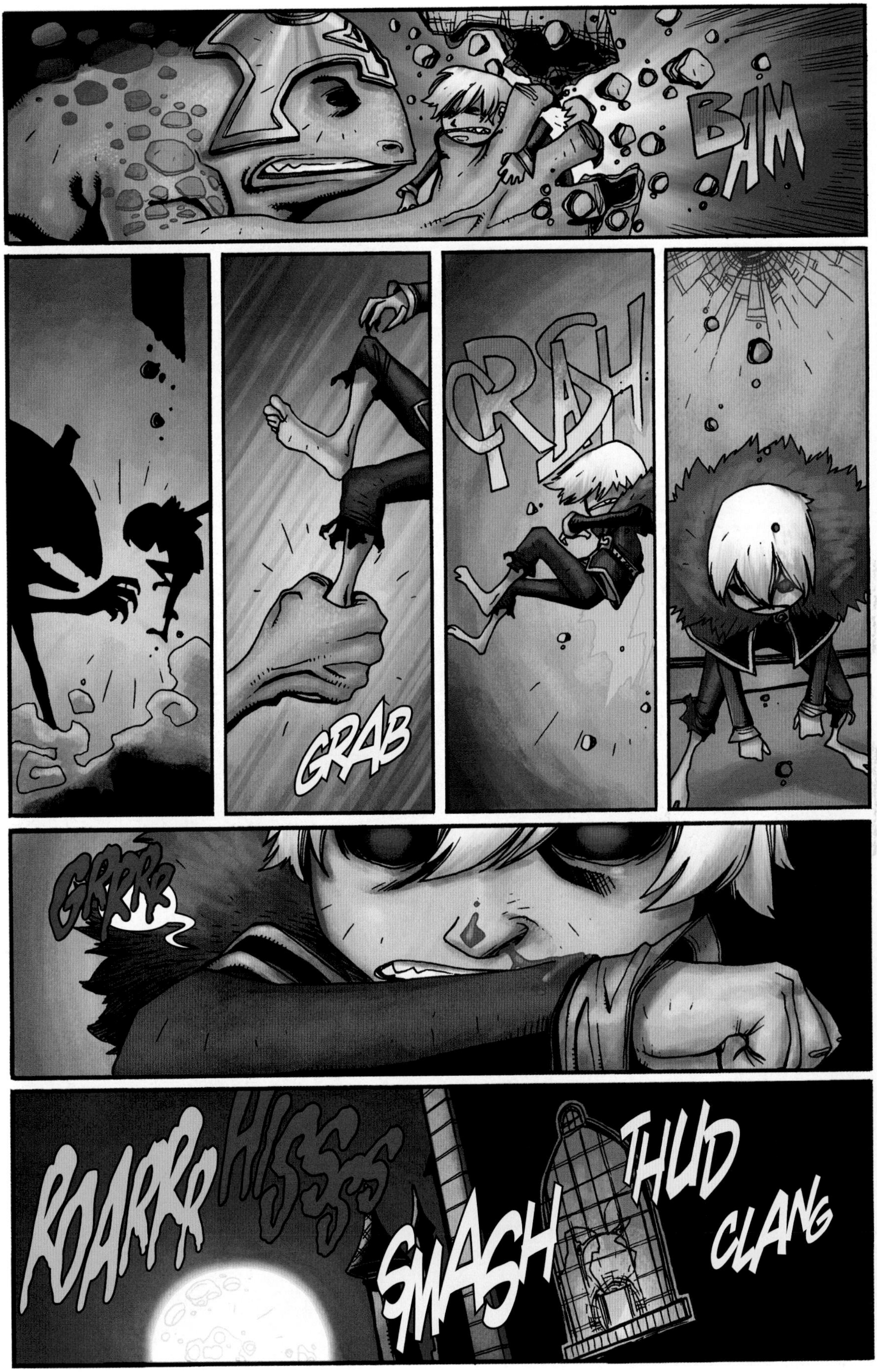
BAM
GRAB
CRASH
GRRRR
ROARRR
HISSSS
SMASH
THUD
CLANG

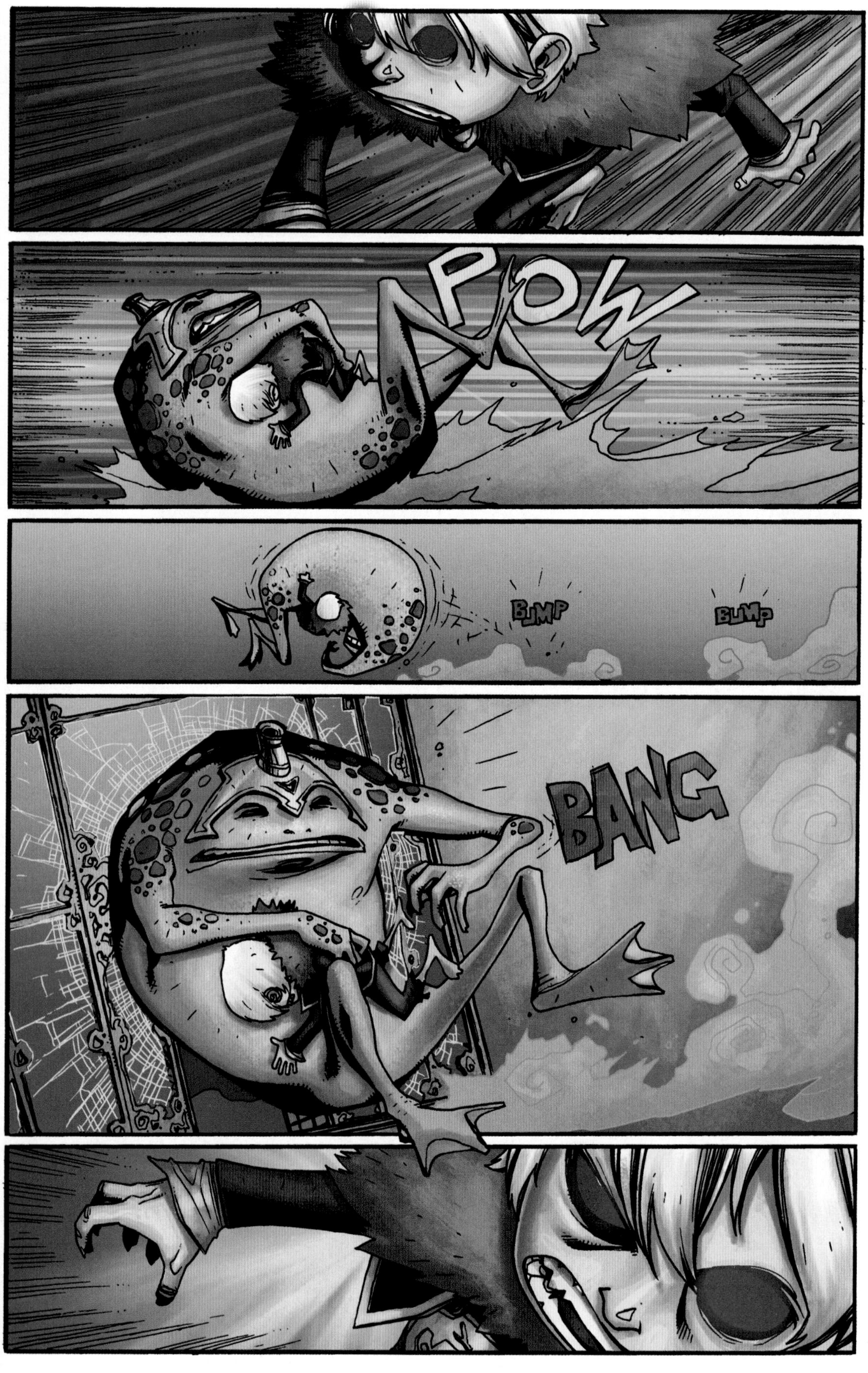
POW
BUMP
BUMP
BANG

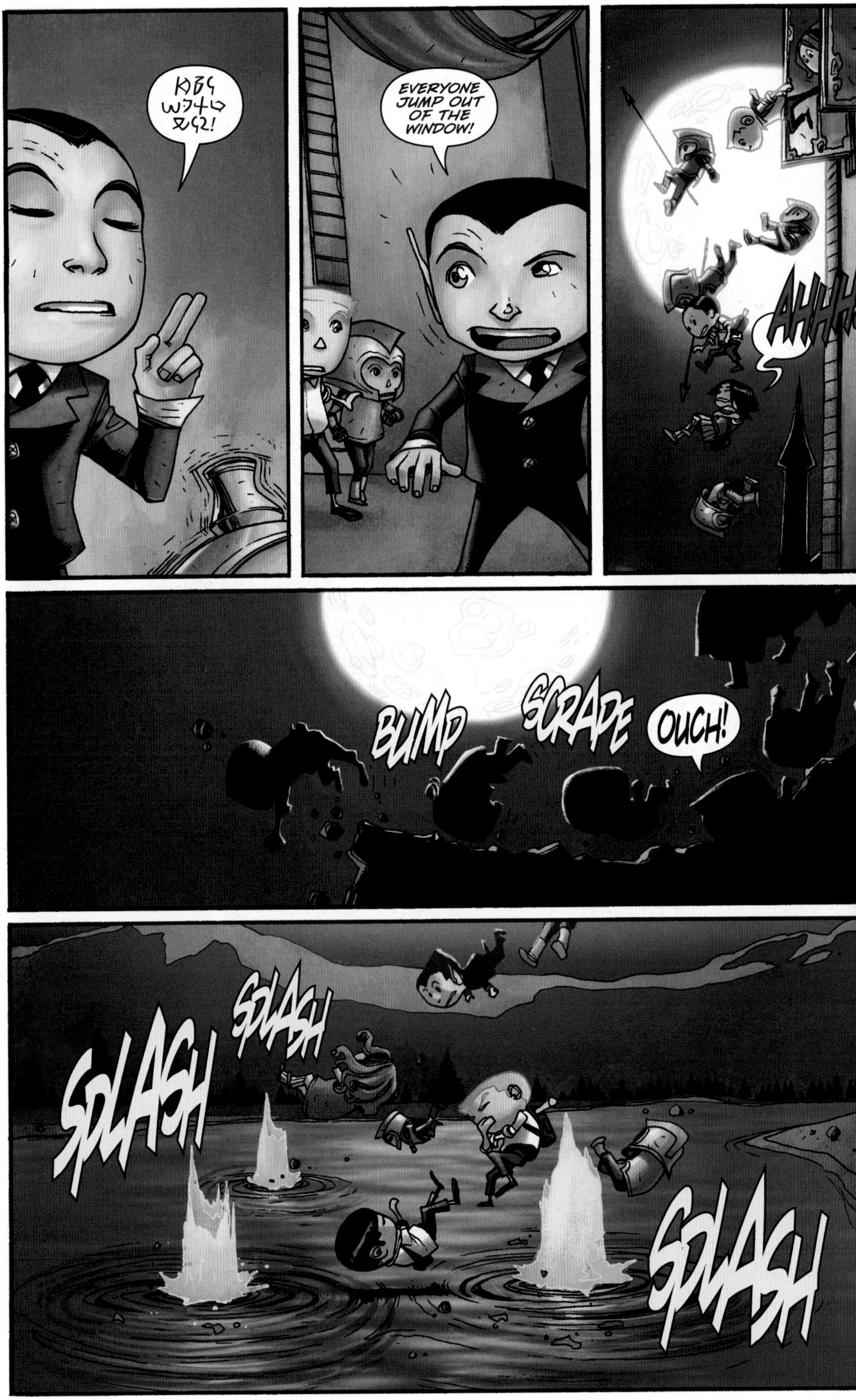
EVERYONE JUMP OUT OF THE WINDOW!
AHHH!
BUMP
SCRAPE
OUCH!
SPLASH
SPLASH
SPLASH

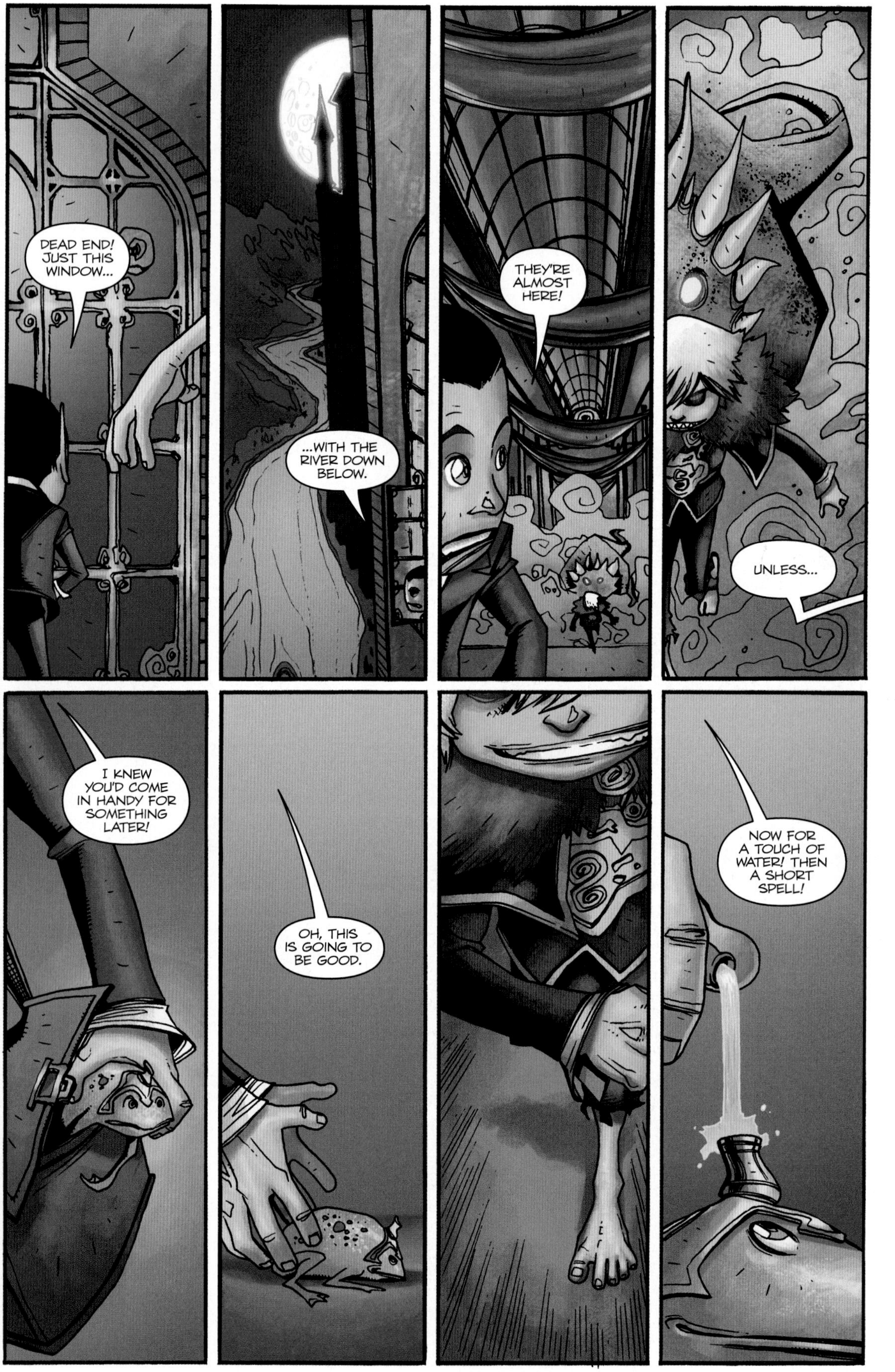
DEAD END! JUST THIS WINDOW...
...WITH THE RIVER DOWN BELOW.
THEY'RE ALMOST HERE!
UNLESS...
I KNEW YOU'D COME IN HANDY FOR SOMETHING LATER!
OH, THIS IS GOING TO BE GOOD.
NOW FOR A TOUCH OF WATER! THEN A SHORT SPELL!

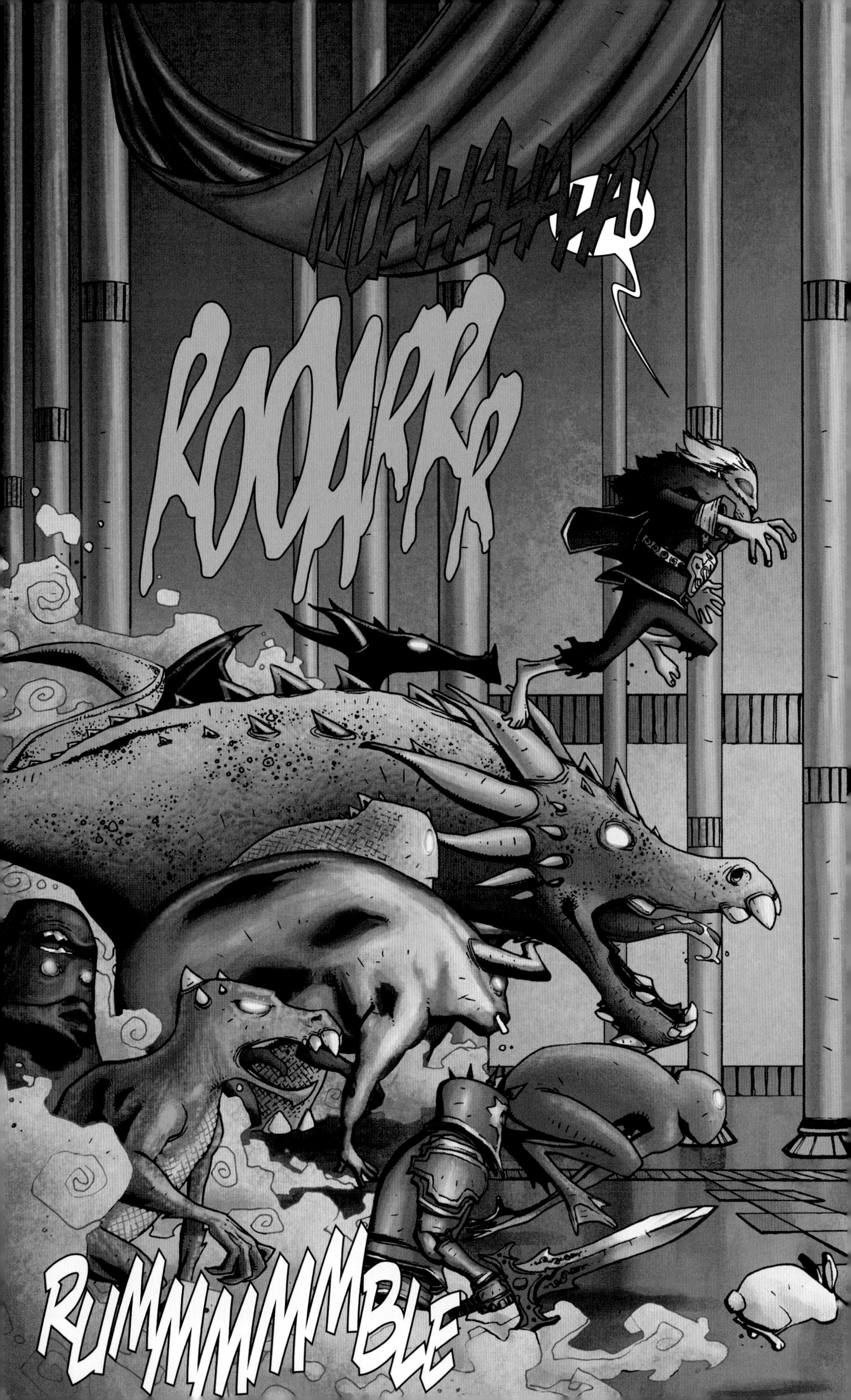
MUAHAHAHAHA!
ROOARRR
RUMMMMMMBLE

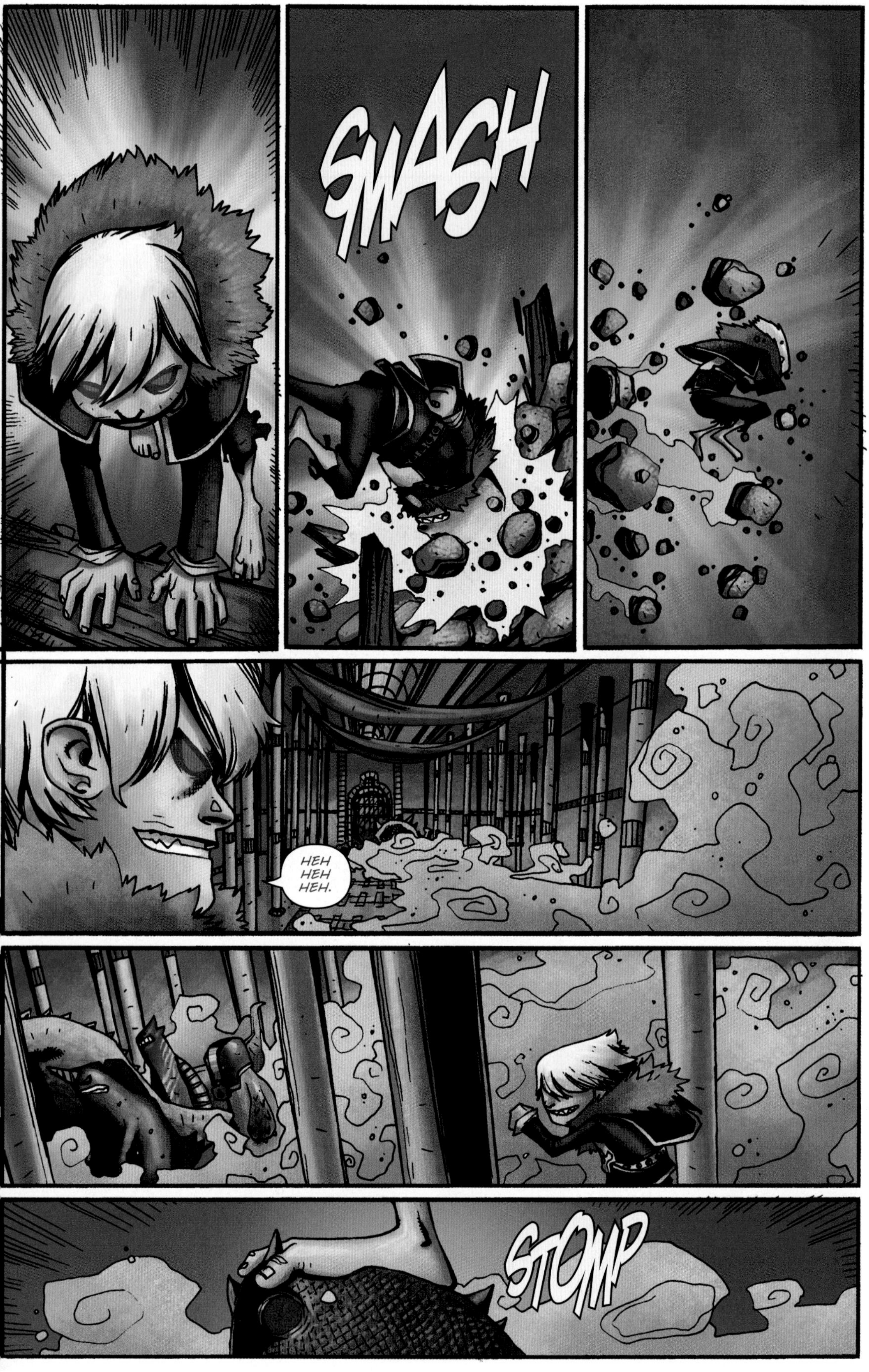
SWASH
HEH HEH HEH.
STOMP

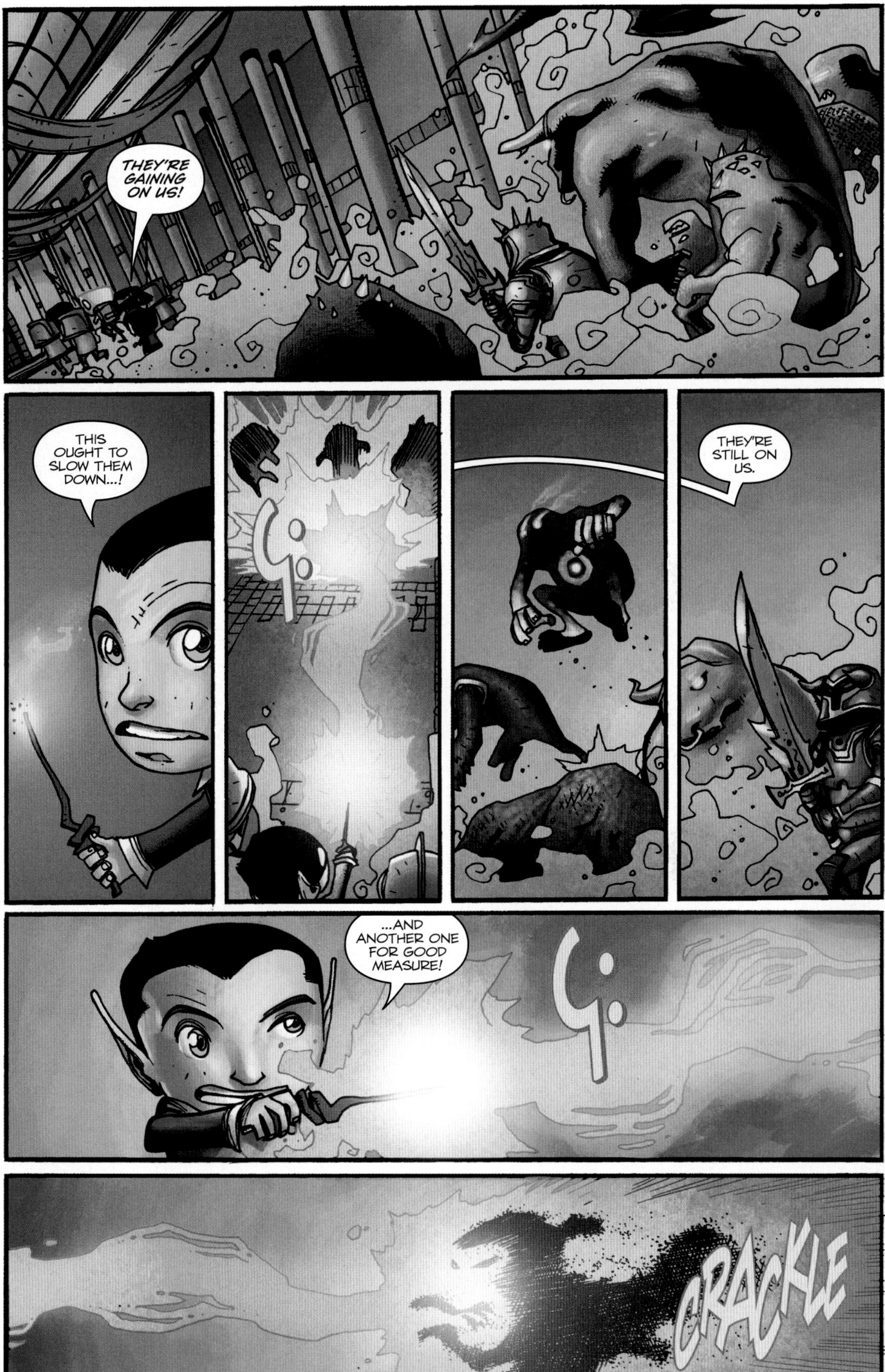
THEY'RE GAINING ON US!
THIS OUGHT TO SLOW THEM DOWN...!
THEY'RE STILL ON US.
...AND ANOTHER ONE FOR GOOD MEASURE!
CRACKLE

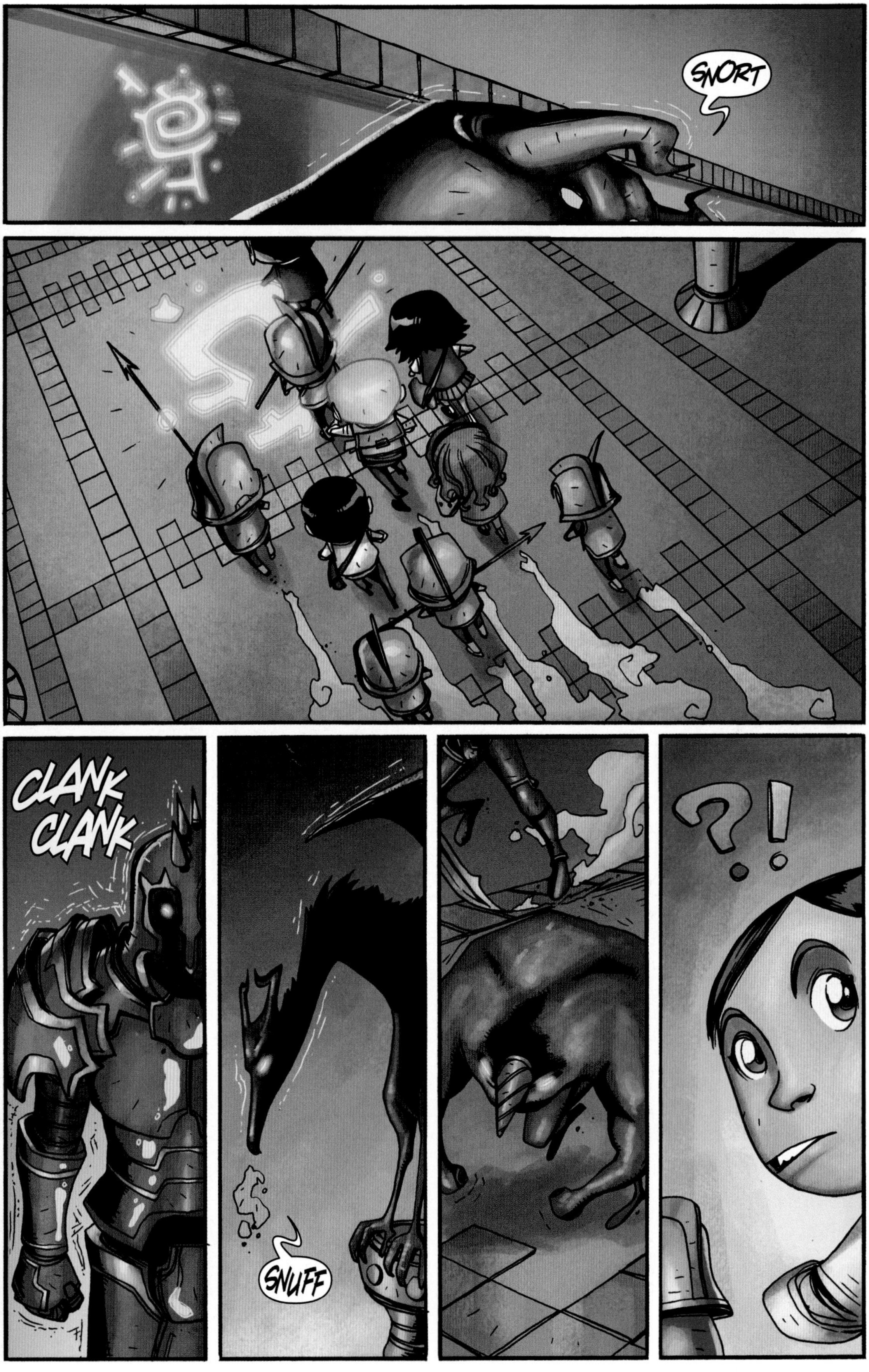
SNORT
CLANK
CLANK
SNUFF
?!

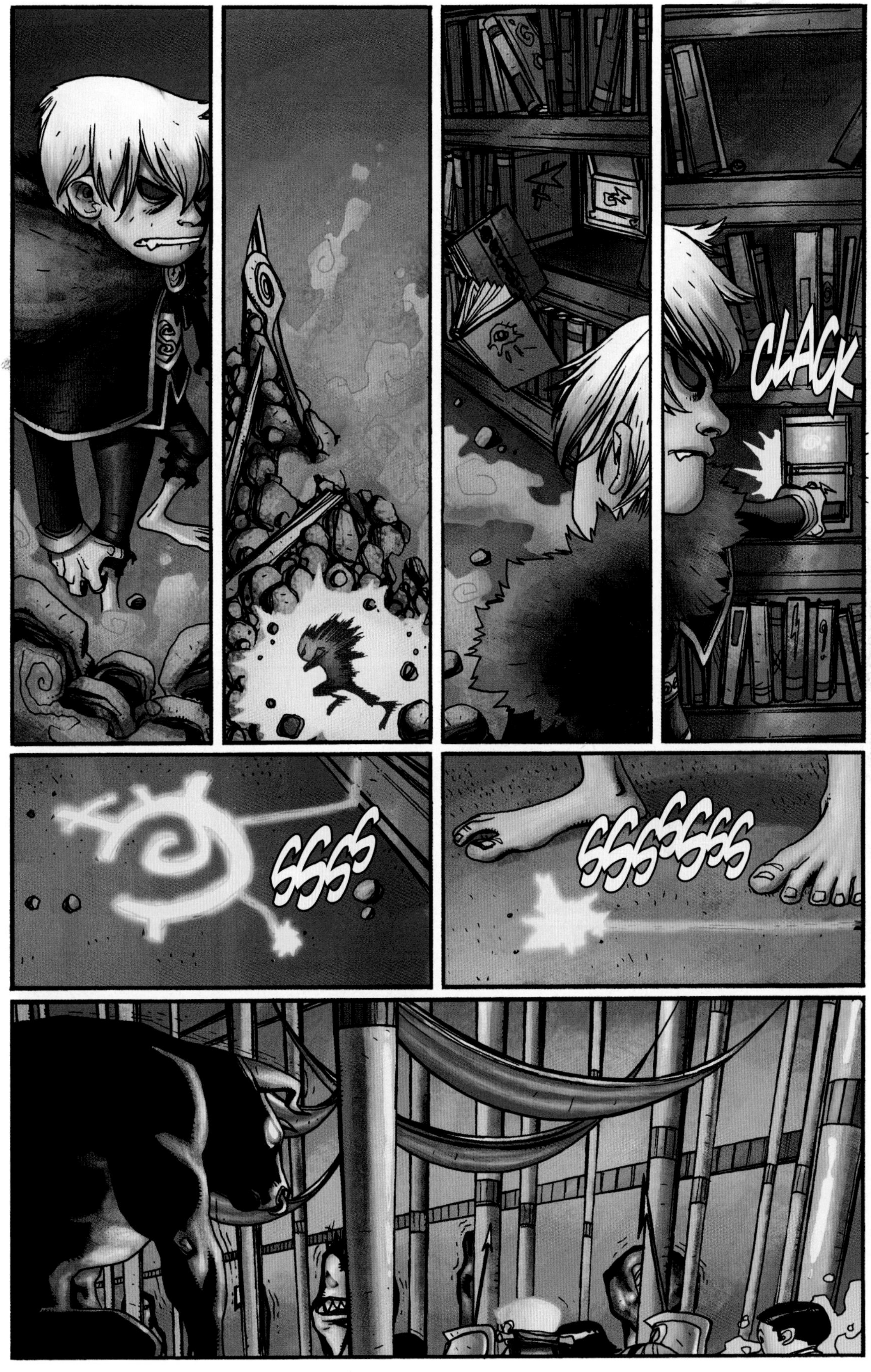
CLACK
SSSS
SSSSSSS

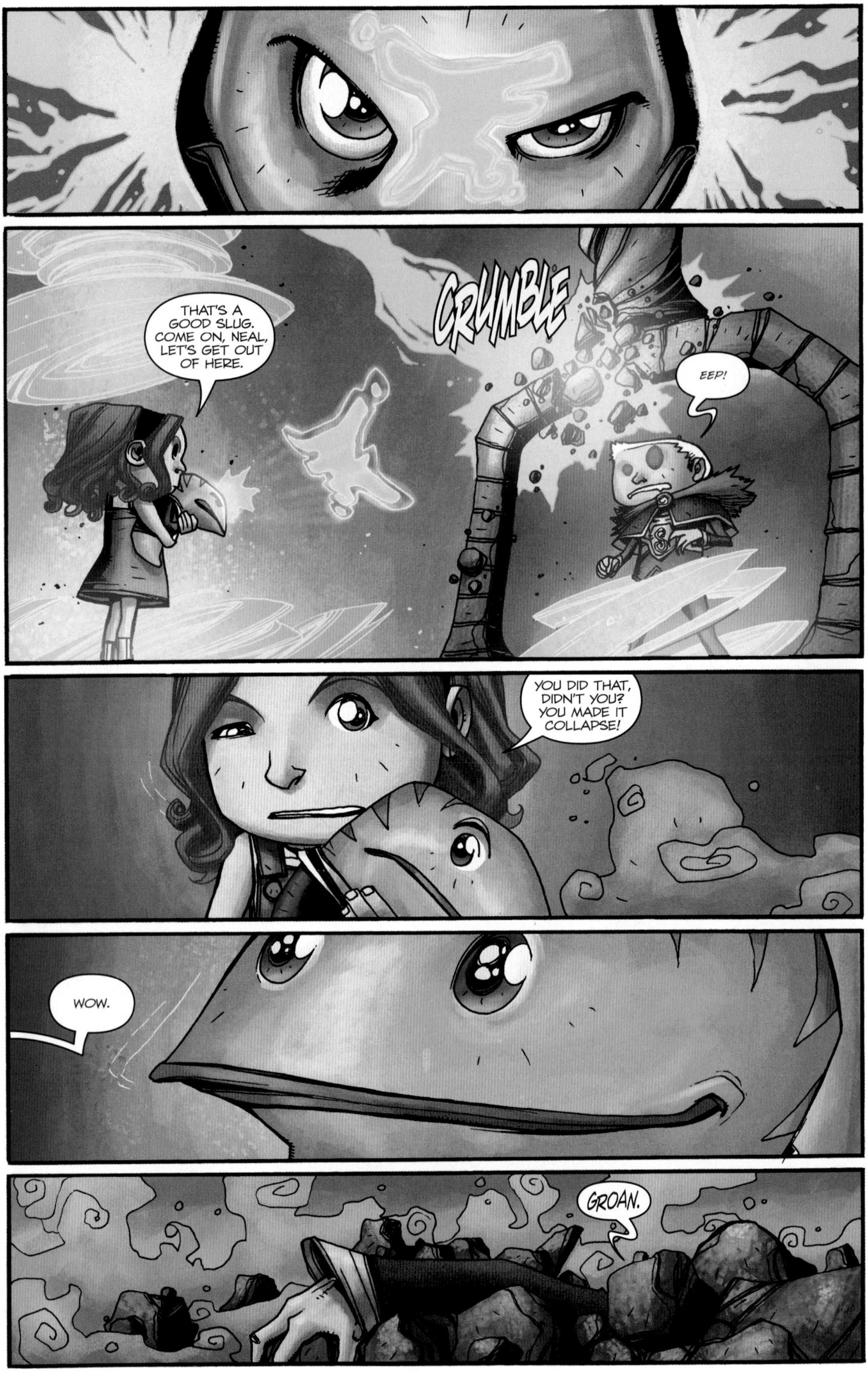
THAT'S A GOOD SLUG. COME ON, NEAL, LET'S GET OUT OF HERE.
CRUMBLE
EEP!
YOU DID THAT, DIDN'T YOU? YOU MADE IT COLLAPSE!
WOW.
GROAN.

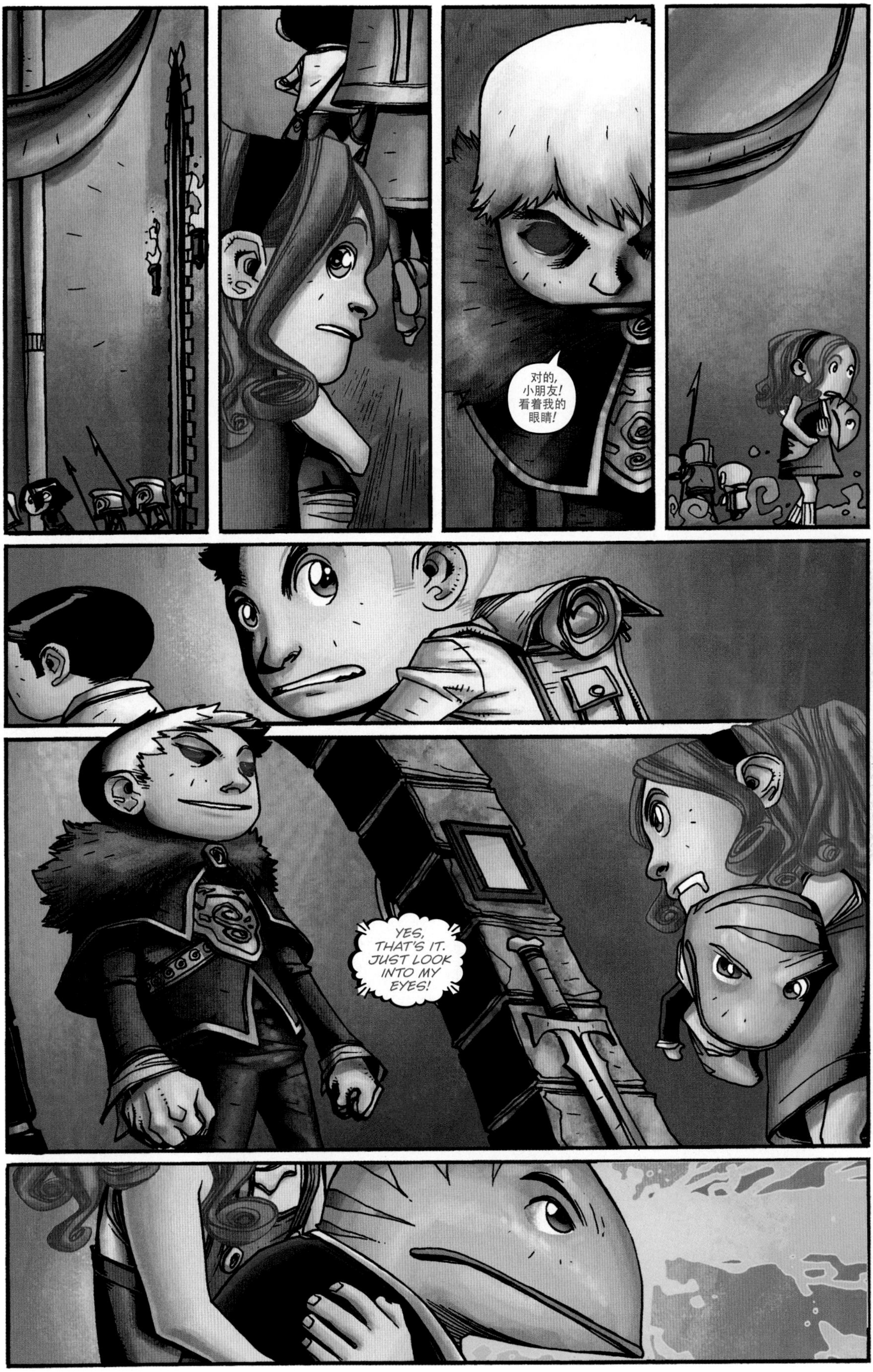
对的,
小朋友!
看着我的
眼睛!
YES, THAT'S IT. JUST LOOK INTO MY EYES!

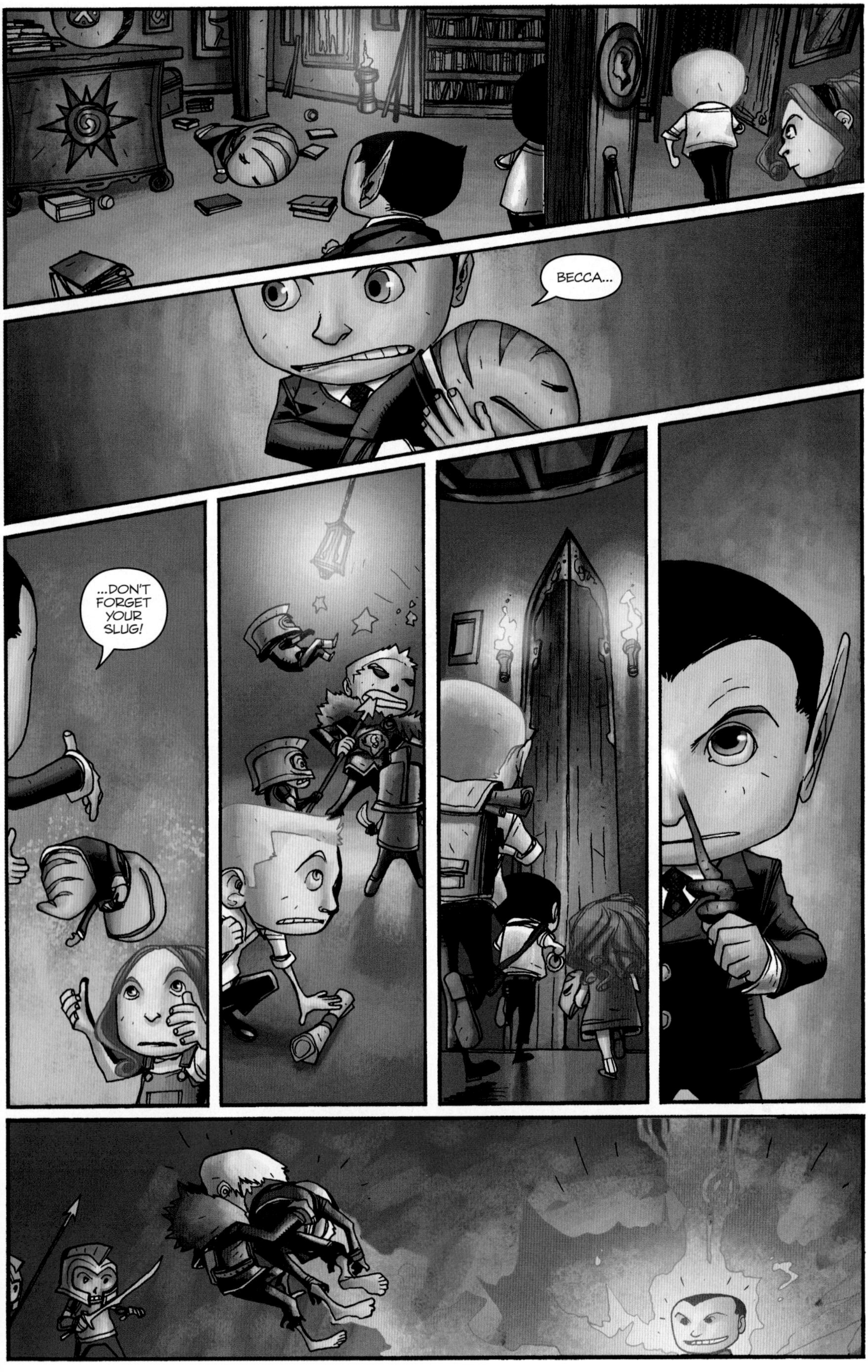
BECCA...
...DON'T FORGET YOUR SLUG!

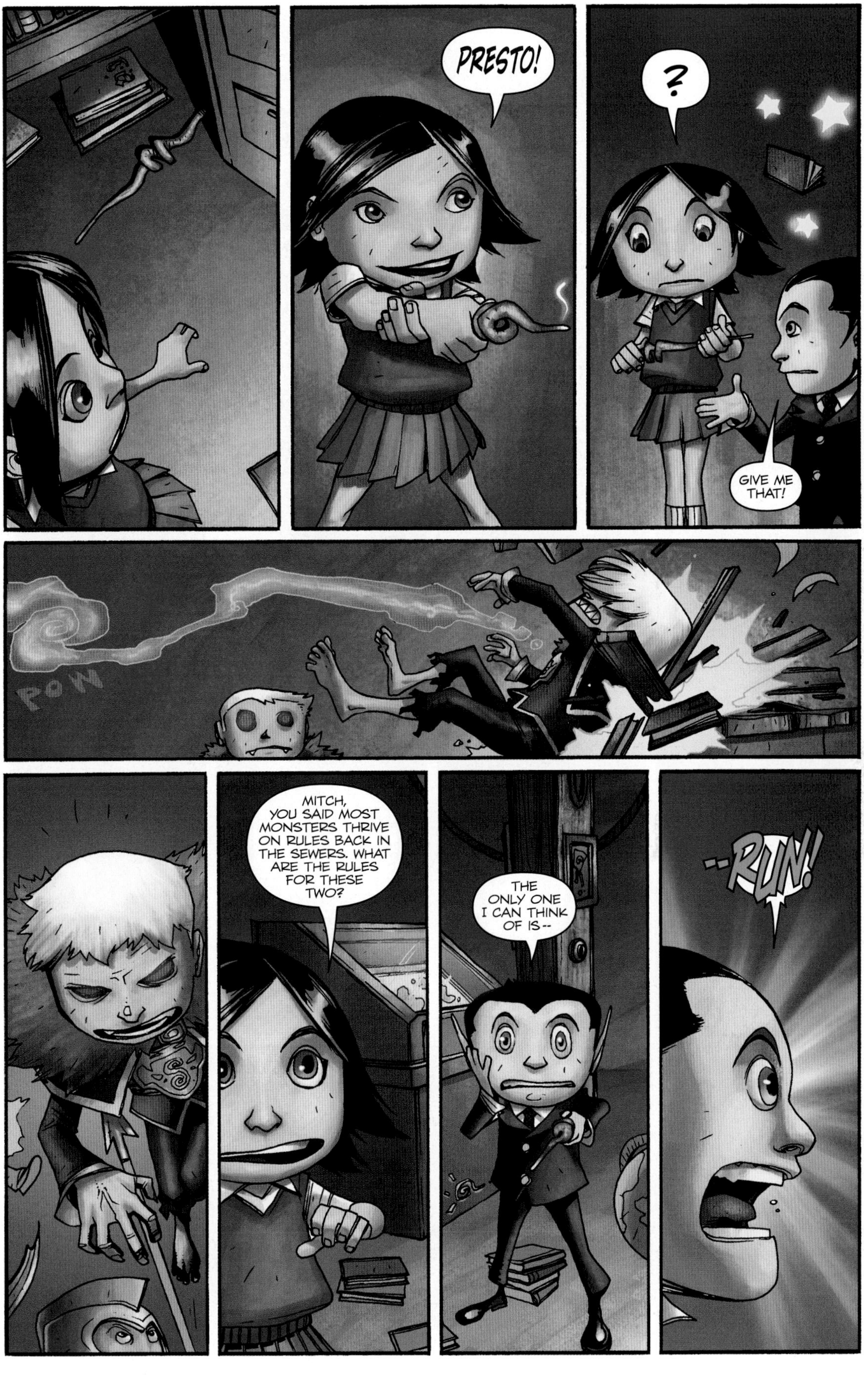
PRESTO!
?
GIVE ME THAT!
POW
MITCH, YOU SAID MOST MONSTERS THRIVE ON RULES BACK IN THE SEWERS. WHAT ARE THE RULES FOR THESE TWO?
THE ONLY ONE I CAN THINK OF IS--
--RUN!

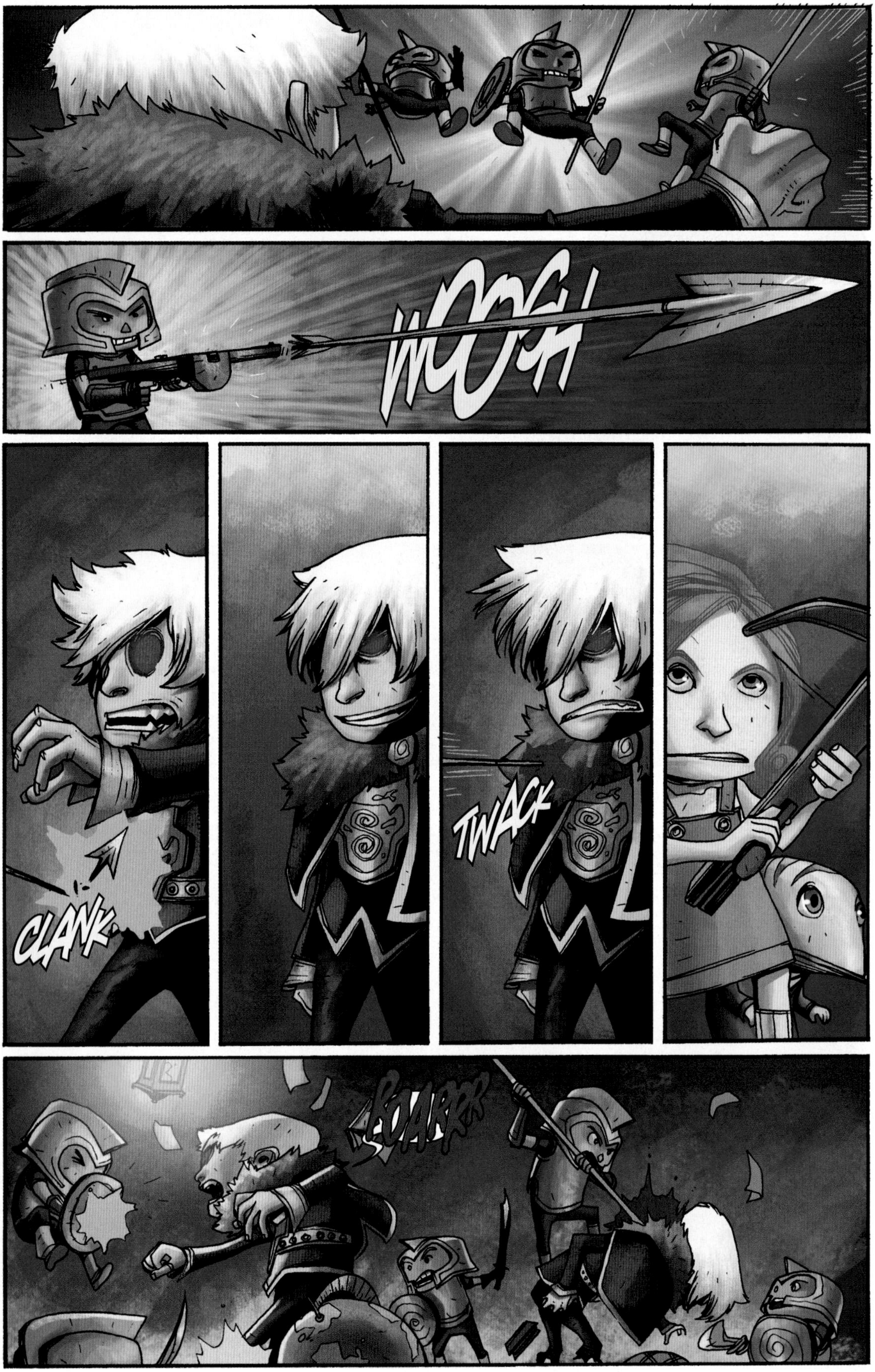
WOOSH
CLANK
TWACK
ROARRR

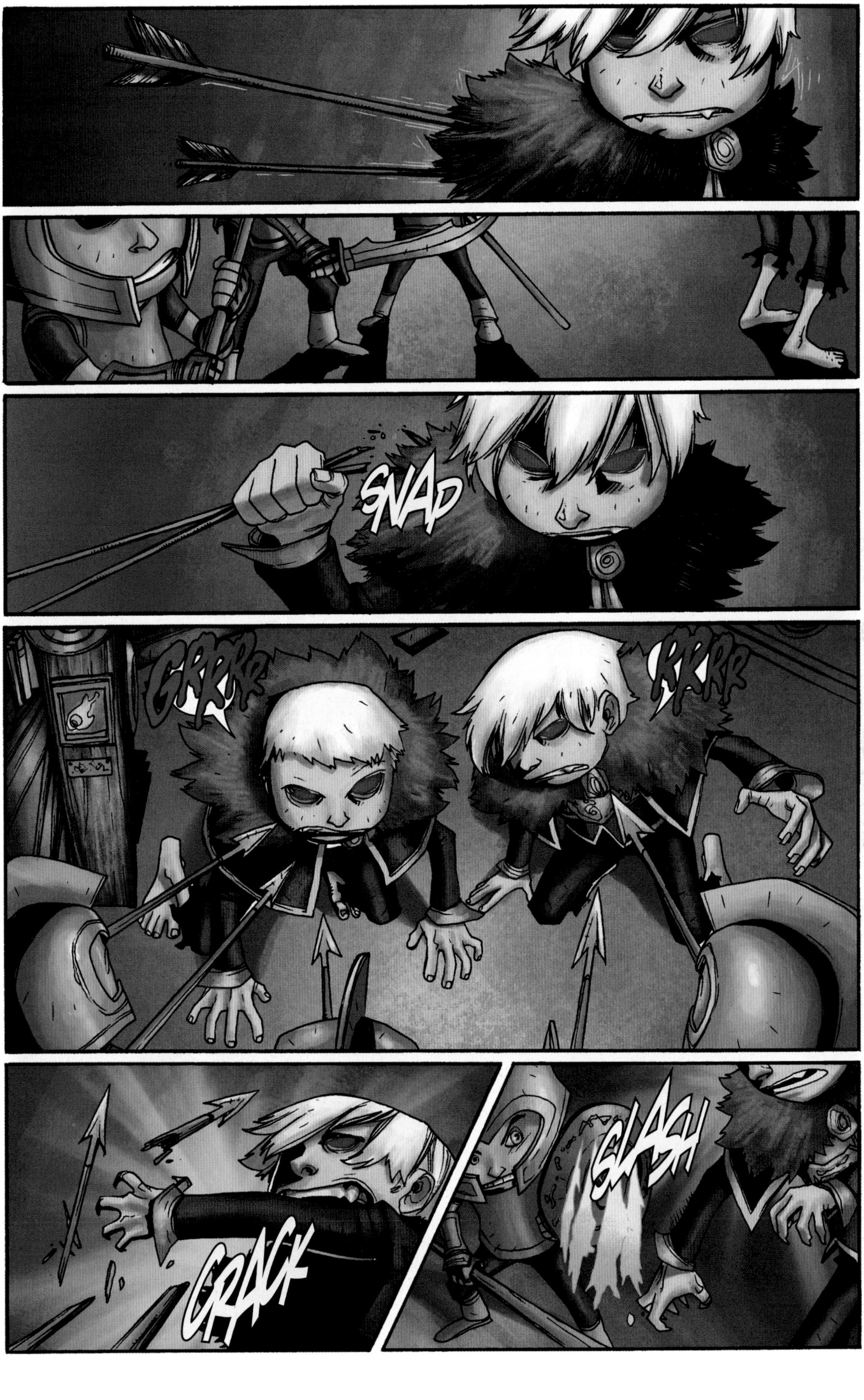
SNAP
GRRRR
RRRR
CRACK
SLASH

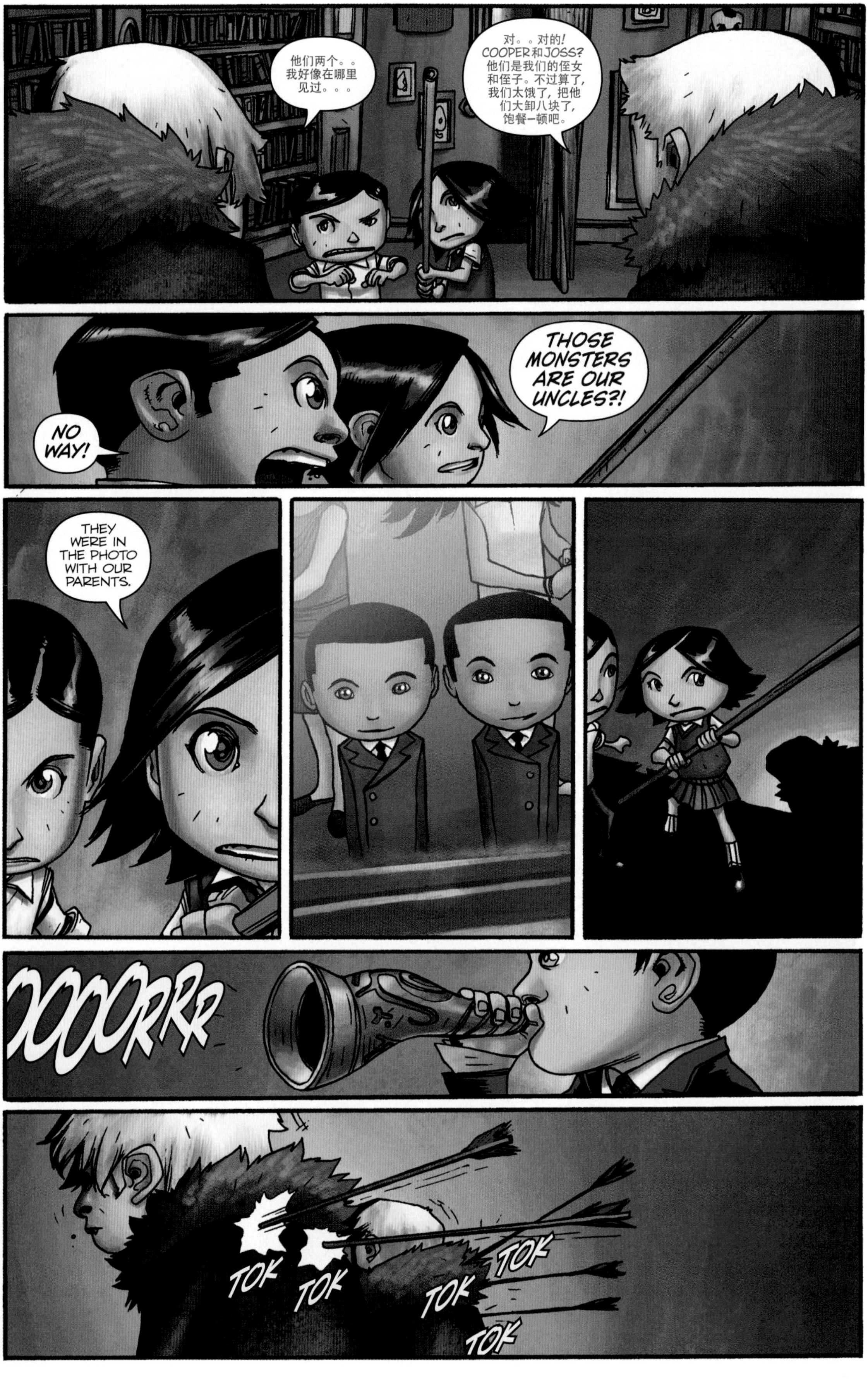

他们两个。。我好像在哪里见过。。。
对。。对的! COOPER和JOSS? 他们是我们的侄女和侄子。不过算了，我们太饿了，把他们大卸八块了，饱餐一顿吧。
THOSE MONSTERS ARE OUR UNCLES?!
NO WAY!
THEY WERE IN THE PHOTO WITH OUR PARENTS.
OOOORRR
TOK
TOK
TOK
TOK
TOK

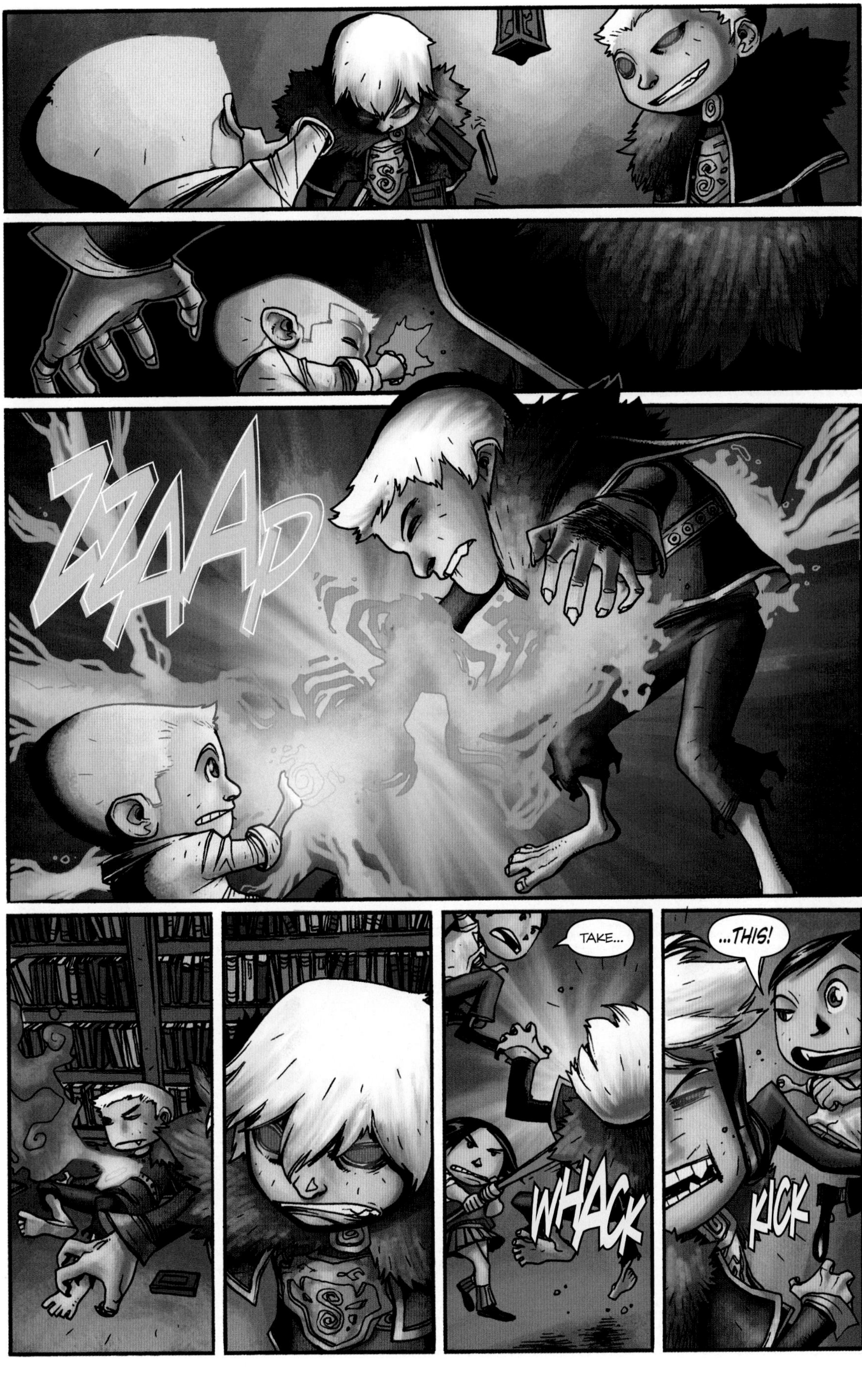

ZZZAAP
TAKE...
WHACK
...THIS!
KICK

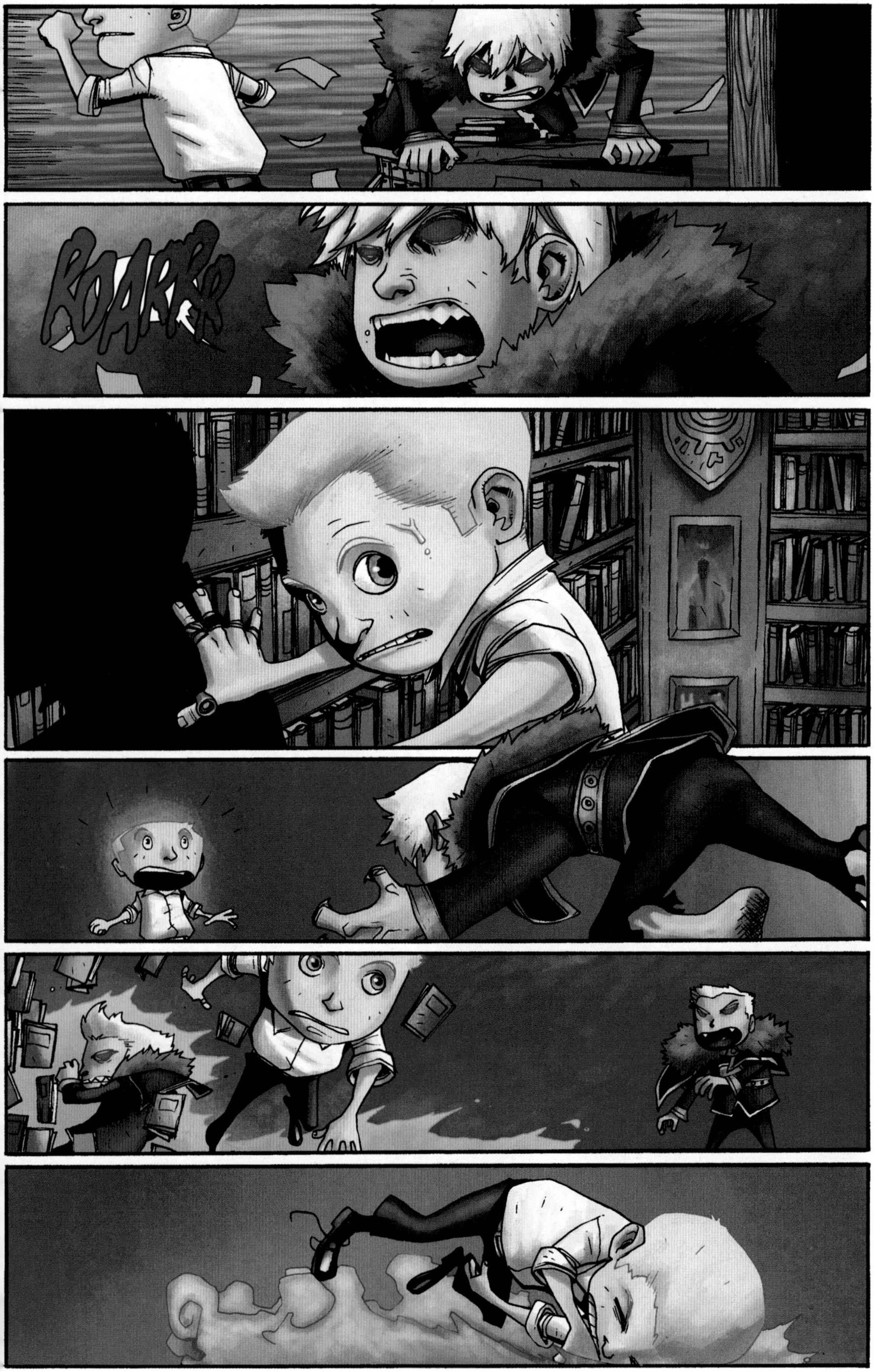
ROARRR

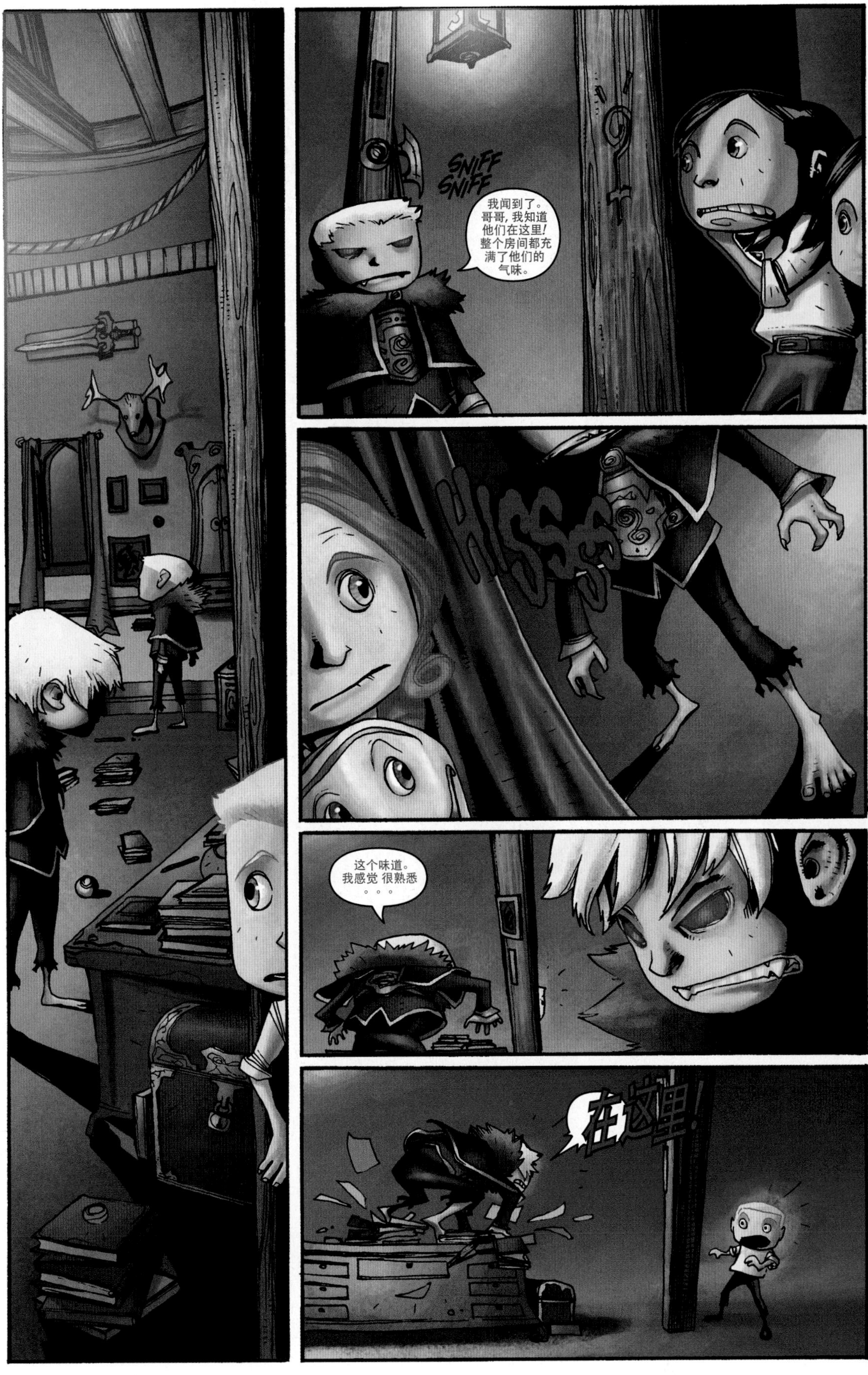
SNIFF SNIFF
我闻到了。哥哥，我知道他们在这里！整个房间都充满了他们的气味。
HISSSS
这个味道。我感觉 很熟悉。。。
在这里！

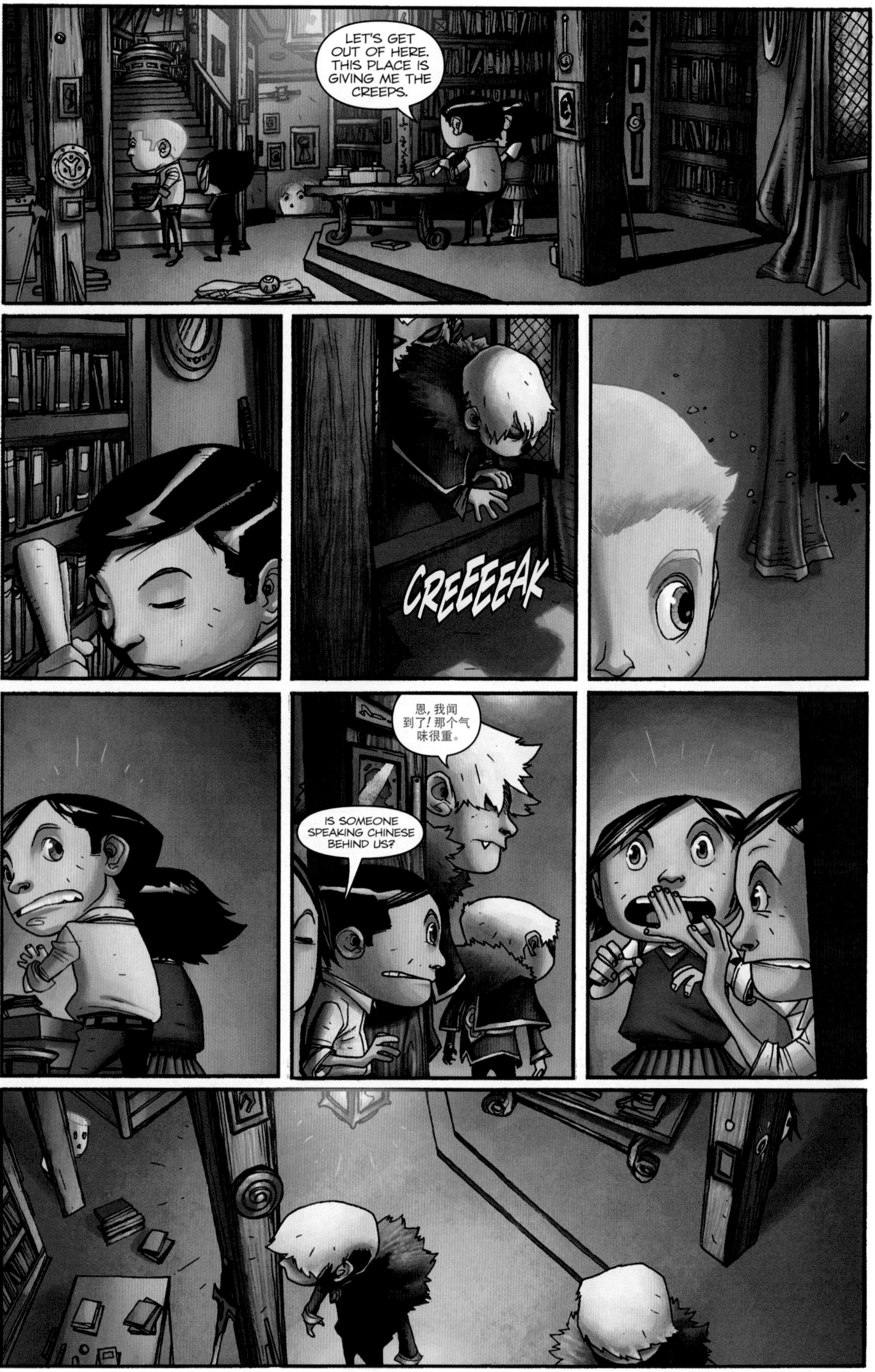
LET'S GET OUT OF HERE. THIS PLACE IS GIVING ME THE CREEPS.
CREEEEAK
恩，我闻到了！那个气味很重。
IS SOMEONE SPEAKING CHINESE BEHIND US?

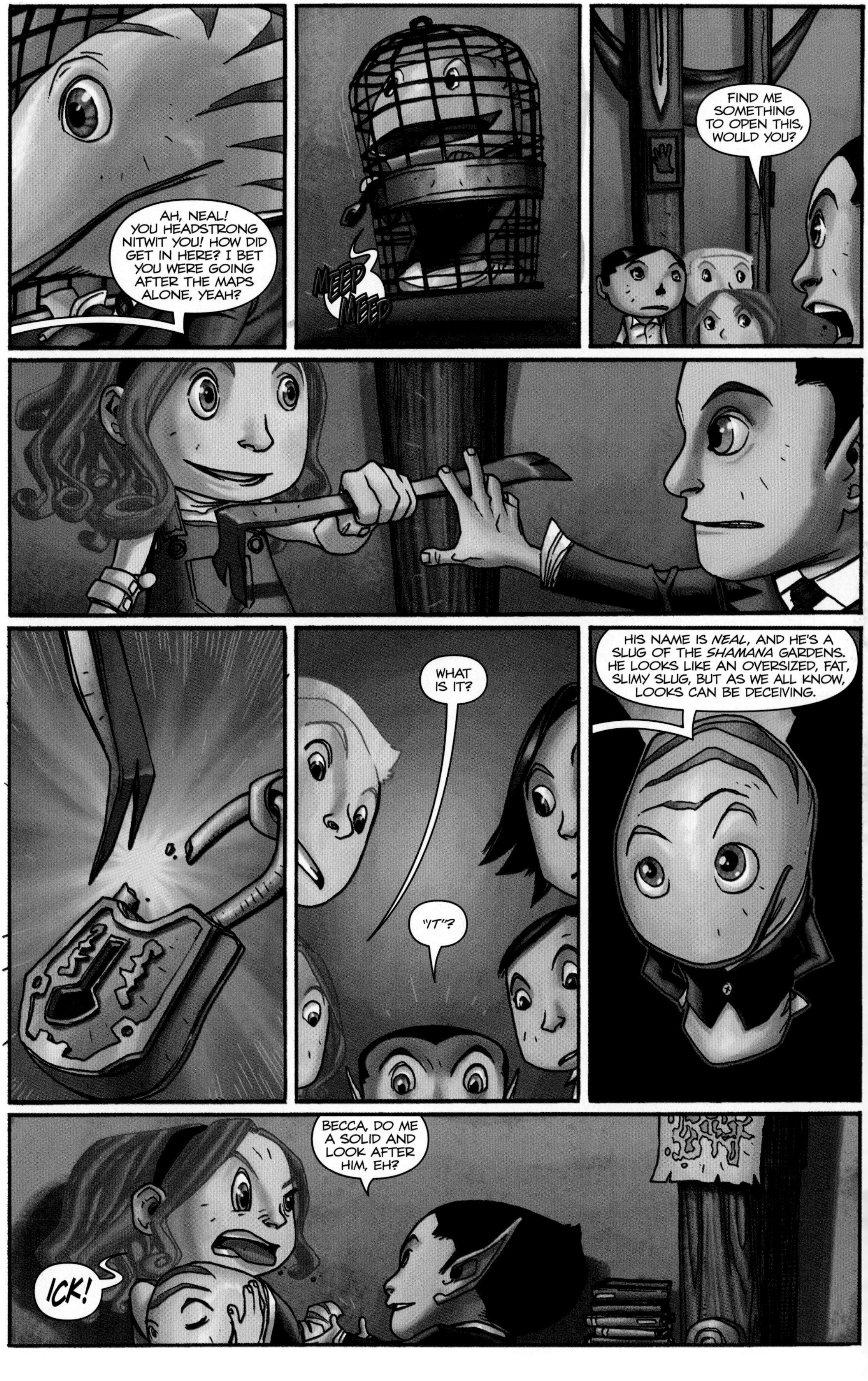
AH, NEAL! YOU HEADSTRONG NITWIT YOU! HOW DID GET IN HERE? I BET YOU WERE GOING AFTER THE MAPS ALONE, YEAH?
MEEP MEEP
FIND ME SOMETHING TO OPEN THIS, WOULD YOU?
WHAT IS IT?
"IT"?
HIS NAME IS NEAL, AND HE'S A SLUG OF THE SHAMANA GARDENS. HE LOOKS LIKE AN OVERSIZED, FAT, SLIMY SLUG, BUT AS WE ALL KNOW, LOOKS CAN BE DECEIVING.
BECCA, DO ME A SOLID AND LOOK AFTER HIM, EH?
ICK!

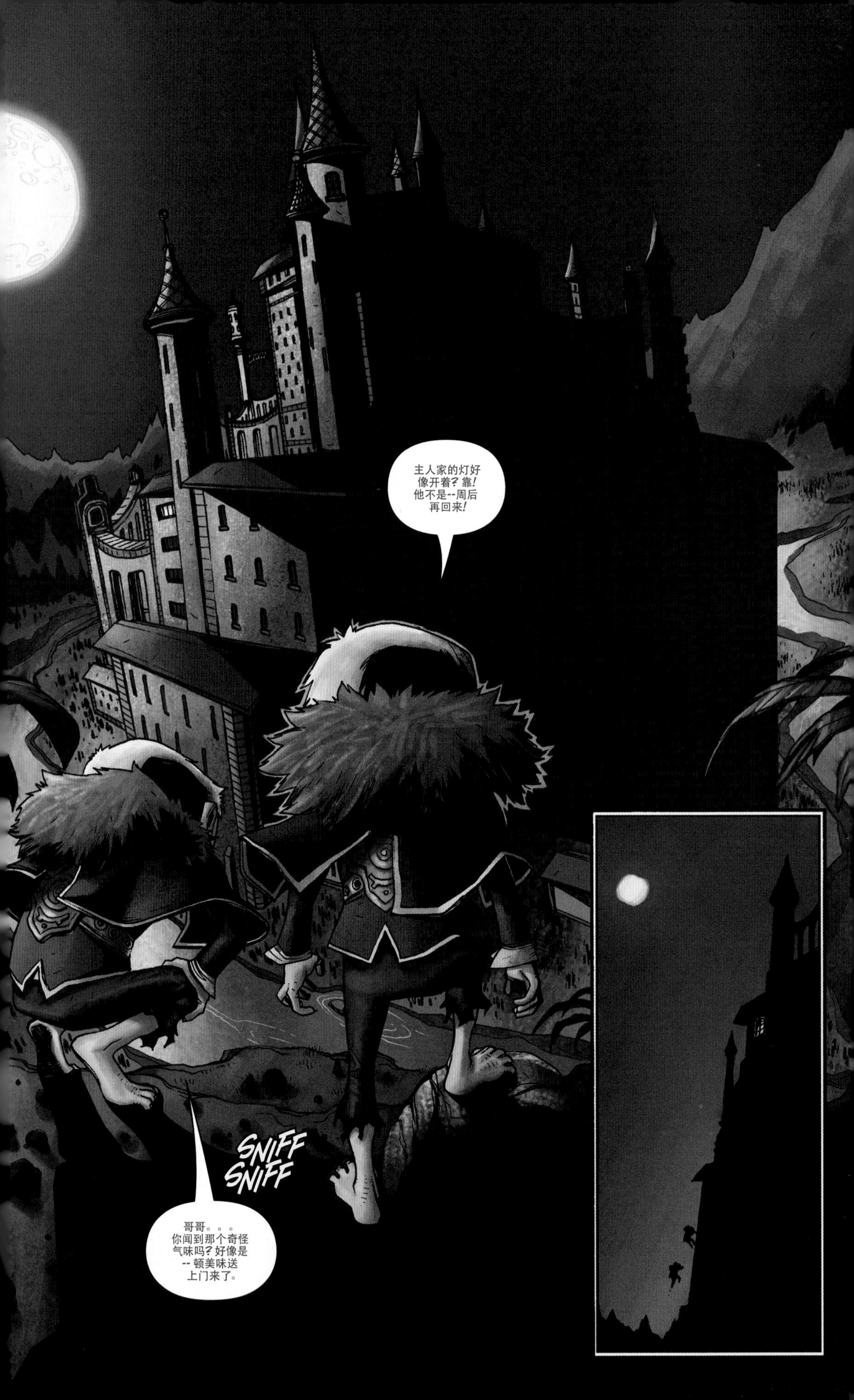
主人家的灯好像开着? 靠! 他不是--周后再回来!
SNIFF SNIFF
哥哥。。。你闻到那个奇怪气味吗? 好像是-- 顿美味送上门来了。

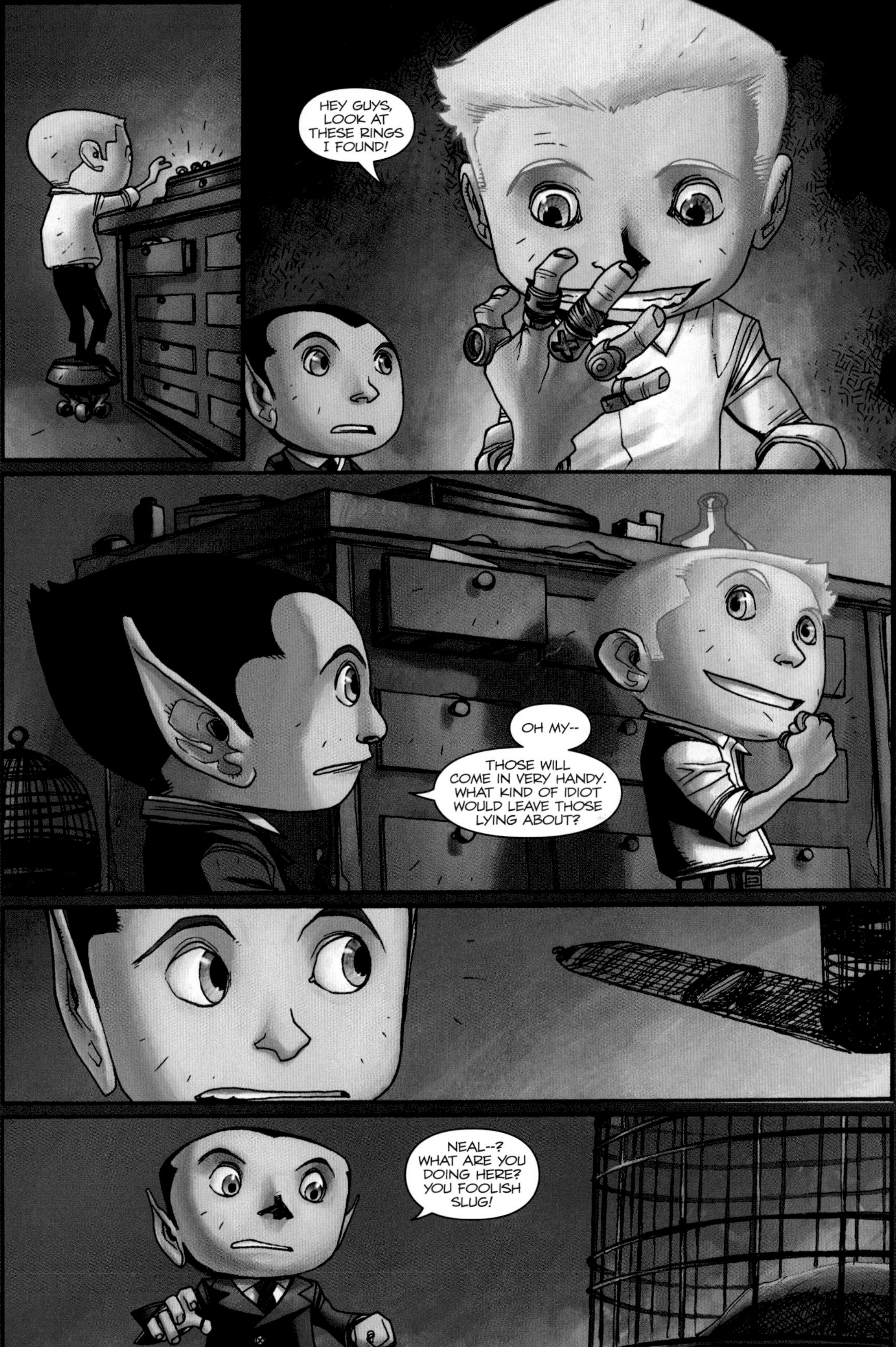
HEY GUYS, LOOK AT THESE RINGS I FOUND!
OH MY--
THOSE WILL COME IN VERY HANDY. WHAT KIND OF IDIOT WOULD LEAVE THOSE LYING ABOUT?
NEAL--? WHAT ARE YOU DOING HERE? YOU FOOLISH SLUG!

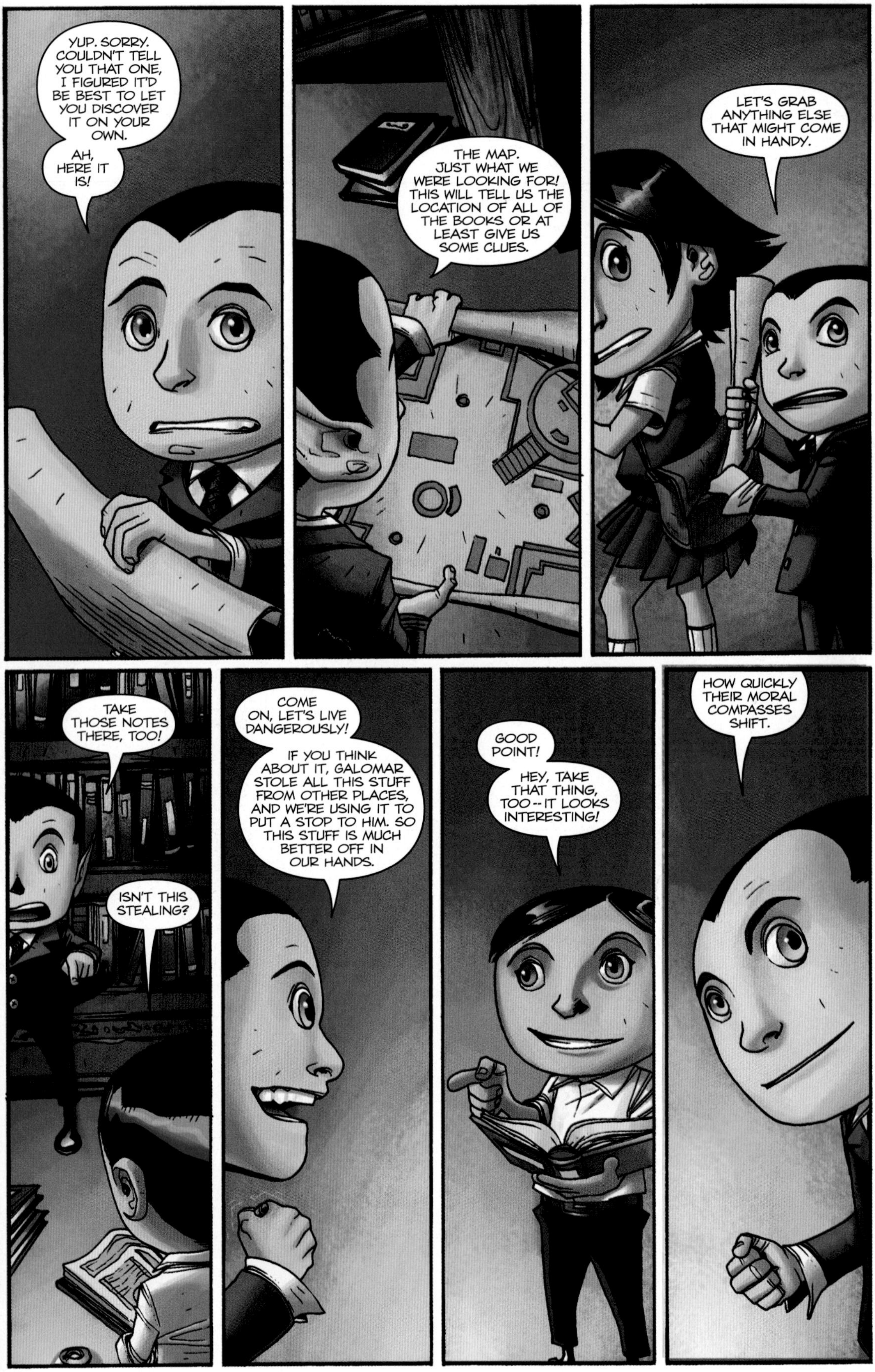
YUP. SORRY. COULDN'T TELL YOU THAT ONE, I FIGURED IT'D BE BEST TO LET YOU DISCOVER IT ON YOUR OWN.
AH, HERE IT IS!
THE MAP. JUST WHAT WE WERE LOOKING FOR! THIS WILL TELL US THE LOCATION OF ALL OF THE BOOKS OR AT LEAST GIVE US SOME CLUES.
LET'S GRAB ANYTHING ELSE THAT MIGHT COME IN HANDY.
TAKE THOSE NOTES THERE, TOO!
ISN'T THIS STEALING?
COME ON, LET'S LIVE DANGEROUSLY!
IF YOU THINK ABOUT IT, GALOMAR STOLE ALL THIS STUFF FROM OTHER PLACES, AND WE'RE USING IT TO PUT A STOP TO HIM. SO THIS STUFF IS MUCH BETTER OFF IN OUR HANDS.
GOOD POINT!
HEY, TAKE THAT THING, TOO -- IT LOOKS INTERESTING!
HOW QUICKLY THEIR MORAL COMPASSES SHIFT.

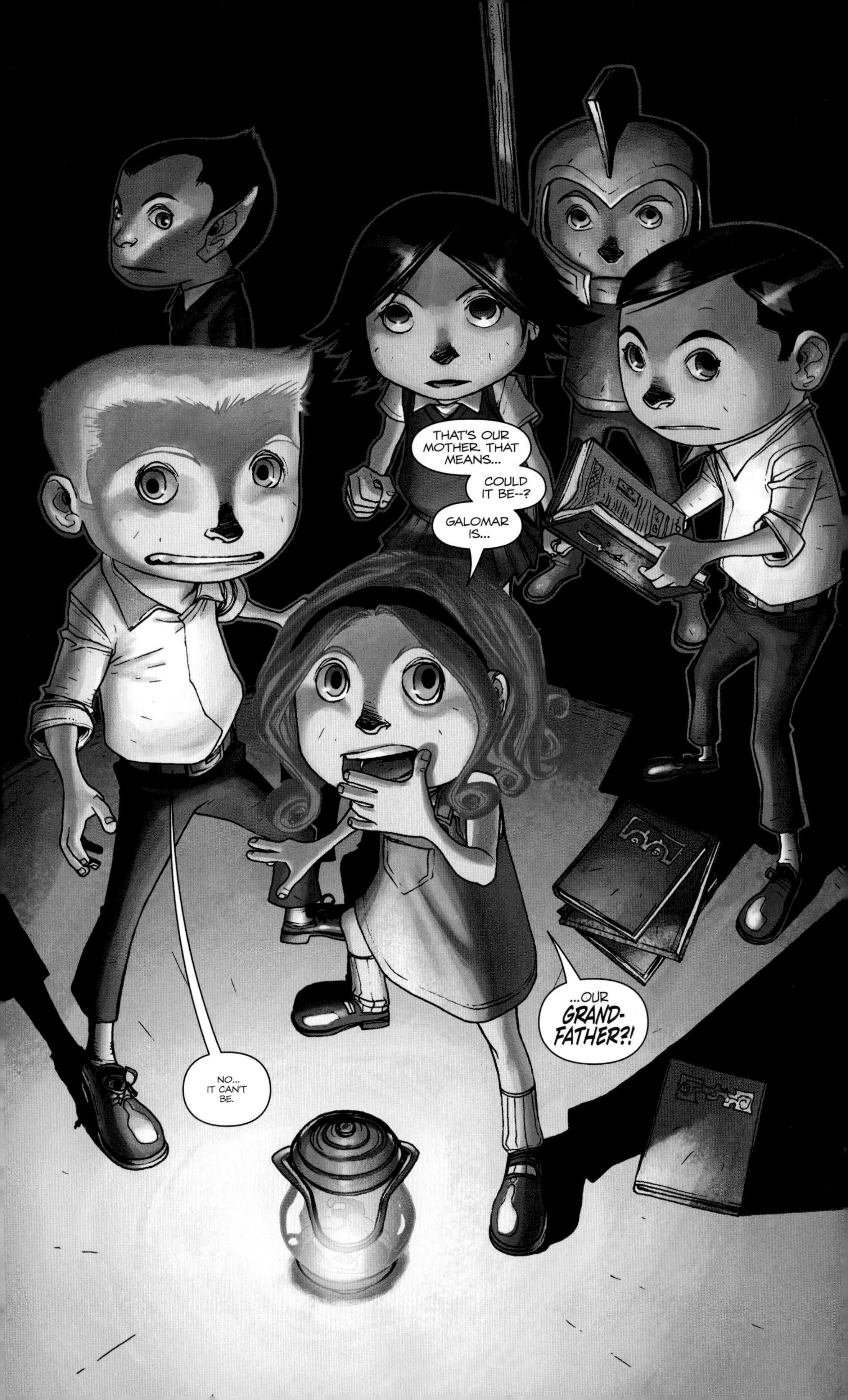
THAT'S OUR MOTHER. THAT MEANS...
COULD IT BE--?
GALOMAR IS...
NO... IT CAN'T BE.
...OUR GRAND-FATHER?!

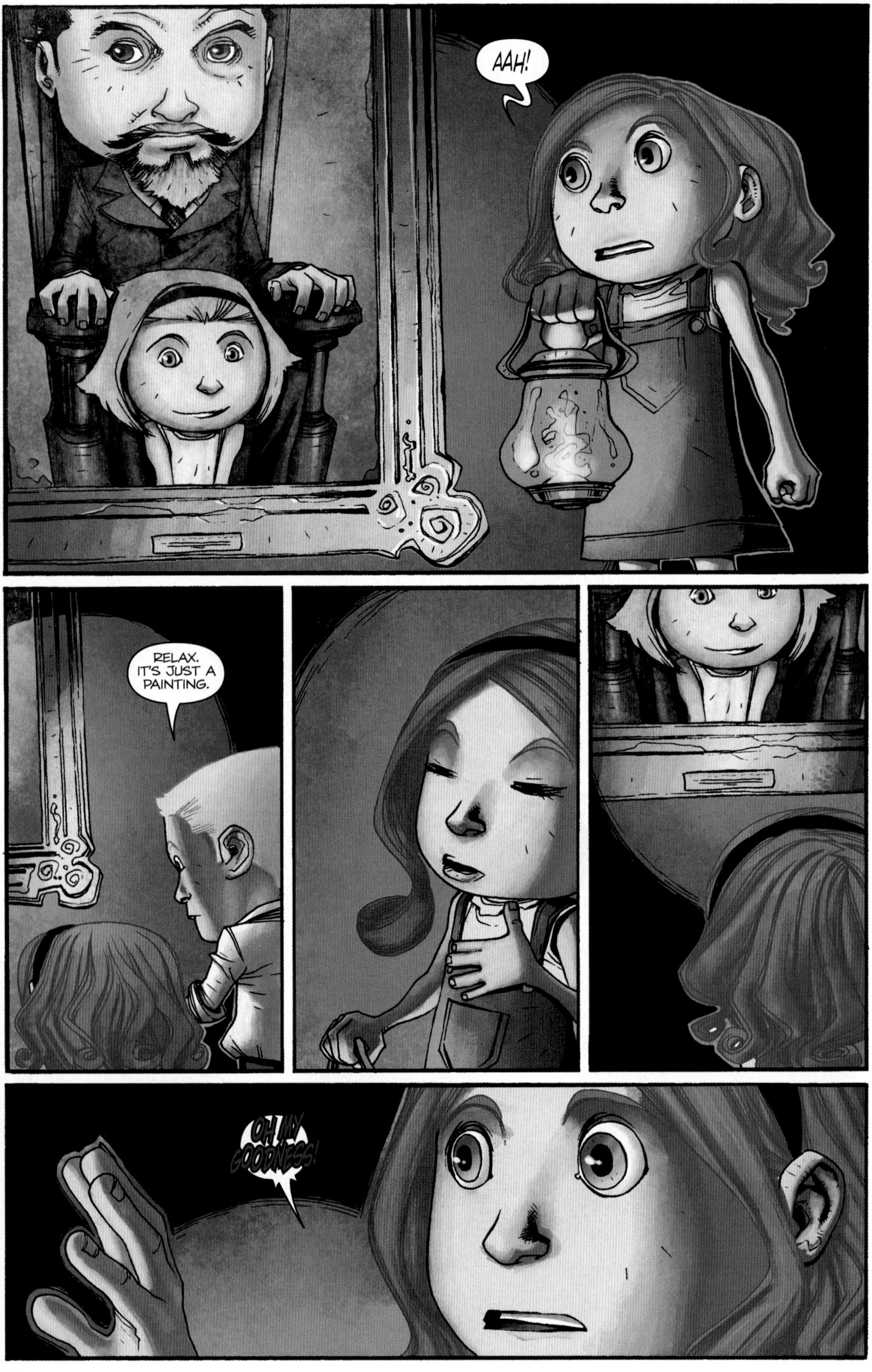
AAH!
RELAX. IT'S JUST A PAINTING.
OH MY GOODNESS!

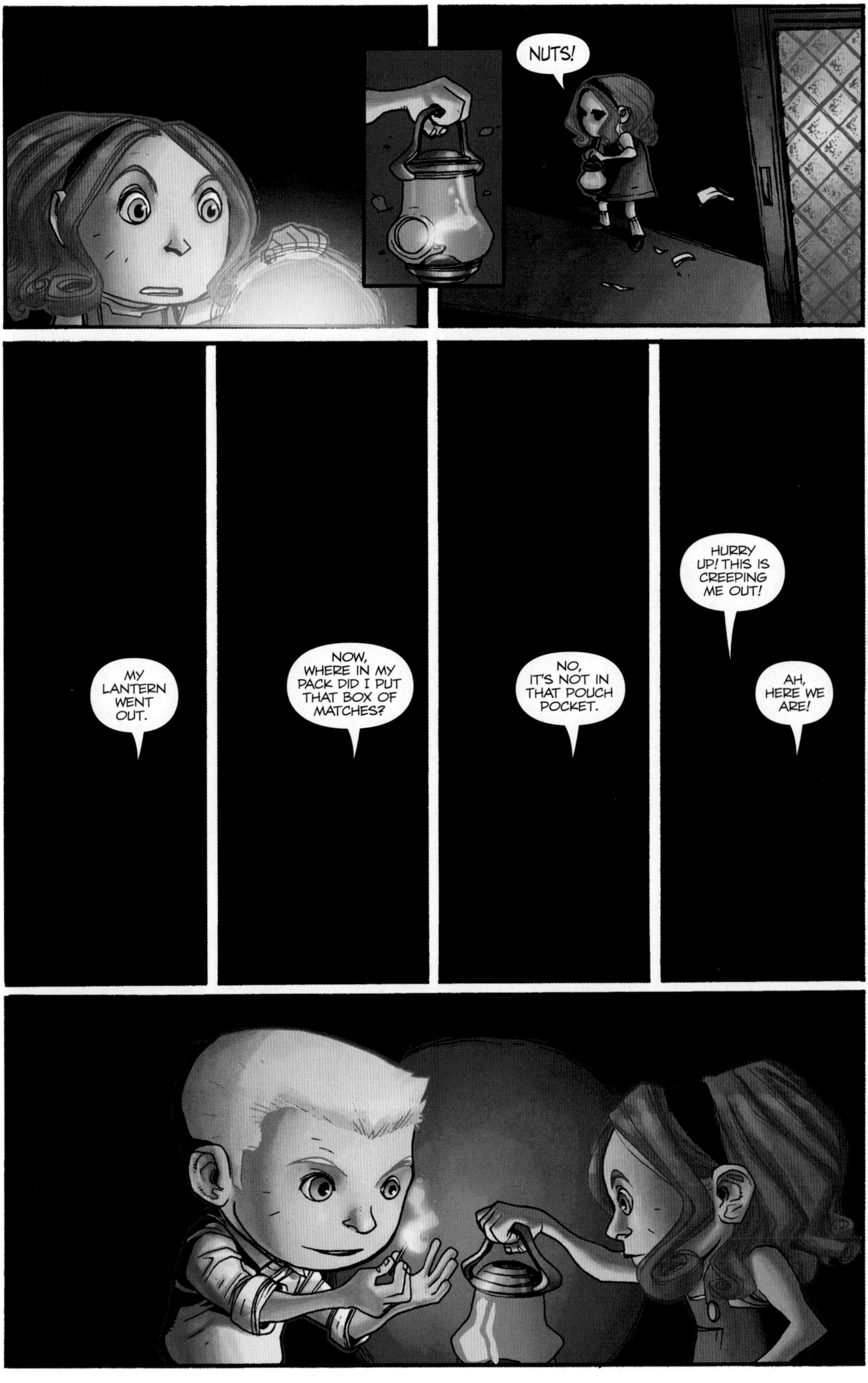

NUTS!
MY LANTERN WENT OUT.
NOW, WHERE IN MY PACK DID I PUT THAT BOX OF MATCHES?
NO, IT'S NOT IN THAT POUCH POCKET.
HURRY UP! THIS IS CREEPING ME OUT!
AH, HERE WE ARE!

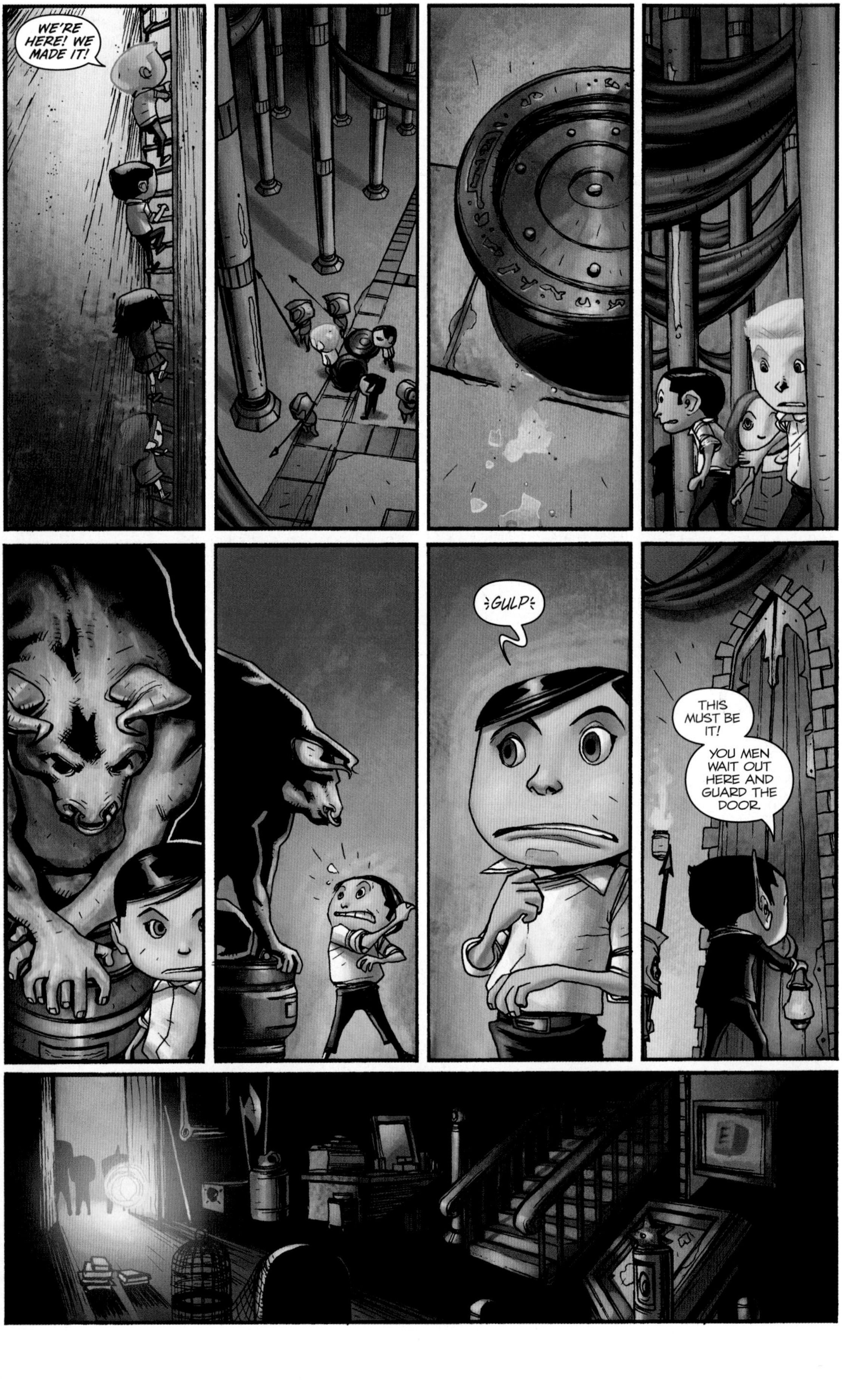
WE'RE HERE! WE MADE IT!
GULP
THIS MUST BE IT!
YOU MEN WAIT OUT HERE AND GUARD THE DOOR.

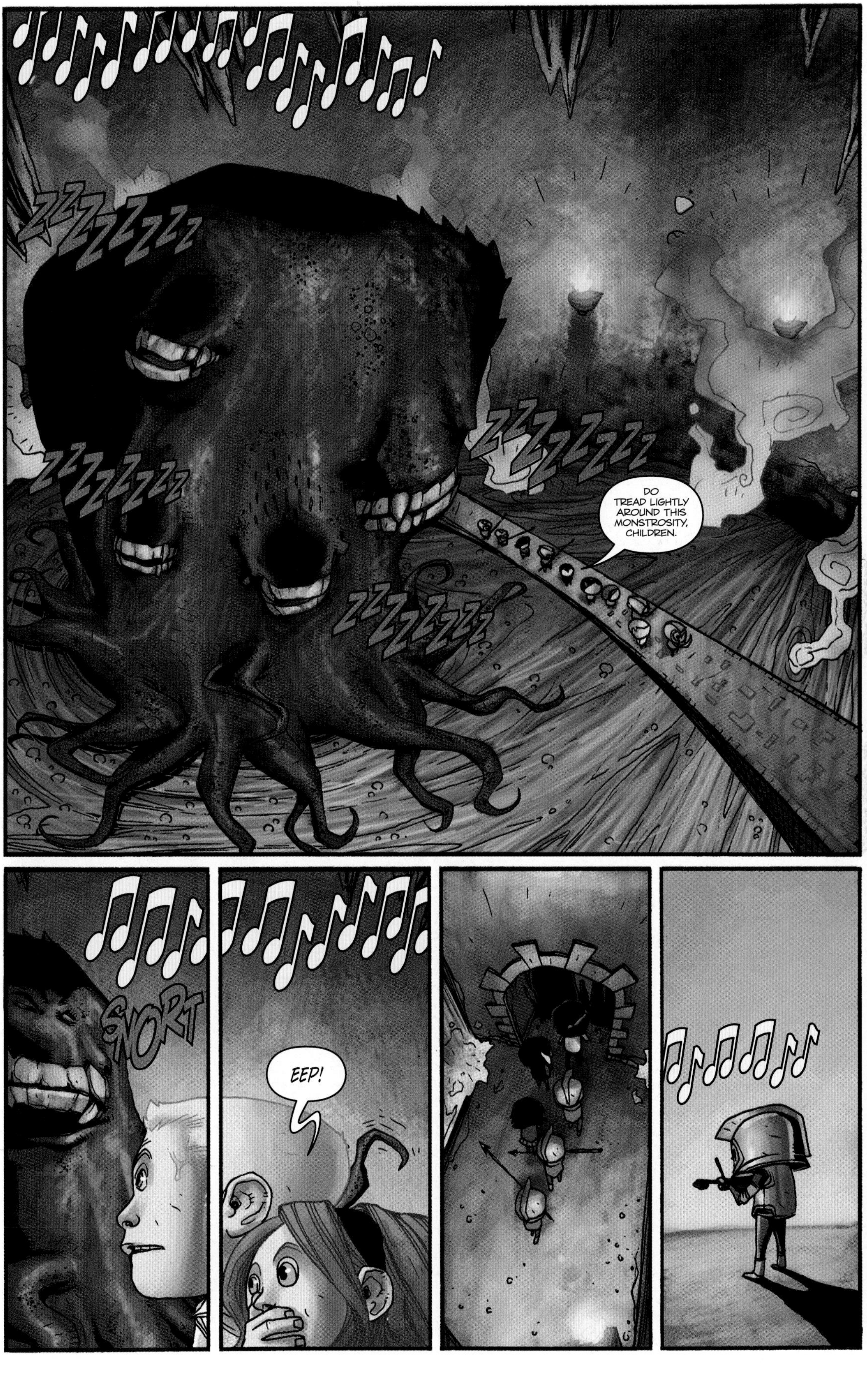
ZZZZZZZZZ
ZZZZZZZZZ
ZZZZZZZZZ
ZZZZZZZZZ
DO TREAD LIGHTLY AROUND THIS MONSTROSITY, CHILDREN.
SNORT
EEP!

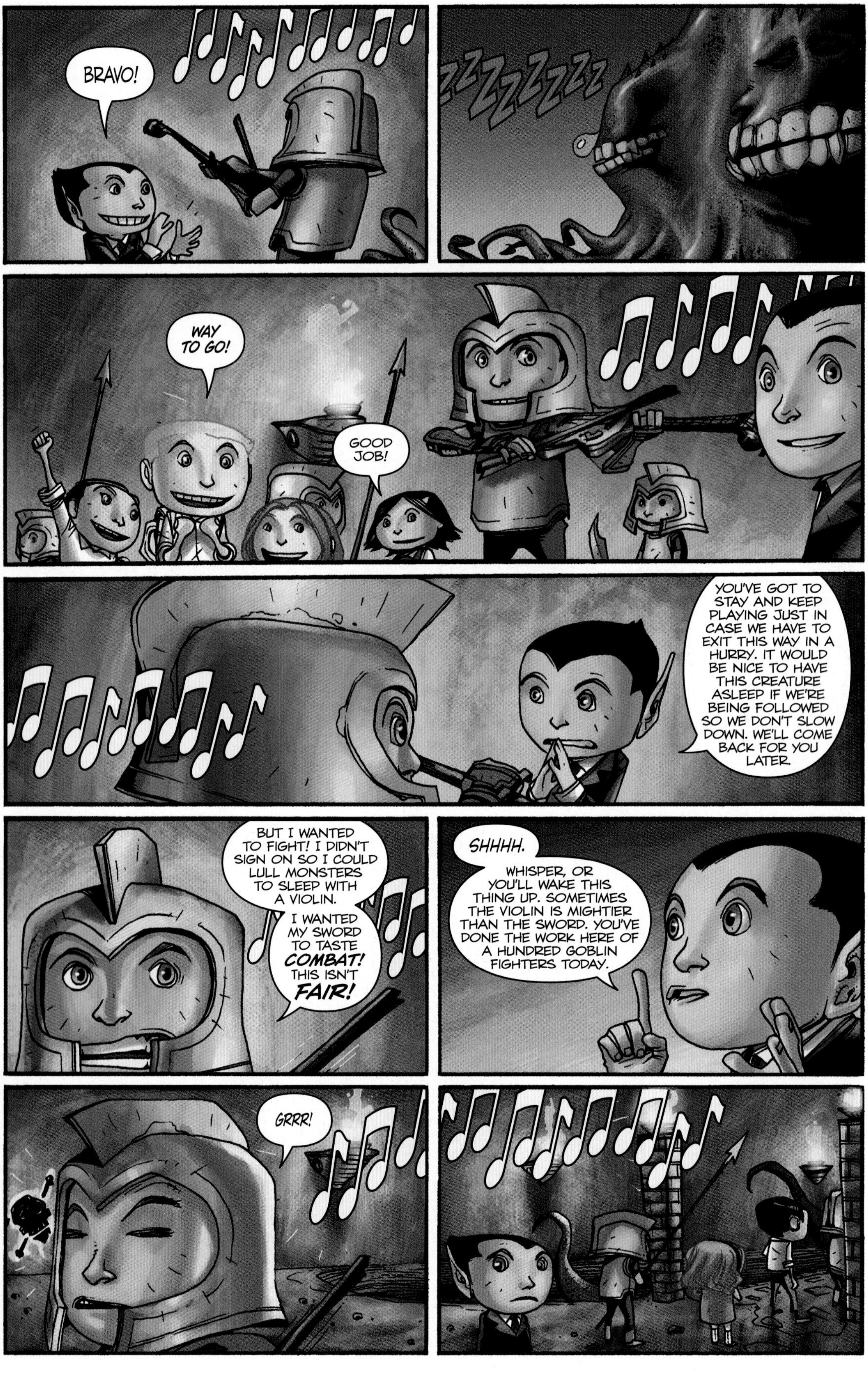
BRAVO!
ZZZZZZZZ
WAY TO GO!
GOOD JOB!
YOU'VE GOT TO STAY AND KEEP PLAYING JUST IN CASE WE HAVE TO EXIT THIS WAY IN A HURRY. IT WOULD BE NICE TO HAVE THIS CREATURE ASLEEP IF WE'RE BEING FOLLOWED SO WE DON'T SLOW DOWN. WE'LL COME BACK FOR YOU LATER.
BUT I WANTED TO FIGHT! I DIDN'T SIGN ON SO I COULD LULL MONSTERS TO SLEEP WITH A VIOLIN.
I WANTED MY SWORD TO TASTE COMBAT! THIS ISN'T FAIR!
SHHHH.
WHISPER, OR YOU'LL WAKE THIS THING UP. SOMETIMES THE VIOLIN IS MIGHTIER THAN THE SWORD. YOU'VE DONE THE WORK HERE OF A HUNDRED GOBLIN FIGHTERS TODAY.
GRRR!

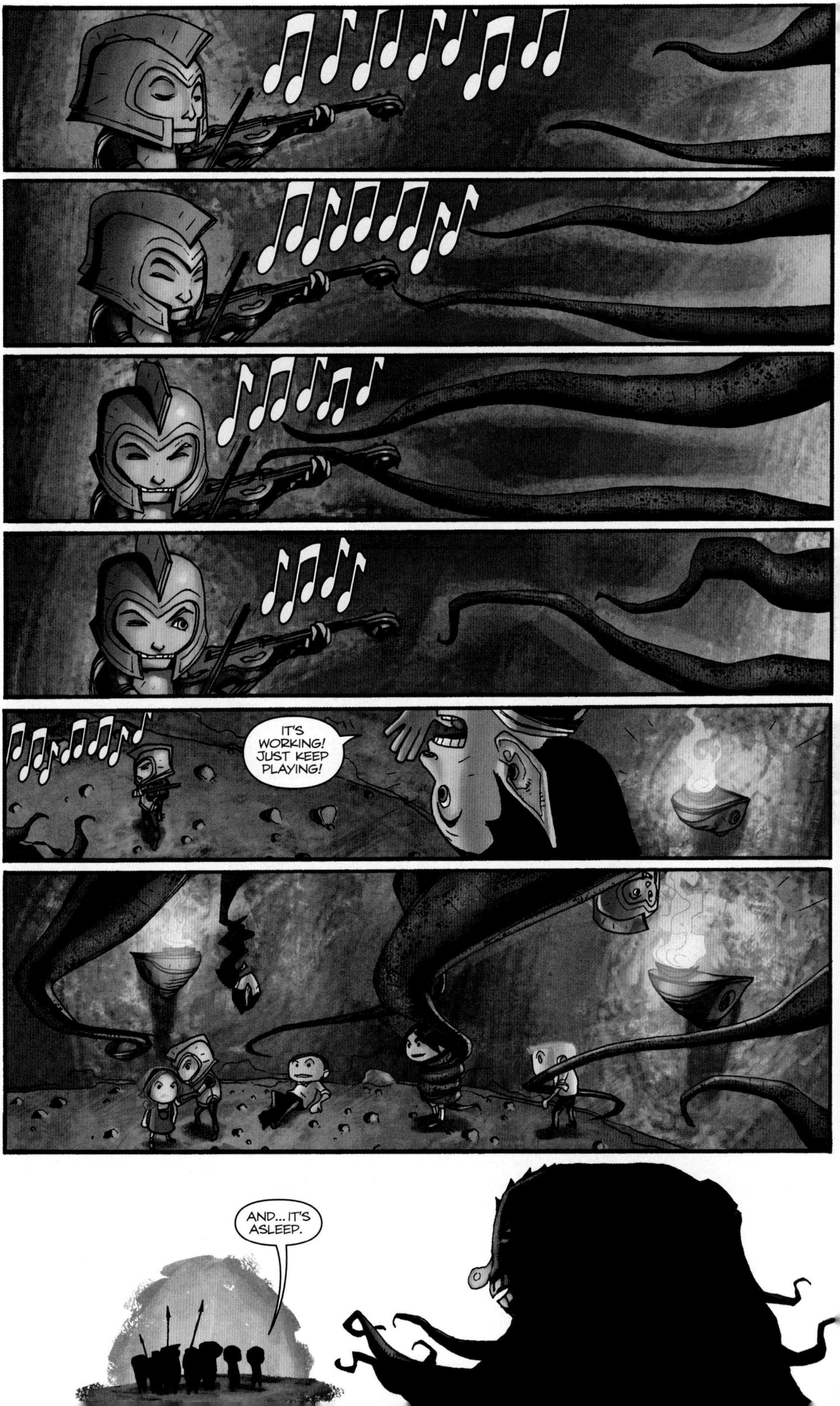
IT'S WORKING! JUST KEEP PLAYING!
AND... IT'S ASLEEP.

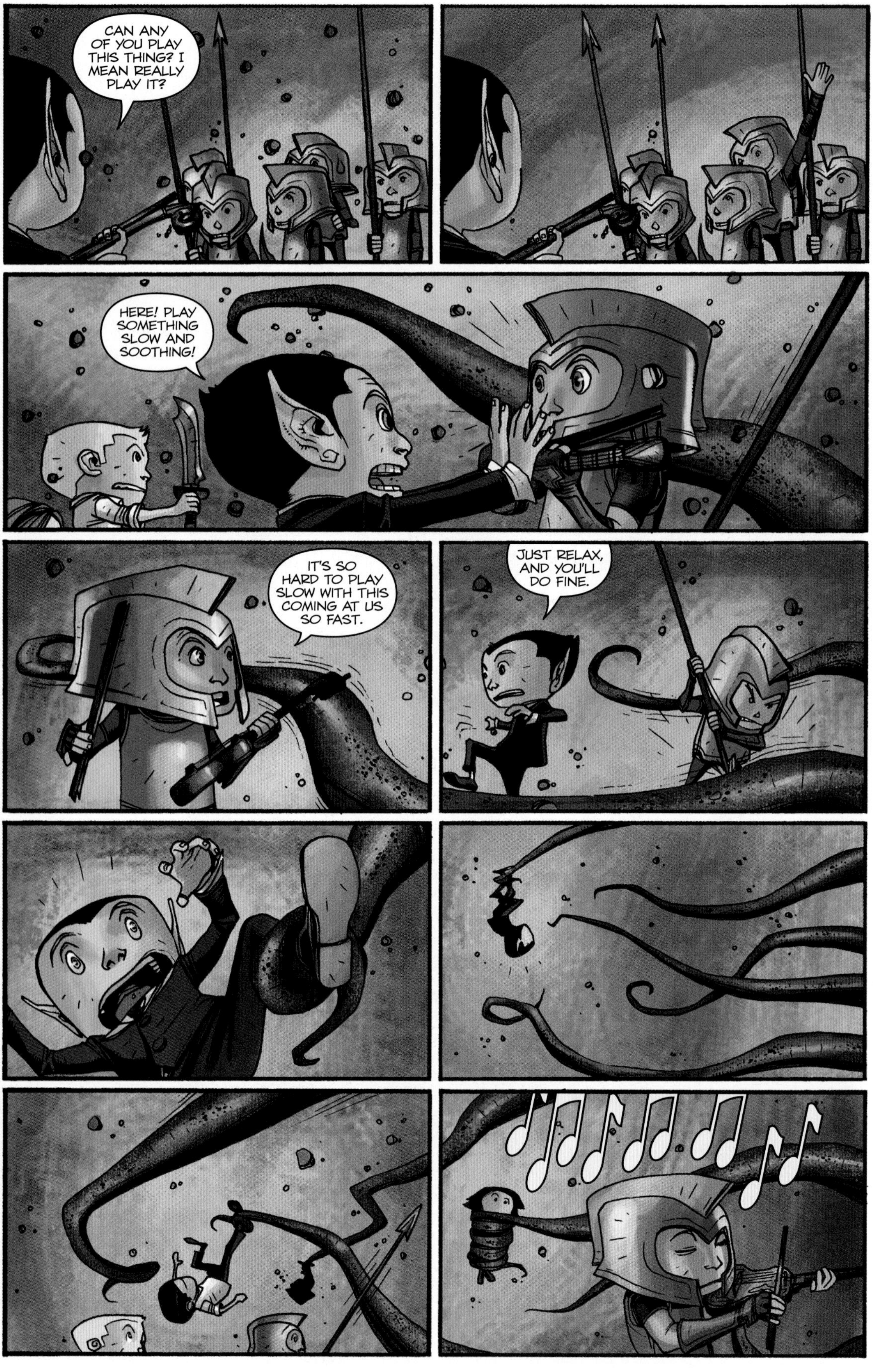
CAN ANY OF YOU PLAY THIS THING? I MEAN REALLY PLAY IT?
HERE! PLAY SOMETHING SLOW AND SOOTHING!
IT'S SO HARD TO PLAY SLOW WITH THIS COMING AT US SO FAST.
JUST RELAX, AND YOU'LL DO FINE.

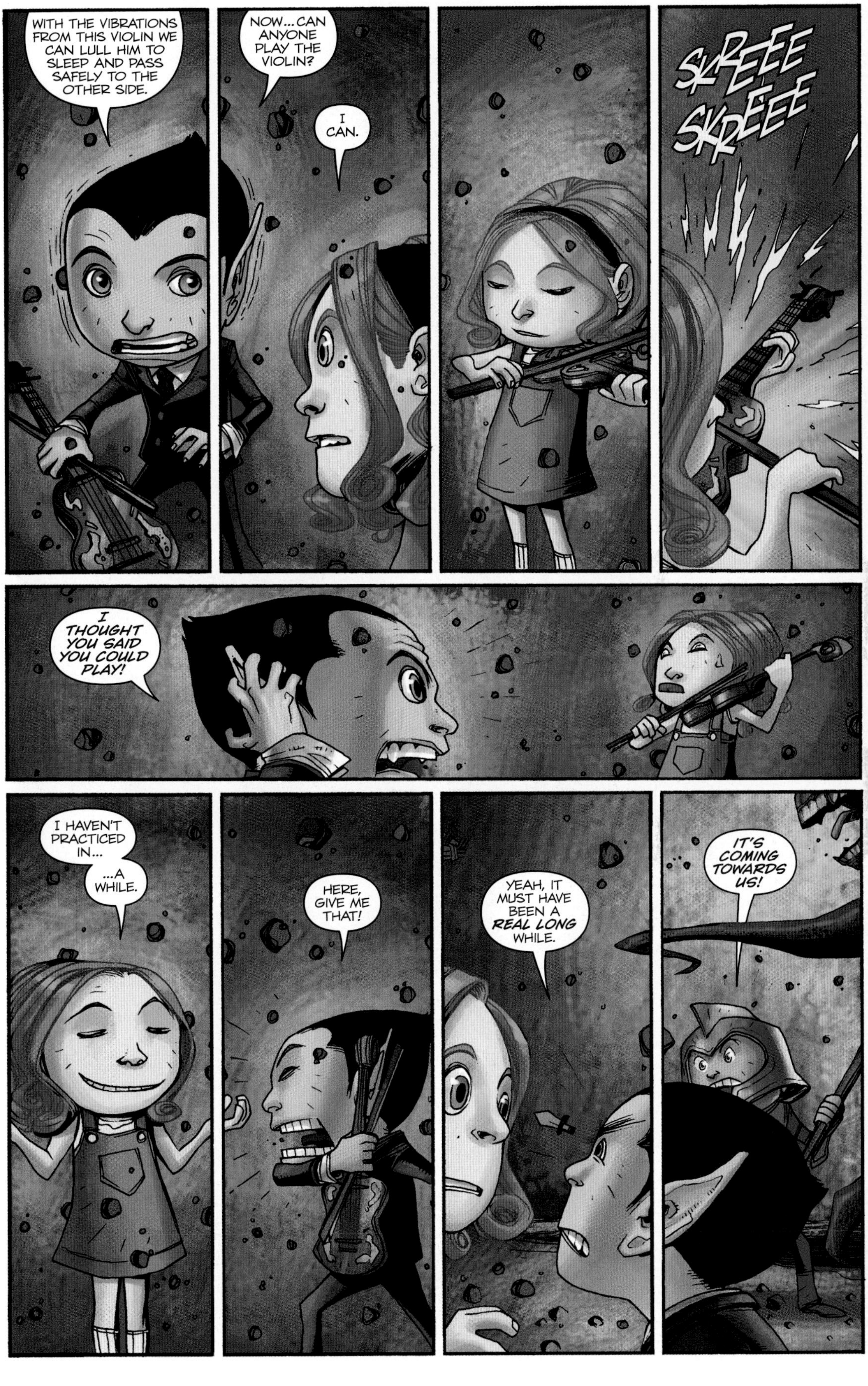
WITH THE VIBRATIONS FROM THIS VIOLIN WE CAN LULL HIM TO SLEEP AND PASS SAFELY TO THE OTHER SIDE.
NOW...CAN ANYONE PLAY THE VIOLIN?
I CAN.
SKREEE SKREEE
I THOUGHT YOU SAID YOU COULD PLAY!
I HAVEN'T PRACTICED IN...
...A WHILE.
HERE, GIVE ME THAT!
YEAH, IT MUST HAVE BEEN A REAL LONG WHILE.
IT'S COMING TOWARDS US!

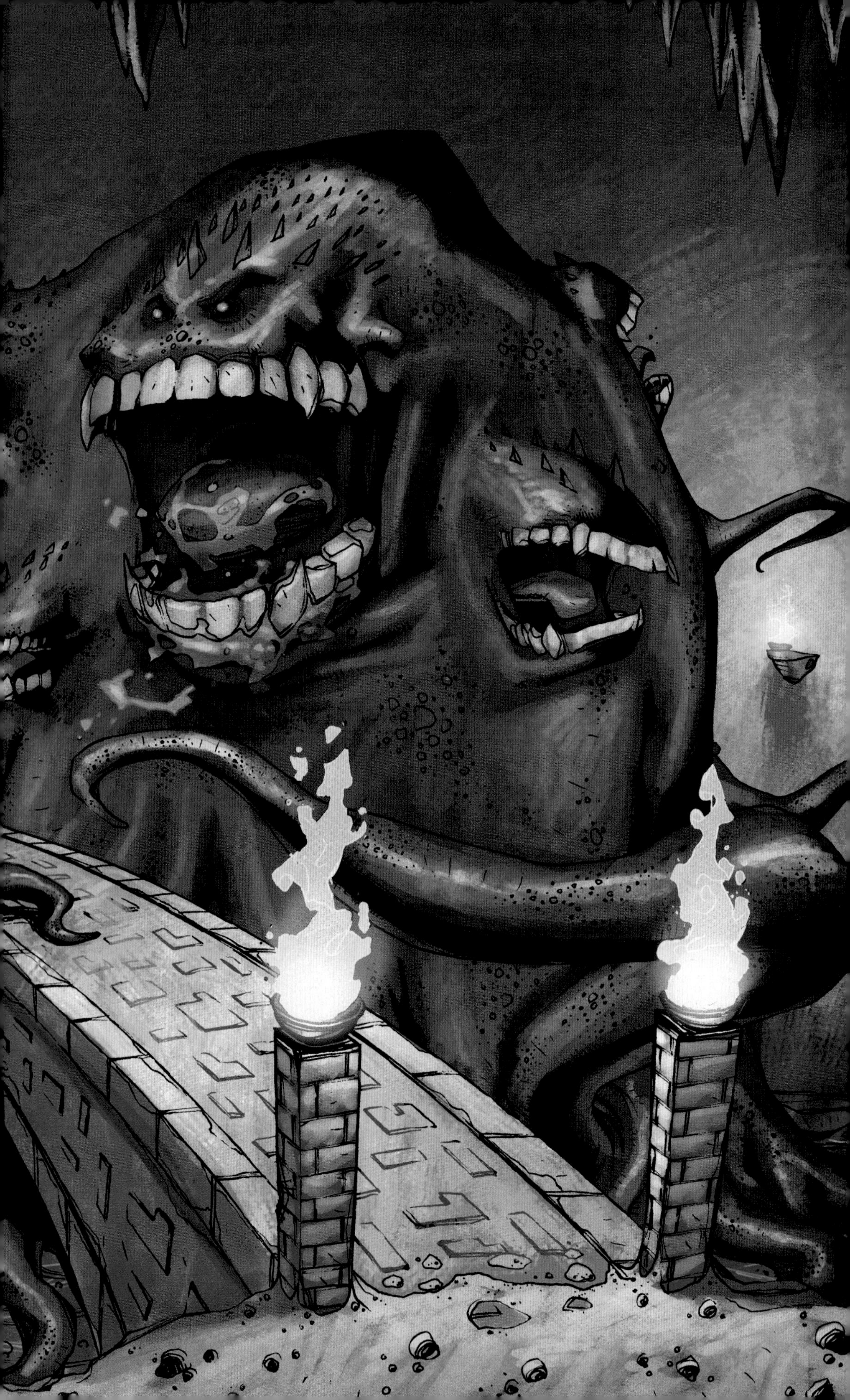

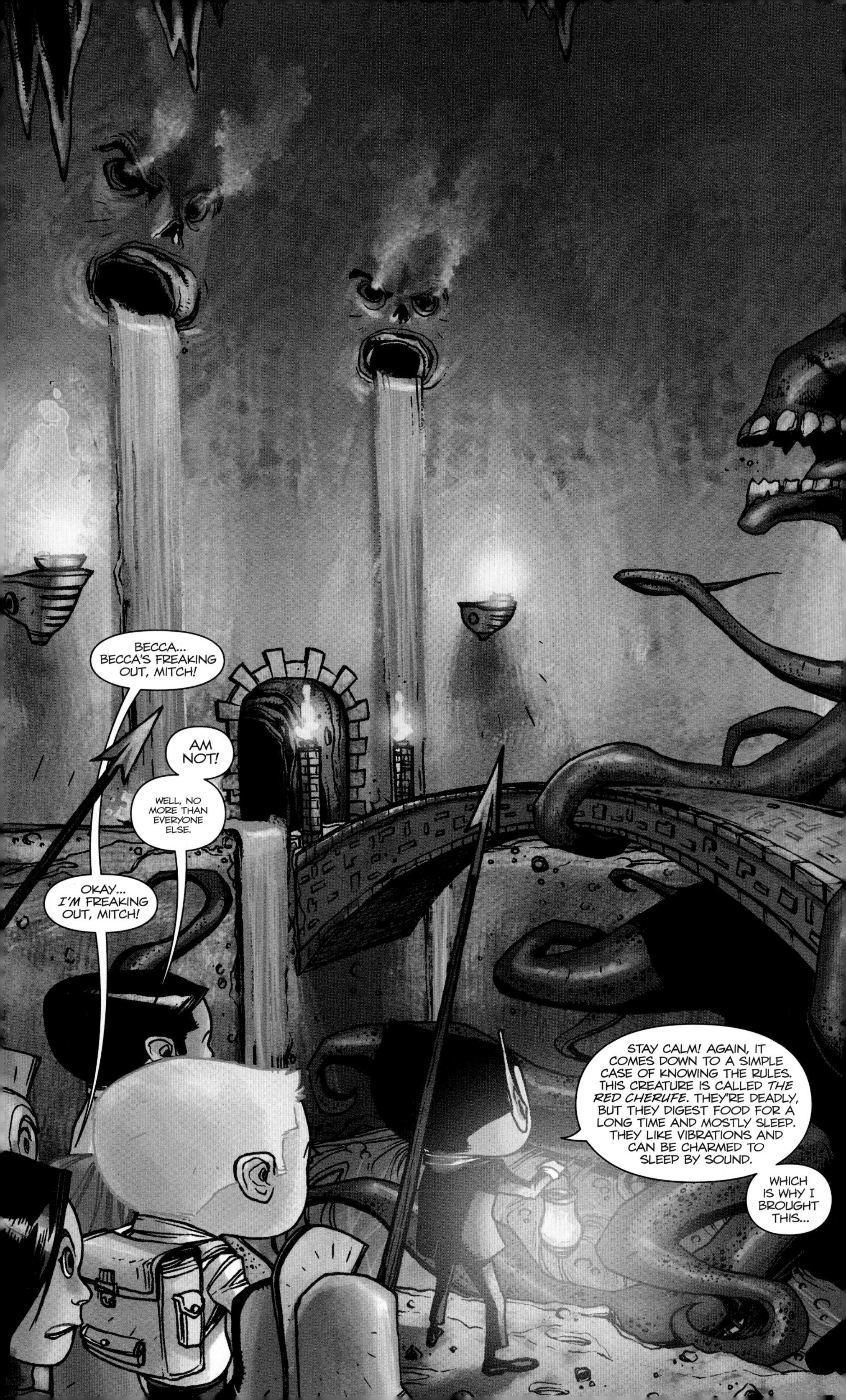
BECCA... BECCA'S FREAKING OUT, MITCH!
AM NOT!
WELL, NO MORE THAN EVERYONE ELSE.
OKAY... I'M FREAKING OUT, MITCH!
STAY CALM! AGAIN, IT COMES DOWN TO A SIMPLE CASE OF KNOWING THE RULES. THIS CREATURE IS CALLED *THE RED CHERUFE*. THEY'RE DEADLY, BUT THEY DIGEST FOOD FOR A LONG TIME AND MOSTLY SLEEP. THEY LIKE VIBRATIONS AND CAN BE CHARMED TO SLEEP BY SOUND.
WHICH IS WHY I BROUGHT THIS...

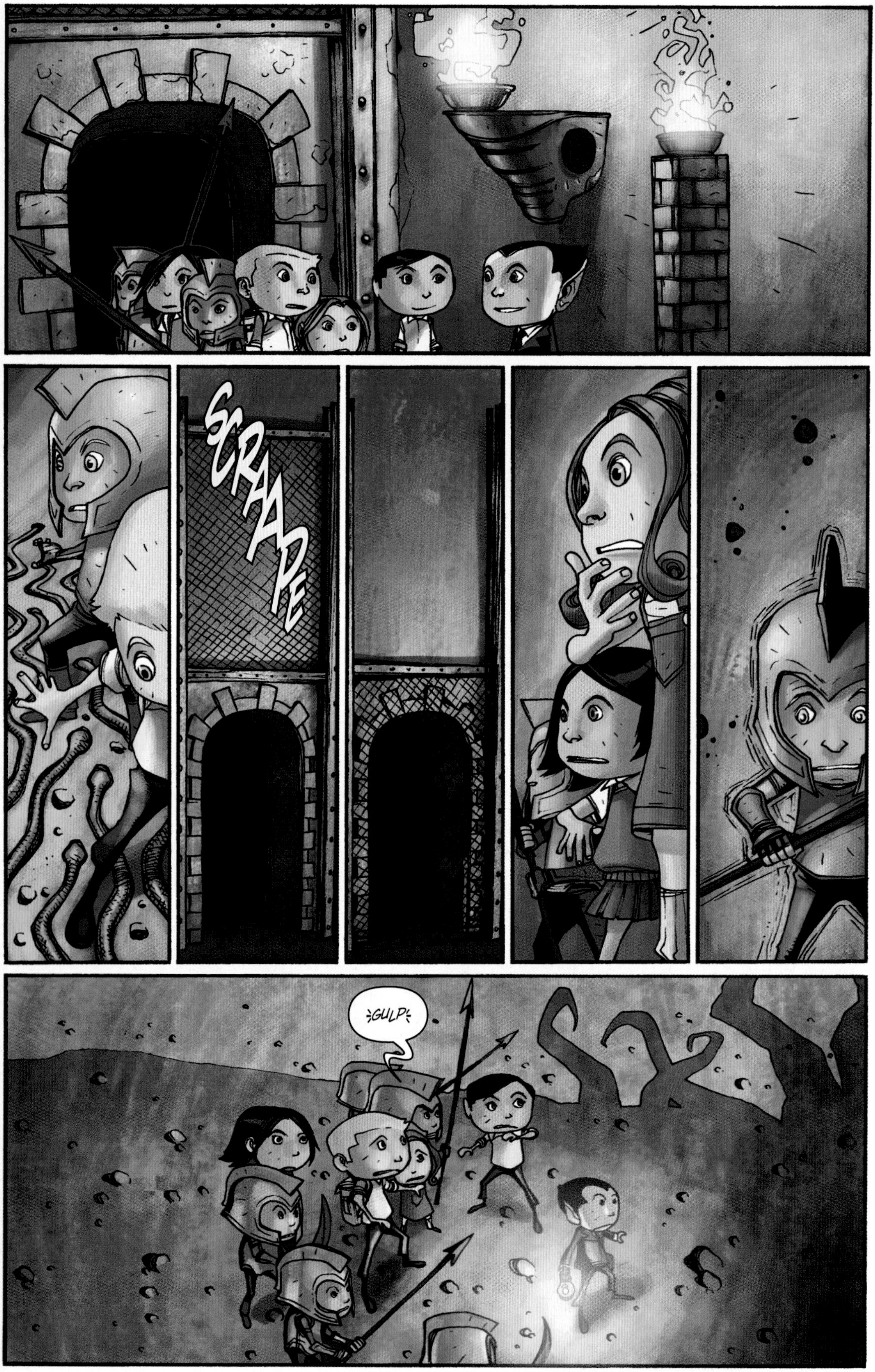
SCRAAPE
GULP

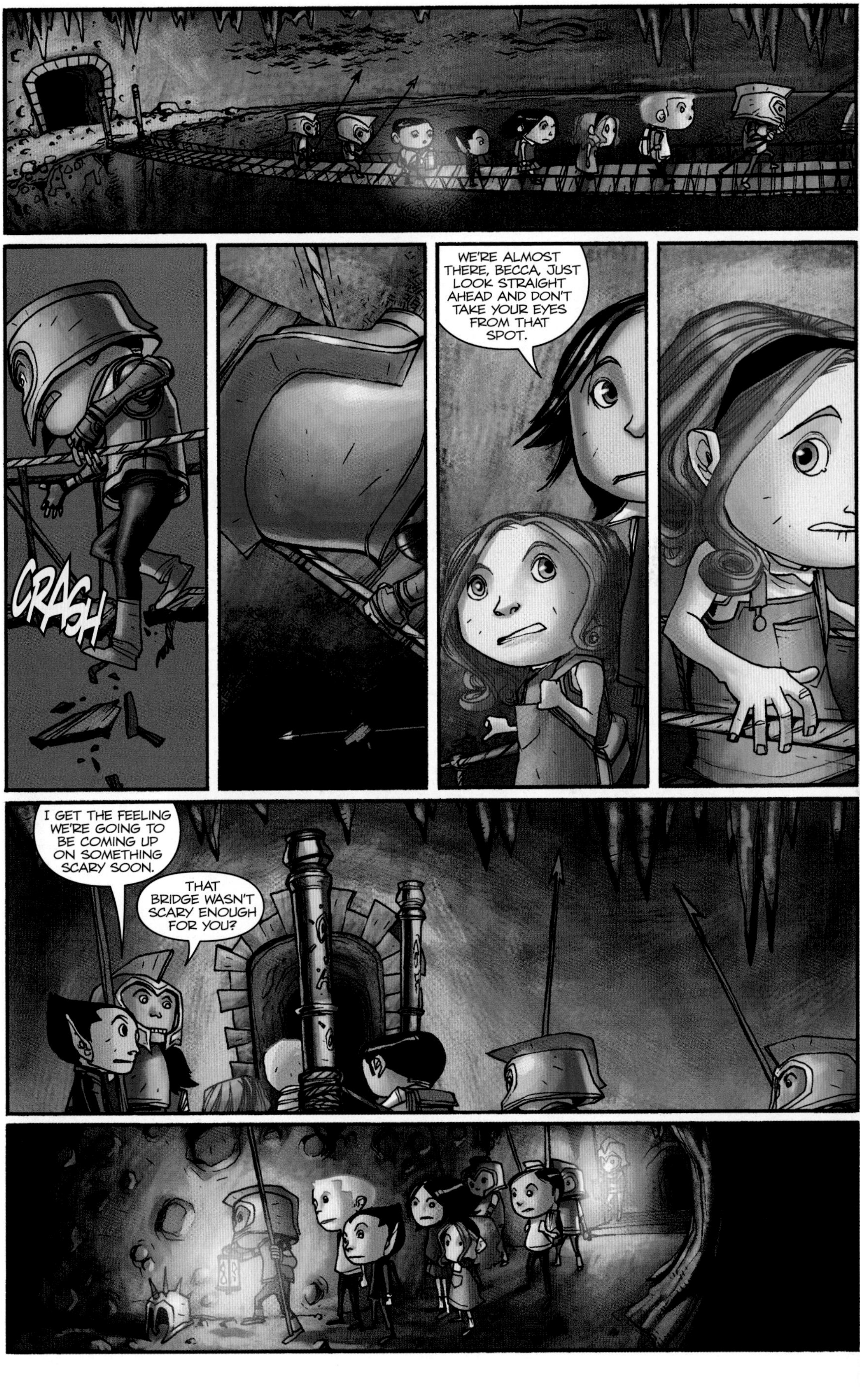
CRASH
WE'RE ALMOST THERE, BECCA, JUST LOOK STRAIGHT AHEAD AND DON'T TAKE YOUR EYES FROM THAT SPOT.
I GET THE FEELING WE'RE GOING TO BE COMING UP ON SOMETHING SCARY SOON.
THAT BRIDGE WASN'T SCARY ENOUGH FOR YOU?

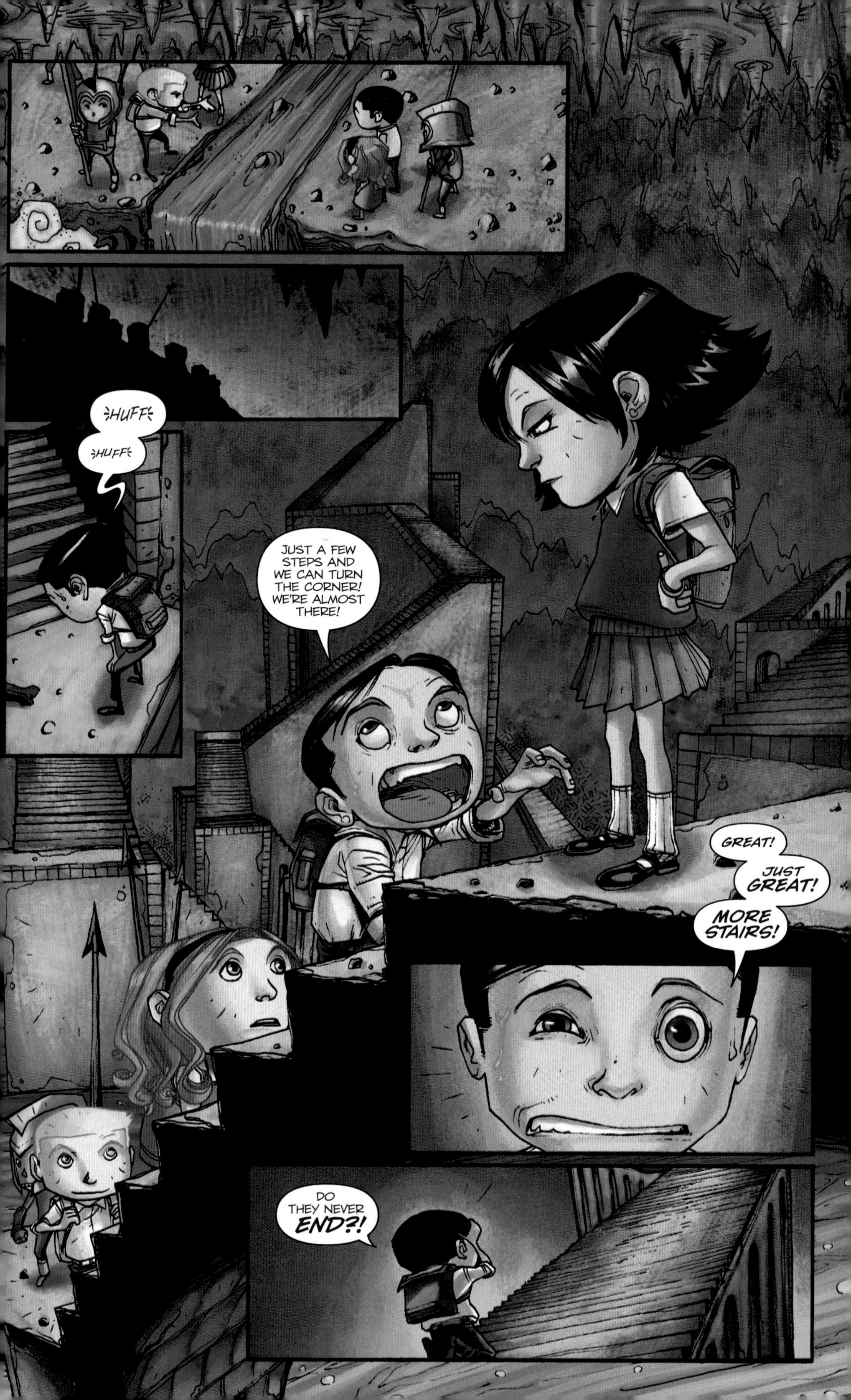
HUFF
HUFF
JUST A FEW STEPS AND WE CAN TURN THE CORNER! WE'RE ALMOST THERE!
GREAT!
JUST GREAT!
MORE STAIRS!
DO THEY NEVER END?!

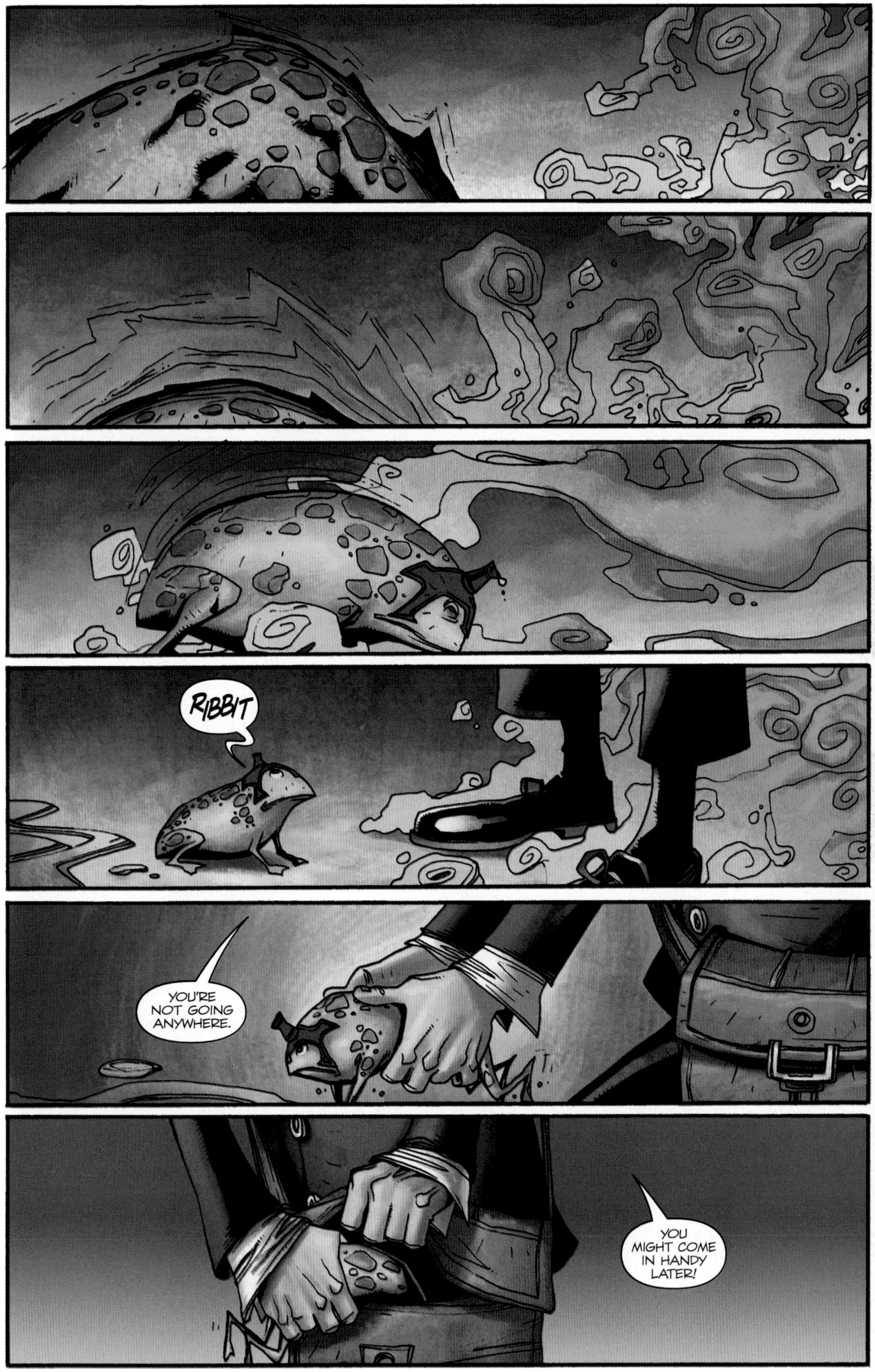
RIBBIT
YOU'RE NOT GOING ANYWHERE.
YOU MIGHT COME IN HANDY LATER!

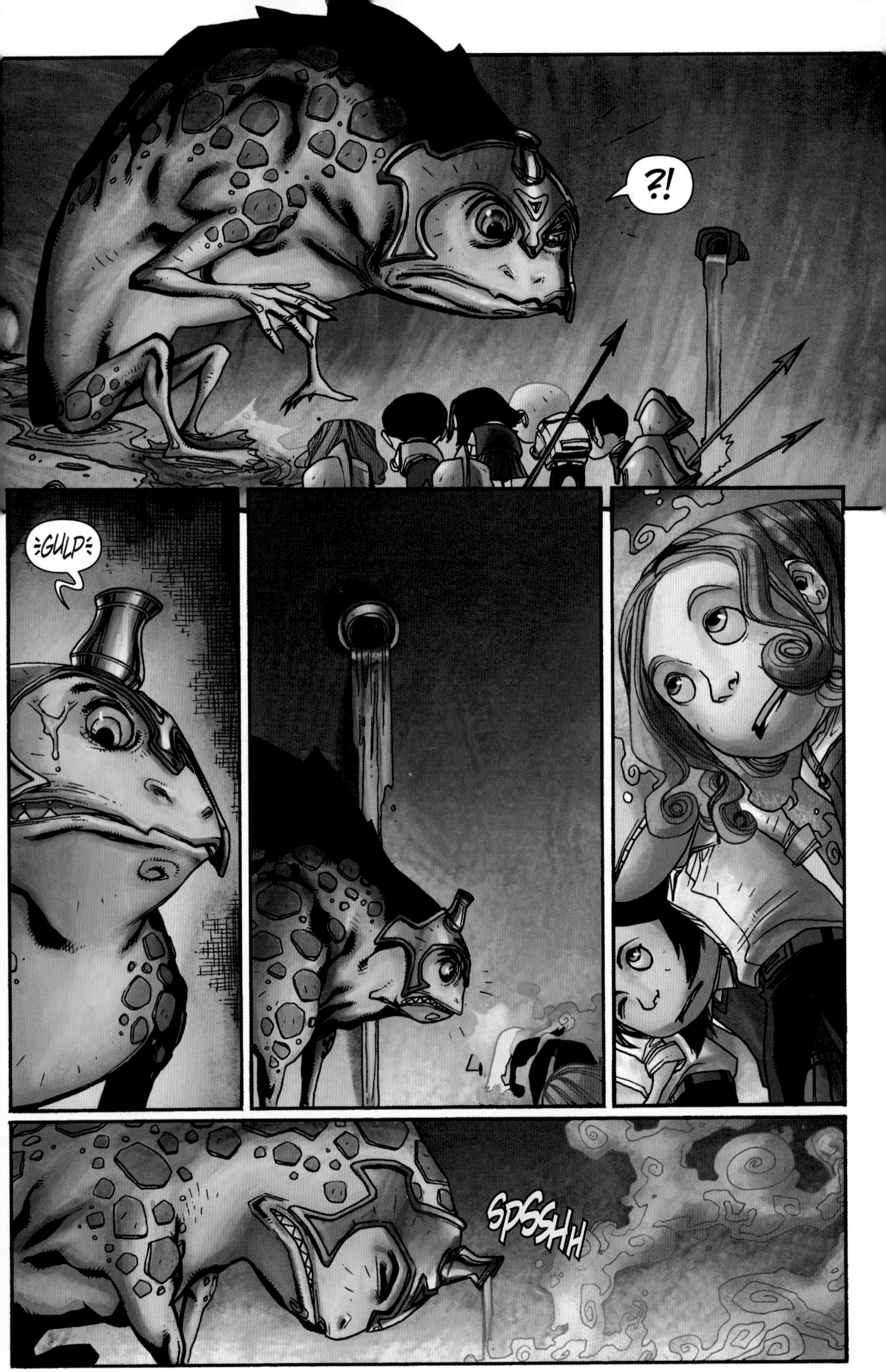
?!
GULP
SPSSHH

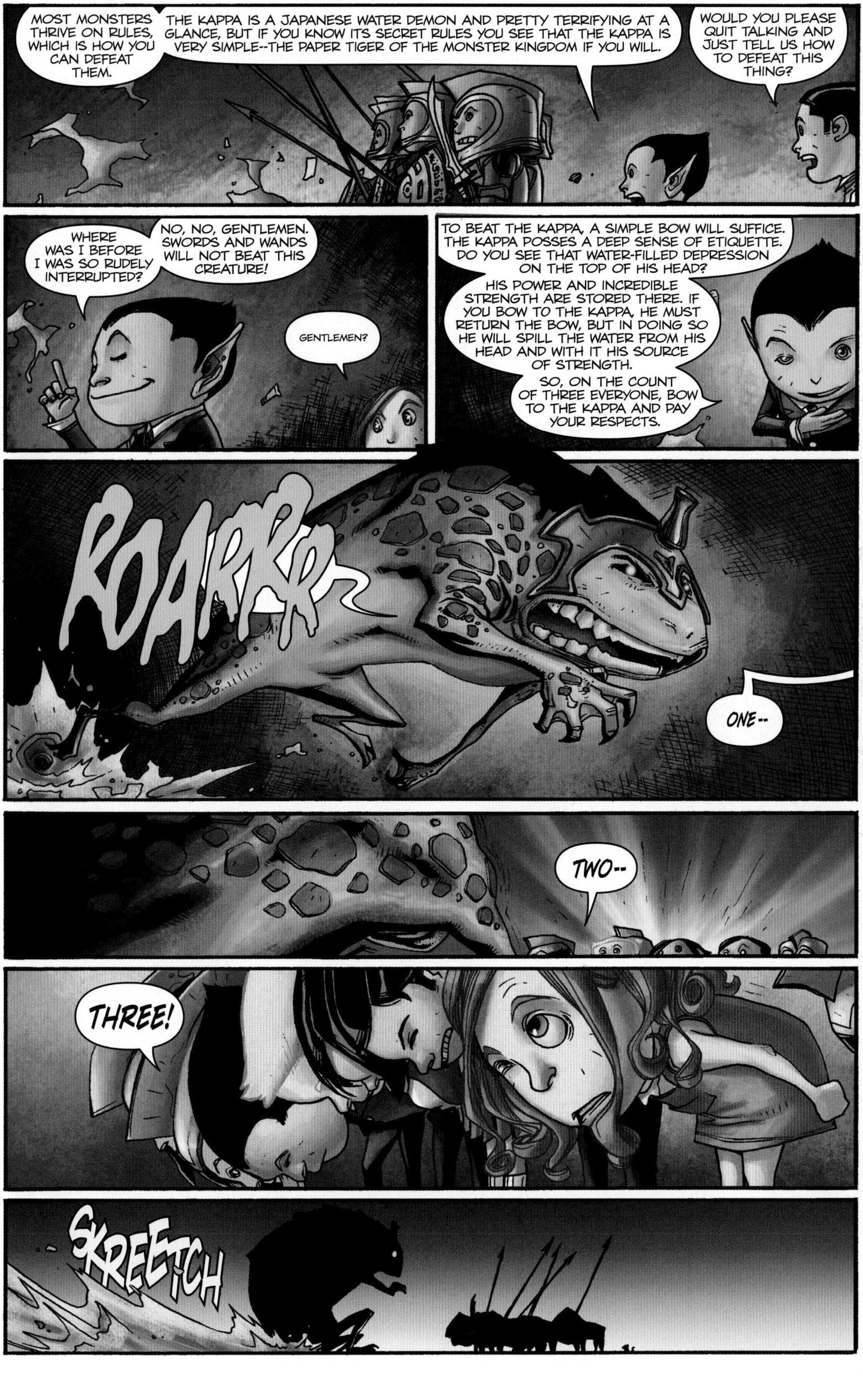
MOST MONSTERS THRIVE ON RULES, WHICH IS HOW YOU CAN DEFEAT THEM.
THE KAPPA IS A JAPANESE WATER DEMON AND PRETTY TERRIFYING AT A GLANCE, BUT IF YOU KNOW ITS SECRET RULES YOU SEE THAT THE KAPPA IS VERY SIMPLE--THE PAPER TIGER OF THE MONSTER KINGDOM IF YOU WILL.
WOULD YOU PLEASE QUIT TALKING AND JUST TELL US HOW TO DEFEAT THIS THING?
WHERE WAS I BEFORE I WAS SO RUDELY INTERRUPTED?
NO, NO, GENTLEMEN. SWORDS AND WANDS WILL NOT BEAT THIS CREATURE!
GENTLEMEN?
TO BEAT THE KAPPA, A SIMPLE BOW WILL SUFFICE. THE KAPPA POSSES A DEEP SENSE OF ETIQUETTE. DO YOU SEE THAT WATER-FILLED DEPRESSION ON THE TOP OF HIS HEAD?
HIS POWER AND INCREDIBLE STRENGTH ARE STORED THERE. IF YOU BOW TO THE KAPPA, HE MUST RETURN THE BOW, BUT IN DOING SO HE WILL SPILL THE WATER FROM HIS HEAD AND WITH IT HIS SOURCE OF STRENGTH.
SO, ON THE COUNT OF THREE EVERYONE, BOW TO THE KAPPA AND PAY YOUR RESPECTS.
ROARRR
ONE--
TWO--
THREE!
SKREETCH

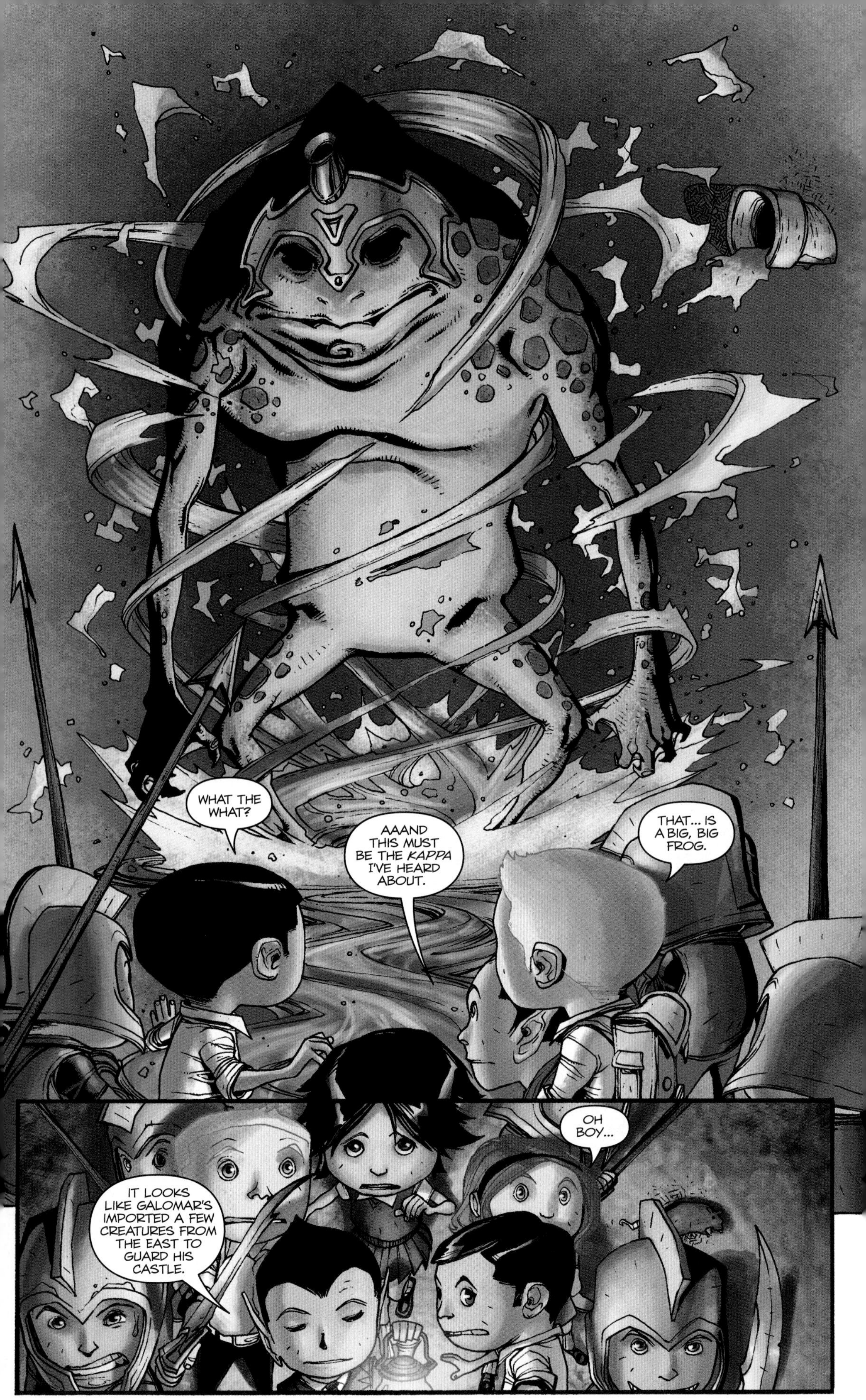
WHAT THE WHAT?
AAAND THIS MUST BE THE *KAPPA* I'VE HEARD ABOUT.
THAT... IS A BIG, BIG FROG.
OH BOY...
IT LOOKS LIKE GALOMAR'S IMPORTED A FEW CREATURES FROM THE EAST TO GUARD HIS CASTLE.

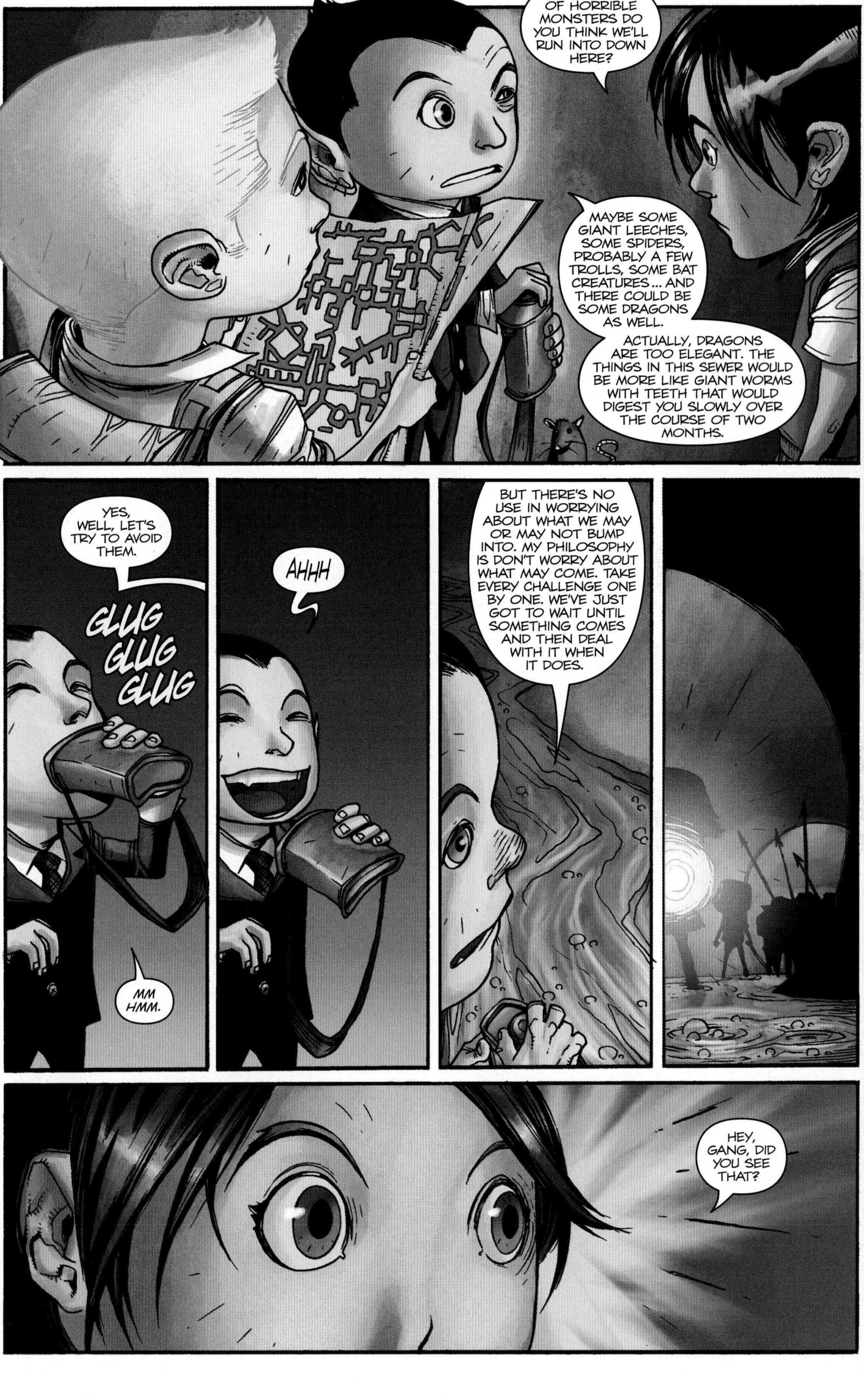
WHAT KIND OF HORRIBLE MONSTERS DO YOU THINK WE'LL RUN INTO DOWN HERE?
MAYBE SOME GIANT LEECHES, SOME SPIDERS, PROBABLY A FEW TROLLS, SOME BAT CREATURES... AND THERE COULD BE SOME DRAGONS AS WELL.
ACTUALLY, DRAGONS ARE TOO ELEGANT. THE THINGS IN THIS SEWER WOULD BE MORE LIKE GIANT WORMS WITH TEETH THAT WOULD DIGEST YOU SLOWLY OVER THE COURSE OF TWO MONTHS.
YES, WELL, LET'S TRY TO AVOID THEM.
GLUG GLUG GLUG
MM HMM.
AHHH
BUT THERE'S NO USE IN WORRYING ABOUT WHAT WE MAY OR MAY NOT BUMP INTO. MY PHILOSOPHY IS DON'T WORRY ABOUT WHAT MAY COME. TAKE EVERY CHALLENGE ONE BY ONE. WE'VE JUST GOT TO WAIT UNTIL SOMETHING COMES AND THEN DEAL WITH IT WHEN IT DOES.
HEY, GANG, DID YOU SEE THAT?

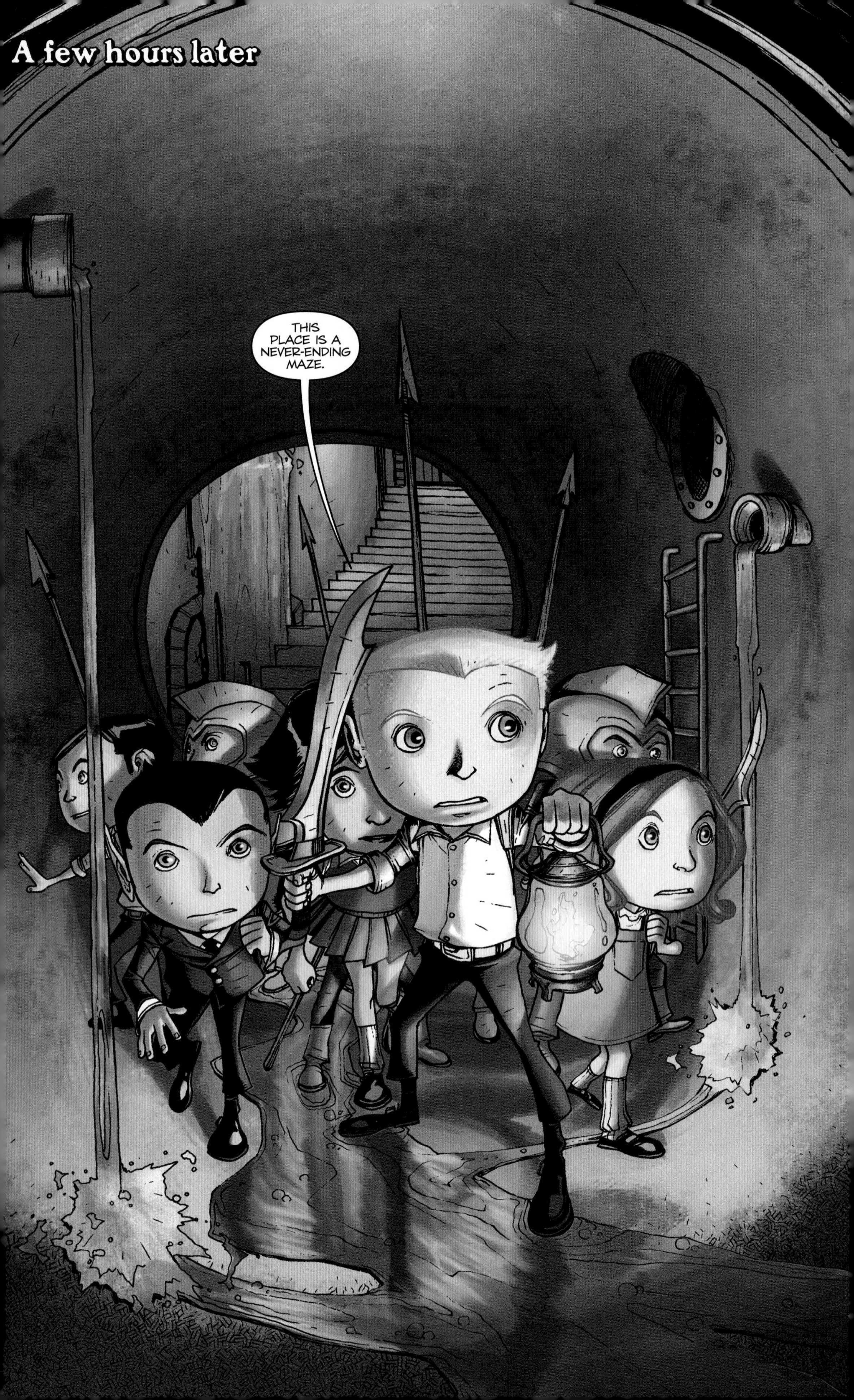
A few hours later
THIS PLACE IS A NEVER-ENDING MAZE.

• The Castle of Galomar •

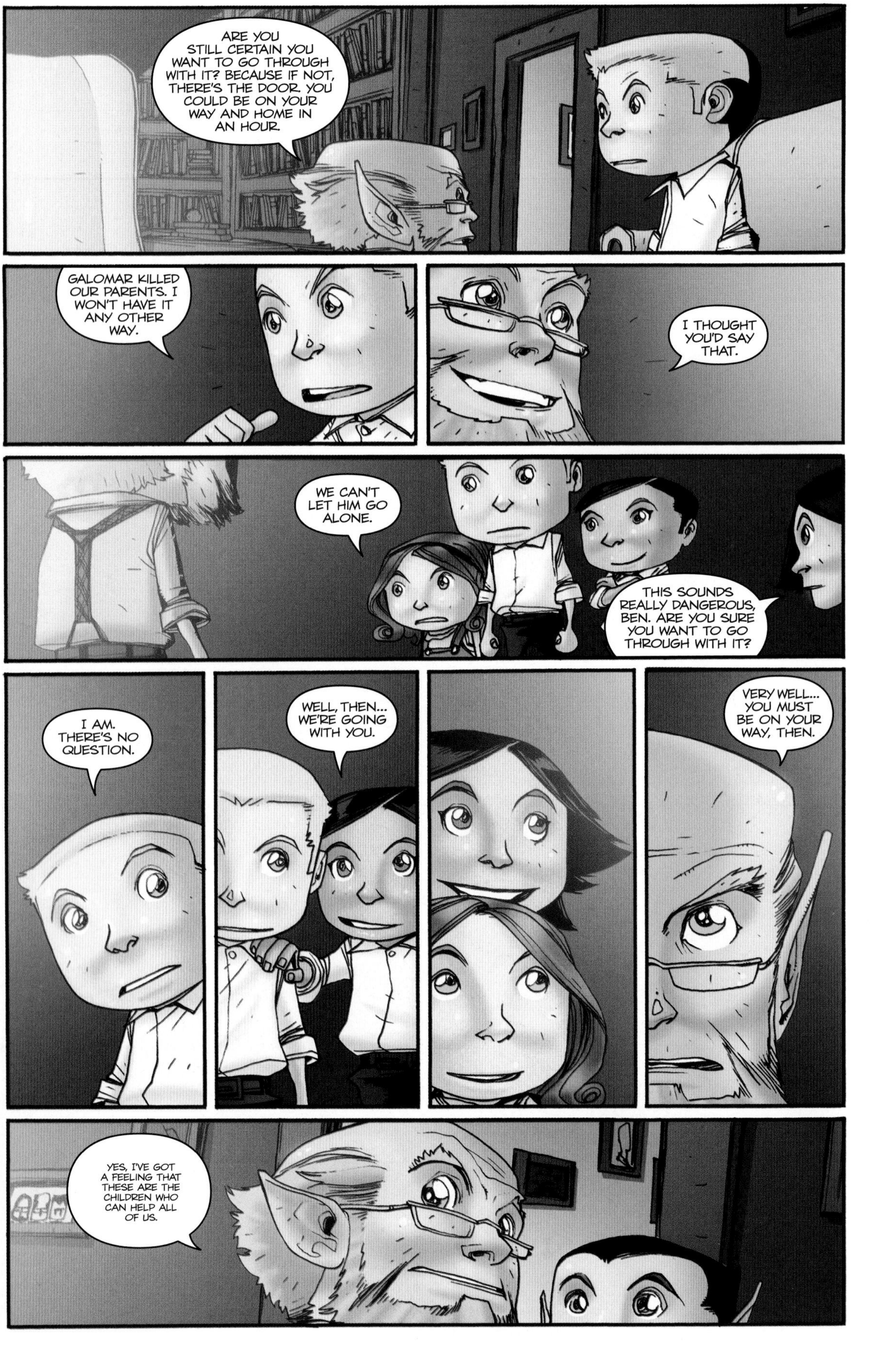
ARE YOU STILL CERTAIN YOU WANT TO GO THROUGH WITH IT? BECAUSE IF NOT, THERE'S THE DOOR. YOU COULD BE ON YOUR WAY AND HOME IN AN HOUR.
GALOMAR KILLED OUR PARENTS. I WON'T HAVE IT ANY OTHER WAY.
I THOUGHT YOU'D SAY THAT.
WE CAN'T LET HIM GO ALONE.
THIS SOUNDS REALLY DANGEROUS, BEN. ARE YOU SURE YOU WANT TO GO THROUGH WITH IT?
I AM. THERE'S NO QUESTION.
WELL, THEN... WE'RE GOING WITH YOU.
VERY WELL... YOU MUST BE ON YOUR WAY, THEN.
YES, I'VE GOT A FEELING THAT THESE ARE THE CHILDREN WHO CAN HELP ALL OF US.

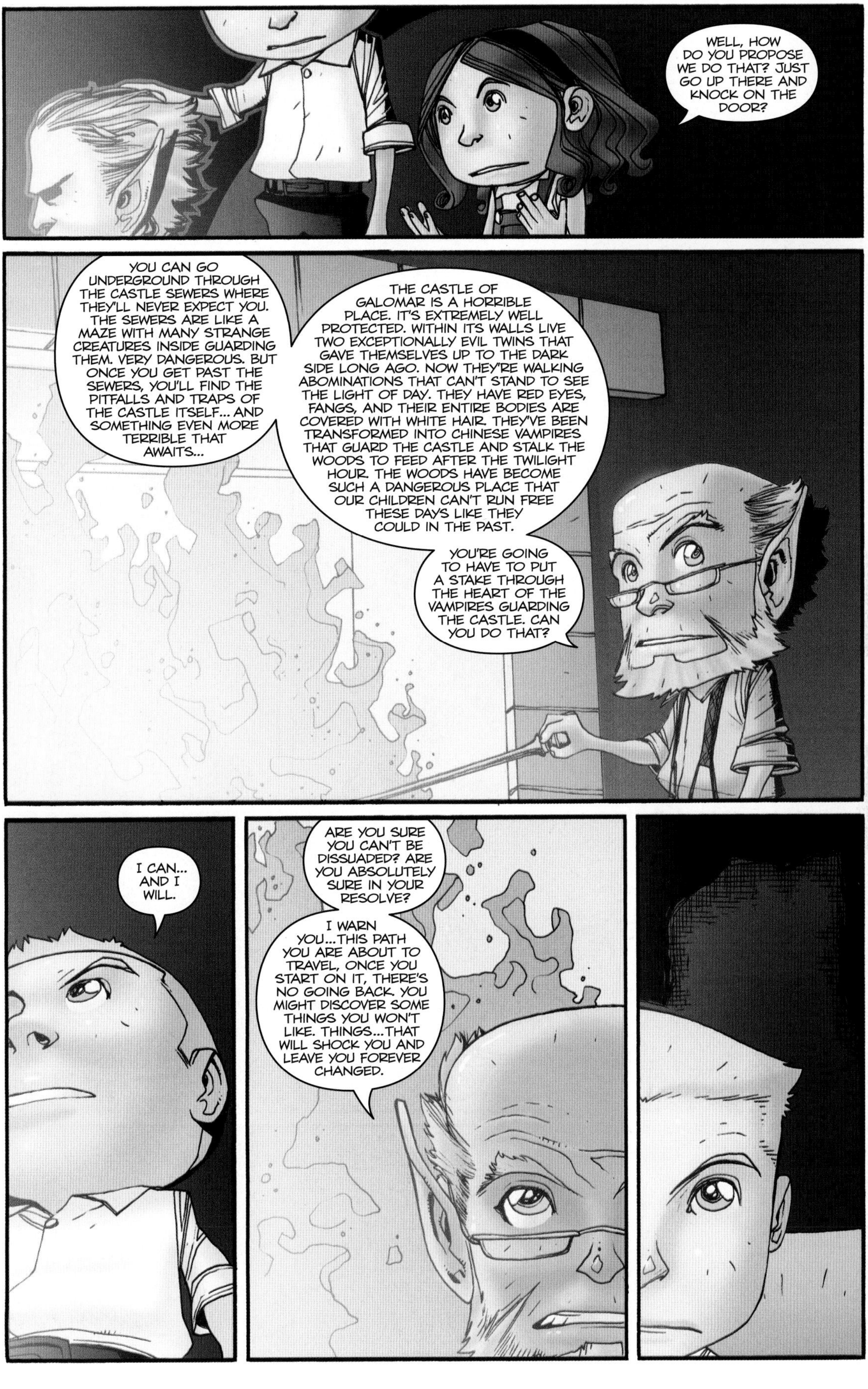
WELL, HOW DO YOU PROPOSE WE DO THAT? JUST GO UP THERE AND KNOCK ON THE DOOR?
THE CASTLE OF GALOMAR IS A HORRIBLE PLACE. IT'S EXTREMELY WELL PROTECTED. WITHIN ITS WALLS LIVE TWO EXCEPTIONALLY EVIL TWINS THAT GAVE THEMSELVES UP TO THE DARK SIDE LONG AGO. NOW THEY'RE WALKING ABOMINATIONS THAT CAN'T STAND TO SEE THE LIGHT OF DAY. THEY HAVE RED EYES, FANGS, AND THEIR ENTIRE BODIES ARE COVERED WITH WHITE HAIR. THEY'VE BEEN TRANSFORMED INTO CHINESE VAMPIRES THAT GUARD THE CASTLE AND STALK THE WOODS TO FEED AFTER THE TWILIGHT HOUR. THE WOODS HAVE BECOME SUCH A DANGEROUS PLACE THAT OUR CHILDREN CAN'T RUN FREE THESE DAYS LIKE THEY COULD IN THE PAST.
YOU'RE GOING TO HAVE TO PUT A STAKE THROUGH THE HEART OF THE VAMPIRES GUARDING THE CASTLE. CAN YOU DO THAT?
YOU CAN GO UNDERGROUND THROUGH THE CASTLE SEWERS WHERE THEY'LL NEVER EXPECT YOU. THE SEWERS ARE LIKE A MAZE WITH MANY STRANGE CREATURES INSIDE GUARDING THEM. VERY DANGEROUS. BUT ONCE YOU GET PAST THE SEWERS, YOU'LL FIND THE PITFALLS AND TRAPS OF THE CASTLE ITSELF... AND SOMETHING EVEN MORE TERRIBLE THAT AWAITS...
I CAN... AND I WILL.
ARE YOU SURE YOU CAN'T BE DISSUADED? ARE YOU ABSOLUTELY SURE IN YOUR RESOLVE?
I WARN YOU...THIS PATH YOU ARE ABOUT TO TRAVEL, ONCE YOU START ON IT, THERE'S NO GOING BACK. YOU MIGHT DISCOVER SOME THINGS YOU WON'T LIKE. THINGS...THAT WILL SHOCK YOU AND LEAVE YOU FOREVER CHANGED.

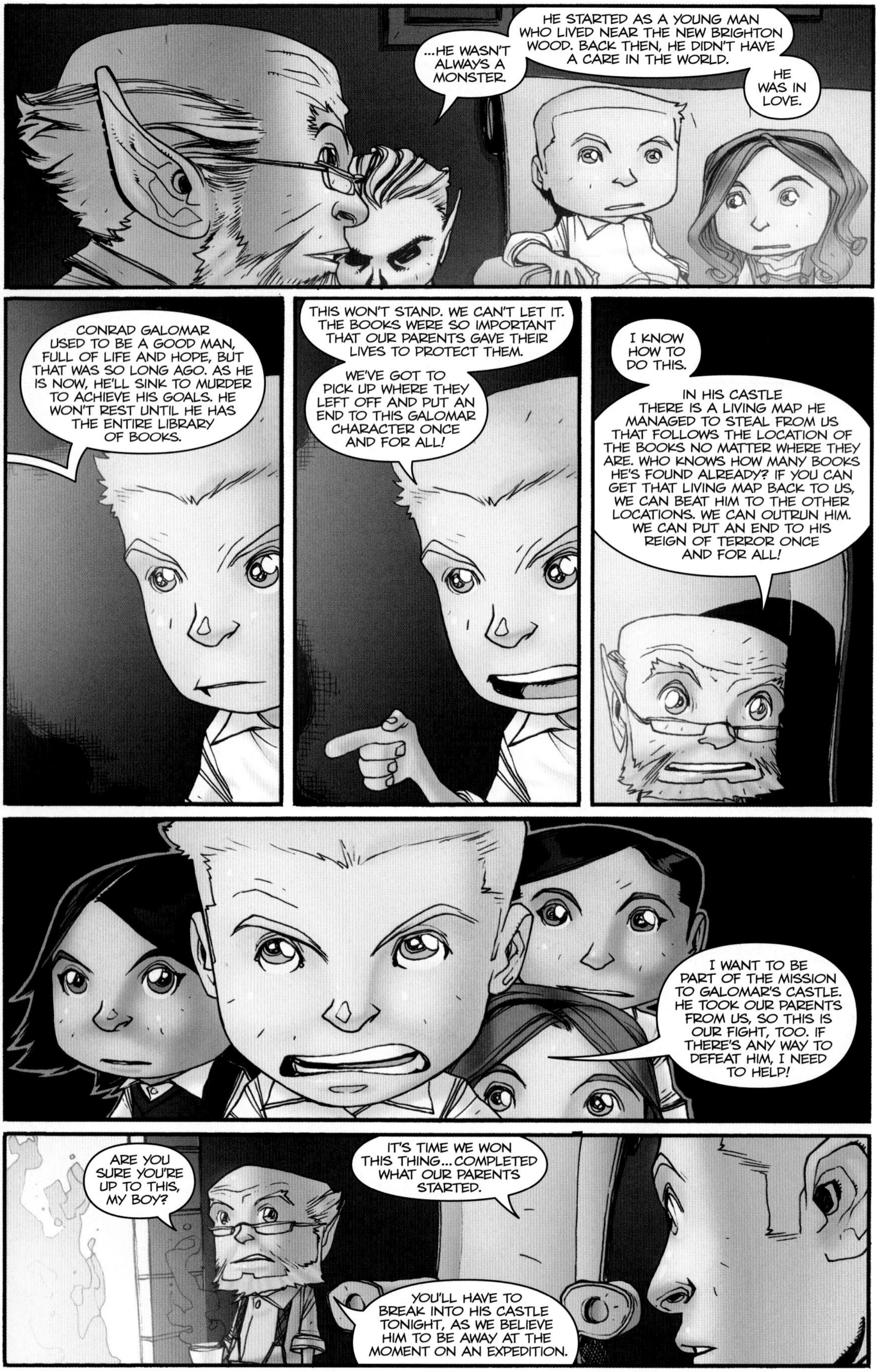
...HE WASN'T ALWAYS A MONSTER.
HE STARTED AS A YOUNG MAN WHO LIVED NEAR THE NEW BRIGHTON WOOD. BACK THEN, HE DIDN'T HAVE A CARE IN THE WORLD.
HE WAS IN LOVE.
CONRAD GALOMAR USED TO BE A GOOD MAN, FULL OF LIFE AND HOPE, BUT THAT WAS SO LONG AGO. AS HE IS NOW, HE'LL SINK TO MURDER TO ACHIEVE HIS GOALS. HE WON'T REST UNTIL HE HAS THE ENTIRE LIBRARY OF BOOKS.
THIS WON'T STAND. WE CAN'T LET IT. THE BOOKS WERE SO IMPORTANT THAT OUR PARENTS GAVE THEIR LIVES TO PROTECT THEM.
WE'VE GOT TO PICK UP WHERE THEY LEFT OFF AND PUT AN END TO THIS GALOMAR CHARACTER ONCE AND FOR ALL!
I KNOW HOW TO DO THIS.
IN HIS CASTLE THERE IS A LIVING MAP HE MANAGED TO STEAL FROM US THAT FOLLOWS THE LOCATION OF THE BOOKS NO MATTER WHERE THEY ARE. WHO KNOWS HOW MANY BOOKS HE'S FOUND ALREADY? IF YOU CAN GET THAT LIVING MAP BACK TO US, WE CAN BEAT HIM TO THE OTHER LOCATIONS. WE CAN OUTRUN HIM. WE CAN PUT AN END TO HIS REIGN OF TERROR ONCE AND FOR ALL!
I WANT TO BE PART OF THE MISSION TO GALOMAR'S CASTLE. HE TOOK OUR PARENTS FROM US, SO THIS IS OUR FIGHT, TOO. IF THERE'S ANY WAY TO DEFEAT HIM, I NEED TO HELP!
ARE YOU SURE YOU'RE UP TO THIS, MY BOY?
IT'S TIME WE WON THIS THING...COMPLETED WHAT OUR PARENTS STARTED.
YOU'LL HAVE TO BREAK INTO HIS CASTLE TONIGHT, AS WE BELIEVE HIM TO BE AWAY AT THE MOMENT ON AN EXPEDITION.

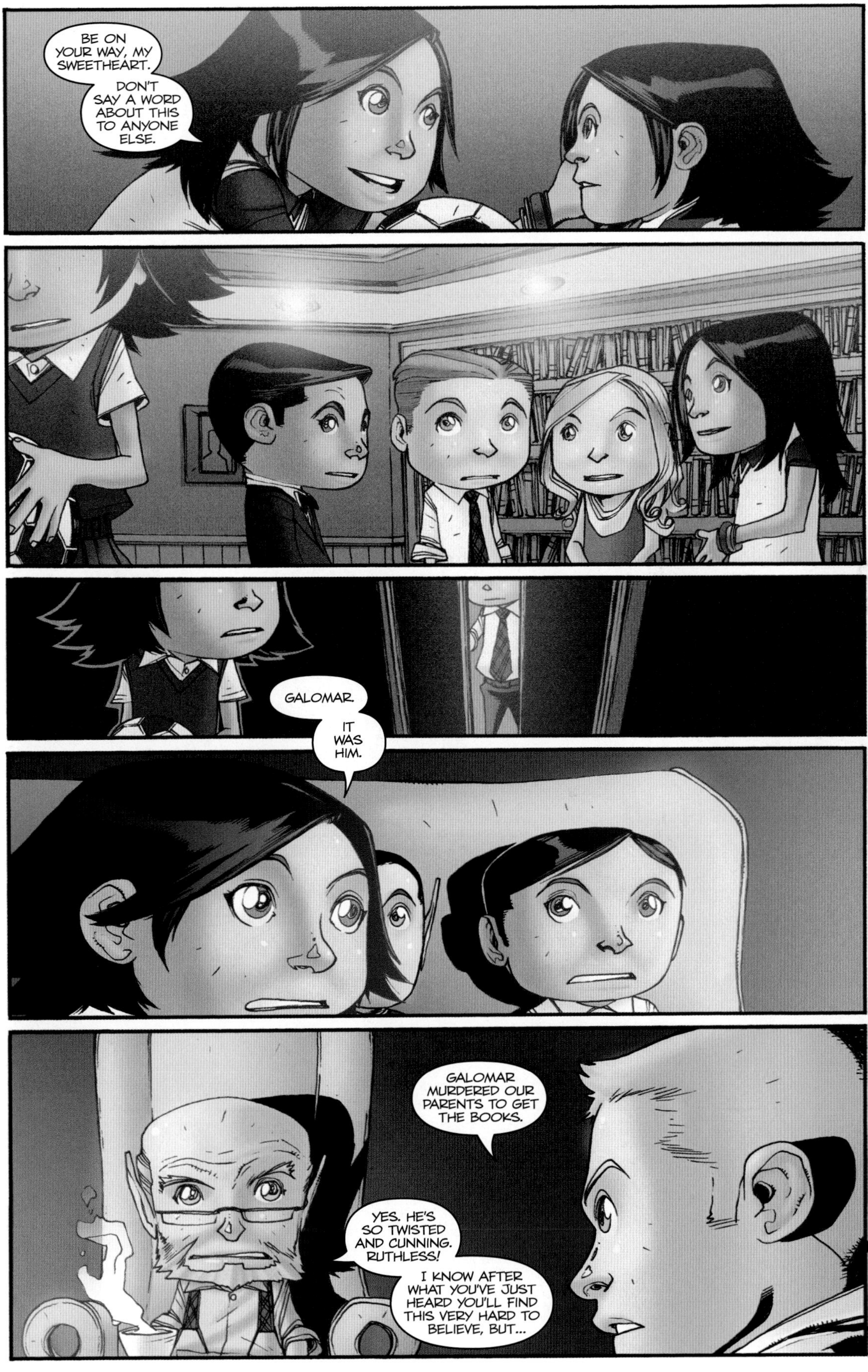
BE ON YOUR WAY, MY SWEETHEART.
DON'T SAY A WORD ABOUT THIS TO ANYONE ELSE.
GALOMAR.
IT WAS HIM.
GALOMAR MURDERED OUR PARENTS TO GET THE BOOKS.
YES. HE'S SO TWISTED AND CUNNING. RUTHLESS!
I KNOW AFTER WHAT YOU'VE JUST HEARD YOU'LL FIND THIS VERY HARD TO BELIEVE, BUT...

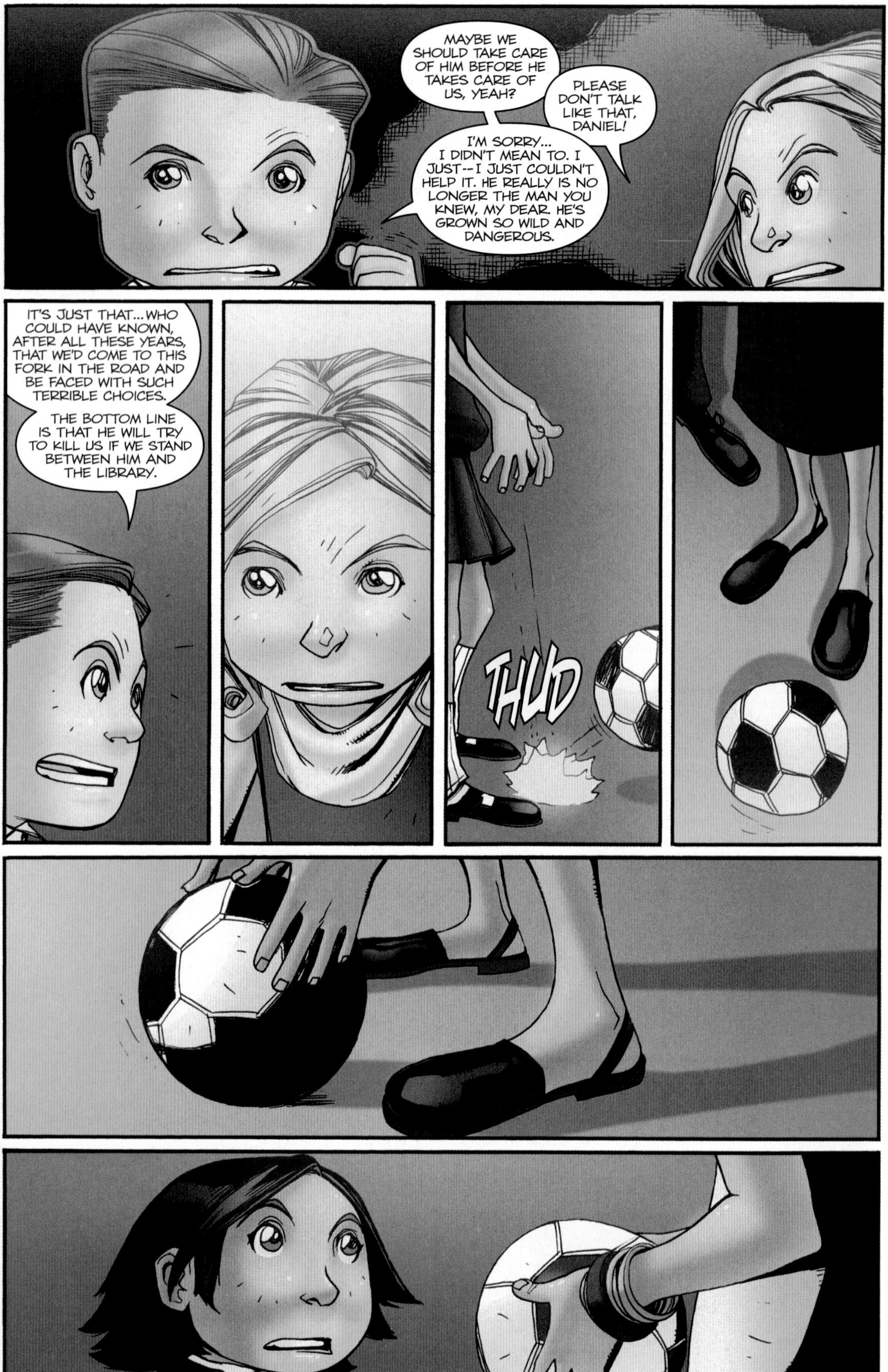

MAYBE WE SHOULD TAKE CARE OF HIM BEFORE HE TAKES CARE OF US, YEAH?
PLEASE DON'T TALK LIKE THAT, DANIEL!
I'M SORRY... I DIDN'T MEAN TO. I JUST--I JUST COULDN'T HELP IT. HE REALLY IS NO LONGER THE MAN YOU KNEW, MY DEAR. HE'S GROWN SO WILD AND DANGEROUS.
IT'S JUST THAT...WHO COULD HAVE KNOWN, AFTER ALL THESE YEARS, THAT WE'D COME TO THIS FORK IN THE ROAD AND BE FACED WITH SUCH TERRIBLE CHOICES.
THE BOTTOM LINE IS THAT HE WILL TRY TO KILL US IF WE STAND BETWEEN HIM AND THE LIBRARY.
THUD

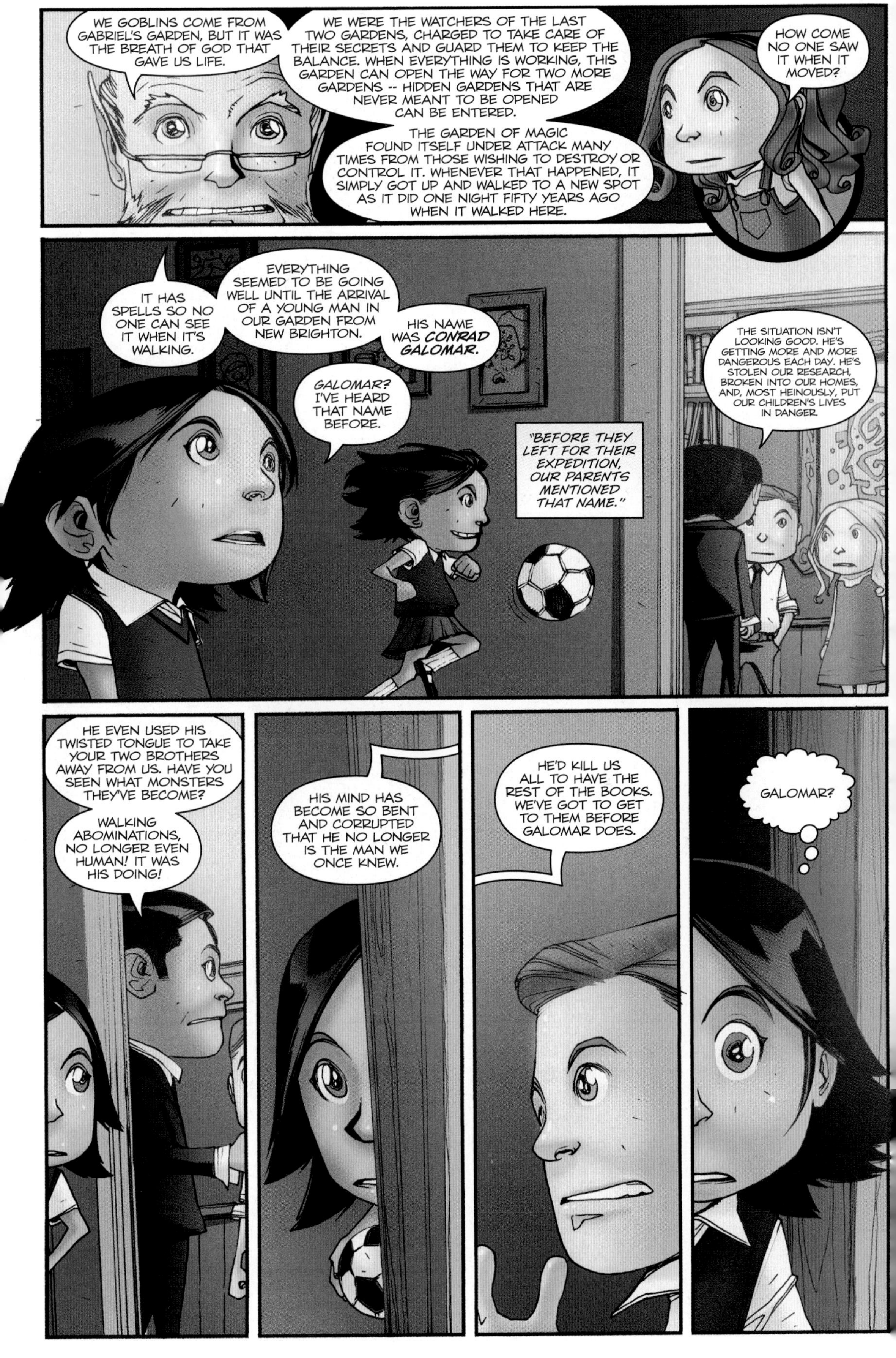

WE GOBLINS COME FROM GABRIEL'S GARDEN, BUT IT WAS THE BREATH OF GOD THAT GAVE US LIFE.
WE WERE THE WATCHERS OF THE LAST TWO GARDENS, CHARGED TO TAKE CARE OF THEIR SECRETS AND GUARD THEM TO KEEP THE BALANCE. WHEN EVERYTHING IS WORKING, THIS GARDEN CAN OPEN THE WAY FOR TWO MORE GARDENS -- HIDDEN GARDENS THAT ARE NEVER MEANT TO BE OPENED CAN BE ENTERED.
THE GARDEN OF MAGIC FOUND ITSELF UNDER ATTACK MANY TIMES FROM THOSE WISHING TO DESTROY OR CONTROL IT. WHENEVER THAT HAPPENED, IT SIMPLY GOT UP AND WALKED TO A NEW SPOT AS IT DID ONE NIGHT FIFTY YEARS AGO WHEN IT WALKED HERE.
HOW COME NO ONE SAW IT WHEN IT MOVED?
IT HAS SPELLS SO NO ONE CAN SEE IT WHEN IT'S WALKING.
EVERYTHING SEEMED TO BE GOING WELL UNTIL THE ARRIVAL OF A YOUNG MAN IN OUR GARDEN FROM NEW BRIGHTON.
HIS NAME WAS **CONRAD GALOMAR.**
GALOMAR? I'VE HEARD THAT NAME BEFORE.
"BEFORE THEY LEFT FOR THEIR EXPEDITION, OUR PARENTS MENTIONED THAT NAME."
THE SITUATION ISN'T LOOKING GOOD. HE'S GETTING MORE AND MORE DANGEROUS EACH DAY. HE'S STOLEN OUR RESEARCH, BROKEN INTO OUR HOMES, AND, MOST HEINOUSLY, PUT OUR CHILDREN'S LIVES IN DANGER.
HE EVEN USED HIS TWISTED TONGUE TO TAKE YOUR TWO BROTHERS AWAY FROM US. HAVE YOU SEEN WHAT MONSTERS THEY'VE BECOME?
WALKING ABOMINATIONS, NO LONGER EVEN HUMAN! IT WAS HIS DOING!
HIS MIND HAS BECOME SO BENT AND CORRUPTED THAT HE NO LONGER IS THE MAN WE ONCE KNEW.
HE'D KILL US ALL TO HAVE THE REST OF THE BOOKS. WE'VE GOT TO GET TO THEM BEFORE GALOMAR DOES.
GALOMAR?

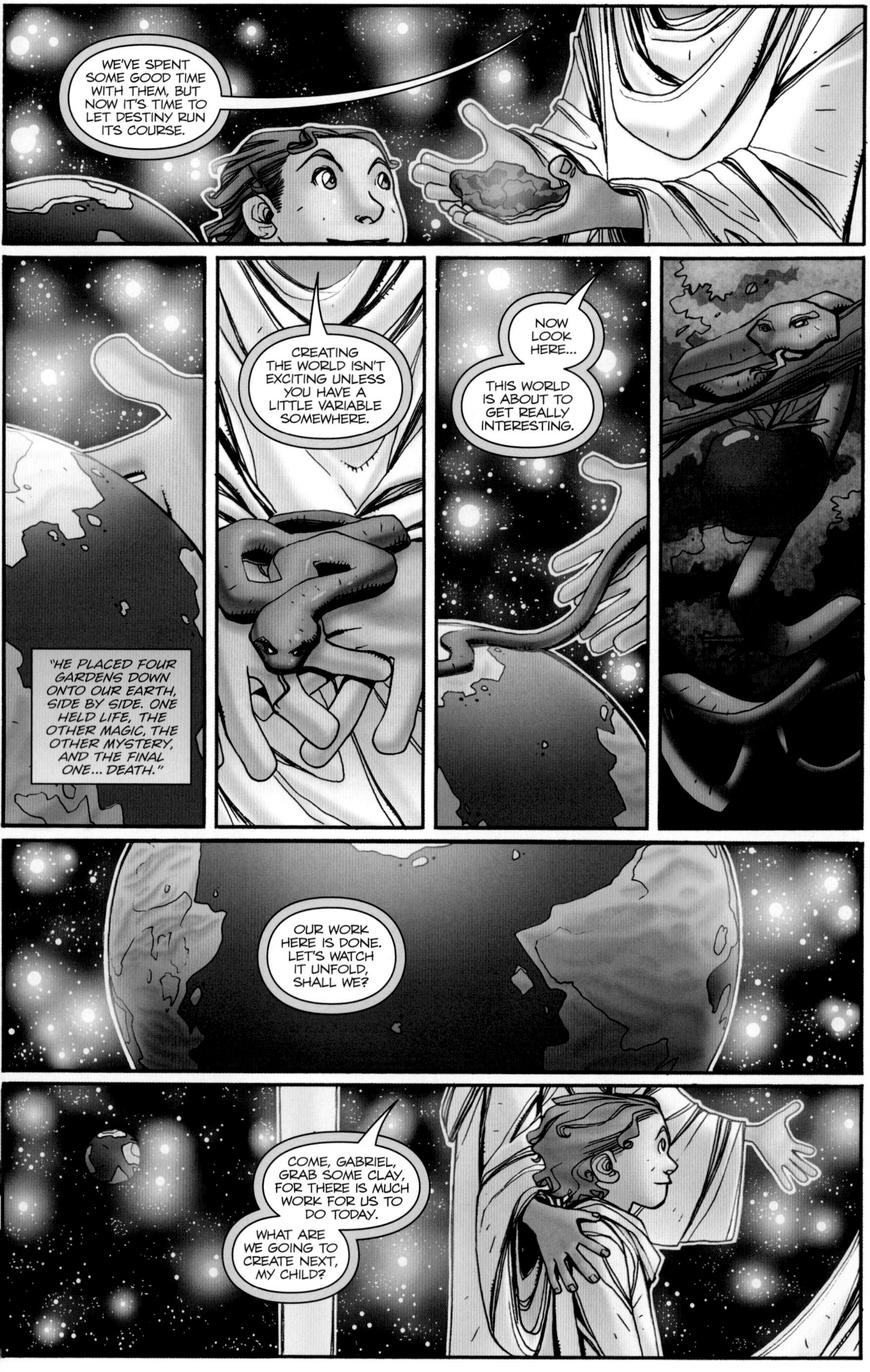
WE'VE SPENT SOME GOOD TIME WITH THEM, BUT NOW IT'S TIME TO LET DESTINY RUN ITS COURSE.
"HE PLACED FOUR GARDENS DOWN ONTO OUR EARTH, SIDE BY SIDE. ONE HELD LIFE, THE OTHER MAGIC, THE OTHER MYSTERY, AND THE FINAL ONE... DEATH."
CREATING THE WORLD ISN'T EXCITING UNLESS YOU HAVE A LITTLE VARIABLE SOMEWHERE.
NOW LOOK HERE...
THIS WORLD IS ABOUT TO GET REALLY INTERESTING.
OUR WORK HERE IS DONE. LET'S WATCH IT UNFOLD, SHALL WE?
COME, GABRIEL, GRAB SOME CLAY, FOR THERE IS MUCH WORK FOR US TO DO TODAY.
WHAT ARE WE GOING TO CREATE NEXT, MY CHILD?

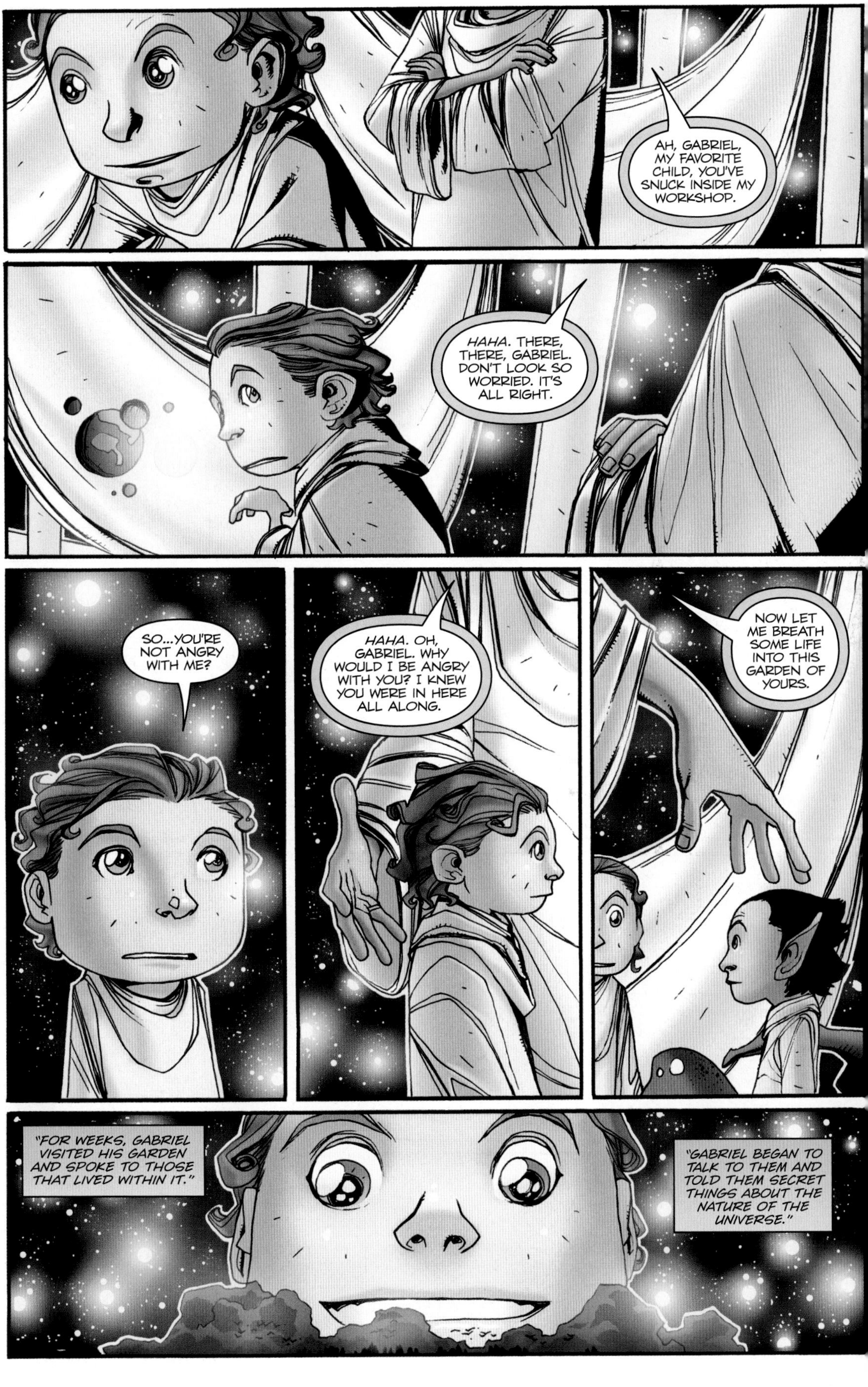
AH, GABRIEL, MY FAVORITE CHILD, YOU'VE SNUCK INSIDE MY WORKSHOP.
HAHA. THERE, THERE, GABRIEL. DON'T LOOK SO WORRIED. IT'S ALL RIGHT.
SO...YOU'RE NOT ANGRY WITH ME?
HAHA. OH, GABRIEL. WHY WOULD I BE ANGRY WITH YOU? I KNEW YOU WERE IN HERE ALL ALONG.
NOW LET ME BREATH SOME LIFE INTO THIS GARDEN OF YOURS.
"FOR WEEKS, GABRIEL VISITED HIS GARDEN AND SPOKE TO THOSE THAT LIVED WITHIN IT."
"GABRIEL BEGAN TO TALK TO THEM AND TOLD THEM SECRET THINGS ABOUT THE NATURE OF THE UNIVERSE."

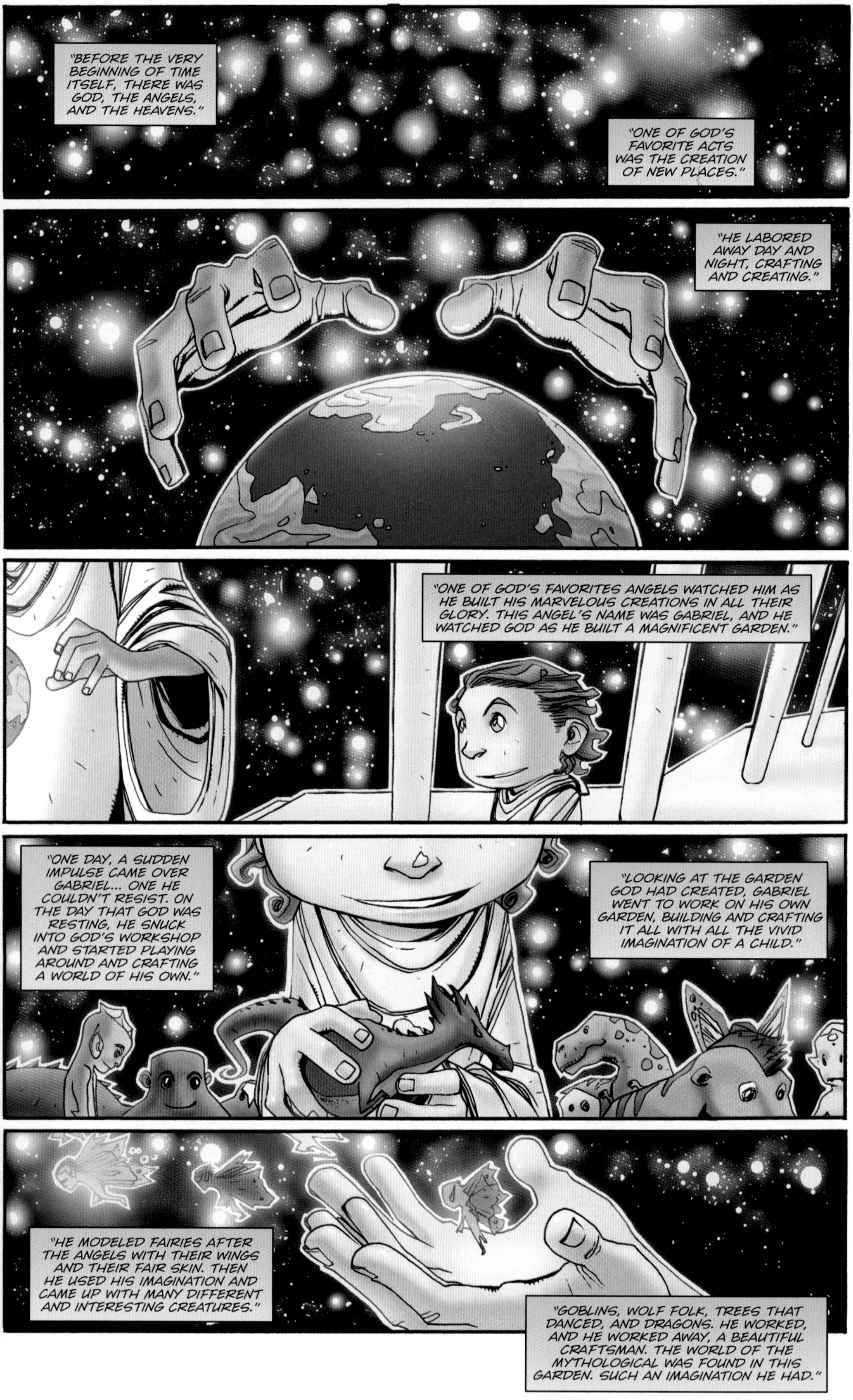
"BEFORE THE VERY BEGINNING OF TIME ITSELF, THERE WAS GOD, THE ANGELS, AND THE HEAVENS."
"ONE OF GOD'S FAVORITE ACTS WAS THE CREATION OF NEW PLACES."
"HE LABORED AWAY DAY AND NIGHT, CRAFTING AND CREATING."
"ONE OF GOD'S FAVORITES ANGELS WATCHED HIM AS HE BUILT HIS MARVELOUS CREATIONS IN ALL THEIR GLORY. THIS ANGEL'S NAME WAS GABRIEL, AND HE WATCHED GOD AS HE BUILT A MAGNIFICENT GARDEN."
"ONE DAY, A SUDDEN IMPULSE CAME OVER GABRIEL... ONE HE COULDN'T RESIST. ON THE DAY THAT GOD WAS RESTING, HE SNUCK INTO GOD'S WORKSHOP AND STARTED PLAYING AROUND AND CRAFTING A WORLD OF HIS OWN."
"LOOKING AT THE GARDEN GOD HAD CREATED, GABRIEL WENT TO WORK ON HIS OWN GARDEN, BUILDING AND CRAFTING IT ALL WITH ALL THE VIVID IMAGINATION OF A CHILD."
"HE MODELED FAIRIES AFTER THE ANGELS WITH THEIR WINGS AND THEIR FAIR SKIN. THEN HE USED HIS IMAGINATION AND CAME UP WITH MANY DIFFERENT AND INTERESTING CREATURES."
"GOBLINS, WOLF FOLK, TREES THAT DANCED, AND DRAGONS. HE WORKED, AND HE WORKED AWAY, A BEAUTIFUL CRAFTSMAN. THE WORLD OF THE MYTHOLOGICAL WAS FOUND IN THIS GARDEN. SUCH AN IMAGINATION HE HAD."

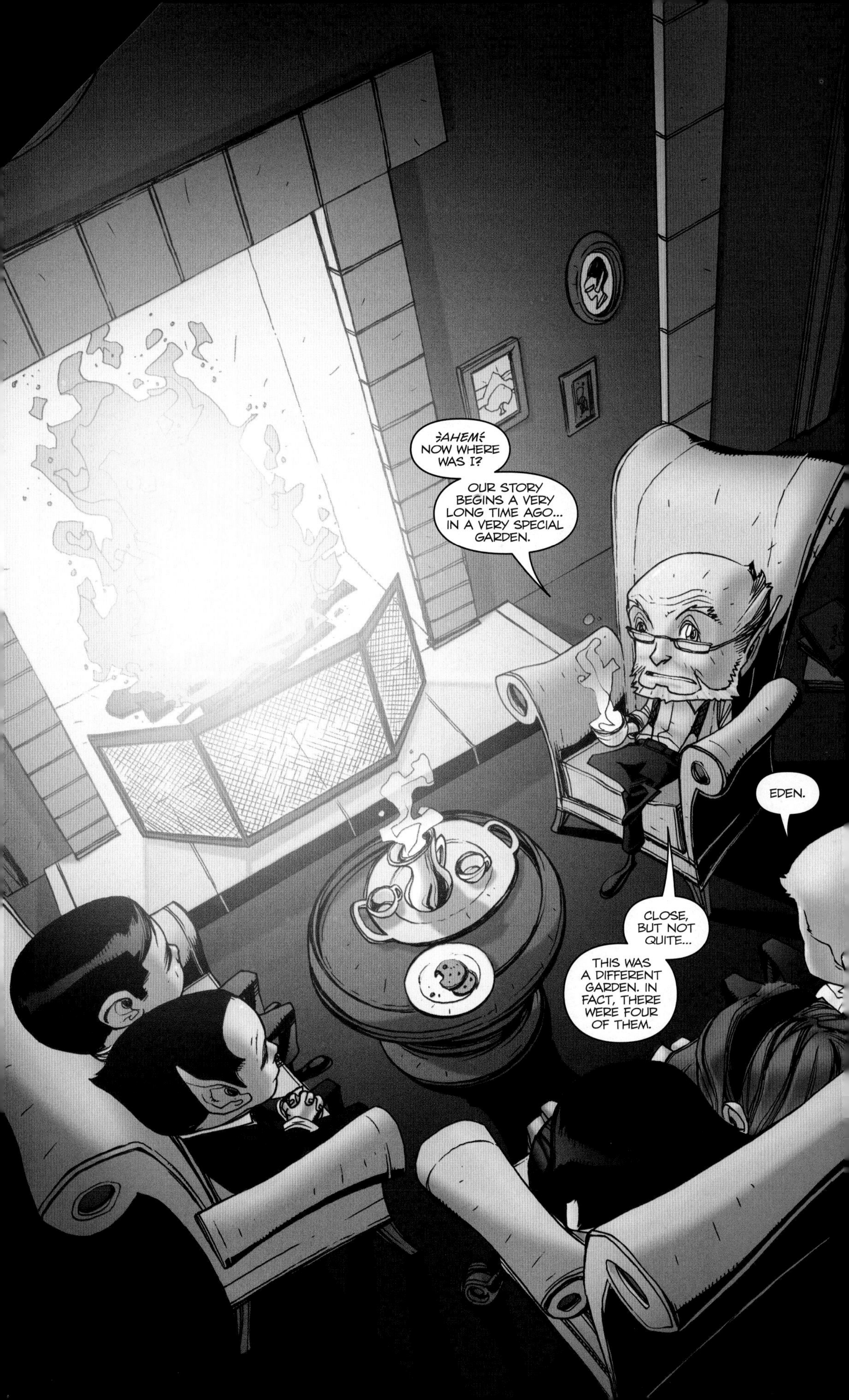
AHEM NOW WHERE WAS I?
OUR STORY BEGINS A VERY LONG TIME AGO... IN A VERY SPECIAL GARDEN.
EDEN.
CLOSE, BUT NOT QUITE...
THIS WAS A DIFFERENT GARDEN. IN FACT, THERE WERE FOUR OF THEM.

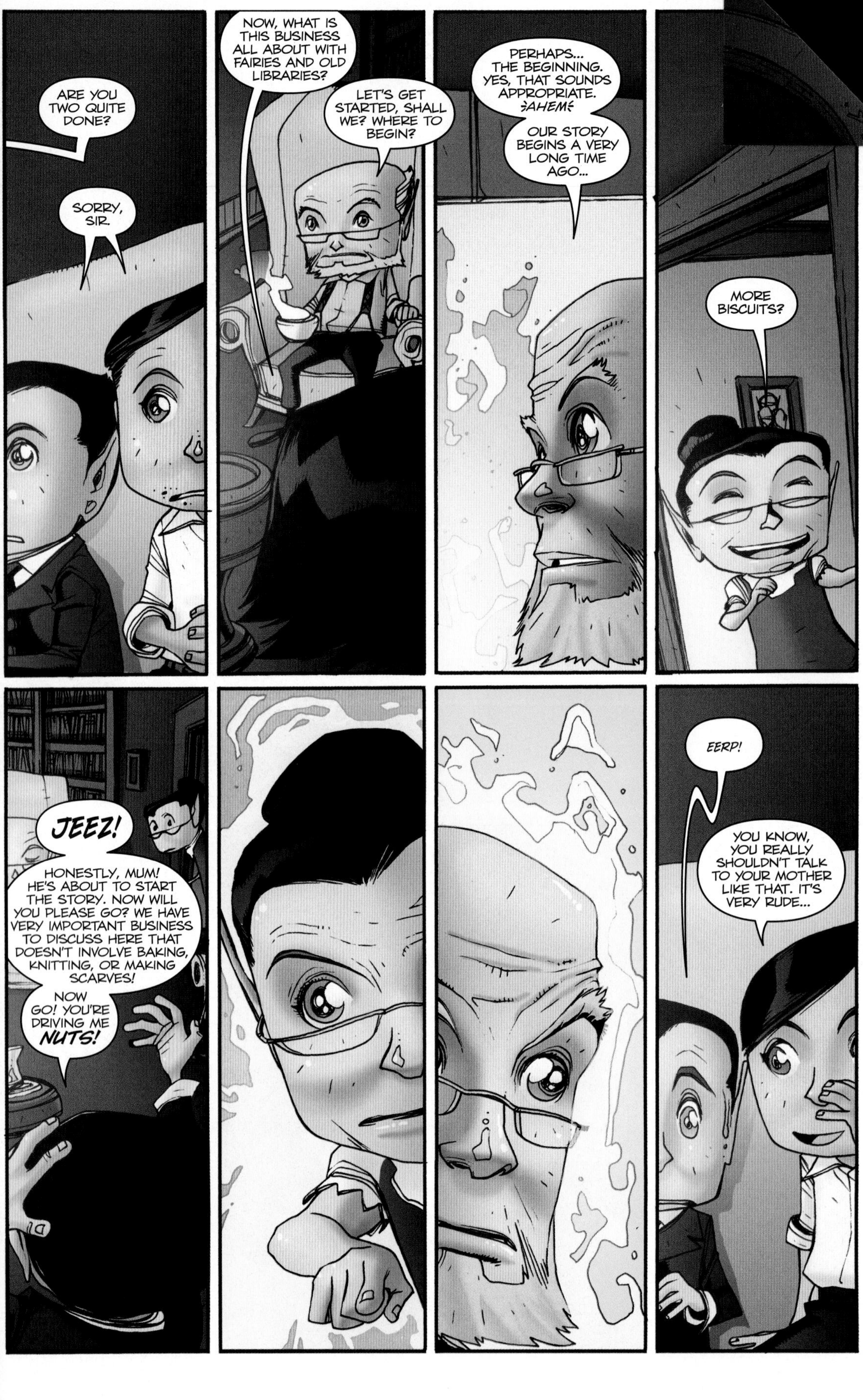

ARE YOU TWO QUITE DONE?
SORRY, SIR.
NOW, WHAT IS THIS BUSINESS ALL ABOUT WITH FAIRIES AND OLD LIBRARIES?
LET'S GET STARTED, SHALL WE? WHERE TO BEGIN?
PERHAPS... THE BEGINNING. YES, THAT SOUNDS APPROPRIATE.
AHEM
OUR STORY BEGINS A VERY LONG TIME AGO...
MORE BISCUITS?
JEEZ!
HONESTLY, MUM! HE'S ABOUT TO START THE STORY. NOW WILL YOU PLEASE GO? WE HAVE VERY IMPORTANT BUSINESS TO DISCUSS HERE THAT DOESN'T INVOLVE BAKING, KNITTING, OR MAKING SCARVES!
NOW GO! YOU'RE DRIVING ME NUTS!
EERP!
YOU KNOW, YOU REALLY SHOULDN'T TALK TO YOUR MOTHER LIKE THAT. IT'S VERY RUDE...

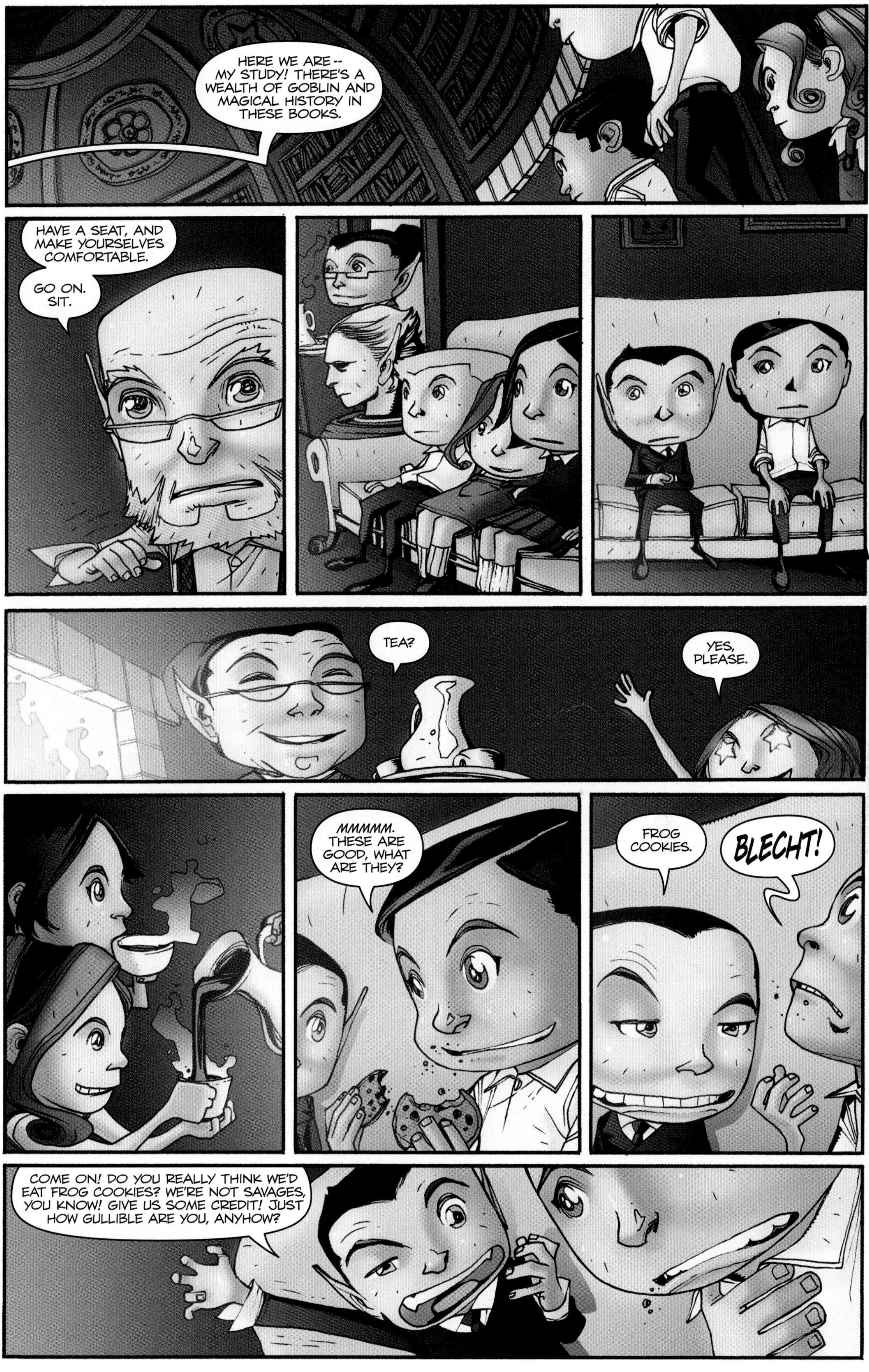
HERE WE ARE -- MY STUDY! THERE'S A WEALTH OF GOBLIN AND MAGICAL HISTORY IN THESE BOOKS.
HAVE A SEAT, AND MAKE YOURSELVES COMFORTABLE.
GO ON. SIT.
TEA?
YES, PLEASE.
MMMMM. THESE ARE GOOD, WHAT ARE THEY?
FROG COOKIES.
BLECHT!
COME ON! DO YOU REALLY THINK WE'D EAT FROG COOKIES? WE'RE NOT SAVAGES, YOU KNOW! GIVE US SOME CREDIT! JUST HOW GULLIBLE ARE YOU, ANYHOW?

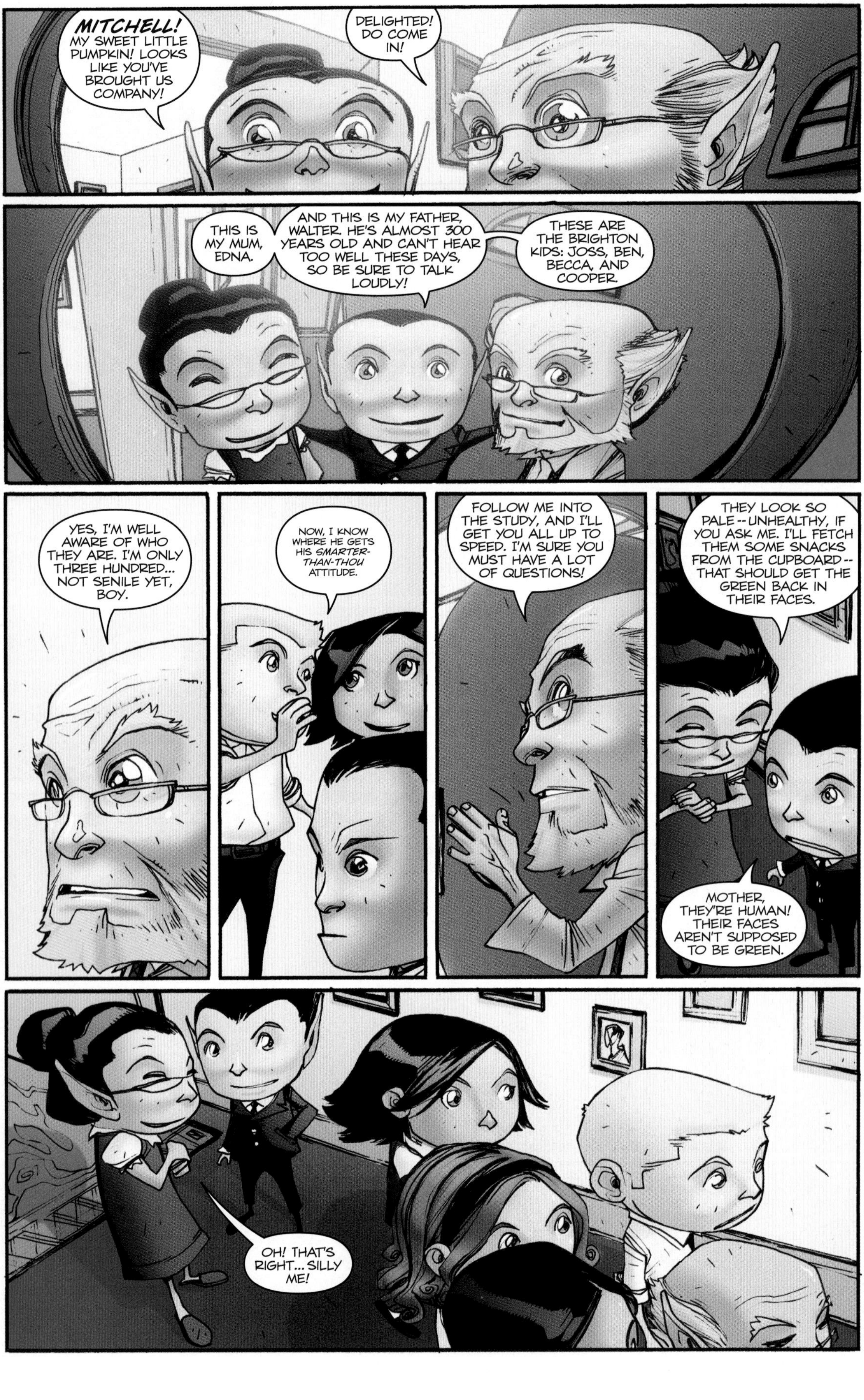
MITCHELL! MY SWEET LITTLE PUMPKIN! LOOKS LIKE YOU'VE BROUGHT US COMPANY!
DELIGHTED! DO COME IN!
THIS IS MY MUM, EDNA.
AND THIS IS MY FATHER, WALTER. HE'S ALMOST 300 YEARS OLD AND CAN'T HEAR TOO WELL THESE DAYS, SO BE SURE TO TALK LOUDLY!
THESE ARE THE BRIGHTON KIDS: JOSS, BEN, BECCA, AND COOPER.
YES, I'M WELL AWARE OF WHO THEY ARE. I'M ONLY THREE HUNDRED... NOT SENILE YET, BOY.
NOW, I KNOW WHERE HE GETS HIS SMARTER-THAN-THOU ATTITUDE.
FOLLOW ME INTO THE STUDY, AND I'LL GET YOU ALL UP TO SPEED. I'M SURE YOU MUST HAVE A LOT OF QUESTIONS!
THEY LOOK SO PALE--UNHEALTHY, IF YOU ASK ME. I'LL FETCH THEM SOME SNACKS FROM THE CUPBOARD--THAT SHOULD GET THE GREEN BACK IN THEIR FACES.
MOTHER, THEY'RE HUMAN! THEIR FACES AREN'T SUPPOSED TO BE GREEN.
OH! THAT'S RIGHT... SILLY ME!

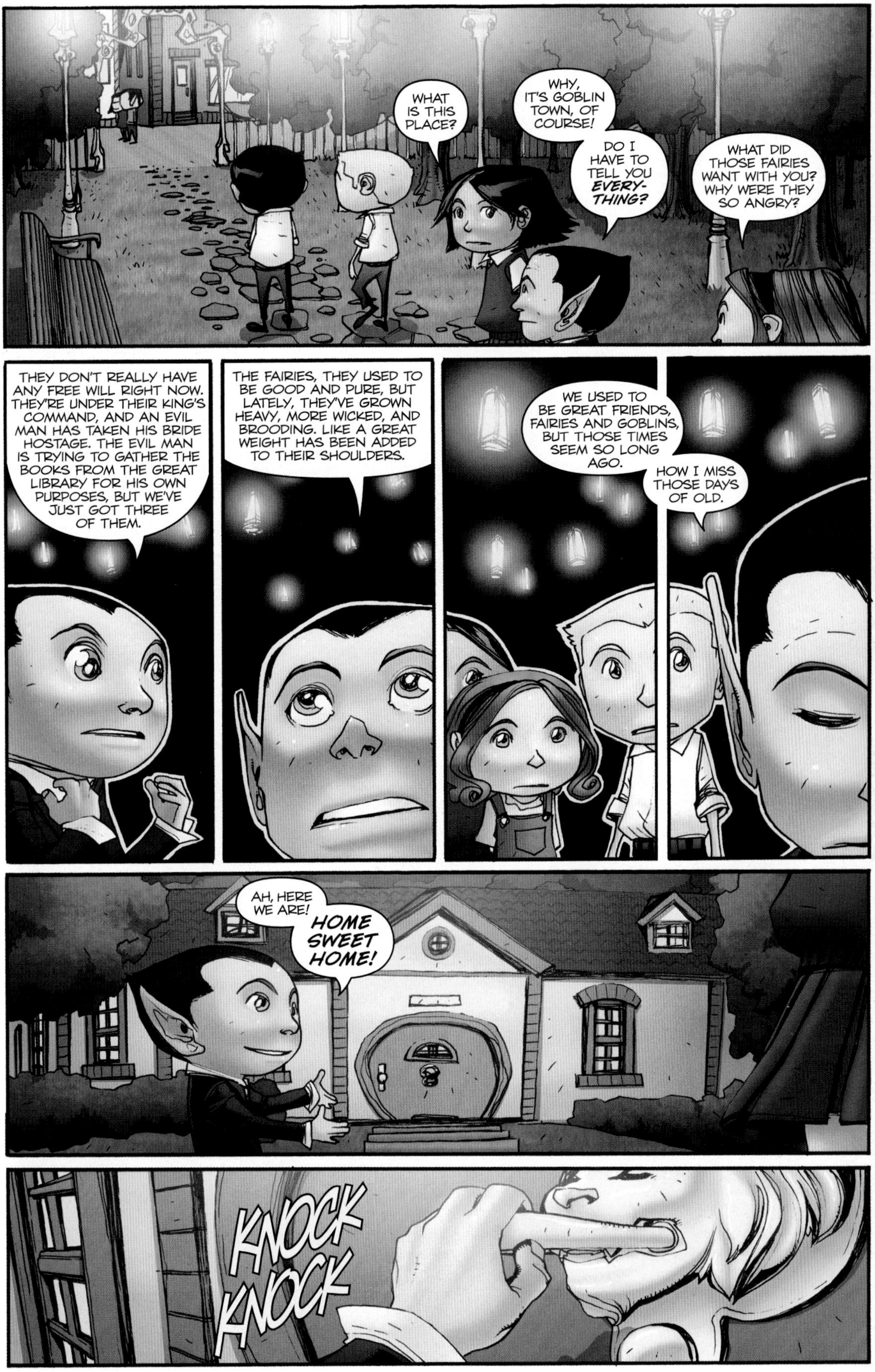
WHAT IS THIS PLACE?
WHY, IT'S GOBLIN TOWN, OF COURSE!
DO I HAVE TO TELL YOU *EVERYTHING?*
WHAT DID THOSE FAIRIES WANT WITH YOU? WHY WERE THEY SO ANGRY?
THEY DON'T REALLY HAVE ANY FREE WILL RIGHT NOW. THEY'RE UNDER THEIR KING'S COMMAND, AND AN EVIL MAN HAS TAKEN HIS BRIDE HOSTAGE. THE EVIL MAN IS TRYING TO GATHER THE BOOKS FROM THE GREAT LIBRARY FOR HIS OWN PURPOSES, BUT WE'VE JUST GOT THREE OF THEM.
THE FAIRIES, THEY USED TO BE GOOD AND PURE, BUT LATELY, THEY'VE GROWN HEAVY, MORE WICKED, AND BROODING. LIKE A GREAT WEIGHT HAS BEEN ADDED TO THEIR SHOULDERS.
WE USED TO BE GREAT FRIENDS, FAIRIES AND GOBLINS, BUT THOSE TIMES SEEM SO LONG AGO.
HOW I MISS THOSE DAYS OF OLD.
AH, HERE WE ARE!
HOME SWEET HOME!
KNOCK KNOCK

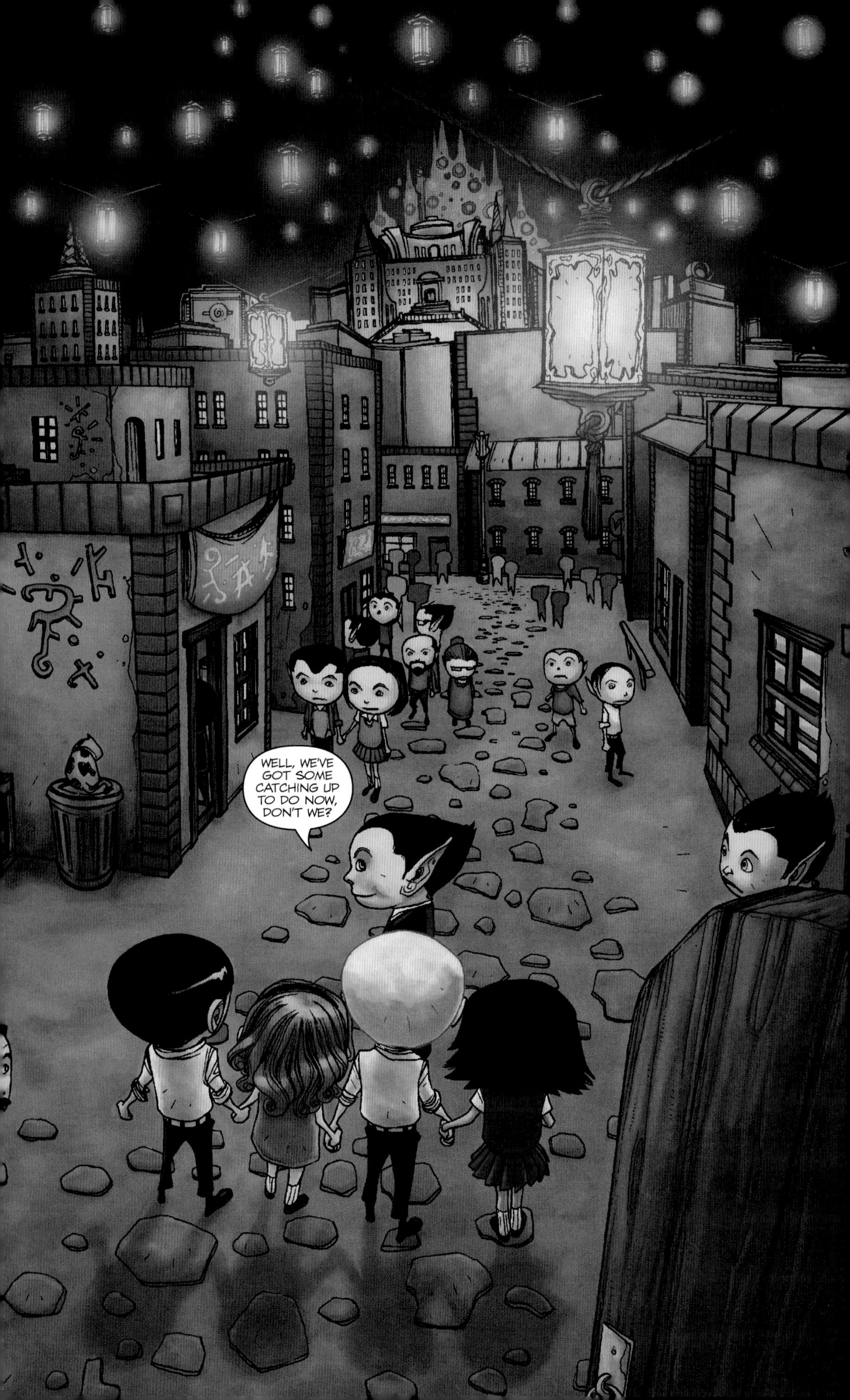
WELL, WE'VE GOT SOME CATCHING UP TO DO NOW, DON'T WE?

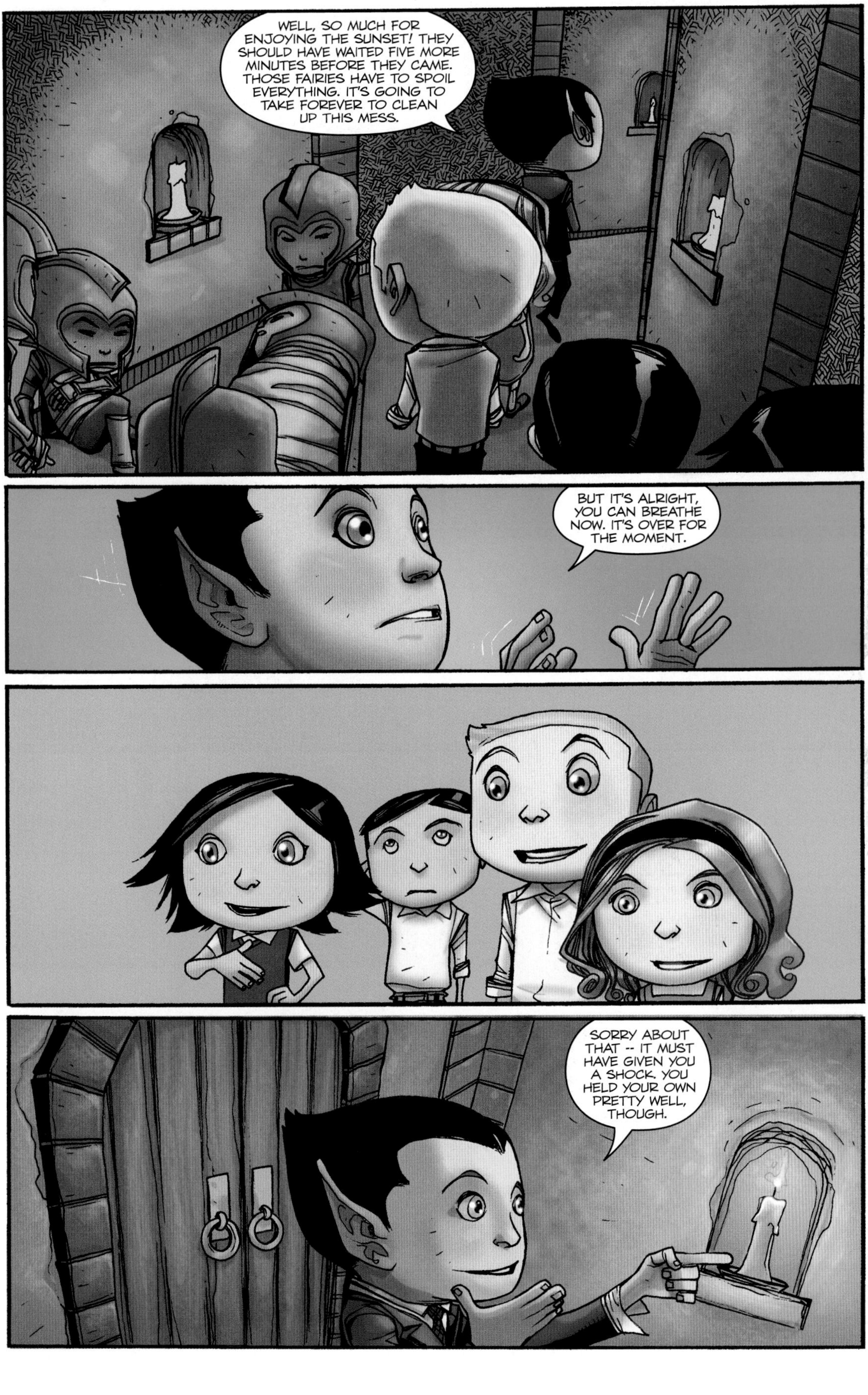
WELL, SO MUCH FOR ENJOYING THE SUNSET! THEY SHOULD HAVE WAITED FIVE MORE MINUTES BEFORE THEY CAME. THOSE FAIRIES HAVE TO SPOIL EVERYTHING. IT'S GOING TO TAKE FOREVER TO CLEAN UP THIS MESS.
BUT IT'S ALRIGHT, YOU CAN BREATHE NOW. IT'S OVER FOR THE MOMENT.
SORRY ABOUT THAT -- IT MUST HAVE GIVEN YOU A SHOCK. YOU HELD YOUR OWN PRETTY WELL, THOUGH.

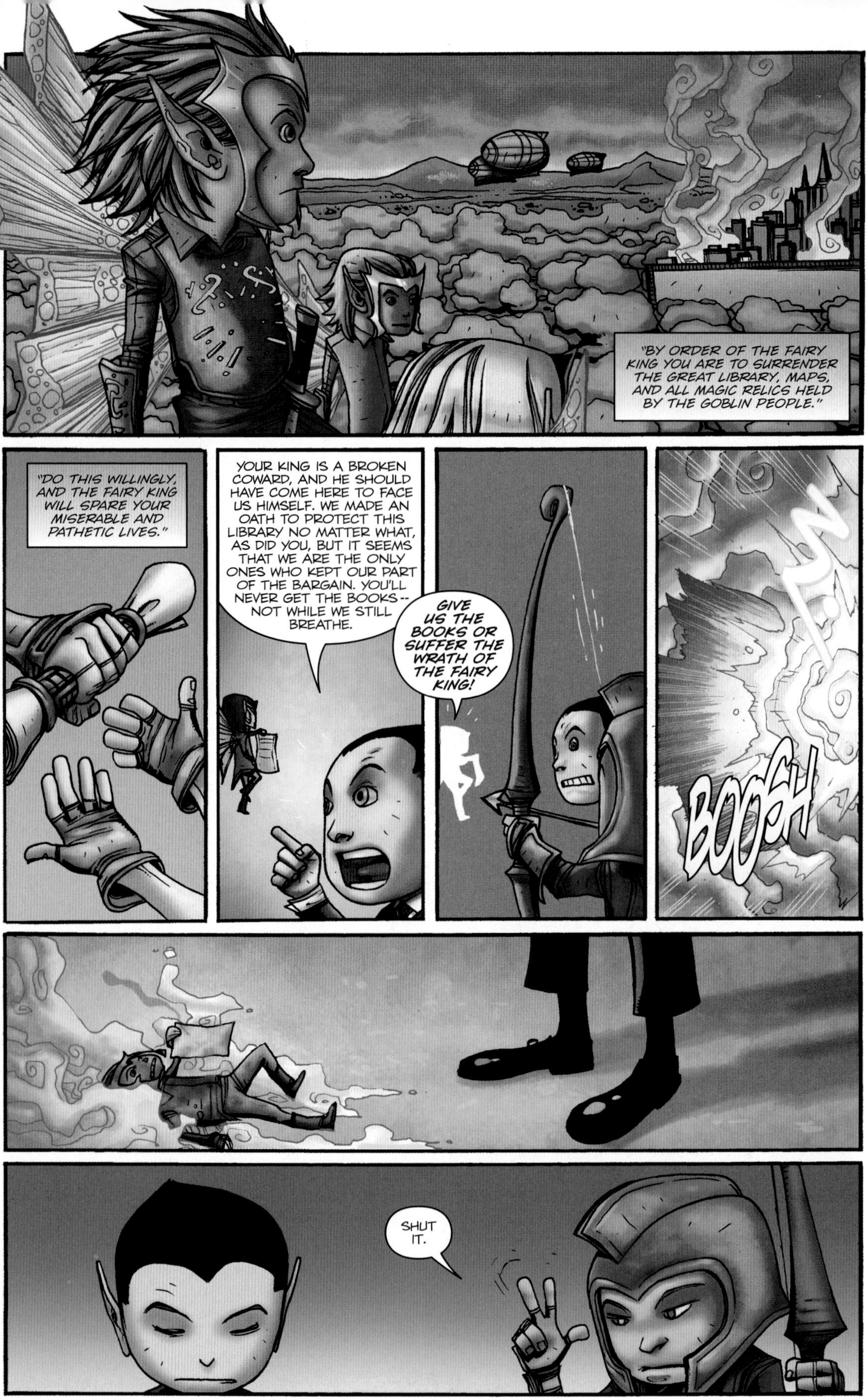
"BY ORDER OF THE FAIRY KING YOU ARE TO SURRENDER THE GREAT LIBRARY, MAPS, AND ALL MAGIC RELICS HELD BY THE GOBLIN PEOPLE."
"DO THIS WILLINGLY, AND THE FAIRY KING WILL SPARE YOUR MISERABLE AND PATHETIC LIVES."
YOUR KING IS A BROKEN COWARD, AND HE SHOULD HAVE COME HERE TO FACE US HIMSELF. WE MADE AN OATH TO PROTECT THIS LIBRARY NO MATTER WHAT, AS DID YOU, BUT IT SEEMS THAT WE ARE THE ONLY ONES WHO KEPT OUR PART OF THE BARGAIN. YOU'LL NEVER GET THE BOOKS-- NOT WHILE WE STILL BREATHE.
GIVE US THE BOOKS OR SUFFER THE WRATH OF THE FAIRY KING!
BOOSH
SHUT IT.

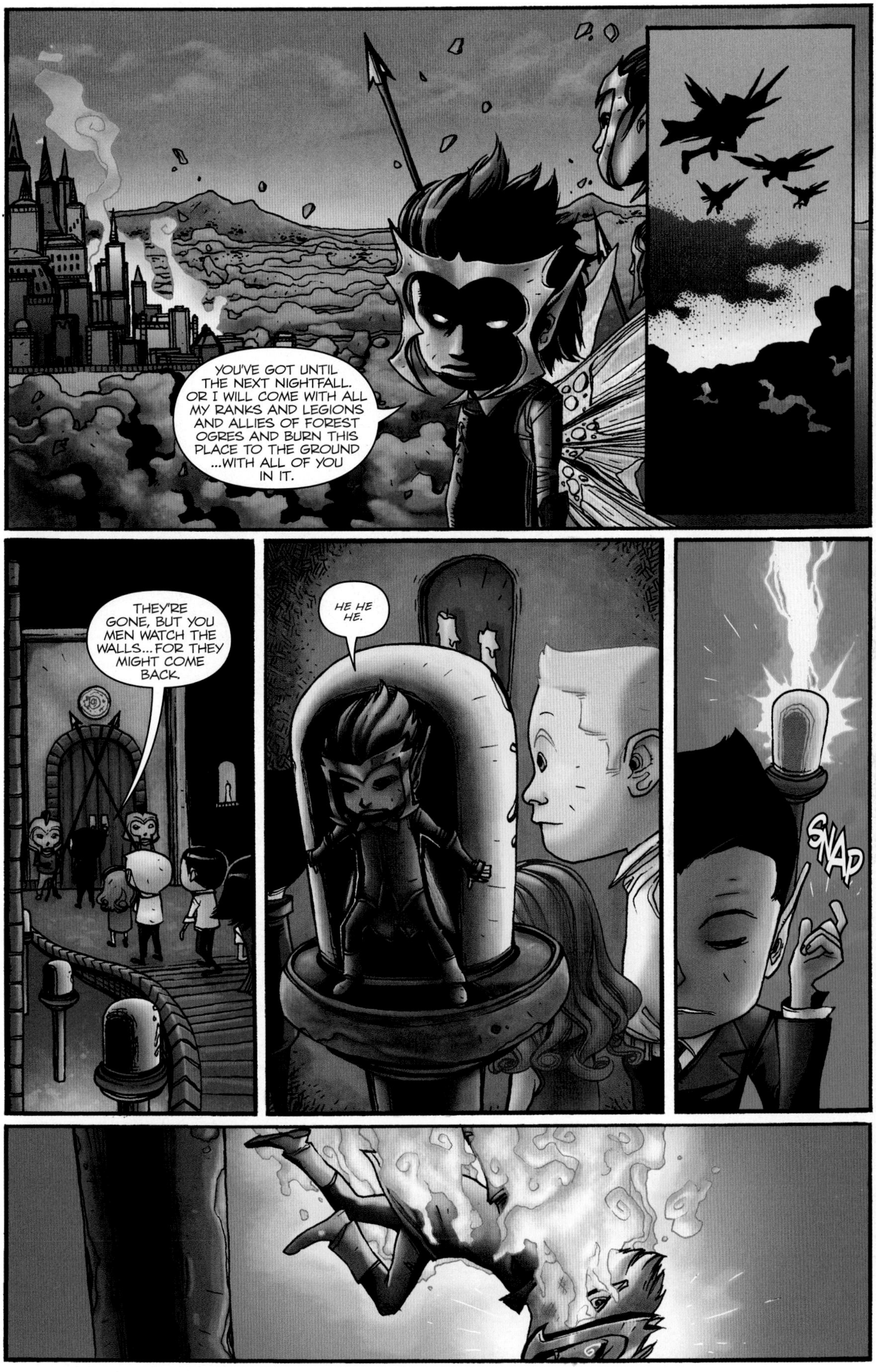
YOU'VE GOT UNTIL THE NEXT NIGHTFALL. OR I WILL COME WITH ALL MY RANKS AND LEGIONS AND ALLIES OF FOREST OGRES AND BURN THIS PLACE TO THE GROUND ...WITH ALL OF YOU IN IT.
THEY'RE GONE, BUT YOU MEN WATCH THE WALLS...FOR THEY MIGHT COME BACK.
HE HE HE.
SNAP

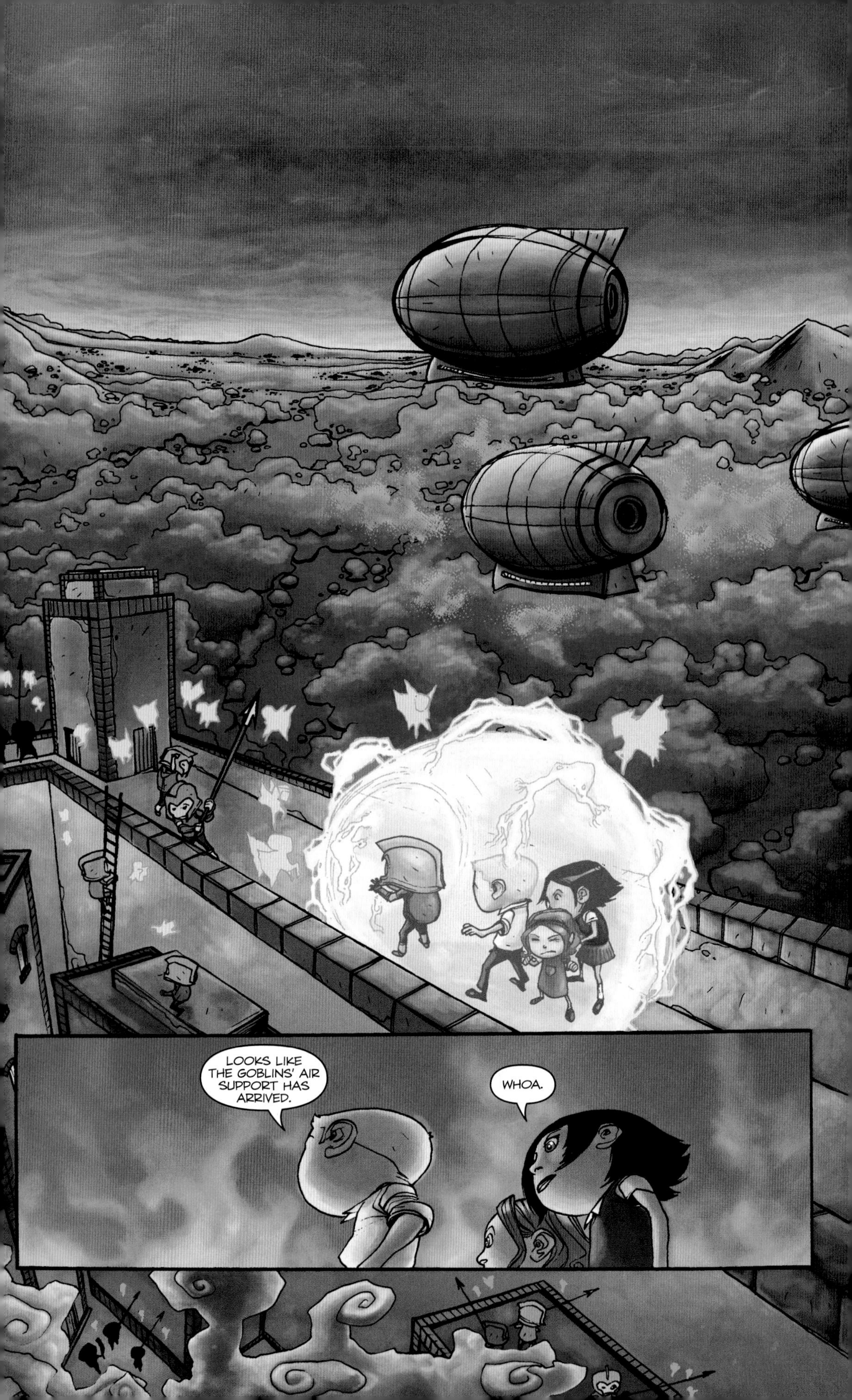
LOOKS LIKE THE GOBLINS' AIR SUPPORT HAS ARRIVED.
WHOA.

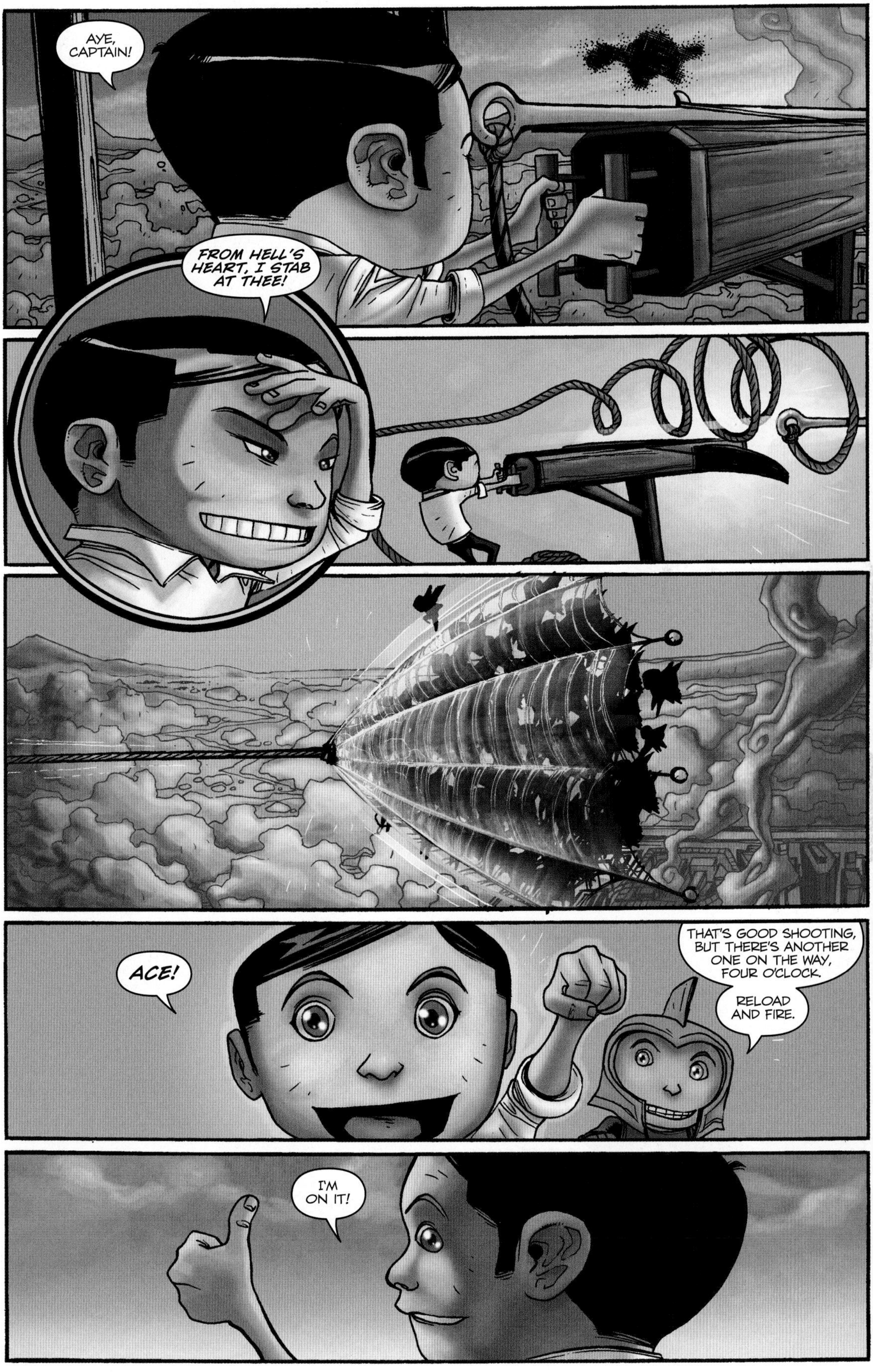
AYE, CAPTAIN!
FROM HELL'S HEART, I STAB AT THEE!
ACE!
THAT'S GOOD SHOOTING, BUT THERE'S ANOTHER ONE ON THE WAY, FOUR O'CLOCK.
RELOAD AND FIRE.
I'M ON IT!

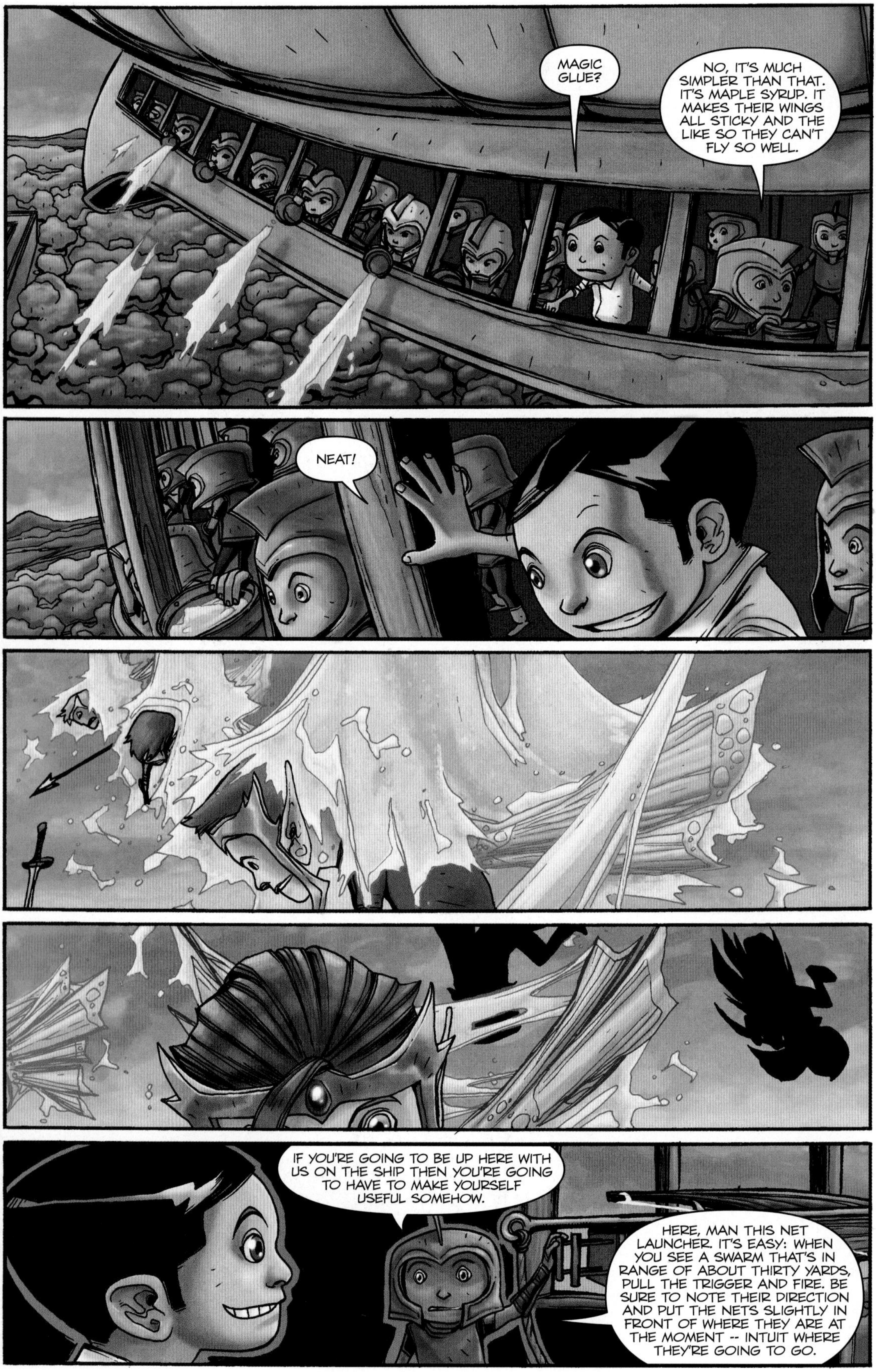
MAGIC GLUE?
NO, IT'S MUCH SIMPLER THAN THAT. IT'S MAPLE SYRUP. IT MAKES THEIR WINGS ALL STICKY AND THE LIKE SO THEY CAN'T FLY SO WELL.
NEAT!
IF YOU'RE GOING TO BE UP HERE WITH US ON THE SHIP THEN YOU'RE GOING TO HAVE TO MAKE YOURSELF USEFUL SOMEHOW.
HERE, MAN THIS NET LAUNCHER. IT'S EASY: WHEN YOU SEE A SWARM THAT'S IN RANGE OF ABOUT THIRTY YARDS, PULL THE TRIGGER AND FIRE. BE SURE TO NOTE THEIR DIRECTION AND PUT THE NETS SLIGHTLY IN FRONT OF WHERE THEY ARE AT THE MOMENT -- INTUIT WHERE THEY'RE GOING TO GO.

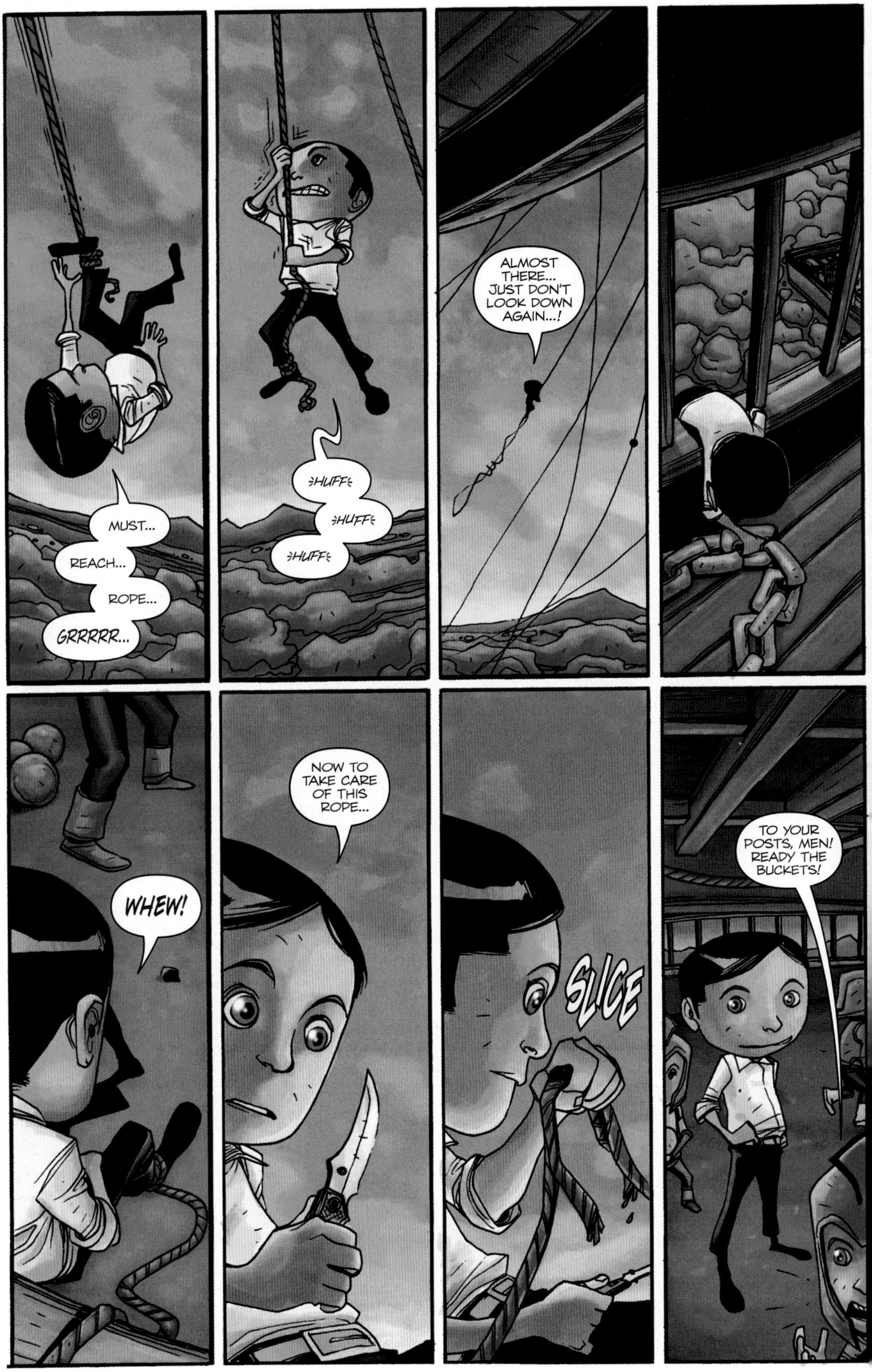
MUST...
REACH...
ROPE...
GRRRRR...
HUFF
HUFF
HUFF
ALMOST THERE... JUST DON'T LOOK DOWN AGAIN...!
WHEW!
NOW TO TAKE CARE OF THIS ROPE...
SLICE
TO YOUR POSTS, MEN! READY THE BUCKETS!

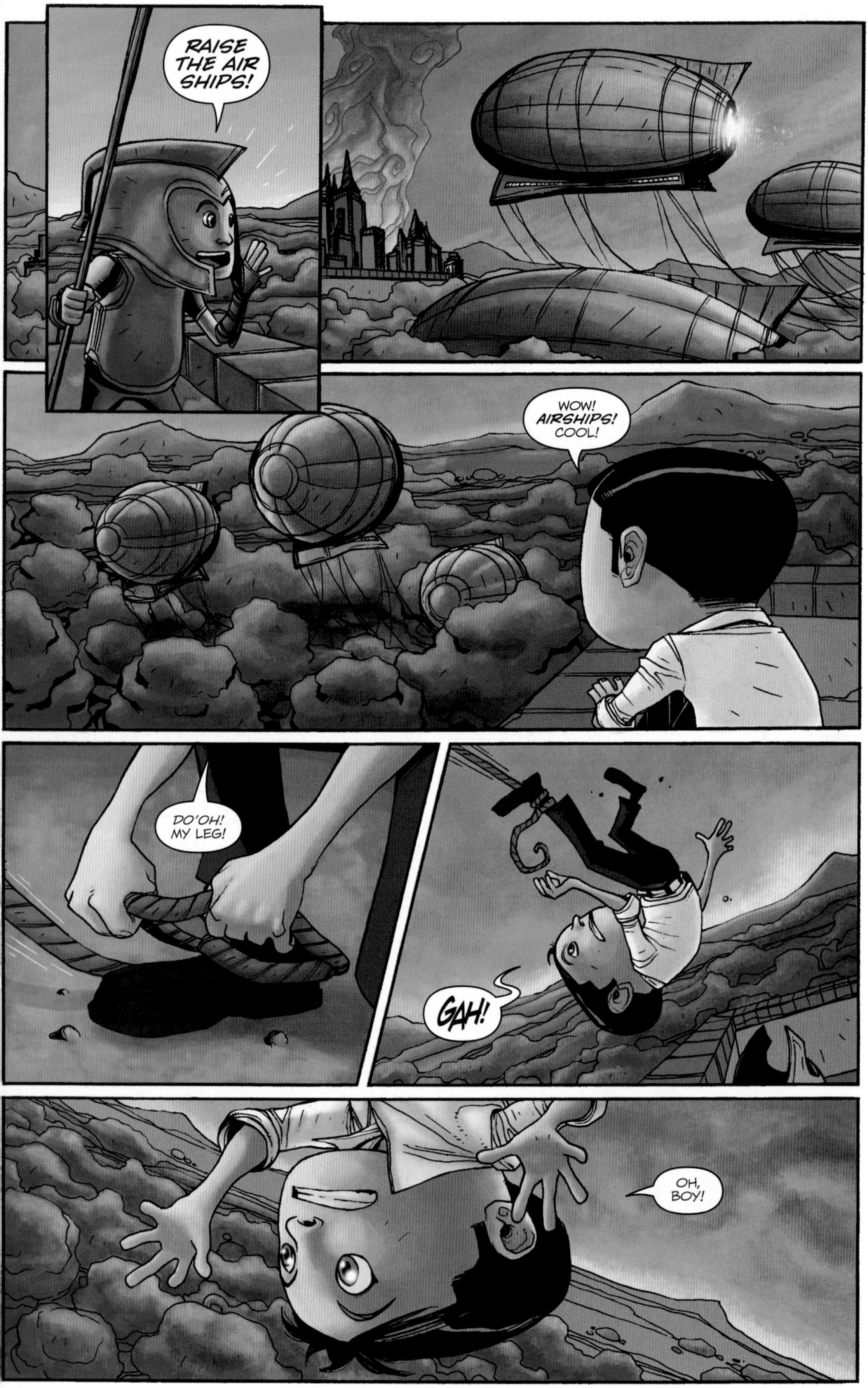
RAISE THE AIR SHIPS!
WOW! AIRSHIPS! COOL!
DO'OH! MY LEG!
GAH!
OH, BOY!

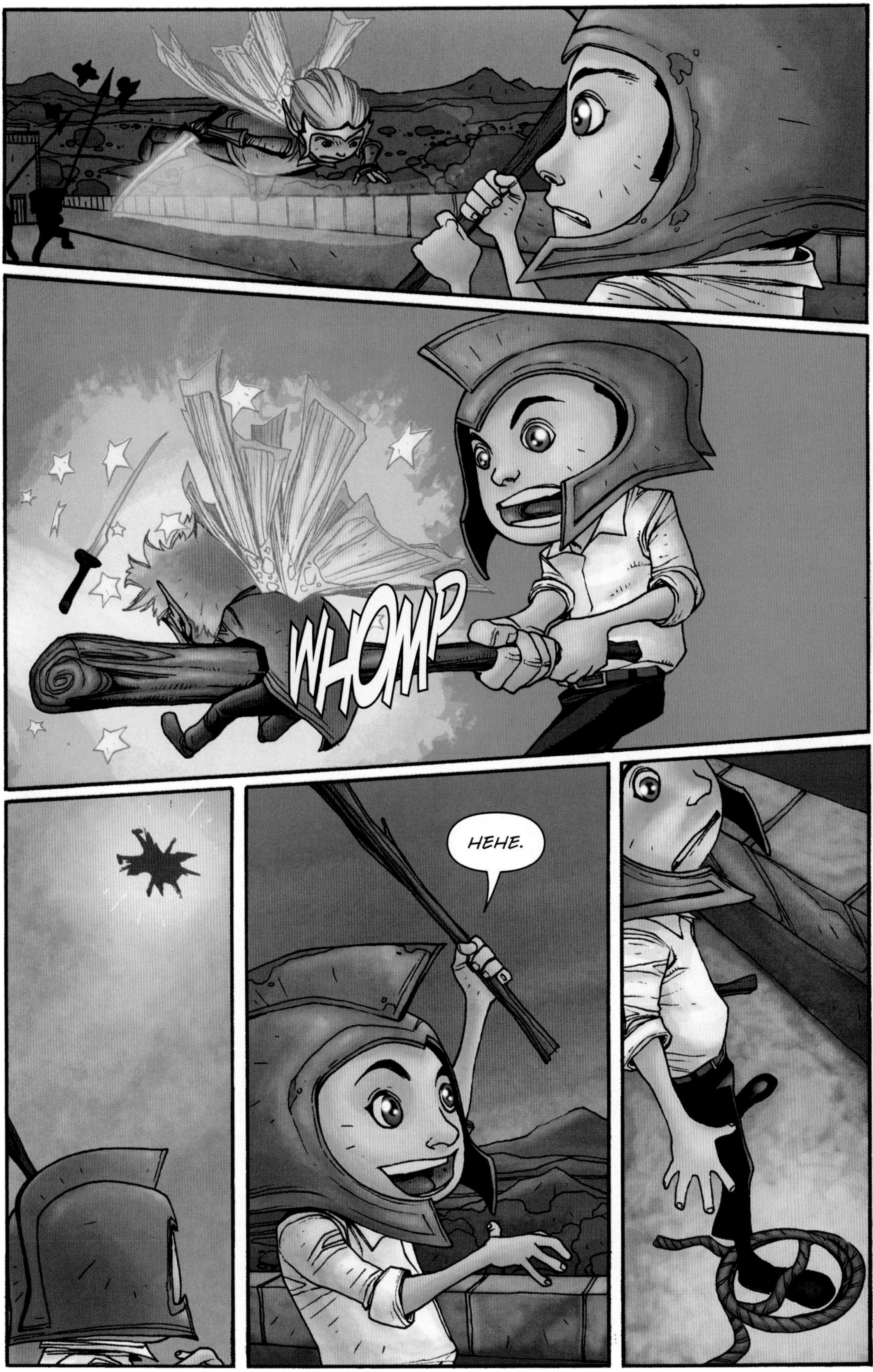
WHOMP
HEHE.

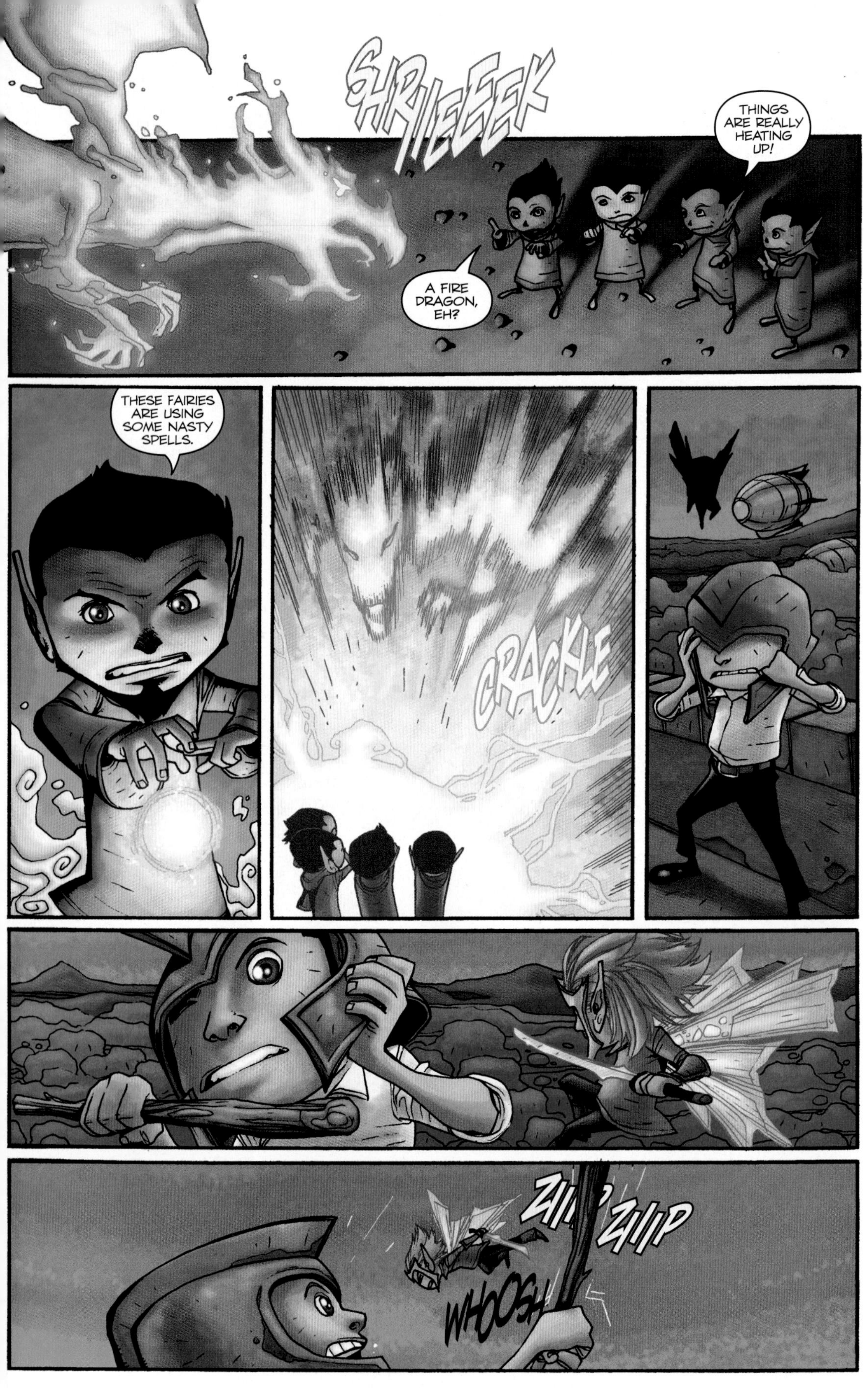
SHRIEEEEK
THINGS ARE REALLY HEATING UP!
A FIRE DRAGON, EH?
THESE FAIRIES ARE USING SOME NASTY SPELLS.
CRACKLE
ZIIIP ZIIIP
WHOOSH

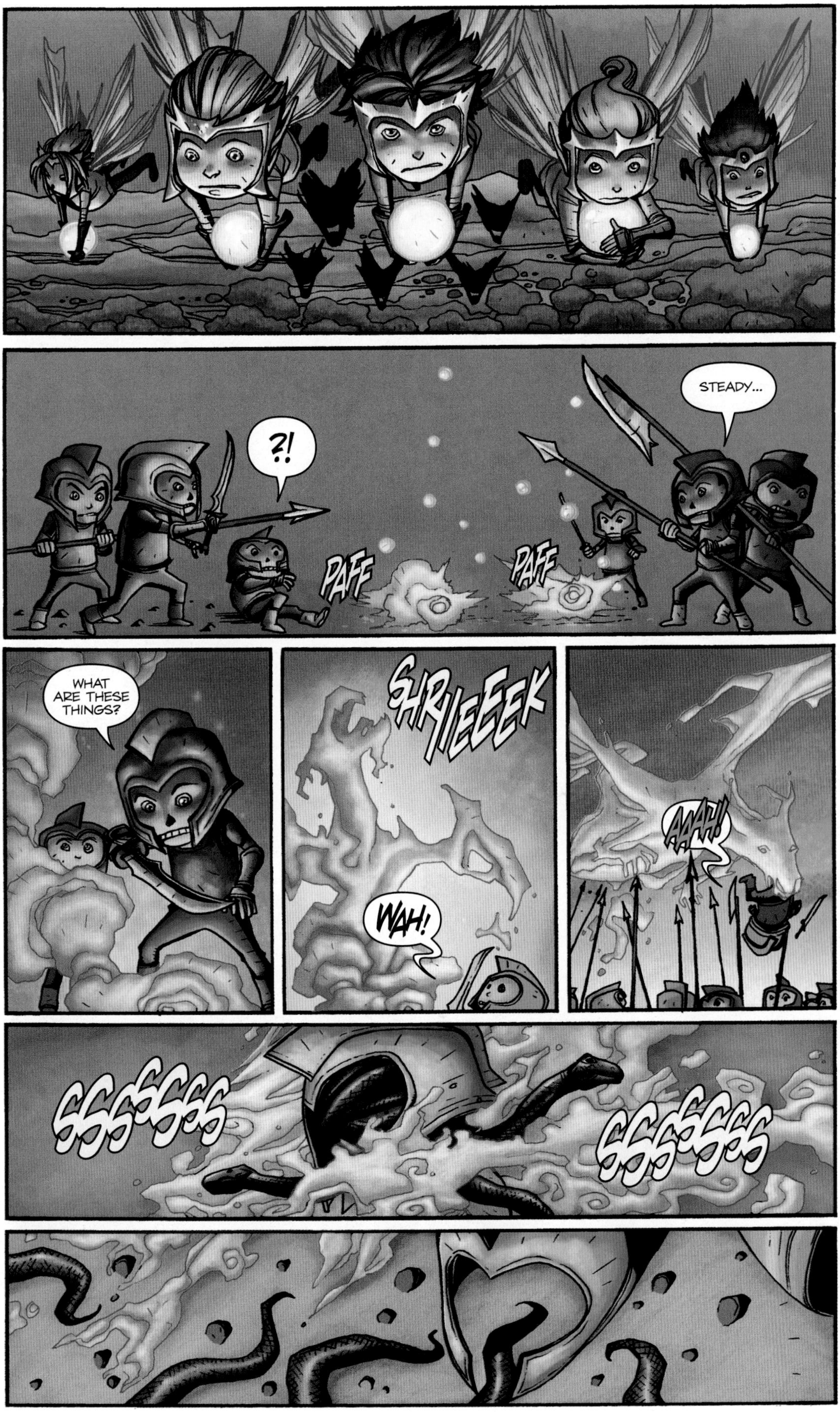

STEADY...
?!
PAFF
PAFF
WHAT ARE THESE THINGS?
SHRIEEEEK
WAH!
AAAH!
SSSSSSS
SSSSSSS

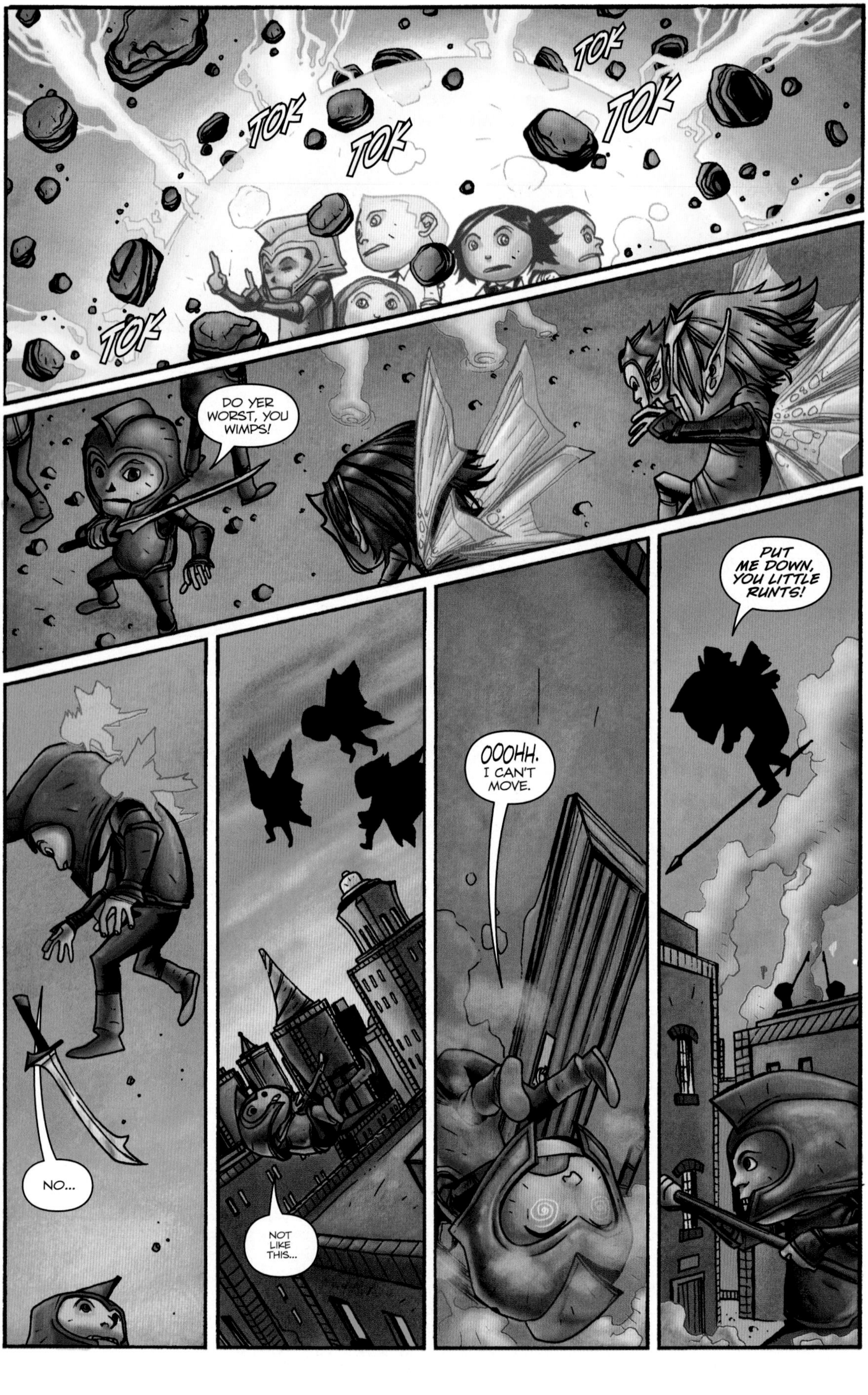
TOK
TOK
TOK
TOK
TOK
DO YER WORST, YOU WIMPS!
PUT ME DOWN, YOU LITTLE RUNTS!
OOOHH. I CAN'T MOVE.
NO...
NOT LIKE THIS...

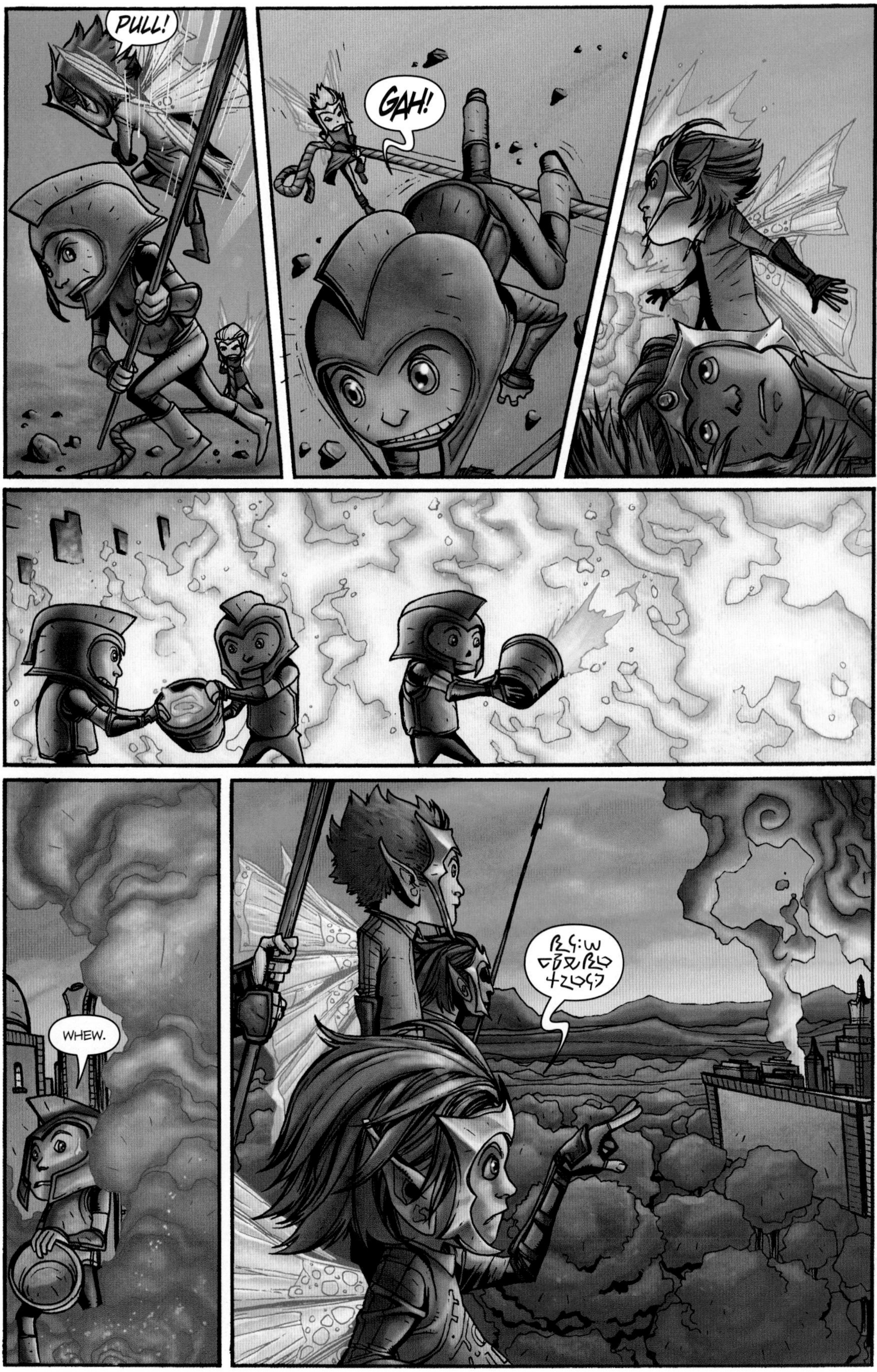
PULL!
GAH!
WHEW.

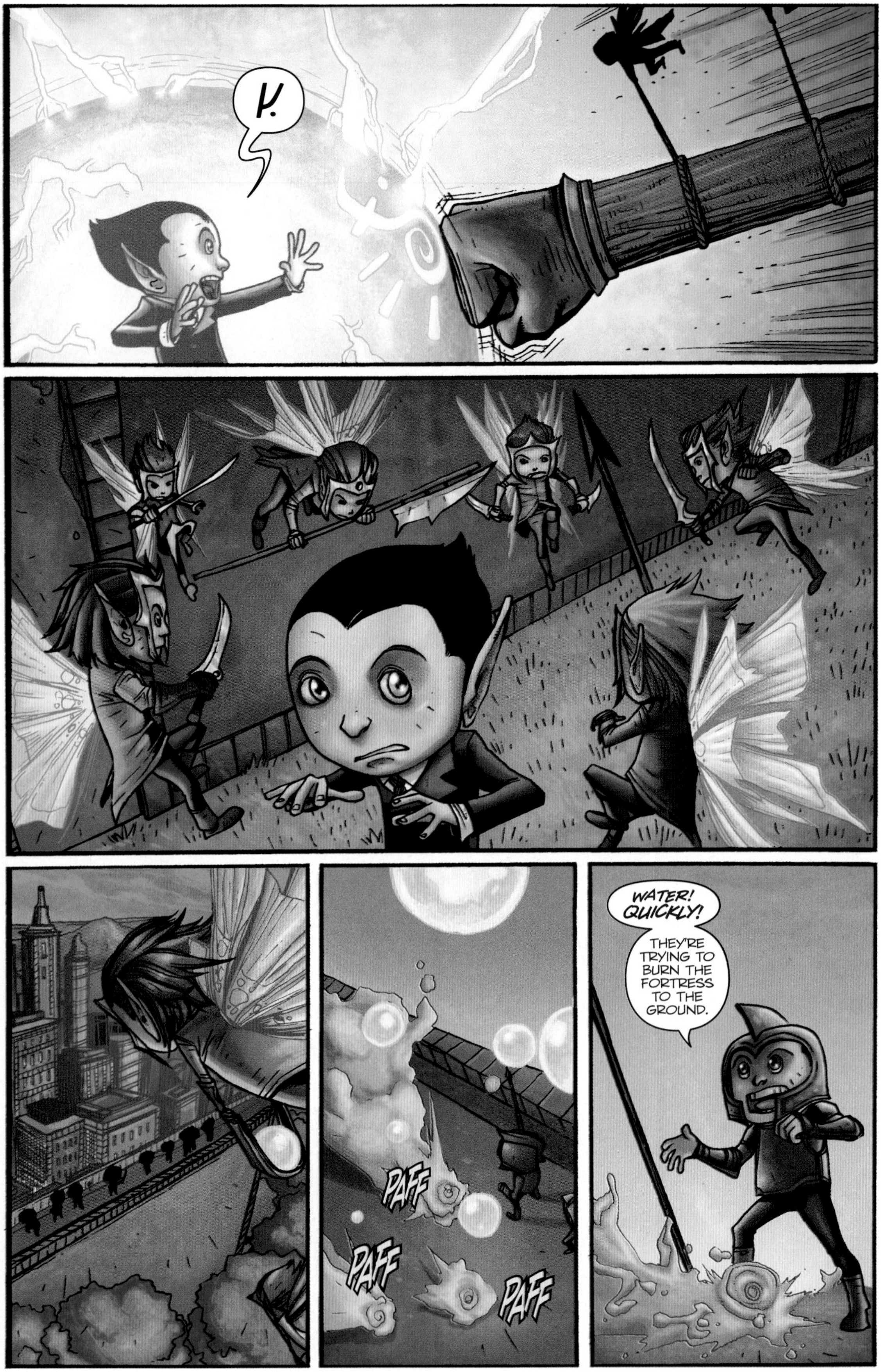
PAFF
PAFF
PAFF
WATER! QUICKLY!
THEY'RE TRYING TO BURN THE FORTRESS TO THE GROUND.

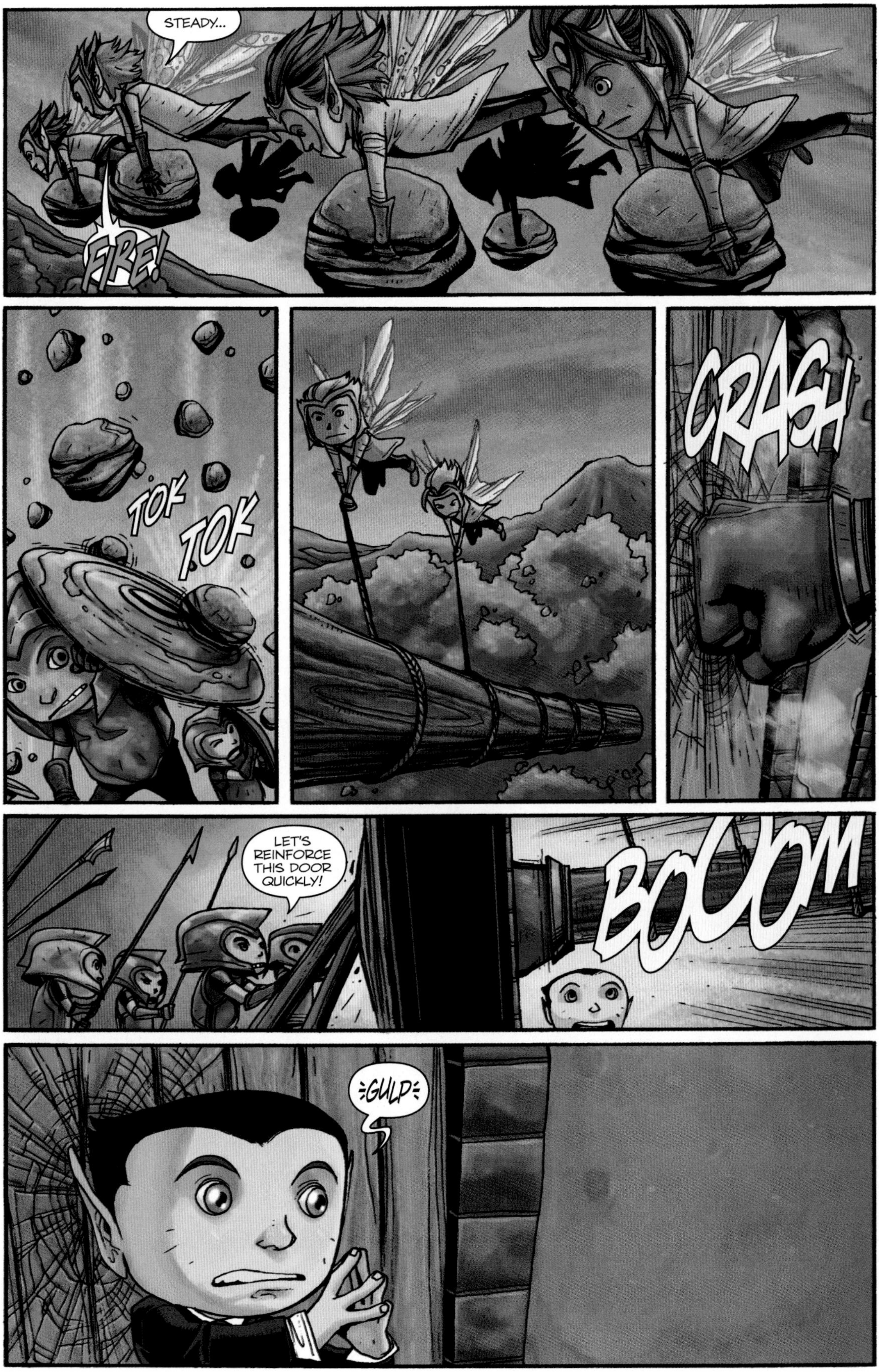
STEADY...
FIRE!
TOK
TOK
CRASH
LET'S REINFORCE THIS DOOR QUICKLY!
BOOOM
GULP

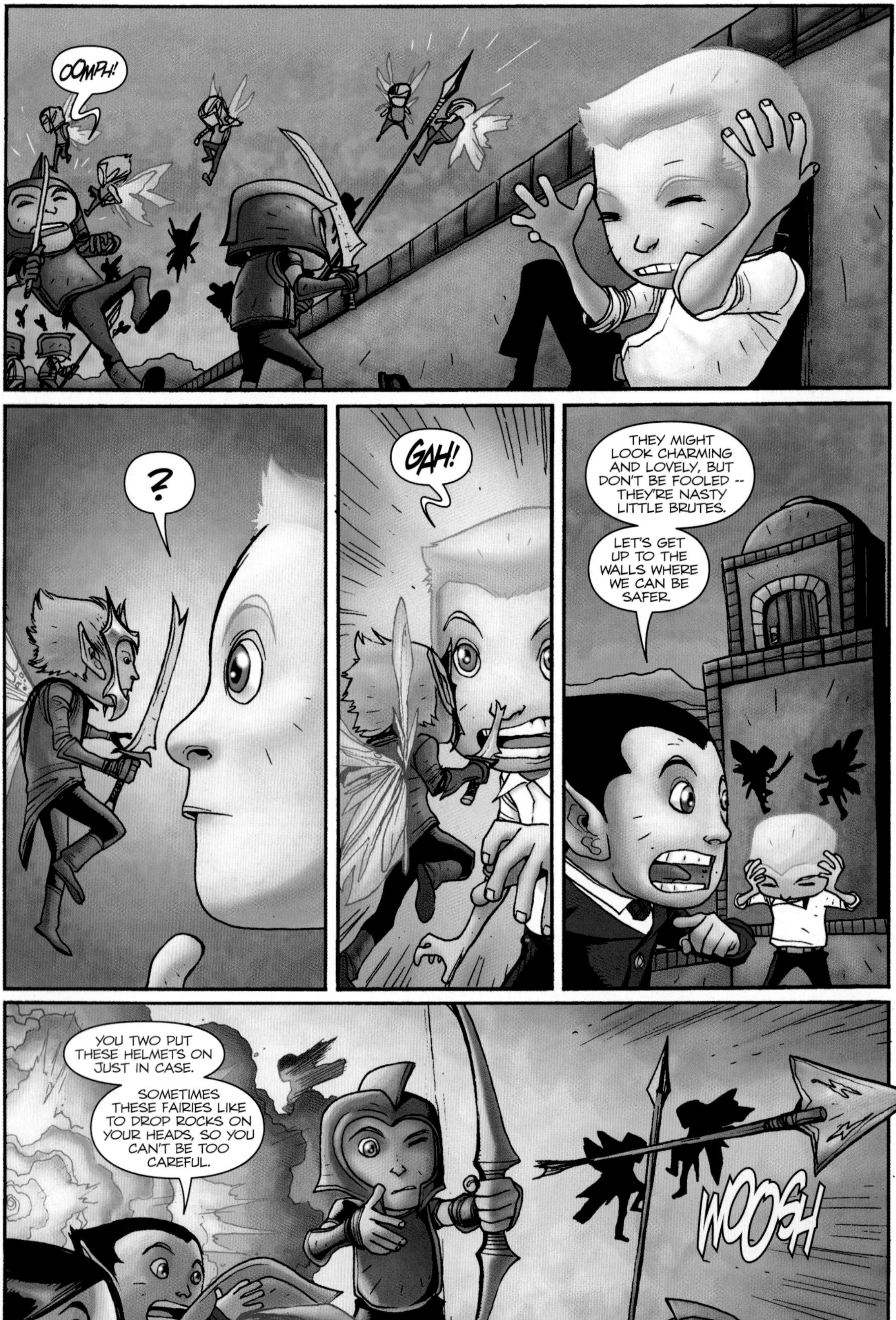
OOMPH!
?
GAH!
THEY MIGHT LOOK CHARMING AND LOVELY, BUT DON'T BE FOOLED -- THEY'RE NASTY LITTLE BRUTES.
LET'S GET UP TO THE WALLS WHERE WE CAN BE SAFER.
YOU TWO PUT THESE HELMETS ON JUST IN CASE.
SOMETIMES THESE FAIRIES LIKE TO DROP ROCKS ON YOUR HEADS, SO YOU CAN'T BE TOO CAREFUL.
WOOSH

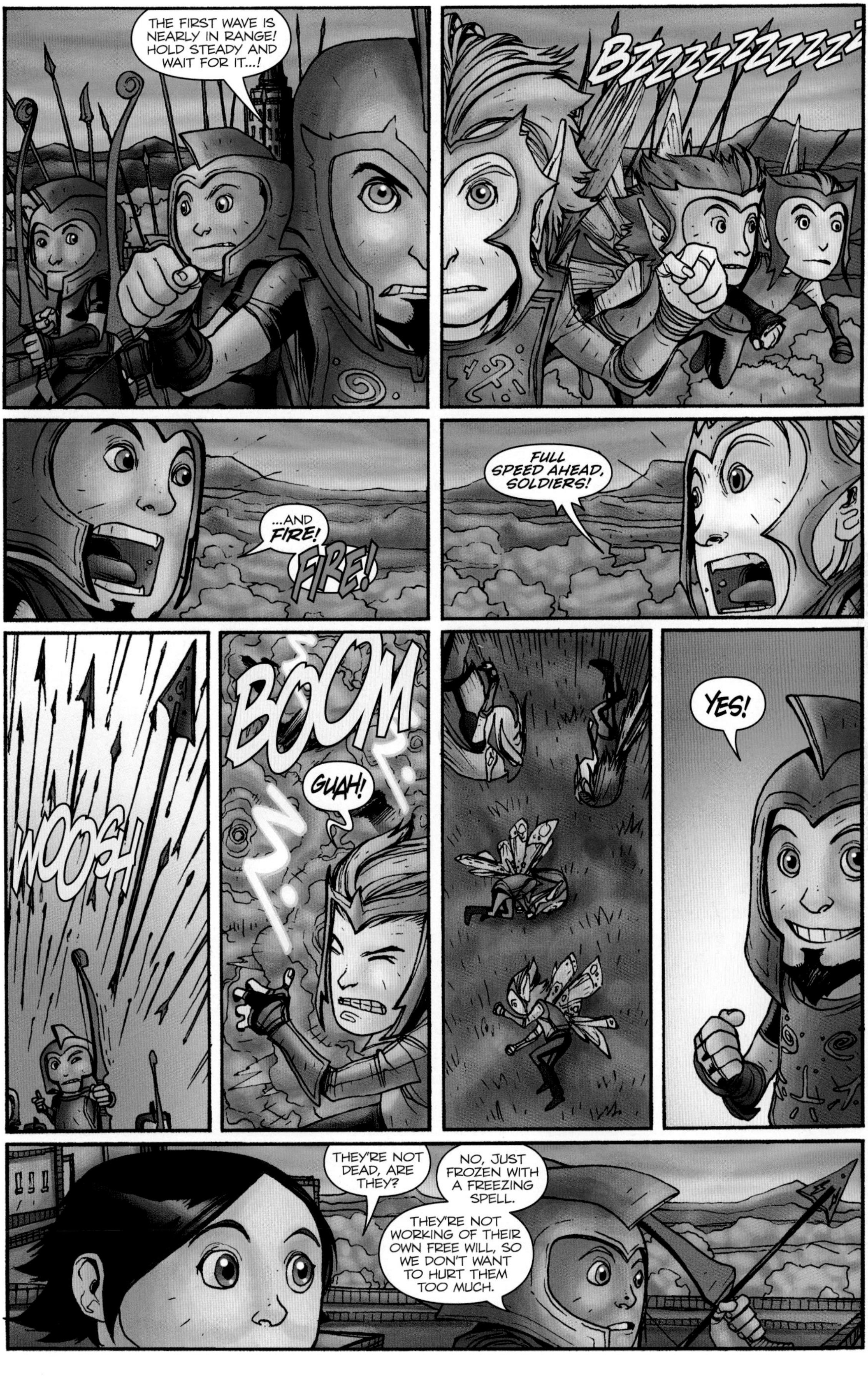
THE FIRST WAVE IS NEARLY IN RANGE! HOLD STEADY AND WAIT FOR IT...!
BZZZZZZZZZZ
...AND FIRE!
FIRE!
FULL SPEED AHEAD, SOLDIERS!
WOOSH
BOOM
GUAH!
YES!
THEY'RE NOT DEAD, ARE THEY?
NO, JUST FROZEN WITH A FREEZING SPELL.
THEY'RE NOT WORKING OF THEIR OWN FREE WILL, SO WE DON'T WANT TO HURT THEM TOO MUCH.

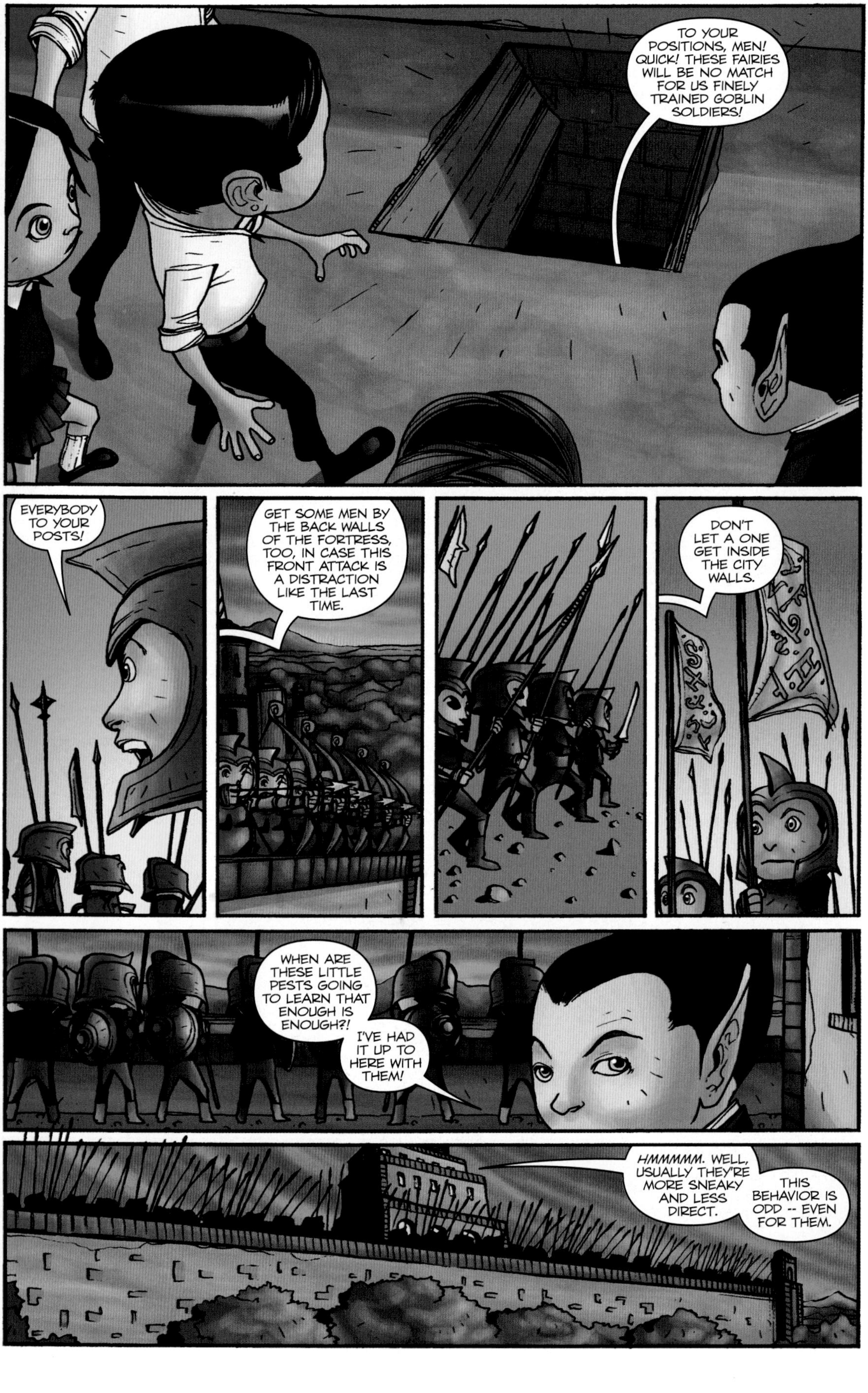
TO YOUR POSITIONS, MEN! QUICK! THESE FAIRIES WILL BE NO MATCH FOR US FINELY TRAINED GOBLIN SOLDIERS!
EVERYBODY TO YOUR POSTS!
GET SOME MEN BY THE BACK WALLS OF THE FORTRESS, TOO, IN CASE THIS FRONT ATTACK IS A DISTRACTION LIKE THE LAST TIME.
DON'T LET A ONE GET INSIDE THE CITY WALLS.
WHEN ARE THESE LITTLE PESTS GOING TO LEARN THAT ENOUGH IS ENOUGH?!
I'VE HAD IT UP TO HERE WITH THEM!
HMMMMM. WELL, USUALLY THEY'RE MORE SNEAKY AND LESS DIRECT.
THIS BEHAVIOR IS ODD -- EVEN FOR THEM.

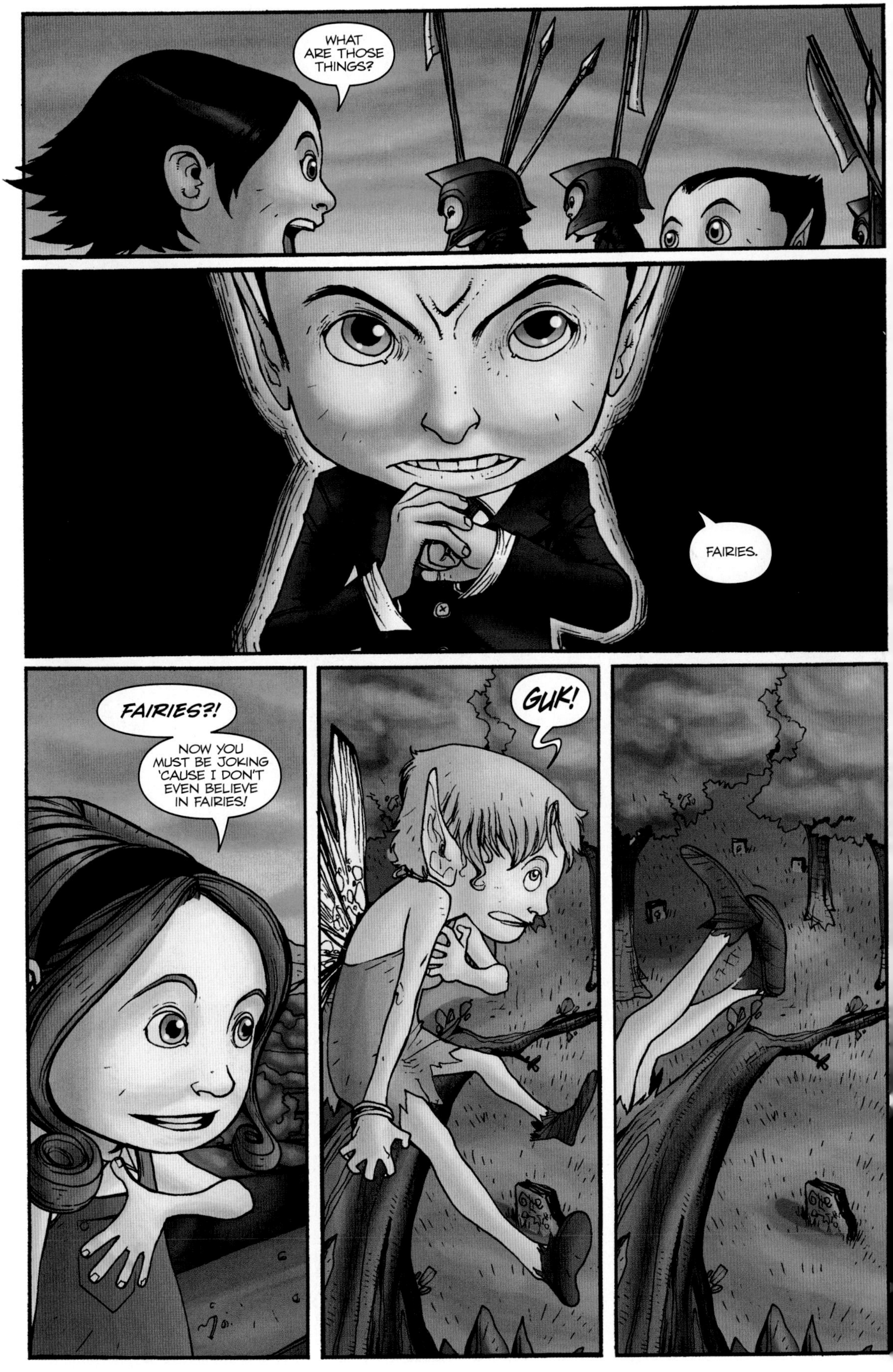
WHAT ARE THOSE THINGS?
FAIRIES.
FAIRIES?!
NOW YOU MUST BE JOKING 'CAUSE I DON'T EVEN BELIEVE IN FAIRIES!
GUK!

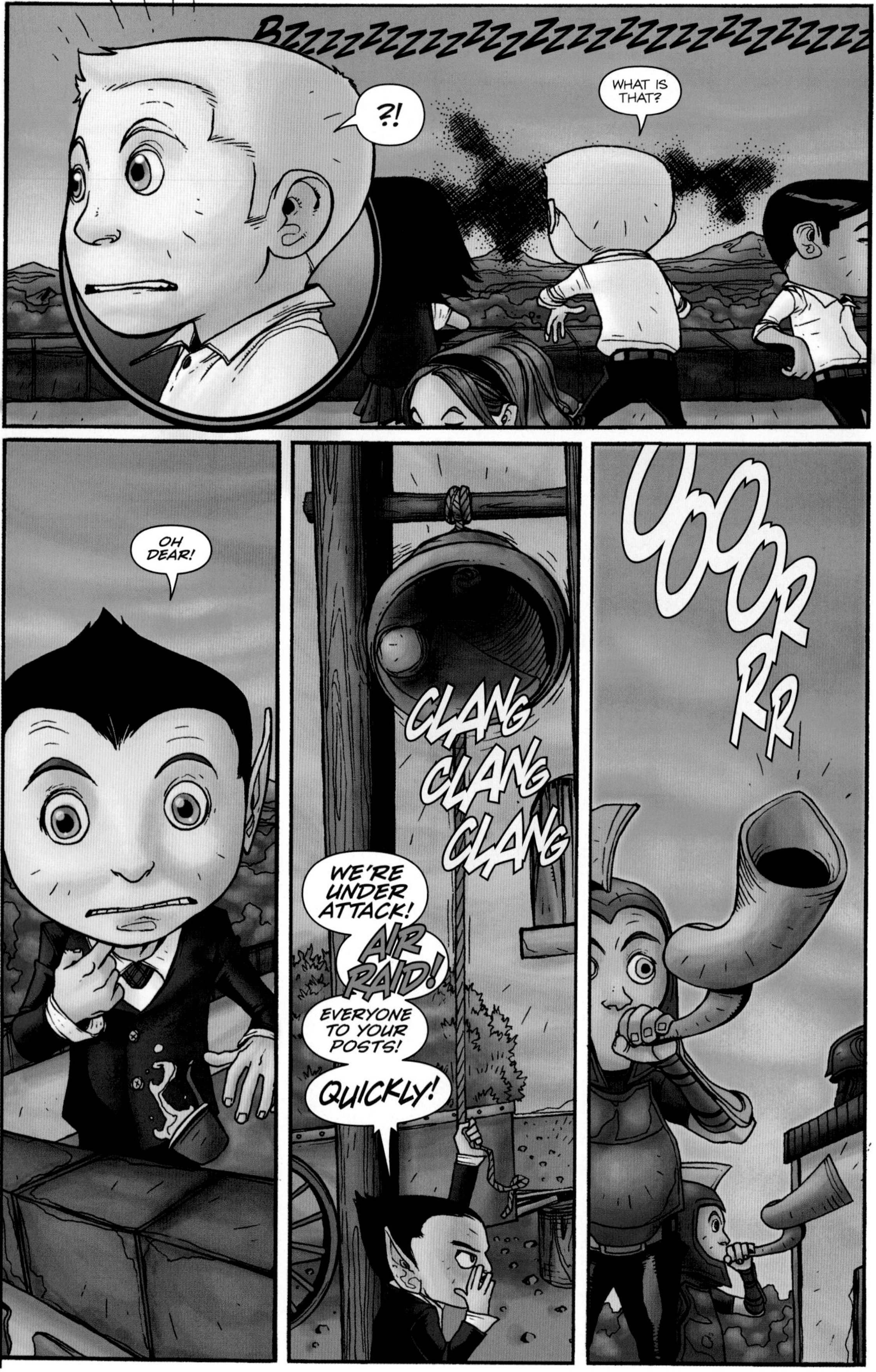
BZZZZZZZZZZZZZZZZZZZZZZZZZZZZZZ
?!
WHAT IS THAT?
OH DEAR!
CLANG CLANG CLANG
WE'RE UNDER ATTACK!
AIR RAID!
EVERYONE TO YOUR POSTS!
QUICKLY!
UOOORRR

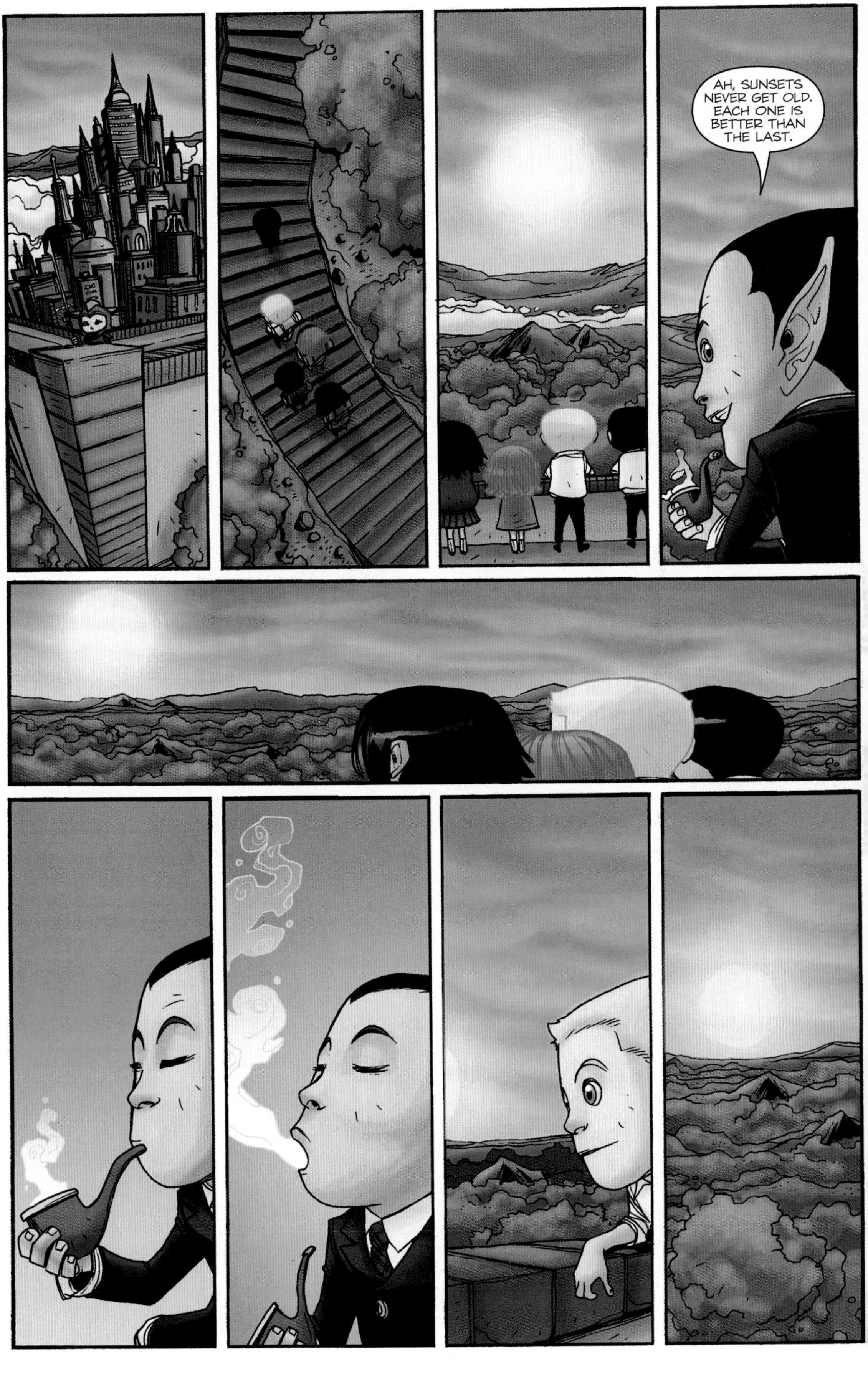
AH, SUNSETS NEVER GET OLD. EACH ONE IS BETTER THAN THE LAST.

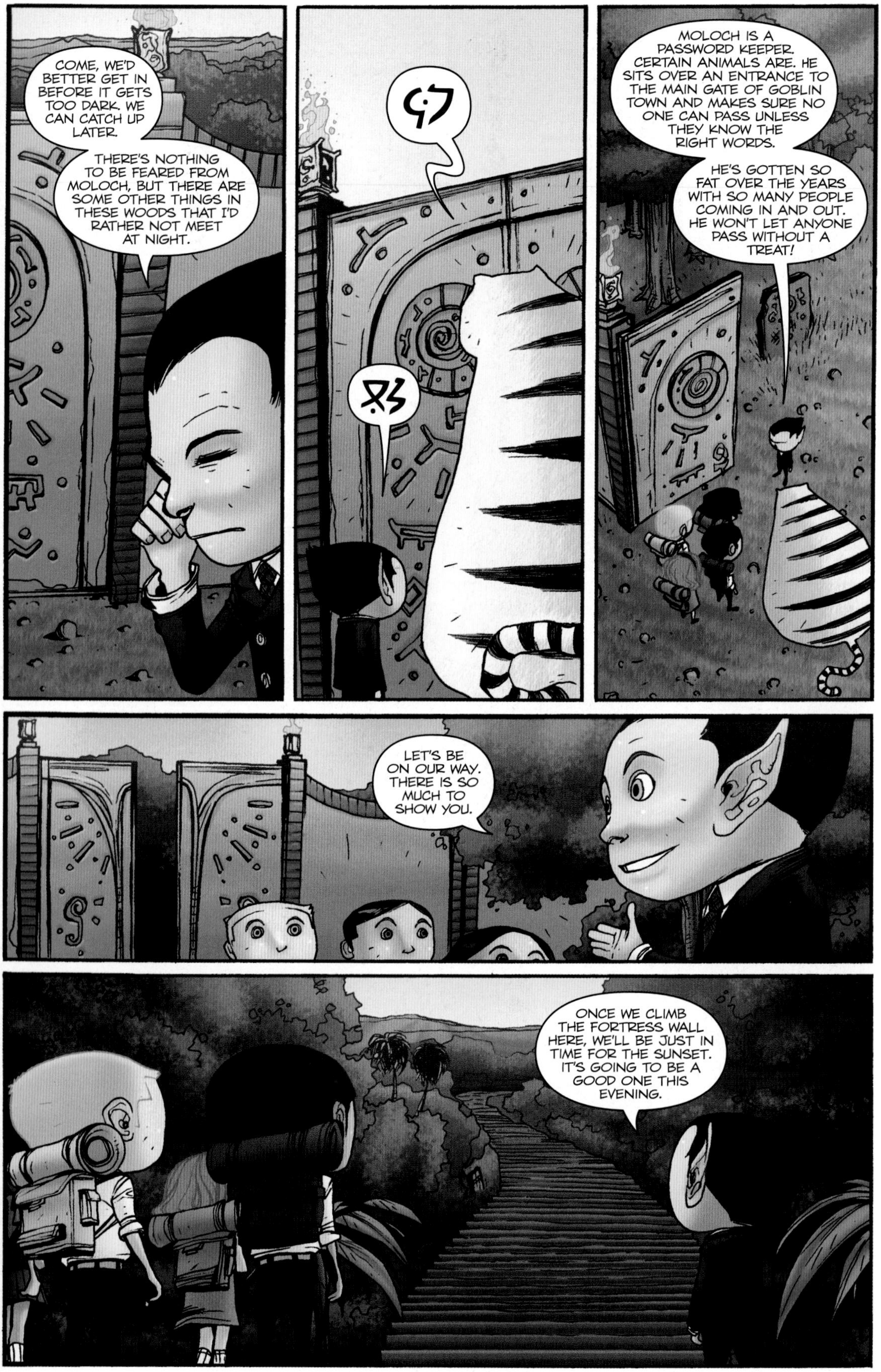

COME, WE'D BETTER GET IN BEFORE IT GETS TOO DARK. WE CAN CATCH UP LATER.
THERE'S NOTHING TO BE FEARED FROM MOLOCH, BUT THERE ARE SOME OTHER THINGS IN THESE WOODS THAT I'D RATHER NOT MEET AT NIGHT.
MOLOCH IS A PASSWORD KEEPER. CERTAIN ANIMALS ARE. HE SITS OVER AN ENTRANCE TO THE MAIN GATE OF GOBLIN TOWN AND MAKES SURE NO ONE CAN PASS UNLESS THEY KNOW THE RIGHT WORDS.
HE'S GOTTEN SO FAT OVER THE YEARS WITH SO MANY PEOPLE COMING IN AND OUT. HE WON'T LET ANYONE PASS WITHOUT A TREAT!
LET'S BE ON OUR WAY. THERE IS SO MUCH TO SHOW YOU.
ONCE WE CLIMB THE FORTRESS WALL HERE, WE'LL BE JUST IN TIME FOR THE SUNSET. IT'S GOING TO BE A GOOD ONE THIS EVENING.

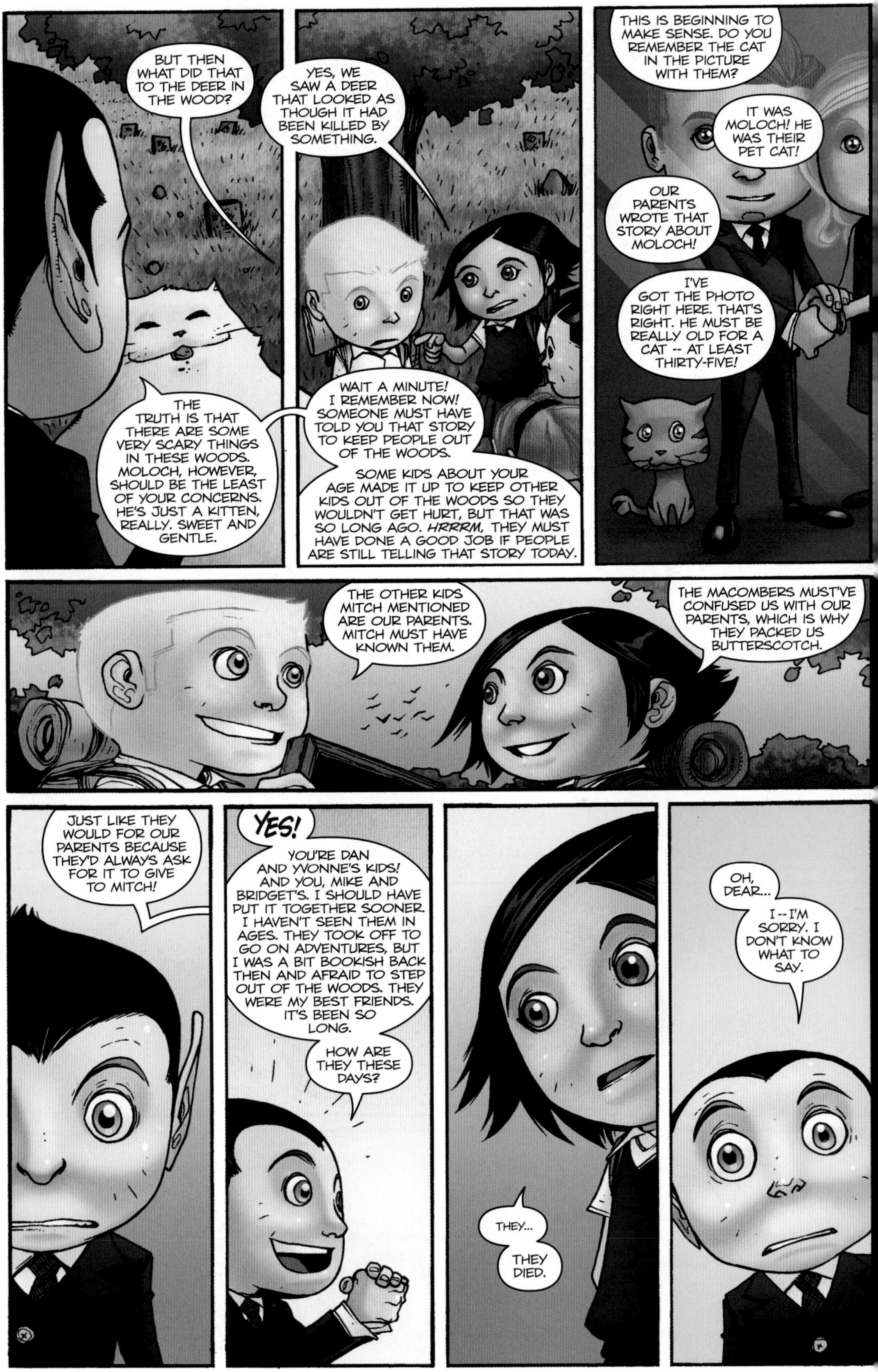
BUT THEN WHAT DID THAT TO THE DEER IN THE WOOD?
THE TRUTH IS THAT THERE ARE SOME VERY SCARY THINGS IN THESE WOODS. MOLOCH, HOWEVER, SHOULD BE THE LEAST OF YOUR CONCERNS. HE'S JUST A KITTEN, REALLY. SWEET AND GENTLE.
YES, WE SAW A DEER THAT LOOKED AS THOUGH IT HAD BEEN KILLED BY SOMETHING.
WAIT A MINUTE! I REMEMBER NOW! SOMEONE MUST HAVE TOLD YOU THAT STORY TO KEEP PEOPLE OUT OF THE WOODS.
SOME KIDS ABOUT YOUR AGE MADE IT UP TO KEEP OTHER KIDS OUT OF THE WOODS SO THEY WOULDN'T GET HURT, BUT THAT WAS SO LONG AGO. *HRRRM,* THEY MUST HAVE DONE A GOOD JOB IF PEOPLE ARE STILL TELLING THAT STORY TODAY.
THIS IS BEGINNING TO MAKE SENSE. DO YOU REMEMBER THE CAT IN THE PICTURE WITH THEM?
IT WAS MOLOCH! HE WAS THEIR PET CAT!
OUR PARENTS WROTE THAT STORY ABOUT MOLOCH!
I'VE GOT THE PHOTO RIGHT HERE. THAT'S RIGHT. HE MUST BE REALLY OLD FOR A CAT -- AT LEAST THIRTY-FIVE!
THE OTHER KIDS MITCH MENTIONED ARE OUR PARENTS. MITCH MUST HAVE KNOWN THEM.
THE MACOMBERS MUST'VE CONFUSED US WITH OUR PARENTS, WHICH IS WHY THEY PACKED US BUTTERSCOTCH.
JUST LIKE THEY WOULD FOR OUR PARENTS BECAUSE THEY'D ALWAYS ASK FOR IT TO GIVE TO MITCH!
YES!
YOU'RE DAN AND YVONNE'S KIDS! AND YOU, MIKE AND BRIDGET'S. I SHOULD HAVE PUT IT TOGETHER SOONER. I HAVEN'T SEEN THEM IN AGES. THEY TOOK OFF TO GO ON ADVENTURES, BUT I WAS A BIT BOOKISH BACK THEN AND AFRAID TO STEP OUT OF THE WOODS. THEY WERE MY BEST FRIENDS. IT'S BEEN SO LONG.
HOW ARE THEY THESE DAYS?
THEY...
THEY DIED.
OH, DEAR...
I -- I'M SORRY. I DON'T KNOW WHAT TO SAY.

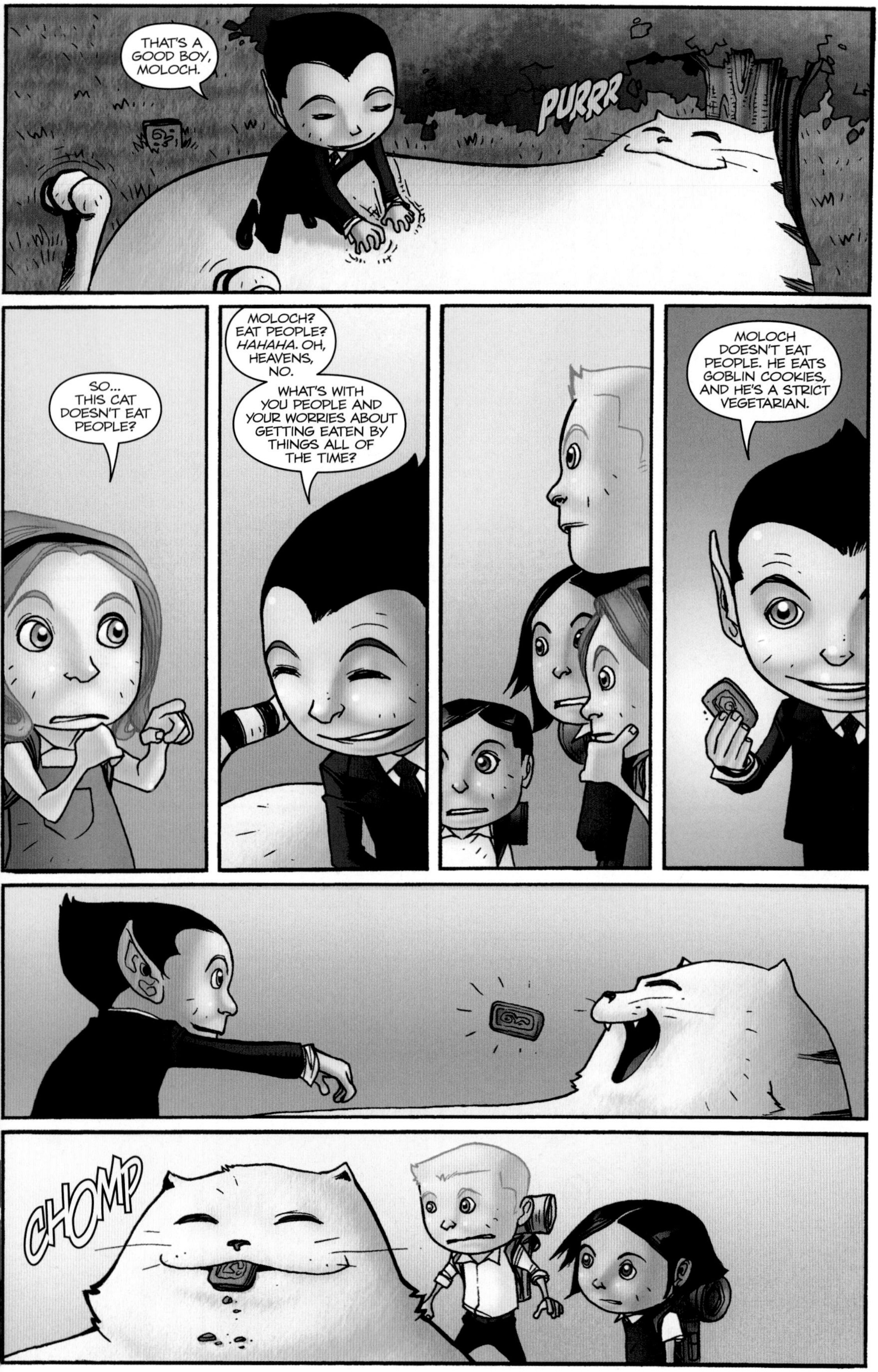
THAT'S A GOOD BOY, MOLOCH.
PURRR
SO... THIS CAT DOESN'T EAT PEOPLE?
MOLOCH? EAT PEOPLE? *HAHAHA.* OH, HEAVENS, NO.
WHAT'S WITH YOU PEOPLE AND YOUR WORRIES ABOUT GETTING EATEN BY THINGS ALL OF THE TIME?
MOLOCH DOESN'T EAT PEOPLE. HE EATS GOBLIN COOKIES, AND HE'S A STRICT VEGETARIAN.
CHOMP

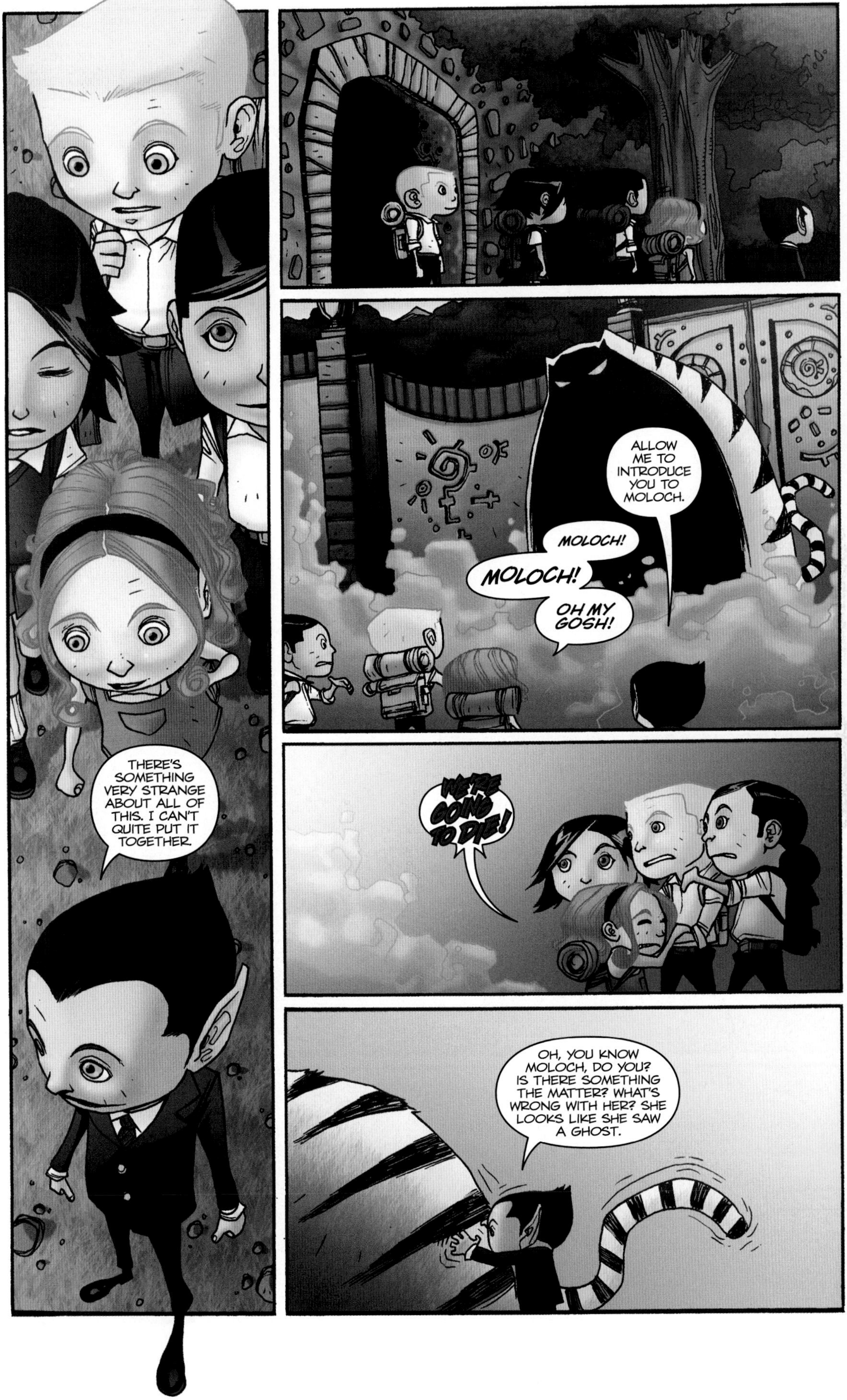

THERE'S SOMETHING VERY STRANGE ABOUT ALL OF THIS. I CAN'T QUITE PUT IT TOGETHER.
ALLOW ME TO INTRODUCE YOU TO MOLOCH.
MOLOCH!
MOLOCH!
OH MY GOSH!
WE'RE GOING TO DIE!
OH, YOU KNOW MOLOCH, DO YOU? IS THERE SOMETHING THE MATTER? WHAT'S WRONG WITH HER? SHE LOOKS LIKE SHE SAW A GHOST.

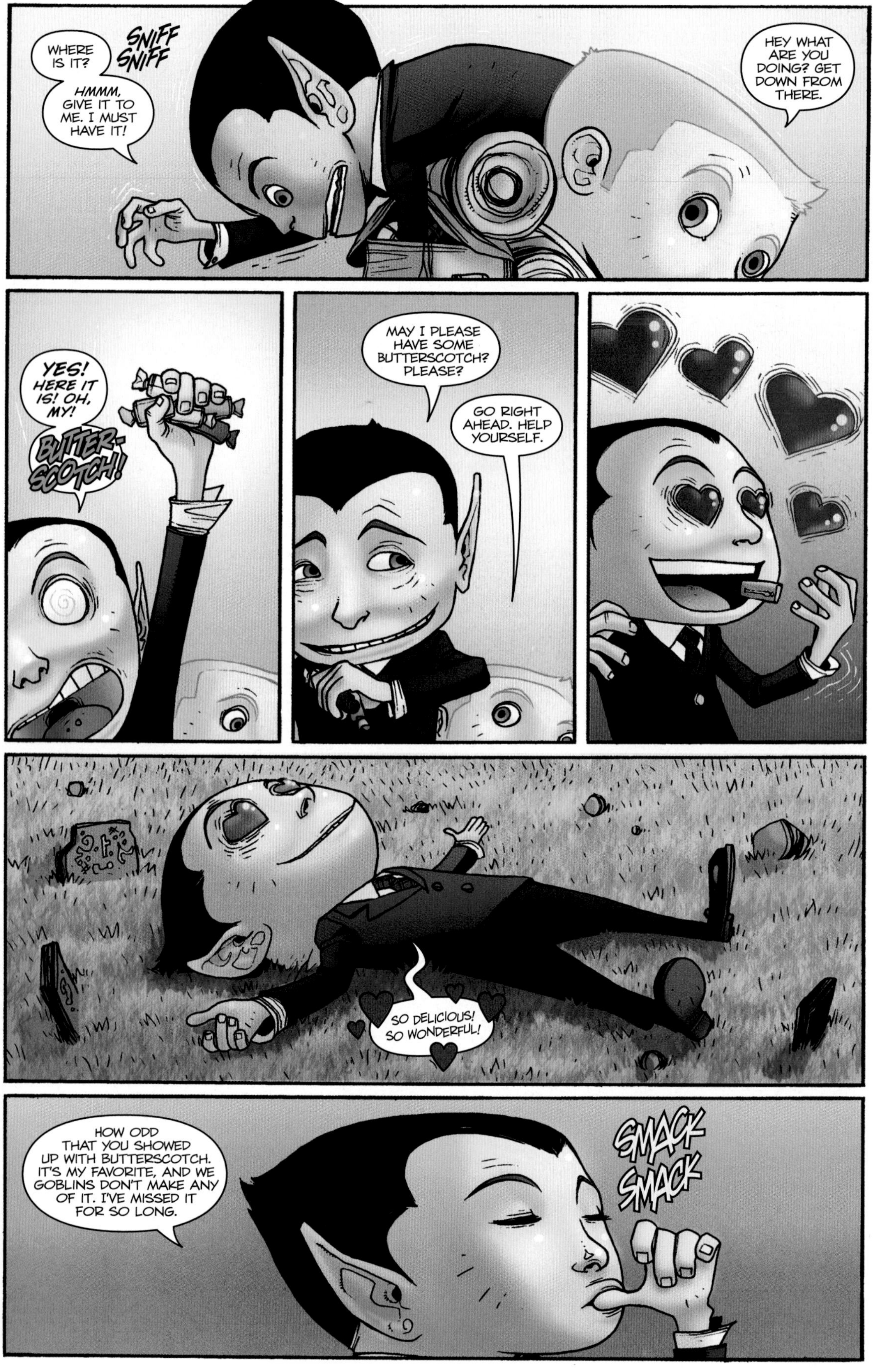
WHERE IS IT?
SNIFF SNIFF
HMMM, GIVE IT TO ME. I MUST HAVE IT!
HEY WHAT ARE YOU DOING? GET DOWN FROM THERE.
YES! HERE IT IS! OH, MY!
BUTTER-SCOTCH!
MAY I PLEASE HAVE SOME BUTTERSCOTCH? PLEASE?
GO RIGHT AHEAD. HELP YOURSELF.
SO DELICIOUS! SO WONDERFUL!
HOW ODD THAT YOU SHOWED UP WITH BUTTERSCOTCH. IT'S MY FAVORITE, AND WE GOBLINS DON'T MAKE ANY OF IT. I'VE MISSED IT FOR SO LONG.
SMACK SMACK

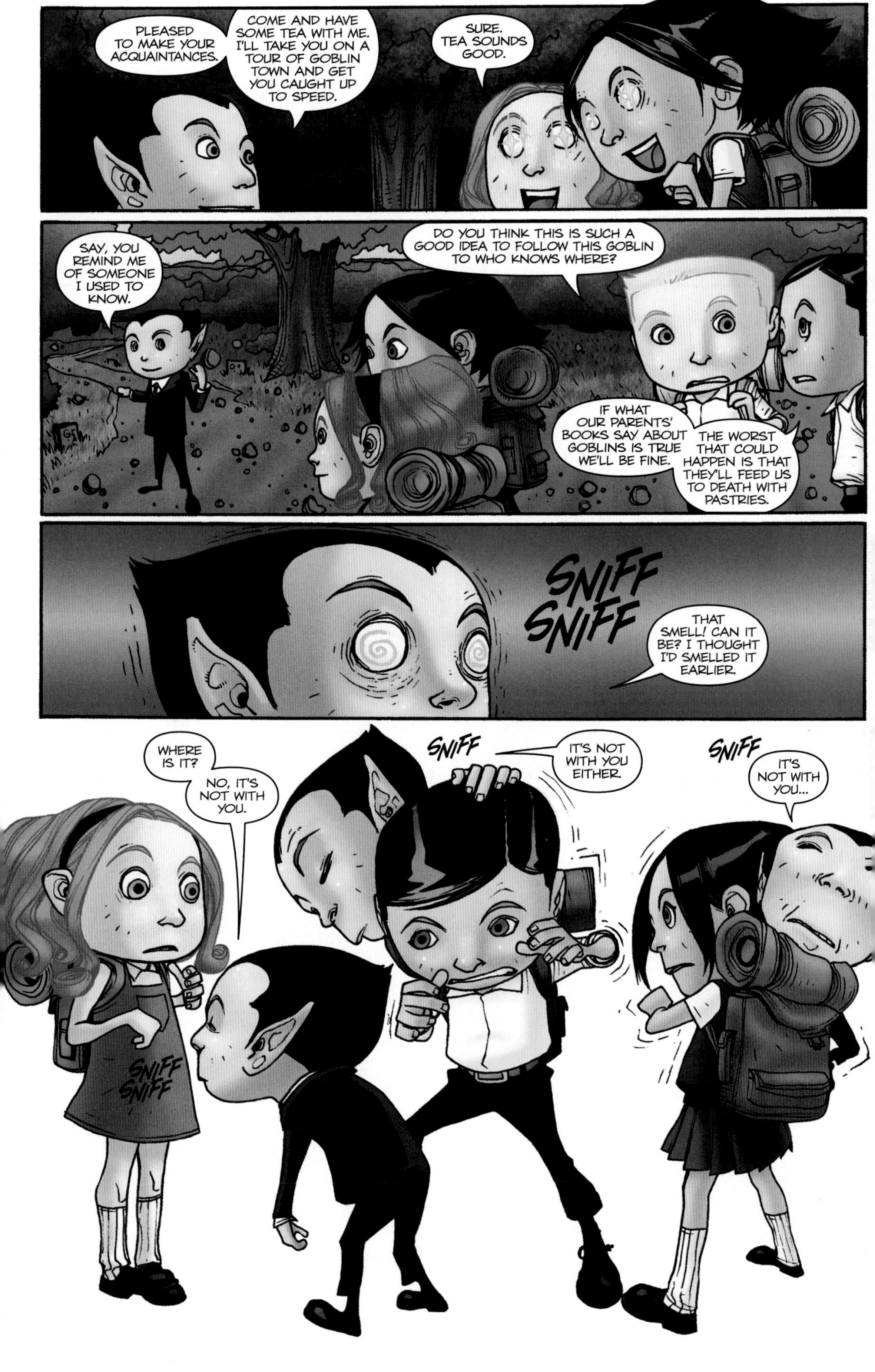
PLEASED TO MAKE YOUR ACQUAINTANCES.
COME AND HAVE SOME TEA WITH ME. I'LL TAKE YOU ON A TOUR OF GOBLIN TOWN AND GET YOU CAUGHT UP TO SPEED.
SURE. TEA SOUNDS GOOD.
SAY, YOU REMIND ME OF SOMEONE I USED TO KNOW.
DO YOU THINK THIS IS SUCH A GOOD IDEA TO FOLLOW THIS GOBLIN TO WHO KNOWS WHERE?
IF WHAT OUR PARENTS' BOOKS SAY ABOUT GOBLINS IS TRUE WE'LL BE FINE.
THE WORST THAT COULD HAPPEN IS THAT THEY'LL FEED US TO DEATH WITH PASTRIES.
SNIFF SNIFF
THAT SMELL! CAN IT BE? I THOUGHT I'D SMELLED IT EARLIER.
WHERE IS IT?
NO, IT'S NOT WITH YOU.
SNIFF SNIFF
SNIFF
IT'S NOT WITH YOU EITHER.
SNIFF
IT'S NOT WITH YOU...

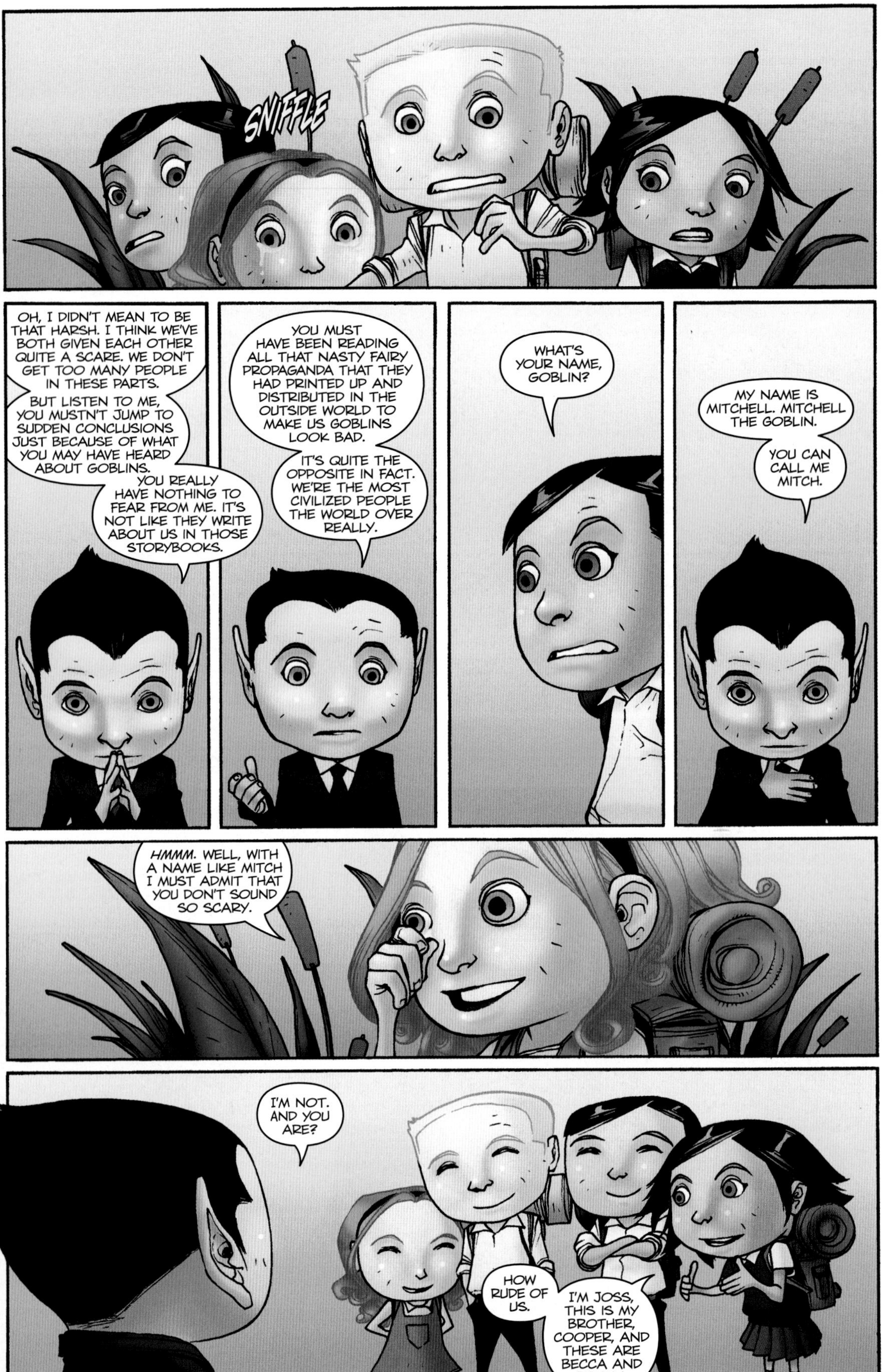
SNIFFLE
OH, I DIDN'T MEAN TO BE THAT HARSH. I THINK WE'VE BOTH GIVEN EACH OTHER QUITE A SCARE. WE DON'T GET TOO MANY PEOPLE IN THESE PARTS.
BUT LISTEN TO ME, YOU MUSTN'T JUMP TO SUDDEN CONCLUSIONS JUST BECAUSE OF WHAT YOU MAY HAVE HEARD ABOUT GOBLINS.
YOU REALLY HAVE NOTHING TO FEAR FROM ME. IT'S NOT LIKE THEY WRITE ABOUT US IN THOSE STORYBOOKS.
YOU MUST HAVE BEEN READING ALL THAT NASTY FAIRY PROPAGANDA THAT THEY HAD PRINTED UP AND DISTRIBUTED IN THE OUTSIDE WORLD TO MAKE US GOBLINS LOOK BAD.
IT'S QUITE THE OPPOSITE IN FACT. WE'RE THE MOST CIVILIZED PEOPLE THE WORLD OVER REALLY.
WHAT'S YOUR NAME, GOBLIN?
MY NAME IS MITCHELL. MITCHELL THE GOBLIN.
YOU CAN CALL ME MITCH.
HMMM. WELL, WITH A NAME LIKE MITCH I MUST ADMIT THAT YOU DON'T SOUND SO SCARY.
I'M NOT. AND YOU ARE?
HOW RUDE OF US.
I'M JOSS, THIS IS MY BROTHER, COOPER, AND THESE ARE BECCA AND BENNY.

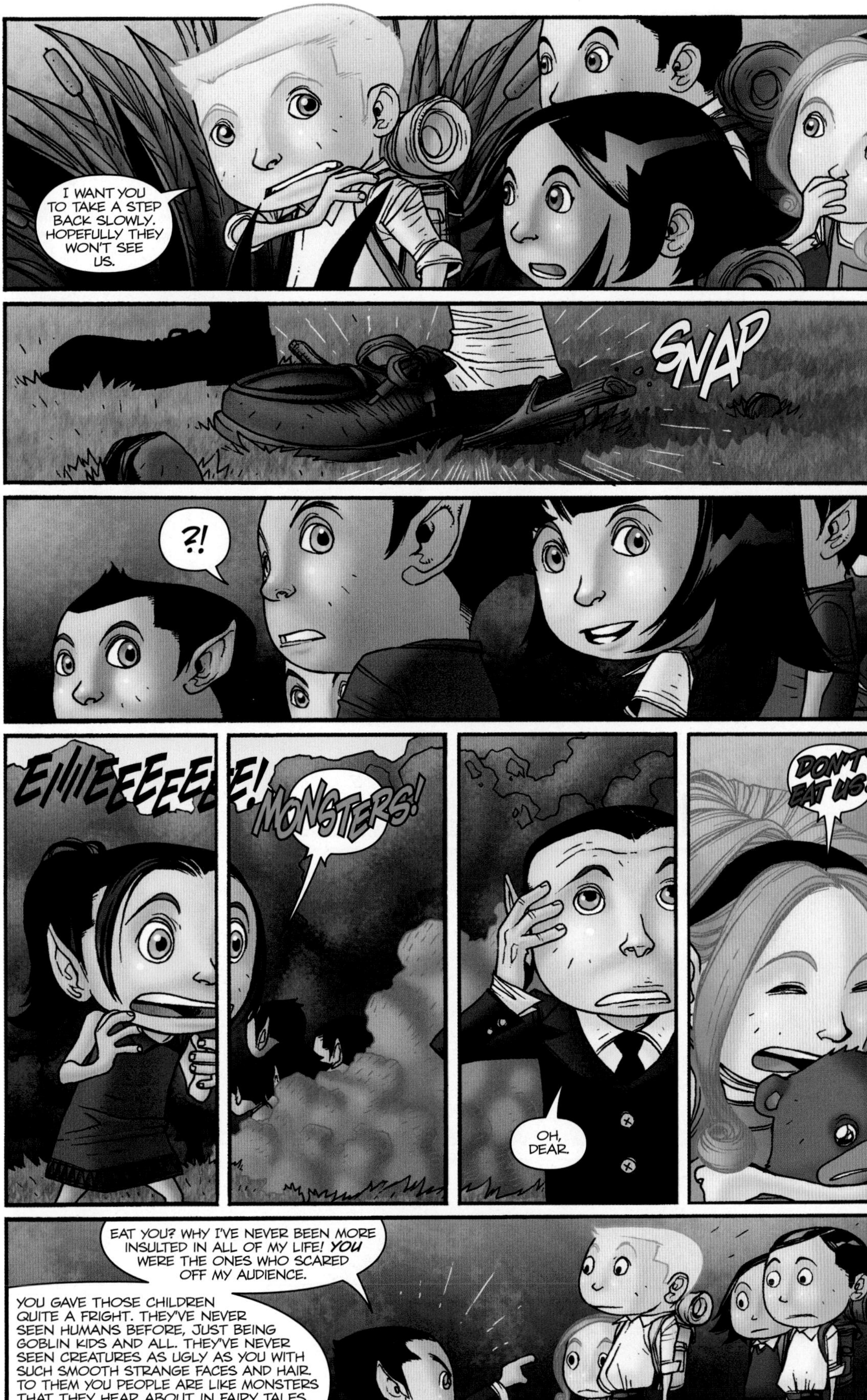
I WANT YOU TO TAKE A STEP BACK SLOWLY. HOPEFULLY THEY WON'T SEE US.
SNAP
?!
EIIIEEEEEEEE!
MONSTERS!
OH, DEAR.
DON'T EAT US!
EAT YOU? WHY I'VE NEVER BEEN MORE INSULTED IN ALL OF MY LIFE! YOU WERE THE ONES WHO SCARED OFF MY AUDIENCE.
YOU GAVE THOSE CHILDREN QUITE A FRIGHT. THEY'VE NEVER SEEN HUMANS BEFORE, JUST BEING GOBLIN KIDS AND ALL. THEY'VE NEVER SEEN CREATURES AS UGLY AS YOU WITH SUCH SMOOTH STRANGE FACES AND HAIR. TO THEM YOU PEOPLE ARE LIKE MONSTERS THAT THEY HEAR ABOUT IN FAIRY TALES.

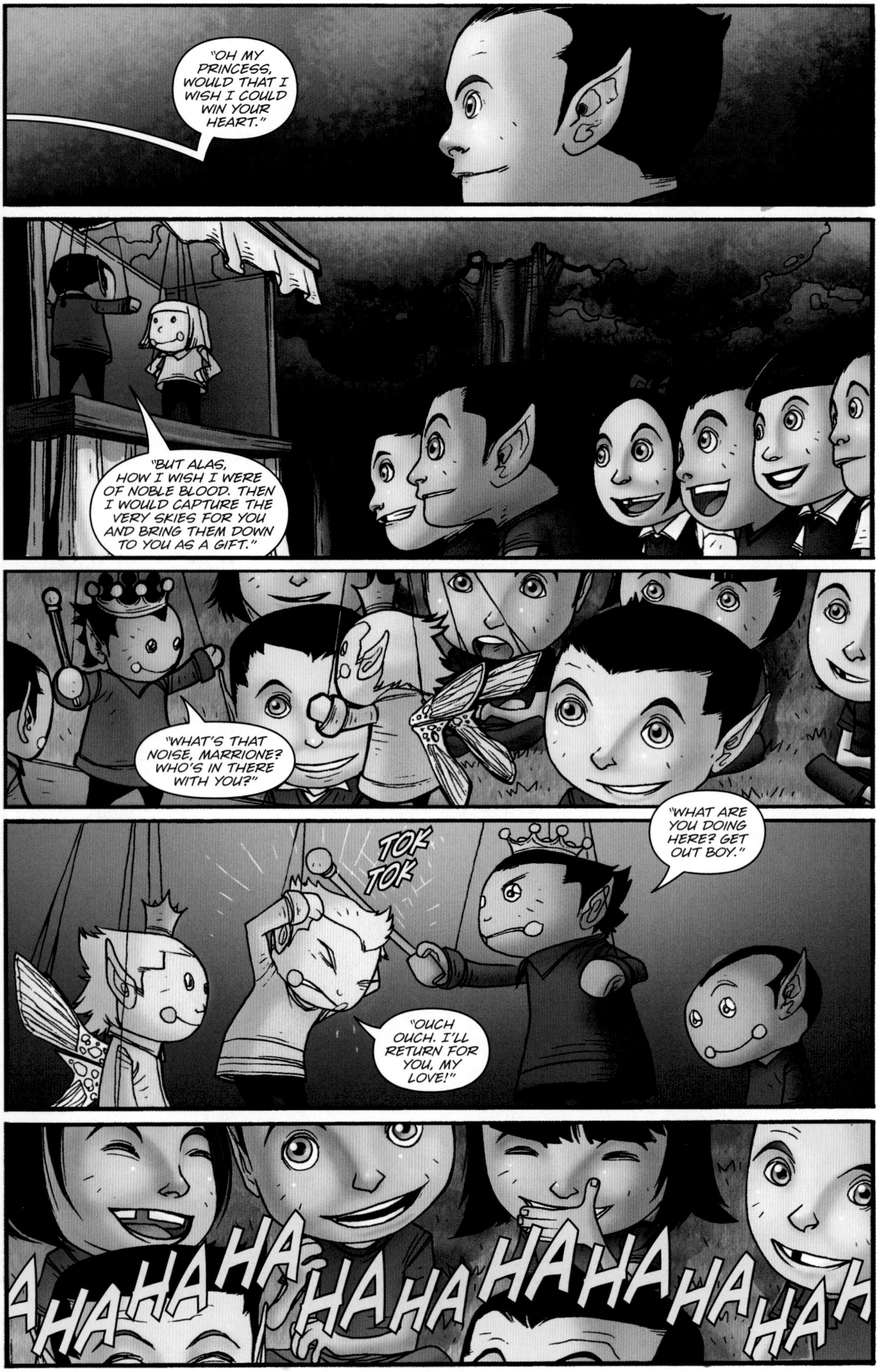
"OH MY PRINCESS, WOULD THAT I WISH I COULD WIN YOUR HEART."
"BUT ALAS, HOW I WISH I WERE OF NOBLE BLOOD. THEN I WOULD CAPTURE THE VERY SKIES FOR YOU AND BRING THEM DOWN TO YOU AS A GIFT."
"WHAT'S THAT NOISE, MARRIONE? WHO'S IN THERE WITH YOU?"
TOK TOK
"WHAT ARE YOU DOING HERE? GET OUT BOY."
"OUCH OUCH. I'LL RETURN FOR YOU, MY LOVE!"
HAHAHAHAHAHAHAHAHAHAHAHAHA

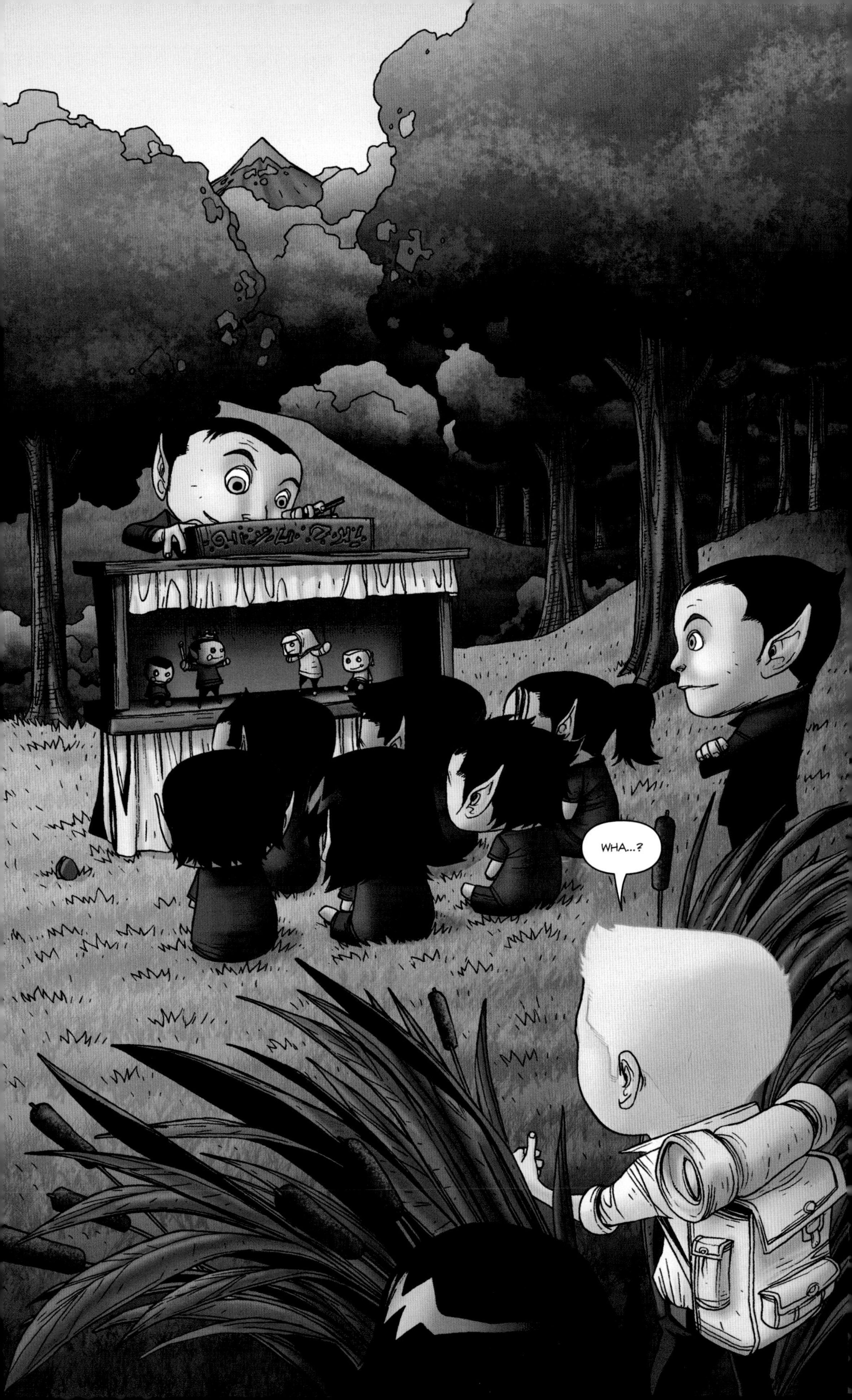
WHA...?

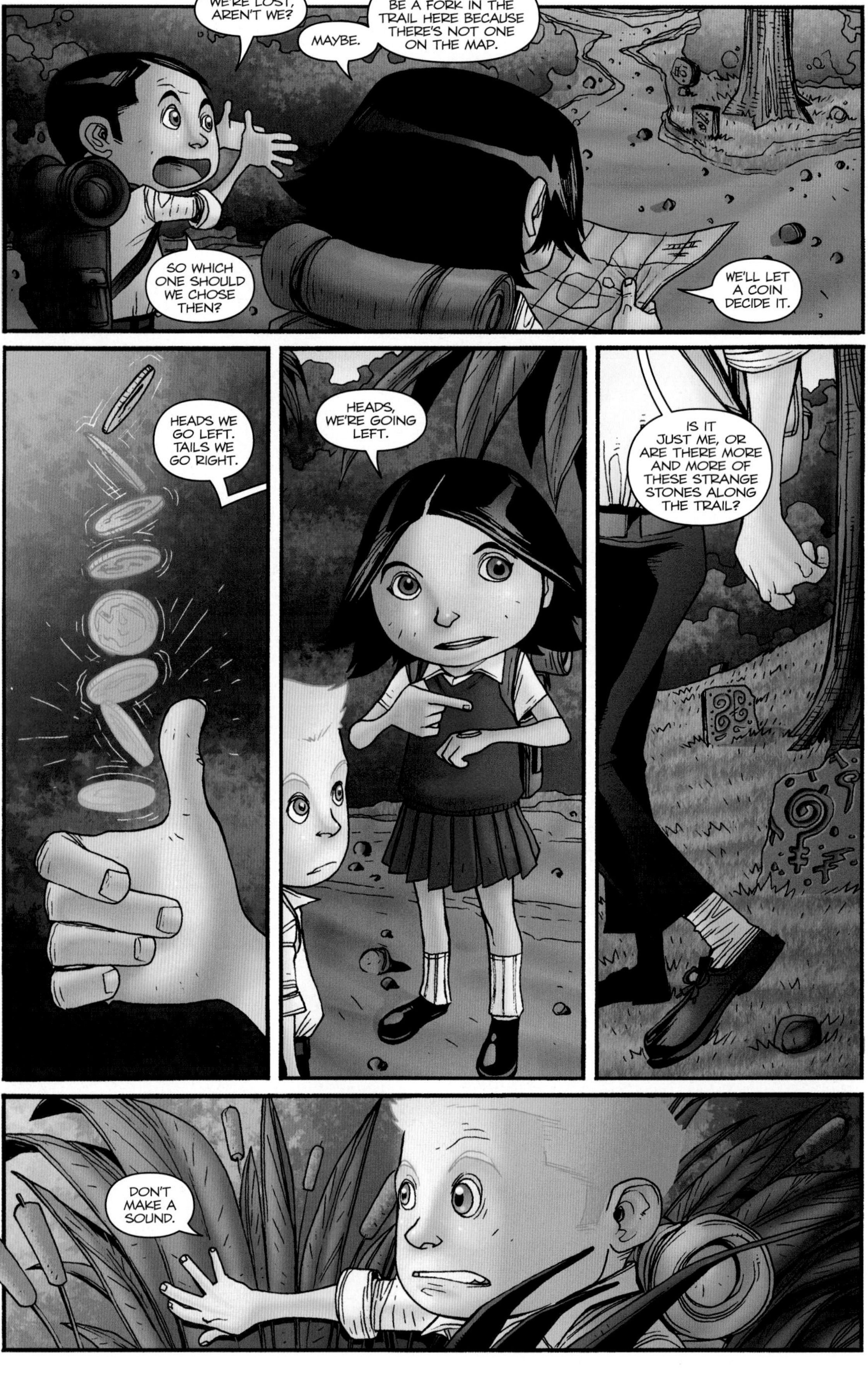
WE'RE LOST, AREN'T WE?
MAYBE.
THERE SHOULDN'T BE A FORK IN THE TRAIL HERE BECAUSE THERE'S NOT ONE ON THE MAP.
SO WHICH ONE SHOULD WE CHOSE THEN?
WE'LL LET A COIN DECIDE IT.
HEADS WE GO LEFT. TAILS WE GO RIGHT.
HEADS, WE'RE GOING LEFT.
IS IT JUST ME, OR ARE THERE MORE AND MORE OF THESE STRANGE STONES ALONG THE TRAIL?
DON'T MAKE A SOUND.

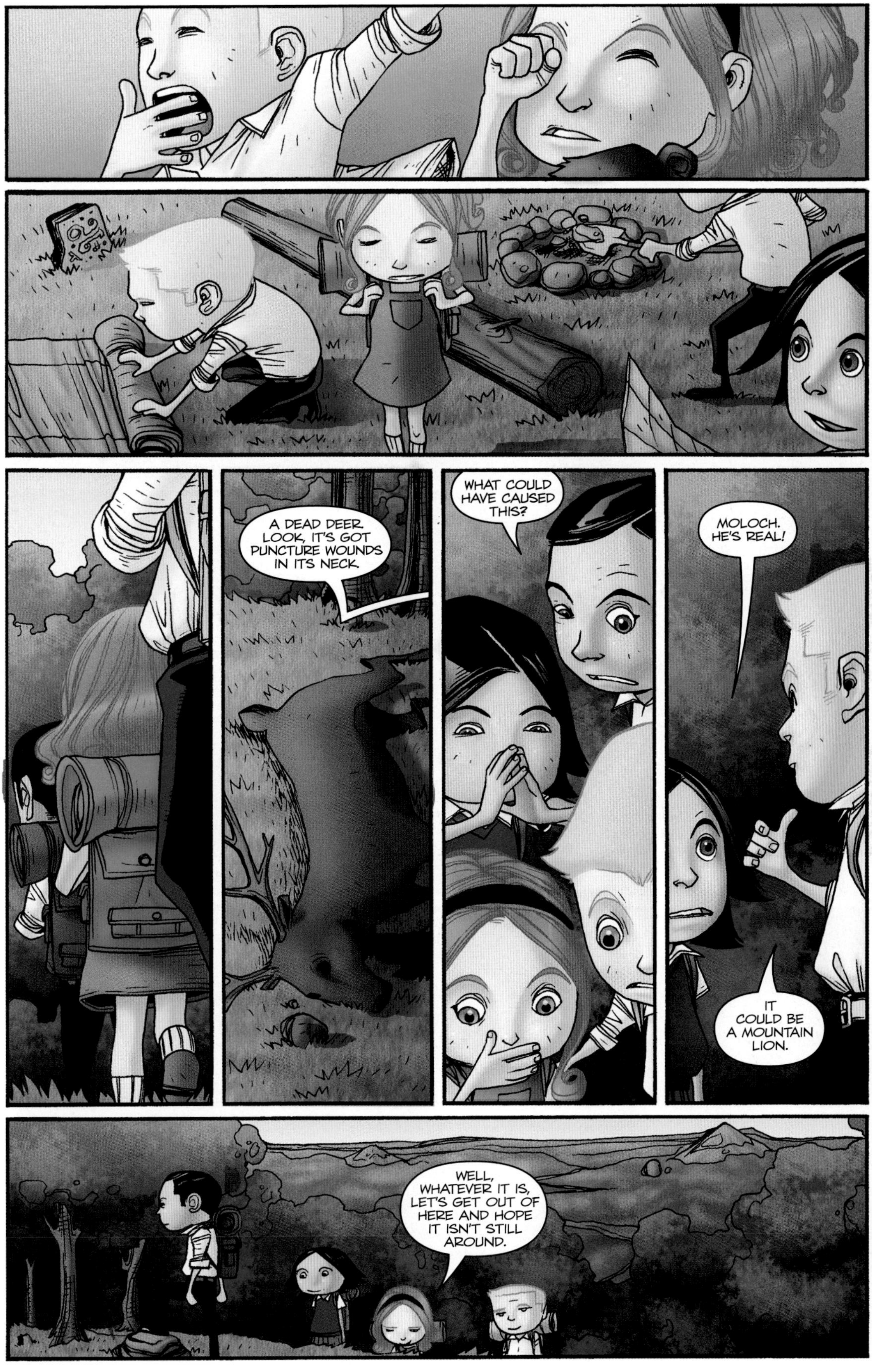
A DEAD DEER
LOOK, IT'S GOT PUNCTURE WOUNDS IN ITS NECK.
WHAT COULD HAVE CAUSED THIS?
MOLOCH. HE'S REAL!
IT COULD BE A MOUNTAIN LION.
WELL, WHATEVER IT IS, LET'S GET OUT OF HERE AND HOPE IT ISN'T STILL AROUND.

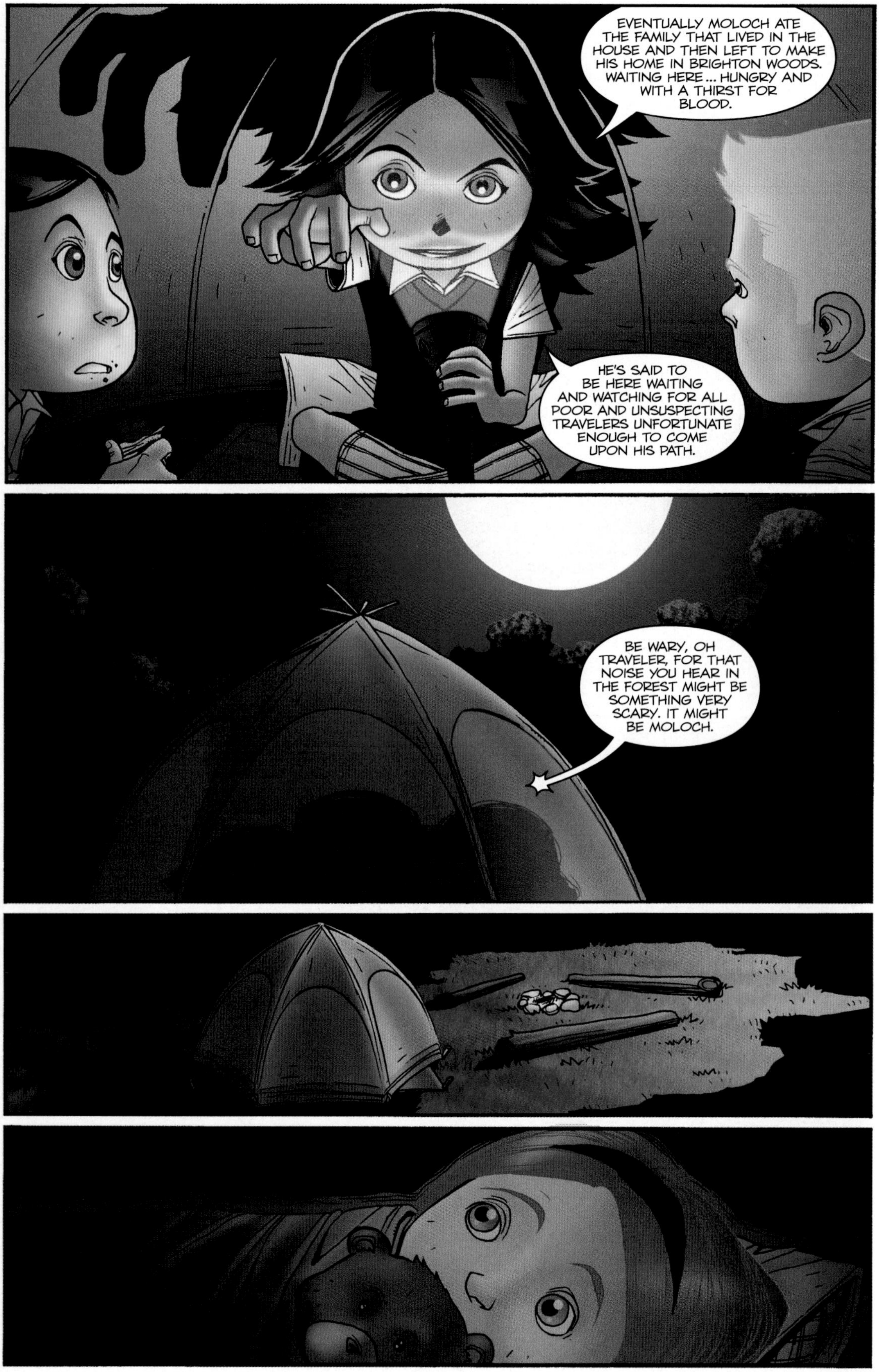
EVENTUALLY MOLOCH ATE THE FAMILY THAT LIVED IN THE HOUSE AND THEN LEFT TO MAKE HIS HOME IN BRIGHTON WOODS. WAITING HERE... HUNGRY AND WITH A THIRST FOR BLOOD.
HE'S SAID TO BE HERE WAITING AND WATCHING FOR ALL POOR AND UNSUSPECTING TRAVELERS UNFORTUNATE ENOUGH TO COME UPON HIS PATH.
BE WARY, OH TRAVELER, FOR THAT NOISE YOU HEAR IN THE FOREST MIGHT BE SOMETHING VERY SCARY. IT MIGHT BE MOLOCH.

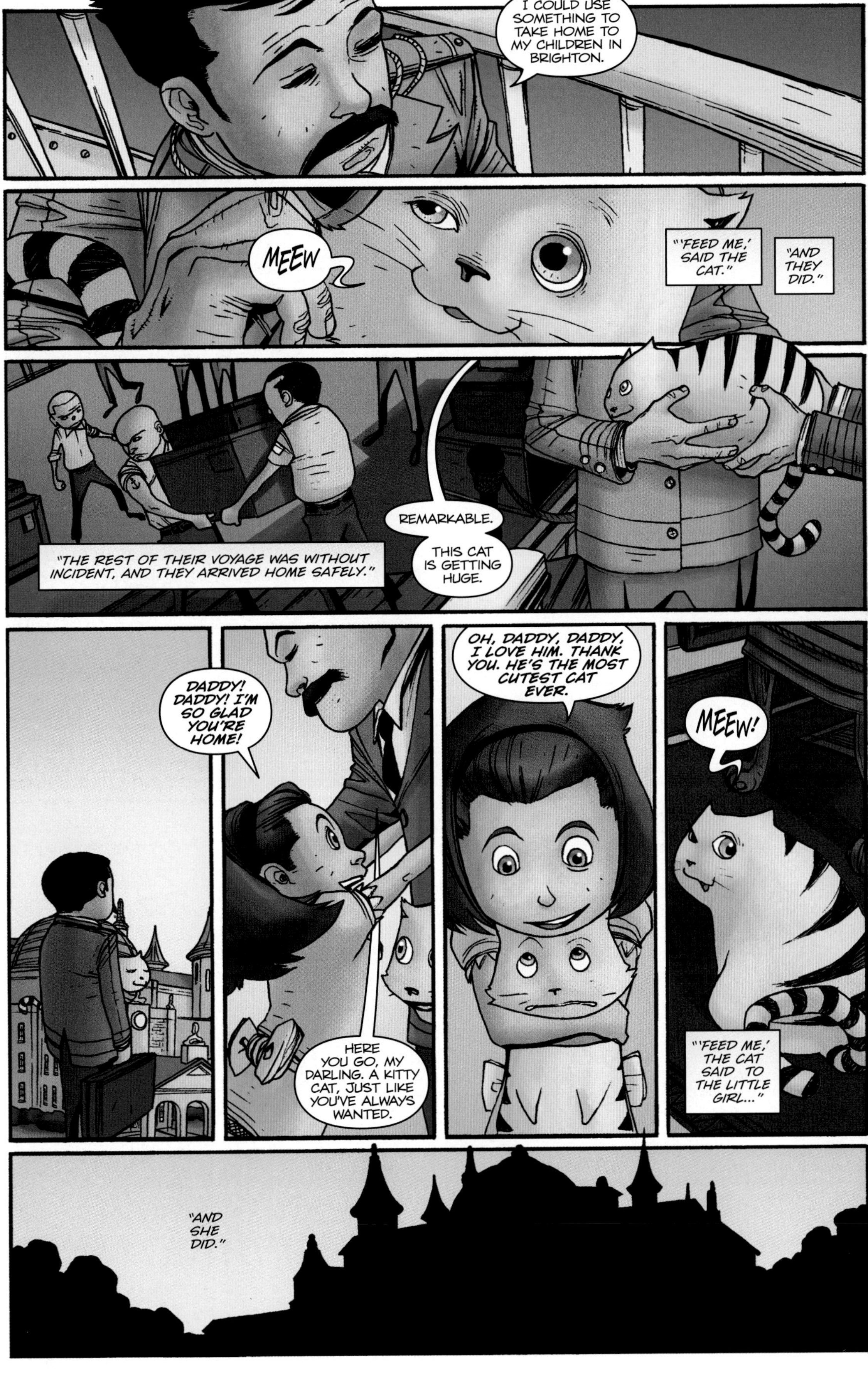
I COULD USE SOMETHING TO TAKE HOME TO MY CHILDREN IN BRIGHTON.
MEEW
"'FEED ME,' SAID THE CAT."
"AND THEY DID."
"THE REST OF THEIR VOYAGE WAS WITHOUT INCIDENT, AND THEY ARRIVED HOME SAFELY."
REMARKABLE.
THIS CAT IS GETTING HUGE.
DADDY! DADDY! I'M SO GLAD YOU'RE HOME!
HERE YOU GO, MY DARLING. A KITTY CAT, JUST LIKE YOU'VE ALWAYS WANTED.
OH, DADDY, DADDY, I LOVE HIM. THANK YOU. HE'S THE MOST CUTEST CAT EVER.
MEEW!
"'FEED ME,' THE CAT SAID TO THE LITTLE GIRL..."
"AND SHE DID."

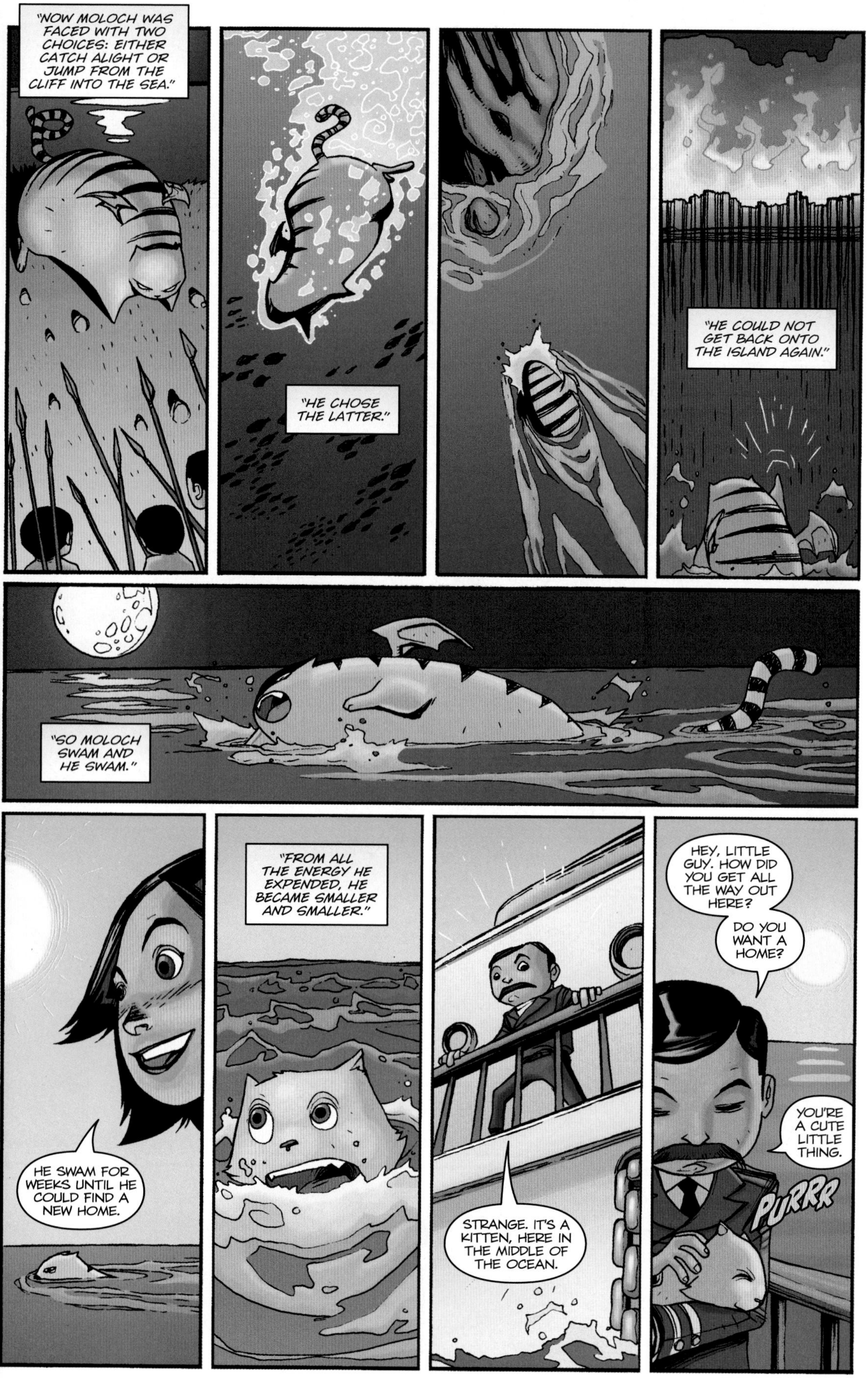
"NOW MOLOCH WAS FACED WITH TWO CHOICES: EITHER CATCH ALIGHT OR JUMP FROM THE CLIFF INTO THE SEA."
"HE CHOSE THE LATTER."
"HE COULD NOT GET BACK ONTO THE ISLAND AGAIN."
"SO MOLOCH SWAM AND HE SWAM."
HE SWAM FOR WEEKS UNTIL HE COULD FIND A NEW HOME.
"FROM ALL THE ENERGY HE EXPENDED, HE BECAME SMALLER AND SMALLER."
STRANGE. IT'S A KITTEN, HERE IN THE MIDDLE OF THE OCEAN.
HEY, LITTLE GUY. HOW DID YOU GET ALL THE WAY OUT HERE?
DO YOU WANT A HOME?
YOU'RE A CUTE LITTLE THING.
PURRR

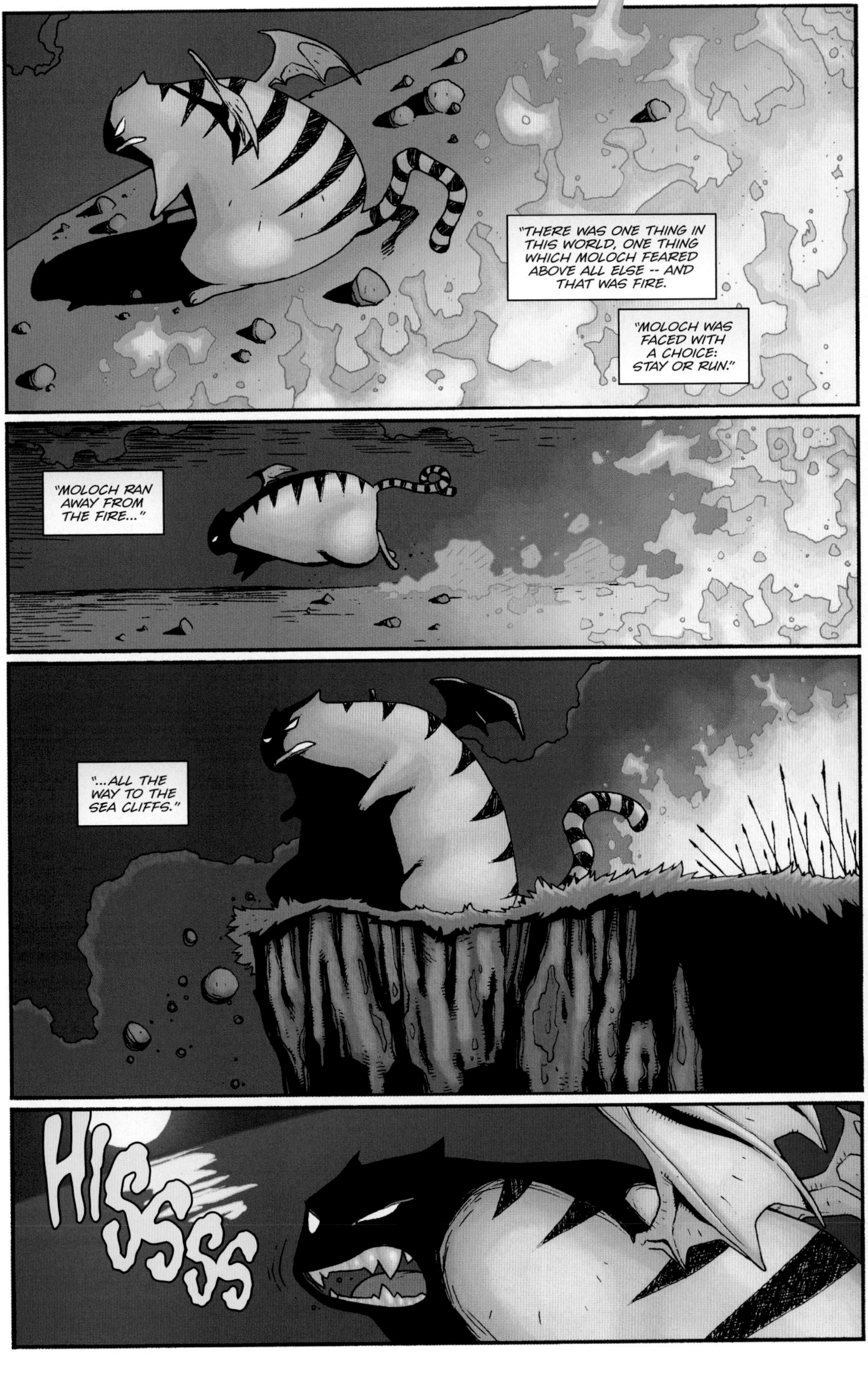
"THERE WAS ONE THING IN THIS WORLD, ONE THING WHICH MOLOCH FEARED ABOVE ALL ELSE -- AND THAT WAS FIRE.
"MOLOCH WAS FACED WITH A CHOICE: STAY OR RUN."
"MOLOCH RAN AWAY FROM THE FIRE..."
"...ALL THE WAY TO THE SEA CLIFFS."
HISSSS

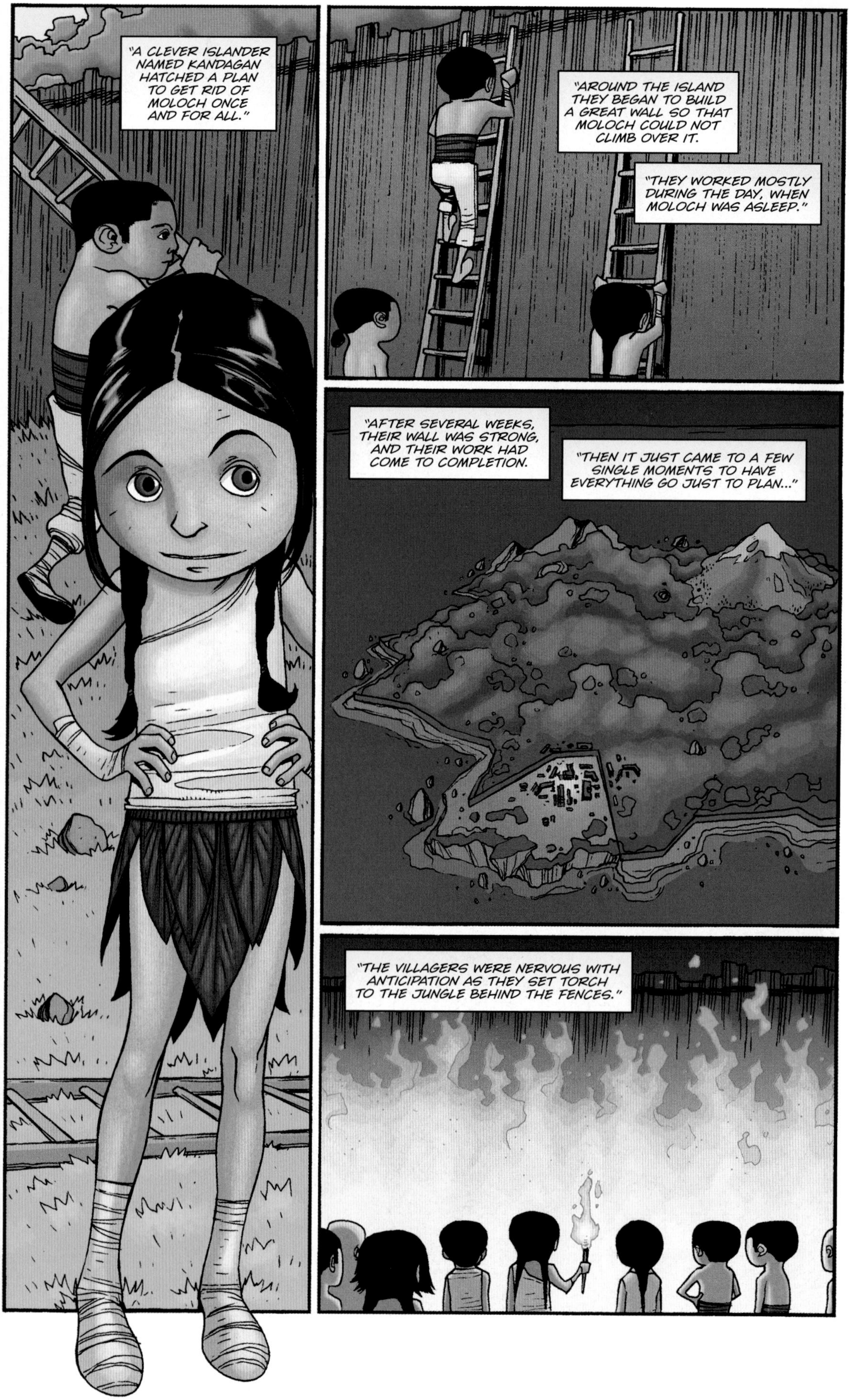
"A CLEVER ISLANDER NAMED KANDAGAN HATCHED A PLAN TO GET RID OF MOLOCH ONCE AND FOR ALL."
"AROUND THE ISLAND THEY BEGAN TO BUILD A GREAT WALL SO THAT MOLOCH COULD NOT CLIMB OVER IT.
"THEY WORKED MOSTLY DURING THE DAY, WHEN MOLOCH WAS ASLEEP."
"AFTER SEVERAL WEEKS, THEIR WALL WAS STRONG, AND THEIR WORK HAD COME TO COMPLETION.
"THEN IT JUST CAME TO A FEW SINGLE MOMENTS TO HAVE EVERYTHING GO JUST TO PLAN..."
"THE VILLAGERS WERE NERVOUS WITH ANTICIPATION AS THEY SET TORCH TO THE JUNGLE BEHIND THE FENCES."